ELLEN GUNDERSON TRAYLOR

HARVEST HOUSE PUBLISHERS
Eugene, Oregon 97402

Other Books by
Ellen Gunderson Traylor

Song of Abraham
John—Son of Thunder
Mary Magdalene
Noah
Ruth—A Love Story
Jonah
Mark
Joseph
Moses
Joshua
Samson

ESTHER

Copyright © 1994 by Harvest House Publishers
Eugene, Oregon 97402

ISBN 1-56865-138-4

Printed in the United States of America.

To Eric,
who loved beauty.

Contents

Thy lovingkindness, O LORD,
extends to the heavens,
Thy faithfulness reaches to the skies.
The righteousness is like
the mountains of God;
Thy judgments are like a great deep.

Psalm 36:5,6 NASB

A Note to the Reader

In a tiny hall of the Oriental Institute Museum, on the campus of the University of Chicago, there is an enormous artifact—the 20,000-pound black stone head of a guardian bull. Transplanted from the grounds of Persepolis, the ancient Persian ceremonial capital, this cold creature stares down upon tourists and scholars with centuries-old aloofness. Could it speak, it would doubtless tell fabulous tales of the grand empire which once ruled half the world.

Having embroiled myself in the study of Esther, the biblical queen who was for a time first lady of that empire, I was overcome with feeling when I first set eyes upon this heartless creature. Esther herself, fairest woman on earth and pure of heart in devotion to her Jewish heritage, had most likely passed before this very statue, and the sightless rock had glowered down on her, just as it now did on me.

In an instant, I sensed a personal link with the young girl whom I had studied, understanding for the first time how frightened she must have been when carried away to become wife of the despot, Xerxes.

Esther's name does not show up in any secular chronicle. Herodotus, the most meticulous recorder of Xerxes' life and of the Greek-Persian Wars, mentions Amestris (probably the biblical Vashti), who was the rightful queen. Only the Bible tells of Hadassah, the orphaned Jewess who rose to the throne, unhappily taking on a pagan name and filling the place where the first noble lady should have remained.

Although overlooked by secular historians, the tale of Esther is crucial to the story of Israel. For Esther was a savior to her people, raised for a purpose higher than worldly acclaim.

"What was she like?" I would have asked the great bull, if I could. "When you and your brothers in Persepolis and Susa loomed above her, did she tremble?"

Only a novelist's imagination could assist me toward the answer. The Scriptures, though telling us all we know of this obscure queen, are typically scant in revealing the heroine's heart. We see the plot, but must interpret the character's motivations and emotions with the aid of prayer and intuition alone. This is true not only for Esther, but for Vashti, Xerxes, and the host of other people who fill the pages of God's Word.

Fumbling as our reconstruction may be, we will not go far wrong if we remember that these were folk of flesh and blood, who once loved and cried and laughed. And that they, like we, were guided through their steps by the Sovereign God who rules all history and governs each life for his ultimate purpose.

If we can apply this principle as we read of those who lived so long ago, we also can apply it to ourselves. No one's circumstances, no matter how mysterious or confounding, are outside God's grand design. Our Father knows the end from the beginning. Despite our frustrated attempts to understand, he will always be proven the Master Architect of all things.

May you find encouragement for your hard times and the laughter of the Lord in all your triumphs.

—Ellen Traylor

PART I
The King and the Prince

1

Purple dusk had settled over Persia's western desert. A rush of cool wind swept through Susa on its way to the Gulf, bearing the scent of lilies across the housetops.

It was Spring. Tomorrow would begin a new imperial year.

Amestris Vashti, daughter of Otanes, shivered and glanced south toward Persepolis, the distant ceremonial capital, where the revelry of New Year's Eve would be even more boisterous than in this northern citadel.

Vashti's private balcony afforded an expansive view across Susa's southern wall, and in this sanctum of her father's home she was free for a moment from the din in the streets beyond the river.

One of the mansions of the seven noblest families in Persia, the house of her childhood stood safely tucked atop Susa's acropolis. Rarely had Vashti found it necessary to mingle with the commoners who lived in the shadow of the royal mount, but New Year's Eve required it.

Vashti, along with her royal sisters (girls born to the highest homes in the land), had ridden through town this day in open carriages, bearing long-stemmed lilies in their hands and wearing pink irises in their hair. Though they had been cheered and praised by adoring masses, Vashti had not enjoyed it.

She would have preferred to accompany her cousins, the young princes of King Darius, to Persepolis.

But that journey was for boys alone.

Pushing slender fingers through a tousle of long black curls, she lifted her face to the wind and let the cool air spill over her bare arms. As she wrapped her fringed shawl about her shoulders, she remembered that Prince Xerxes had once stood with her upon this very balcony.

They had been mere children and very innocent. But when the chamberlain had found them, he had rebuked them soundly. "It is dark, and you are alone!" he had glowered. "This is indiscretion!"

At the time, being but a young girl, she had not known what "indiscretion" meant. It must be something dreadful, she deduced, and so did Xerxes when they spoke of it in the garden the next day.

That had been a decade ago. Vashti was 16 now, and most of her training for the past ten years had been concerned with discretion and indiscretion. She had come to love being a lady and behaving the part.

And she had come to love Xerxes too, if indeed she had ever *not* loved him.

In truth, she could not remember ever feeling neutral toward the third son of Darius. And she could not recall ever feeling anything for him but admiration.

Certainly her circle of childhood playmates and adolescent companions had been carefully chosen. She had known only a few boys in her growing-up years—sons of nobility and sons of Darius. Well before she had reached puberty, she had been limited in socializing even with these.

But Xerxes had won her heart before she knew she could give it. And being rarely allowed to see him had only bound her to him more surely.

Closing her eyes, she leaned against a fluted column of her lofty porch and tried to envision what he might be doing just now. In a few hours it would be midnight, the first day of the new year, and twelve years since Xerxes' ascension to the office of viceroy. He was 18 now, but he had stood behind his father's throne since he was less than half that old.

Though he was not the monarch's eldest son, he was the first since his coronation. Hence he would one day succeed to the throne.

And should all go as planned, Vashti would be queen.

At midnight in Persepolis the sacred dice would be cast, the "purim," which would determine the appointed dates of special events for the empire's coming year.

"The priests, when they cast the dice, will speak of you and me," the prince had promised her. "On New Year's Eve they will decide our wedding day."

It was fully possible that a quirk of the dice or an interpretation of accompanying omens could throw the date into a later year. But Vashti and Xerxes had prayed to Ahura-Mazda and had taken a second drink from the cup of haoma, pleading that no such delay would take place.

Rarely since their earliest days of childish play had the prince been alone with Vashti. As a small boy and girl they had touched often, had held hands, and had skipped through the mammoth hallways of Susa's palace.

But their encounters were more guarded now. Those fleeting occasions when the prince had brushed her arm in passing or had touched her fingertips at a banquet table were stored in her memory like hallowed gems.

Bronze-skinned and tall, he was a striking figure now—a man and not a boy. Were he to bend over her with his strong neck and able arms, she would tremble, she knew. For she had done so this very morning, when in a stolen moment he had kissed her.

Had that been indiscretion? The chamberlain would have said so. But Vashti was Xerxes' betrothed, his soon-to-be-wife. No one could have kept him from seeking her in the garden and pressing his promises to her.

Vashti opened her eyes. The din in the streets was clearly audible now, even at this far side of the mount. Below wound the Shapur River through the center of town, and beyond the city wall stretched the night-cold desert.

Small strings of light here and there along the sandy expanse marked feudal villages, where proud farmers and craftsmen derived a tolerable living from the irrigated soil. Though Susa was dominated by Persians, every nationality in the empire, from Indian to Ethiopian, composed its population and its suburbs. Tonight the people were free to come and go through the city's open gates, and a constant line of traffic traced the highway between the citadel and the nearby Gulf.

Vashti had often tried to comprehend the enormity of Darius' realm. Susa was only a small fraction of the whole, of the dominions which stretched over three thousand miles across the world and which included 127 provinces from India to Africa.

All this would one day belong to Xerxes. The greatest names on earth, from Babylon to Egypt, bowed the knee to Persia.

And if Darius had his way, even Greece would eventually succumb.

Greece, alone of all civilized nations, had managed to resist tribute to Darius. Its native tongue had not yielded to the Aramaic language. Even Xerxes, properly known as Ahasuerus, was called by the more popular Greek variation.

One day, Darius was determined, he would usurp Grecian hold over southern Europe. He would bring away captive Greek slaves, just as his Babylonian predecessor, Nebuchadnezzar, had done with the Israelites.

But that was *Darius'* plan. *Vashti's* was to marry Xerxes. This was all she cared for.

She would have closed her eyes again, to contemplate him, had her gaze not been caught by certain pedestrians along the desert highway.

Hundreds came and went upon the road, all in festive mood, singing, dancing, reeling from drink.

But the little group which caught her attention was strangely huddled, bent about an elderly man and the bundle he carried in his arms. A couple and a younger fellow walked with the old one, intent on helping him along and watching the little parcel with care.

"Peculiar," Vashti thought; "always they are peculiar."

She had recognized them immediately as Jews, and designated them strange not only because of their dress but because of their typically somber attitude.

Though all Persia partied tonight, these folk, like many of their race, kept to themselves, observing the holiday independently and quietly.

These, of all the folk in Persia's realm, were hardest for her to understand. She neither loved nor hated them, but found them curious oddities.

Were she at hand, she might have asked them why they behaved so strangely, and what was concealed in the wrapper.

But when they disappeared through the city gate she forgot them, and her eyes grew heavy with the dark.

Turning for her chamber, she slipped to bed and hoped the midnight cacophony would not rouse her.

She wished to dream of Xerxes.

2

When the little band of Jews entered the city, they did not turn toward the center of common festivity, the marketplace, but instead crossed the elegant bridge leading toward the acropolis.

Along the foot of the mount stood fine homes amid imperial office buildings and treasuries. These houses and apartments were not so elaborate as those of the Persian nobility but were more handsome than the box-shaped residences of the lower class. These fine homes spoke of success and upward mobility. If a Jew lived in Susa, it was not unlikely that he would live here.

The close-knit folk whom Vashti had observed from her balcony traversed several broad avenues fronting such abodes. The youngest of the group, a slender fellow with smooth features and well-trimmed beard, seemed most anxious to move along but was hindered by the eldest, who was not so spry as he.

"We are almost there, Uncle," the young man spurred him. "Just around the next corner."

"You have done well for yourself, Mordecai," the elder observed, studying his surroundings with proud eyes. "To dwell in a foreign land in finery—that is a task for a Jew. And you have accomplished it!"

The idea of Persia being a "foreign" place, after more than two centuries of his ancestors' residing here, had always struck Mordecai as strange. But he nodded graciously, having heard such assessments all his life.

True, the ancestral Israelites had not come to Mesopotamia willingly. They had been taken captive by Nebuchadnezzar 200 years before—"exiled," as they put it, by the hand of God. But Cyrus the Great had emancipated them. There were no longer Jewish slaves in Babylon or any part of Persia. They had been free to return to Israel, just as all captive people of the realm had been free to return to their homelands.

Since then, of course, other slaves had been taken by Cyrus' successors—but never again the Israelites. The many Jews who had chosen to remain in Persia were free to pursue all the empire had to offer, and they, being industrious and creative, had carved many niches of success for themselves.

Certainly in Susa, as in every Persian quarter, there were ghettos—impoverished, hovel-lined pockets where less fortunate Hebrews dwelt. Perhaps Abihail, the elder, had envisioned such a neighborhood when Mordecai had encouraged him to come for a visit. But he was seeing now, as he surveyed these well-kept housefronts, that his nephew was not among the poor.

"I tried to tell you that Mordecai has climbed high in Susa," the young woman of the group objected. With a worried sigh she reached for the old man's bundle, which wriggled now in his arms. "Please, Uncle, let me carry the baby," she pleaded. "You could stumble . . . you could . . ."

"It is all right, Leah," said her husband, Moshe, who steadied the elder's uneasy gait. "Do not press him."

Abihail had been a farmer all his life, in one of Susa's small village suburbs. So had his son, as well as his brother, both of whom had died of plague many years before. Left with no family of their own, Abihail and his wife had taken in the brother's orphaned children, Mordecai and Leah, rearing them as off-spring of their own love.

Never had they dreamed that the five nephews and nieces born to Leah, and whom they loved as grandchildren, would not be their last "gifts from the Lord." Like Sarah of old, who had given Abraham his Isaac, Abihail's wife became pregnant in advanced age. The swaddled infant in the wrapper was the result.

Just seven days ago the old man's wife had died while giving birth to the child. Had Abihail not seen hope for tomorrow in the newborn's perfect form and face, his heart would have died as well.

"A daughter of Israel," he whispered as he cradled the tiny girl to his bosom. "Is she not a myrtle blossom?" he crooned as he peeked between the folds of the homespun blanket, his long patriarchal beard tickling her chin.

"Hadassah," he had named her: "Myrtle," for her creamy skin, white like the bush's fragrant flowers, and her shock of deep-brown hair, dark as evergreen boughs.

Mordecai wondered at the elder's fond behavior. He had always marveled at the old man's love of tradition and heritage. Now that he saw it had a forward thrust, as well as a backward, he marveled all the more.

As for himself, if Mordecai esteemed Israel it was for personal advantage. He had learned in youth that the line of Kish, from whom he was descended, had been Hebrew nobility. Nebuchadnezzar had imported the cream of Israelite society, bringing the highest leaders and families into exile with the Jewish king, Jeconiah. The line of Kish could be traced back to King Saul himself, and many men of the clan had been notable administrators, scribes, clerks, and accountants in Israel and Judah.

Educated in the village synagogue school, Mordecai had been praised at a young age for his finesse with figures and mathematics. He would be a financial wizard, he had decided in his youthful dreams. He would sit one day in the palace gate at Susa or Persepolis, where all the greatest consultants sat. And he would make himself famous for brilliant manipulation of the market.

But Mordecai was not without a sentimental side. Though he had been promoted beyond the village walls and had now come to reside in the city, first as a merchant's bookkeeper and now as his executive stockkeeper, he had not forgotten his kin. He loved them all devoutly, and when he thought of Judaism, he considered it best expressed by close attachment to his people.

Abihail wished he saw it more spiritually than that. He had rankled when his brother named the lad Mordecai, after Marduk, god of storm. The brother had insisted that it meant nothing to do so—that he simply liked the name, and that it was a common one in the land.

"But there is much *meaning* in a name," Abihail had insisted. "The Scriptures bear this out. The lad will have much to overcome with a name like that."

To this day it rolled awkwardly off Abihail's tongue. Though proud of his nephew, he still wished the young man had an Israelite name.

The infant was beginning to whimper. Mordecai saw his sister reach anxiously for her, accustomed to mothering as she was. It had been for this very reason that he had insisted Abihail and Hadassah stay with him for a time. Leah had too many mouths to feed and too many little ones to tend. An aging and bereaved uncle along with a tiny newborn would be an unwieldy burden.

"There are women servants at home, and we are almost there now," he reminded her. "I even hired a nurse to suckle the child. Never you mind."

Leah sighed again and shook her head. She could not imagine a confirmed bachelor like her brother long enduring the trouble a baby would bring. She had tried to warn him of the nighttime crying, the colic, the diaper changes. But he had insisted.

"Abihail needs a shift of scene," Mordecai had determined. "If he grows homesick, he will return to you. But give him a few weeks."

Fireworks imported from the Indus Valley lit the New Year's sky. It was close to midnight as the little family turned the last corner for home. The palace gate was not far from here, and folk in royal chariots were descending the winding road which led from the king's house toward town. Since the king himself, his sons, and his closest companions celebrated in Persepolis, and since women of the court would not leave the acropolis at night, the ones hastening for the market square were underlings, administrative assistants, household eunuchs, and valets. They would not miss the climax of merrymaking which would follow the light display at midnight.

Most of them were already half-drunk. The little group of Jews stepped into the shadows as they went by, watching them quietly. Mordecai's lips curled in a covert smile at their frivolity. He had known a share of high times himself since abiding in Susa, but he was careful not to let Abihail know about it.

When the courtiers were nearly past, and only a band of rowdy stragglers followed, Mordecai led his people back into the street.

Perhaps it was the Jews' simple garb, shawled heads, or downcast eyes, but something in their demeanor enraged the besotted gang who stumbled into the trail of the regal parade. Mordecai would not have recognized them had they not called to him. When they hissed his name, following it with a racial epithet, he instantly knew their voices.

Assistants to the king's grand vizier, they were. Assistants to Haman, highest counselor in the land. Mordecai knew them because his own master had enrolled him in accounting courses at the vizier's royal academy.

They had never lived up to their respectable positions. Mordecai often wondered why Haman had selected them for himself. But, of course, they were very bright—and it did not hurt them that they came from monied families.

He would have ignored the racial slur, but they would not allow it. Stopping directly before his group, they impeded passage down the walkway and began to hurl more insults at him.

"Jew boy," they taunted. "Sheep trap, sand flea!" Then, spying the elderly one behind him, as well as his attractive sister, they made crude gestures with their hands.

"What's in the bundle, old man?" one laughed. "A little lamb for New Year's dinner?"

"Of course, Drusal!" another shouted. "It wouldn't be a pig. Jews don't eat 'unclean' beasts!"

The rowdies elbowed one another, doubling over with guffaws, and Abihail shielded the baby anxiously.

"Ah!" a third cried, seeing his protective action. "It must be a treasure! Let's see, Grandpa!"

When the young men grasped at the bundle, Leah shrieked and her husband pulled her to him.

"Leave us be!" Mordecai growled. "This is nothing to you."

But suddenly, spurred to violence by hours of drink, the men shot forward, pushing Leah's husband aside and pressing Abihail to the wall.

Held tightly to her old father's chest, the baby began to cry, disclosing the secret of herself. With wicked leers the men reached for the bundle, laughing "Jew baby!" and seeming ready to toss her from hand to hand.

Abihail slumped to his knees, still clutching the infant, as Mordecai and Moshe did their best to ward off Haman's boys.

Though they had no love for Jews, in a more sober mood they never would have harmed these people. The leader would never have thrown the piercing kick to the old man's head which sent Abihail sprawling to the pavement.

Leah shrieked again and grabbed the baby, who now lay squalling on the curb. The two Jewish brothers rushed at the attackers with clenched fists.

Suddenly another chariot could be heard coming down the acropolis hill. It would prove to be only the vehicle of a tardy courtier, racing to catch up with those who had passed by earlier.

But Haman's assistants, fearing the authorities, scrambled down the avenue. Though they were drunk, they were not so addlepated as to be caught in a street brawl.

Mordecai and Moshe bent down to help the uncle to his feet. Blood trickled from the old man's forehead, and an ugly bruise throbbed at his temple.

"Help is on its way," Mordecai assured him. "A chariot approaches."

But the Persian vehicle did not slow as it drew near. If the driver even noticed the stranded Jews, he did not stop to help.

There were fireworks to see, and wine to drink in the center of town. The tall white horses shot past, pulling their regal passengers to the sting of an eager whip.

Nothing could be more important than a party.

3

A princely wedding was like practice for a coronation. It would be nine more years before young Xerxes took the throne, but his prayer to marry Vashti before another 12 months elapsed had been granted. It was an auspicious occasion, calling for all the grandeur and pomp the empire could muster, and it evoked images of the day he would be crowned.

Processionals featured the elitist corps of Darius' army, machines and weapons of war, flower-strewn carriages, bevies of dancers and high-stepping horses, orchestras and bands, and wagons of gifts for the bride and groom.

The festivities would last for weeks. Though only the most privileged friends of the palace would actually witness the nuptial rites, Darius had proclaimed a reduction in taxes, release of all but the most criminal of prisoners, and a six-month rest for his troops in training.

But Mordecai was not prone to celebrate. In the darkened chamber which had once been his own bedroom, his uncle lay in a fitful sleep, unable to walk steadily or even sit for long since the blow to his head.

The accountant had seen to it that the best physicians outside the palace of Susa were made available to Abihail. But the man was old, and had only recently sustained a great loss. Though he had much to live for in his new daughter, without his wife life was bitter. The jolt of a head wound made recovery unlikely.

Leah and Moshe had returned reluctantly to their village, leaving Mordecai in charge of both the ailing uncle and the infant. But considering their limited resources, they knew Mordecai was better able to carry the burden.

Blasts of trumpets from a marching band roused Abihail. As always, his first waking thought was of Hadassah.

"She is well," the nephew assured him. "She is with the nurse."

"She should be with her mother," the elder groaned. "God above, why has my little one been put in such a strait?"

Mordecai rarely addressed the Almighty personally. Religion was best left to the rabbis and the synagogues, he reasoned. His uncle's bold conviction that Jehovah really heard, and furthermore cared, had always intrigued him. But it was good that Abihail had his faith, since he had little else in this world.

The nephew stepped near the elder's bed. Noting his perplexed glance toward the window, he was quick to explain the sounds rising from the street.

"Prince Xerxes is getting married today," he said with a smile. "All of Susa celebrates."

Abihail was not impressed with the events of Persian royalty. "A marriage of convenience, I suppose," he muttered. "Some nobleman social-climbing on the head of his daughter."

"Not this time, I hear," Mordecai laughed. "It seems that Xerxes truly loves his bride. They have been betrothed since childhood."

Abihail leaned his head back with a sigh. "Well, and what of you, son?" he asked. "Have you ever loved a woman?"

"Not to my knowledge," the bachelor grinned. "I have had no time for such things."

"You should marry," Abihail insisted. "It would do you good. And Hadassah . . . she needs a mother."

Mordecai knew he alluded to the possibility of her being orphaned. He had tried not to admit the eventuality. He had tried not to think of his own responsibility toward the child should she be left alone.

Changing the subject, Mordecai referred to the men who had put the child's future in jeopardy.

"I have reported to the palace police what happened on New Year's Eve, Uncle. I am assured that they will look into the matter, although since the culprits were Haman's boys we may never see justice."

The old man was not surprised. "It is futile to hope we could. Tell me, who is this Haman?"

"The highest of the king's advisers. And yet he is not even a Persian, I hear. He is an Agagite, a crafty one, who has won his way to the top through many lucrative decisions."

Abihail sat up suddenly, pricked by something in the revelation.

"An Agagite?" he scowled. "He calls himself this?"

"Yes," Mordecai shrugged. "He seems proud enough of the fact."

Wondering why Abihail should take the information so seriously, he listened as the old Jew recounted a bit of Israelite lore.

"King Saul, your ancestor, once had a run-in with an Amalekite named Agag. Do you recall the incident?"

Mordecai shook his head, hoping that the history lesson would be brief.

"The father of the Agagites, Haman's ancestor, he would be."

Again the younger Jew nodded. The story would be a long one, he feared, and how it could possibly bear on their own time he could not imagine.

"The Lord Jehovah had told Saul to utterly destroy the Amalekites—men, women, children, cattle, and all. But Saul took mercy on Agag, their king, and even took the spoil from the vanquished enemy—something which God said he must not do."

Mordecai stifled a yawn. The day was very hot, and he wished he might be with the other Susaites, observing the parade outside the window.

As the musicians of Darius' court marched past, row upon row of them, Abihail's voice droned on, mixing with the rhythmic drums and lulling Mordecai half asleep.

"No end of trouble have the Amalekites been all these years!" he insisted. "The blood-feud has never ceased, except for those who do not remember."

The young accountant supposed he referred to his like, for he had never known this tale. Most Jews of his generation cared little for such matters. Only Abihail and his kind, the rabid orthodox, clung to such particulars as though they still mattered.

"I doubt that Haman knows the story either," he objected, rising from his lethargy. "So what difference does it make? If the animosity is gone from both camps, there is no war."

"Ah," Abihail argued, "but there you are wrong! This shows your shortsightedness. For Jehovah sees things in a timeless frame. He has never forgotten His promises to Abraham, though many of Abraham's children have done so. Nor has He forgotten that he swore enmity against Amalek, and that Israel is obliged to stamp him out."

Mordecai frowned incredulously. "Can you possibly believe that the command given to an ancient Israelite king devolves to his descendants?" he marveled. "Saul is dead, and Agag is dead. So it is ended!"

But Abihail was not dissuaded. Rising up from his bed, he declared, as though it were self-evident, "Saul failed! Therefore the order has been unfulfilled."

Mordecai paced the room now. Such reasoning was preposterous—the product of senility. But he would not argue impersonal theology with a sick old man.

"I think I hear the baby crying," he lied. "Rest, Uncle. The parade will be over soon, and you will be able to sleep."

With a knit brow, Abihail watched Mordecai's exit. Even in the hall beyond the darkened room, the young accountant could feel the elder's sad gaze against his back.

4

Slaves with large feathered fans stood in each corner of Darius' sumptuous council chamber, trying to keep the heat at bay. No breeze had passed between the columns of the porch all afternoon, nor had any movement of air parted the long linen curtains framing the sunlit veranda.

This was the king's private consultation room, one of several palace sanctums devoted to discussions of state. Today he and two of his generals, along with his vizier, met without his other ministers being present.

His son, Xerxes, was with them, however, just as he often was when they spoke of Persia's future. The prince sat erect in a straight-backed chair, hanging on every syllable of the conversation. For today Darius spoke of Greece.

While their great ancestor, Cyrus, had made an unprecedented move to wrest the Middle East from the Medes and Babylonians, consolidating the empire under one banner and founding what would become the greatest dominion on earth, Darius' genius lay in the fact that he completed the organization of the realm created by his predecessors.

From the extremities of the East to the rim of the Mediterranean he had expanded the empire, constructing a canal from the Nile to the Red Sea and even sending an expedition down the Indus to explore the Indian Ocean. For the first time ever there was a commercial waterway linking India, Persia, and Egypt, so that Darius' sovereignty was more vast than any which had gone before.

It was therefore fitting that he was known as "Darius, one king of many, one lord of many, the great king, king of kings, king of the countries possessing all kinds of people, king of this great earth far and wide."

But he was not content. He never would be until the Aegean and the Hellenistic world lay at his feet.

Some said a demon drove Darius. His forerunners had been great warlords. Cyrus had died fighting a savage Eastern race, and Cambyses had made bold attempts against Ethiopia. But Darius had been the first to invade the West.

Trekking into the Danube territory 22 years ago he had made the first historic attack of Asia on Europe. Sweeping through the Balkan hinterland, he crossed the great river on a bridge of boats, and though revolt among his own men ended the campaign in failure, the Greeks and Scythians could no longer consider the Persian dynasty a slumbering dog.

The men in the room today were privileged with a view of the harem courtyard, spread directly before them at the veranda's foot. Few men on earth were allowed to view the king's women. It was supposedly against the law for anyone to look upon his queen. But, though dozens of concubines and secondary wives sported in the pools and garden, the men rarely glanced their way.

Intensely involved in conversation, the generals leaned forward, riveted by the king's ambition. Otanes, Vashti's father, and Mardonius, the mightiest of Persia's military advisers, had much to gain by being here. And Haman, whose expertise lay not in war and weapons but in finance, could advance himself even further in the emperor's graces by wise contributions regarding the state of Persia's economy.

Years before, Otanes had proven his indispensable worth as a warlord when he had subdued Byzantium and her sister cities, securing the entire border between the Asian and European continents and bringing Persia's frontiers within easy distance of Greece.

In the meantime, several forays at Sardes, Miletus, Cyprus, and Caria had thrown victory from hand to hand between the Persians and Greeks. When a surprise nighttime maneuver had destroyed the entire Persian force at Caria, generals and all, the Westerners won a two-year respite by land and sea. Defeat of the Persian fleet at Cyprus and the army at Caria had forced the Persians into a palsied stance, and months had passed with no retaliation on Darius' part.

Perhaps today's meeting heralded a revival of courage on the king's part. Mardonius was hot for blood, and Otanes itched for the feel of the spear.

"How do you see the Greeks these days?" Darius asked his generals. "What are the reports from the Aegean?"

Mardonius cleared his throat and rubbed his hands upon his tight trousers. "The Greeks lack leadership. They are disunited," he replied.

Otanes nodded, adding eagerly, "They have not used their time well during these two years. There are no signs of movement against the sea. They seem to have been simply resting all these months."

The king smiled and leaned back into his throne. The consultants almost laughed with him, but they would not presume to do so just yet.

"They are at rest? But they won the last skirmish. Why would *they* need to recuperate?"

"Our successes have consistently outnumbered theirs, Your Majesty," Mardonius reminded him. "Their victories have been short-lived, or by surprise advantage. They know we could crush them if we had half a mind . . ."

Otanes fidgeted uneasily at this and Mardonius caught himself before he said too much. His suggestion bordered on the discourteous. No one dared impute cowardice to Darius.

Of course, all present knew the question should not have been why the Greeks had been "resting," but why Persia had made no offensive in the same length of time. This was Darius' matter alone, but all suspected that he had taken his fill of beatings at the hands of the Greeks, and was only now recovering.

The emperor scowled at Mardonius, and the general cast his gaze to the floor. When the king addressed Haman next, the warlord's flushed face began to cool.

"The treasury is adequate to an expedition?" Darius inquired.

Such a question! Did the emperor really wonder if the wealthiest coffers on earth could sustain a venture against the West? The generals glanced at one another covertly as Haman joined the talk.

Of course they knew the vizier had been invited only to give the final seal to the king's desires. Everyone knew there was no financial trouble in Persia. But Haman must make good his reason for being here.

"Your Highness has recently reduced taxes," he began. "They may need to be levied at the higher rate once more."

Xerxes shot a keen look in Haman's direction. The citizens of Persia had been granted a break in tribute and celebration of the prince's recent wedding. Was the vizier suggesting that the court had made a mistake?

Otanes, whose daughter was the object of the celebration, liked the insinuation no more than Xerxes. But he dared say nothing, as Haman was the king's favorite.

Darius did not always agree with Haman, however. Studying the young bridegroom fondly, he shook his head. "Taxes shall remain untouched for the time established," he asserted. And Otanes nodded to Xerxes, very pleased.

Haman kept his silence as Mardonius dealt with matters more important to the moment.

"We can engage a Phoenician fleet," he asserted, "and we can call upon contingents from Egypt, Cilicia, and Cyprus to invade Greek waters. All we need is time."

Xerxes' blood boiled with ambition as the commanders plotted their course. Perhaps one day, when he entered upon the throne, he would rule the Western world as well as the Eastern.

Surveying the harem through the consultants' bent heads, he imagined Vashti crowned with the jewels of Greece and Rome, Athens and Carthage.

He would give her half his kingdom. Whichever half she desired.

5

Mordecai, the Jew, stood upon his little veranda watching as the troops of Darius returned from war. He could see just enough through the narrow grates of his barred gate to tell him it was a sorry scene in the street tonight.

Hadassah, his adopted daughter, played at the feet of her governess, pulling at the tall stalks of lilies bordering Mordecai's modest garden. The music of the small fountain which babbled in his court was drowned out by the slow tramping of soldiers and the rhythm of funeral-like drums proceeding down the avenue. But the little girl, now three years old, was oblivious to the great dishonor received by Persia's troops at the hands of the Greeks.

Her father, were he still alive, would have told her that Darius had been retributed by the hand of God, that it was Jehovah who had seen to Persia's defeat due to its greed and materialism. He would have told her that the 6400 Persian dead at Marathon, versus only 192 lost on the Greek side, was reminiscent of the battles of the Hebrews at Jericho and Abraham at Dan. He would have told her that such things do not happen without supernatural intervention. After numerous victories in the Aegean region, and the taking of whole cities of Greek slaves, the Persians had seemed invincible. God had a way of laughing last, Abihail would have told her. The old man had died shortly after coming to Susa, however. So now there was no one to teach Hadassah the deepest things of Judaism.

But the fact that Mordecai was weak on religious training was no indication of his feelings toward the child. The tiny girl had filled a spot in the stubborn bachelor's heart which he had not known was vacant. With the passing months, as he had seen her take her first steps and learn her first words, his affections had expanded.

Along with this came a distinct antipathy toward Haman, the man whose underlings had orphaned the child. When, as Abihail had predicted, nothing was done by the palace police to bring justice against the young men, Mordecai had found himself increasingly doubtful of Persian policy toward the Jews, and especially skeptical of the grand vizier. Though generations ago King Cyrus had emancipated the Hebrew people, it seemed that justice was still elusive.

Nonetheless, Mordecai rarely considered Abihail's adamant assertions concerning the "sons of Agag." The old man's view of history and nations was too ludicrous to be taken seriously.

The only heritage of value given him by his uncle was the curly-haired child who clutched now at his robe. In her tiny dimpled fist she held forth a long-stemmed lily, offering it to Mordecai.

"A scepter befitting a queen," he said with a grin, as he reached down for her and lofted her to his shoulder. Pointing to the bedraggled spearmen who marched past the gate, he teased, "Poor, poor warriors. Perhaps if you had touched them with your wand, Hadassah, they would have come home victors."

* * *

King Darius longed to revenge the rebuff at Marathon. He longed to annex Greece. His most restless neighbors would have made his most useful subjects. But the king whose empire had spread as far as possible to the east, north, and south would not live to recoup his Western losses.

Five years after the defeat in the Aegean, Darius was dead. Whether he was a good or an evil man would remain forever open to debate. As for Xerxes, he would do well to emulate his father in many things. And from the start, as he watched the funeral procession of the fallen monarch, he determined to do so.

The 27-year-old prince rode this evening in a golden carriage behind the black-shrouded wagon which bore his father's corpse into the Zagros Mountains. Far behind lay the glow of Susa, coral in the setting winter sun. Beside him sat his wife, her hand resting lightly upon his knee.

Before Darius' body would be interred in the ancestral tombs at Persepolis, his spirit would be committed to Ahura-Mazda, god of the sky.

It had to be said of Darius that, though he was devoted to this one deity, he gave amazing latitude to the other religions of his diverse subjects. Imitating Cyrus, he even saw to it that the temples and worship of all gods were subsidized by the state.

But when it came to his private devotions, the god embraced by Zoroaster, famed and obscure prophet of the Zagros, was his sole focus. His religion did not call for much art or architecture. No soaring temples lifted the minds of the faithful to the deity. Sufficient were small fire altars atop lofty peaks in the untamed wilderness of Persia's barbaric ancestors.

Through the dusk Xerxes and Vashti could see the curl of gray smoke ascending from one such pyre lit at the crest of the jagged, snow-covered horizon. The flash of burning coals was visible, and behind the pale light, which intruded even at this distance into the darkness, they could make out the silhouettes of the magi, men of the priestly caste, who would offer up Darius' soul.

Certain elements of Persia's religion lingered from the time before Zoroaster's teachings, from the time of the Aryans, ancient animists who had once inhabited the hinterland. Though Zoroaster had recognized no nature worship, some customs died hard.

In keeping with those old traditions, therefore, Darius' body would be exposed to the mountain frost until sunrise, while the magi spread the flesh of a small sacrifice upon a carpet of herbs and burned it to the chant of a theogony.

Already the haunting drone of the hymn was borne on the cool wind descending from the peak. Xerxes felt a chill cross his shoulders, but would not admit to his wife that he found the priests and their rituals an eerie combination.

The shadow of a hawk crossed the icy moon directly above the prince's path as the carriage driver urged the horses higher. A good omen or bad? he wondered. The priests, who studied such matters, would have known, for they saw omens in everything.

Xerxes lifted his regal face to the mountain. Pale silver light illumined his noble features and played against his crimped beard like the hoarfrost of venerable age. He was, in fact, feeling far older than 27 tonight. The knowledge that tomorrow he would receive the imperial crown was a weighty burden. Perhaps with daylight he would feel the joy of power and prestige unequaled in the world. But tonight, grief and responsibility pressed him down.

Cradling Vashti's small hand in his own, he glanced down at her supple fingers, the warmth of her touch strangely saddening him. Dependent she was, as a bird. His most prized possession, though he possessed all things.

As the refrain of the priestly chorus reached them, tears rose to his eyes.

"Ahura-Mazda, who upholds the earth and the firmament," it rang, "who causes the moon to wax and wane, who yokes swiftness to wind and cloud, who creates light and dark, sleeping and waking, morning, noon, and night . . ."

If there were a god in heaven, a father-god, he would surely fit this description, Xerxes believed. But tonight he knew only emptiness. On the eve of his coronation he felt inadequate to his calling.

At last the little processional reached the zenith of the hill. With careful hands the priests pulled back the dark shroud which concealed Darius' prone form, and then, in memory of the days when a corpse would have been left for the dogs and vultures, they ceremonially tore his neckline.

Xerxes stared into the air above his father's frigid body, almost hoping to see the spirit thus released. Such thoughts he kept to himself, shamed by their childishness.

But when the chant began again, and when the flames of the sacrifice leapt renewed into the coolness, his throat was tight.

"Ahura-Mazda," the chorus swelled, "who created this earth, who created yonder heaven, who created man, who created welfare for man . . ."

Scarcely could he bear to hear more. Though it was not dignified to do so, he clung to Vashti's hand and lifted it to his lips. The nearness of her at this needy moment, the availability of her love, filled him with hope.

Perhaps he could be what he must be.

The priests and the entourage of courtiers were fixed on the spectacle of ritual and invocation. They would not see if the prince were to hold her close.

Pressing her head to his breast, he touched his lips to her soft dark hair.

"Precious," he whispered. "My most precious possession."

PART II
Pride Before a Fall

6

"A tax farmer!" Mordecai bellowed. "I have heard it with my own ears. Haman is a tax farmer!"

Leah stood over the pan of dirty cups and utensils, cleaning up after yet another meal. Her children, all teenagers or nearly so, had accomplished their afternoon chores and had taken off for various parts of the village. She, looking forward to an evening of adult conversation, listened eagerly to Mordecai's palace gossip.

Her brother, within the first two years of the new administration, had risen from merchant's stockkeeper to executive of inventory in the royal house. She had always been proud of Mordecai, but never more than now.

"So how did you learn this?" she marveled. "Do you have access to Haman's books?"

"Not directly," he explained. "But there are few secrets among the management. Haman weaseled his way into Darius' graces years ago by buying up provincial concessions."

"He is a tax collector, then," she sneered.

"More than that. A tax *farmer* actually pays an annual lump sum for the right to bleed the public. He does not just earn a commission. He pays such a high rate for the privilege that he is allowed to keep the entire collection! Can you imagine the returns? Enormous!"

Mordecai slapped his thighs and threw his head back. "Tens of thousands of talents!" he sighed.

Leah shook her head. "Then our tax monies, given by the sweat of our brows, do not even go to the royal treasuries?"

"Oh, be assured, the king makes a haul off the bidders. He does not sell the concessions for a song. With several sharing the rights to each province, he makes as much as or more than the taxes would bring in. And the competition between the concessionaires . . ." Here he pounded a fist into his open palm. "They would kill to beat one another out."

Leah pulled the wet dishes from the suds and rinsed them in another bucket. "Folk have been known to murder for less."

Mordecai knew she referred to the wanton violence directed against Abihail. Rising from the low stool in her kitchen, he walked to the little window which looked across the fields east of the village. The snow-capped Zagros Mountains loomed majestic and protective above the sweeping valley.

Mordecai loved Persia, but often, as Hadassah had grown, he had found his mind turning to the teachings of his uncle, especially to his tales of Israel, passed down from his own father and his before him.

He wondered if Israel were as beautiful as the land of his birth. And he wondered if he had missed out on something wonderful by passing off his heritage so lightly.

In the flowered field beyond the low town gate, village children played. Hadassah, now ten years old, ran with the smallest as they mimicked the adult game of goat-drag, riding sticks like horses and hauling a stuffed burlap bag from stake to stake on a miniature playing field. Never was the girl happier than when she visited her second cousins, the energetic offspring of Mordecai's sister.

As the accountant watched her run through the ankle-high grass, her slender legs kicking up dust and her long raven curls bouncing, he knew he would do best by the child to afford her more exposure to the Jewish community.

"She is nearly a young lady . . ." he mused.

Leah, surprised by the new topic, glanced with him out the window. "You are only now noticing?" she teased. "Look over there," she pointed, indicating her 15-year-old firstborn son, who leaned against the gate cavalierly. "David has certainly noticed already."

Mordecai nodded, a smile working at this lips. "I would like to bring her here more often," he requested.

"Of course!" Leah offered. "You know we all enjoy her!"

"Then it is settled," the brother determined. "It would be good for all of us to keep closer ties. I would like her to visit at least twice a month. She would be no trouble. I will pay you . . ."

"Nonsense!" Leah protested. "*Pay*, for *family*? I won't hear of it. And, of course she is obedient! Docile as a doe!"

Turning for her dishpan again, she bustled to finish her work before sunset, shaking her head and muttering exasperation about brothers and about men in general.

* * *

Indeed David, the eldest of Leah's children, *had* noticed Hadassah. She had always been a comely child, and now, as she approached young womanhood, her charms were of another sort.

Sitting cross-legged on the ground, his back against the gatepost, he watched her keenly as she sported with the younger children of the neighborhood. Mordecai had never allowed her to wear her hair twisted and fettered, as so many of the haughty girls of Susa wore theirs. For this David was never more grateful than at this moment as it swung free in the breeze, glancing against her rosy cheeks and caressing her back with brown-black waves. Where the descending sun caught it, auburn-to-red tones revealed themselves amid the curls tumbling about her shoulders.

Nor had Mordecai ever allowed Hadassah's hair to be cut. Though it was trimmed fashionably about the face, it flowed to her midback and bore no ribbons or pins.

Pale lavender gowns were unusual in the small hamlet where David had been raised. The fact that Hadassah's simple dress was out of this hue, and was girded with a fine linen rope, marked her as one of Susa's upper middle class. Whenever she came to visit the village, younger children stood in awe of her as much for this fact as for her unusual beauty.

Always their star-struck gazes mellowed to open smiles, however, when the gentle girl took them by the hands and began to play with them.

Just now, as the stuffed burlap bag (the pretend goat) was carried by an opponent toward the enemy's goal, she raced after the rider, not as quickly as she might, but fast enough to give him a challenge. From behind came another opponent on chubby legs, grasping for her to take her to the ground.

He succeeded only in snapping the belt about her slender waist, breaking the clasp on her fine-carved alabaster buckle.

Squealing, Hadassah wheeled about and confronted the challenger, feigning more offense than she felt.

As she bent over to pick up the broken treasure, David leapt to his feet and ran to her. "Let me see," he offered, touching her lightly on the arm. When she rose to find her cousin brooding over her, a blush rose to her cheeks.

Handing the buckle to him, she said nothing. As he turned the ornament over and over in his hands, she was struck by the glints of gold within his azure eyes.

"This is a very fine piece," he marveled.

"Papa gave it to me," she said, finding her voice.

David nodded. "It must be a pleasure to give you fine things," he said.

Hadassah was not too young to detect the admiration in his tone. But not being trained in worldly ways, she did not know how to respond.

"It is a Greek design, is it not?" David observed, still contemplating the jewel.

"I believe so," Hadassah replied, surprised at his apparent knowledge of such things, and not really certain herself of the artistic origins.

"We have Greek blood in our veins as well as Jewish," he went on. "Did you know this?"

Hadassah recalled Mordecai's allusions to the family's mixed roots. "Such a thing is not unusual," she replied.

"No," David agreed.

But when Hadassah saw that he was proud of the fact, she quickly added, "Of course, you have acquired the look as well as the blood."

The young man straightened his shoulders and lifted his strong chin. He had hoped she noticed, and that she approved. Blond hair and blue eyes were rare in Persia, and had won him the admiration of many village girls.

"I think I can fix this for you," he asserted. "I am an artist in my own right, though I shall likely always be a farmer."

Hadassah was touched by his youthful frustration. "Papa left the village to work in Susa," she reminded him. "Aunt Leah says you are gifted with carving and painting. Perhaps . . ."

"No," David said again. "I am needed too much here."

The girl looked at the brothers and sisters who had congregated at David's back. They had come out from the house to call the two cousins home.

Darkness was descending quickly now, as it always did in the desert. As the family walked toward Leah's warmly lit house, Hadassah knew that David spoke the truth. His parents would require his assistance for a long time. He might never be able to pursue a career beyond the village gate.

Though she was very young, Hadassah felt a peculiar stirring in her as she followed David's manly lead back to the cottage. It was not the first time she had felt it. She had not failed to notice his ruddy strength and field-hardened physique. His golden hair and eyes only added to his appeal.

He still held the buckle in his artistic fingers. She watched him study it as they walked. No words passed between them, but Hadassah stayed close to his elbow.

7

In following Darius' love of Ahura-Mazda and his prophet, Zoroaster, Xerxes had departed from his father's ways in one unusual respect: He had chosen to have no harem, but to honor a monogamous relationship with his beloved wife, Vashti.

Zoroaster had taught that the highest good was symbolized between humans in faithful love for one's spouse. Where Persian kings turned from this injunction, they deviated from the noblest path.

As soon as Xerxes had taken the throne, he set about to send the women away, seeing to it that they were endowed with gifts of precious metal, fabrics, and spices so that they might have means of support. He could do nothing about the fact that many of them, no matter how lovely they might be, would never find a husband. Virginity was highly prized in a bride, something none of them could claim. And to have lived under the same roof as the king, though supposedly an honor, had marked them as "soiled" women.

Harem girls, once turned away, would not even qualify as widows, but would be considered "scorned" women, rendering them even less valuable.

Still, Xerxes could not help this. It was better to remove them, he reasoned, than to maintain secondary wives against the teachings of his faith.

Hadassah had been allowed this morning to enter the outer rim of buildings in the palace area. Mordecai was in charge of an inventory tour through the storehouses of the acropolis, and he had brought his adopted daughter with him for the day, leaving her to enjoy the sights as he escorted his young accountants about their assignments.

Never had the girl been privileged to see the inner workings of the royal compounds. Of course, nothing private to the king's family transpired in the utilitarian courts enclosing the monarch's private palace. Nonetheless, it was an honor for her to be here.

Mordecai was presently inspecting the second floor of the royal warehouse where the king kept his most prized gold pieces. Resting in cases of velvet were tiny trinkets shaped like striding lions, miniature bulls, and birds of prey. Each was worth more than its weight in artistic beauty alone. Thousands upon thousands of delicate chains, bracelets, rings, and earrings sat unused in cedar boxes, the containers themselves worth a fortune.

Once a year the inventory must be recounted, valued, and polished. This was not the rule of a miser, but rather the wisdom of a long line of Persian kings who, despite their wealth, kept careful books. For the managers of the coffers, the day the accountants came around was a tense time. If any treasure was missing, even the slightest piece, it could mean their lives.

Of course, Hadassah was not privy to her uncle's work. She had been permitted to ascend to the second story, but had been left outside the labyrinth of doors barring strangers from the treasury rooms.

The glory of even the limited area she observed, however, was enough to occupy her for hours. The shiny marble balcony, wide enough for two chariots, and the intricate carvings of the turquoise-inlaid mezzanine filled her with wonder. A small garden below, leading to the outer gate of the compound, dazzled her with poppies, irises, flamingos, and fountains. Were she never to see another inch of the acropolis, her memory would be entertained for a lifetime.

When the sound of soft voices caught her attention, she stood poised at the rail, marveling at beauty even more splendid than the surroundings. Half-a-dozen women had entered the little gateway garden. In flowing silken gowns they passed beneath Hadassah's gaze, slender as flower stalks. The girl had seen lovely ladies in Susa's streets, but none so glamorous as these. Soft hair of various hues framed faces that no artist could have conceived. Yet great art was evident in arched eyebrows, blushed cheeks, and red lips. Paint accentuated eyes already large by nature, shading and highlighting flawless complexions.

While each lady had individual charm, they were more alike than not. Hadassah was not too young to realize that these must be women of the king's harem, all selected to suit the taste of one man.

Long of limb and graceful as willows, most of them were quite tall. In carriage and in form they could have passed for sisters, though their skin tones told that they were of different nationalities. The young girl did not know much about the world, but she had heard of Babylon and Africa and India, and figured that these women represented such farflung places.

Captivated, she observed them with the same fascination that the village children exhibited whenever she herself graced their humble town.

But, while she would have expected great happiness to accompany such beauty, these ladies appeared anything but cheerful.

Tears smudged charcoaled eyes and heavy sorrow contorted winsome lips. A few of the women had locked arms, as though for support, and muffled weeping rose from the group.

As the klatch of women crossed the garden, drawing near the door to the outer world, several began to wail miserably. On the instant, a stern-looking character entered behind them.

"Such clatter will not be tolerated!" he growled, his bald head flushed crimson from ear to ear. It seemed he would strike at them, and Hadassah knew he could send them all sprawling with a blow, for he was a big, meaty man, his bare biceps sporting bracelets which would fit a harem girl's waist.

Falling against each other, the ladies cried out and then stifled themselves.

Suddenly the sound of quick footsteps approaching from the corridor halted the bully. The women dried their eyes, falling to their knees, just as he did.

The footsteps heralded the approach of another woman, who stood now in the doorway. Hadassah, peering down between the banister posts, could not have imagined anyone more beautiful than the girls who huddled together. Yet the newcomer to whom they made obeisance was even more ravishing.

"Your Majesty . . ." the hulking fellow cried, "live forever!"

The young spectator deduced immediately that it was the Queen of Persia who stood beneath her gaze. And her small-girl heart tripped with awe.

All her life she had heard of Vashti. She had heard of her great beauty, but she had never dreamed she would one day see it for herself.

It was not Vashti's clothing, nor the style of her hair, nor the flair of her cosmetics which set her apart. Rather, it was her bearing, her noble demeanor, her look of certainty, which elevated her.

Ignoring the fawning man at her feet, she hastened to the cowering women, whose tears for now were fearfully contained.

"Stand, sisters," she commanded.

The ladies, confounded, did so. Then the queen glared at their keeper, who had not dared to look up from the floor.

"Angus!" she confronted him. "Have I not spoken with you about your handling of the harem? You shall treat these women with the same respect they merited when Darius was their lord."

Since the behemoth was being addressed, he knew he must rise and face the queen. How to account for himself he knew not. Vashti realized that any vulnerable female was a temptation to his cruel nature. But he had been raised to his position, keeper of the concubines, by Darius. And, while this station would terminate as soon as the women were removed, only Xerxes, and not Vashti, could send him from the palace.

Nonetheless, he must treat the queen with respect or else lose his head, if not further employment.

"Your Majesty, the women are contrary," he lied. "They require a firm hand."

At this the ladies, who had done nothing amiss, turned defensive eyes to the queen.

"I think they have done no wrong," Vashti interposed. "See that *you* do nothing but your proper job."

Then, clapping her hands, she went toward the hall door and summoned a small train of servants.

Once again the girl on the balcony had reason to marvel as a cohort of slaves entered the garden, each bearing a trayload of luxuries.

Flasks of jasmine, gold necklaces, cakes of myrrh and aloe, sachets of spices, and jeweled bracelets were piled upon broad silver dishes. Hadassah did not know much about the worth of such finery, but she was sure Mordecai would value it at a very great price.

The women, awestruck as each was handed her own trayful of treasure, reacted as though the offerings were worth a lifetime of acquisition.

Trembling, some of them refused the gifts, scarcely believing the queen could mean such generosity. But at last, as Vashti implored them, they conceded, tears dripping down their faces.

"These should stand you in good stead until you can establish yourselves," she explained.

Establish themselves? Hadassah thought. *They should never have to lift a finger the rest of their lives!*

"Though the king has foregone more than one wife," the queen went on, "he would not send you forth into poverty."

"But, Your Highness," one of the girls objected, "these are from your *own* storehouse! They are not a man's treasures."

"Hush, Darla," another softly warned. "You have not been addressed."

But the queen took no notice. Clapping again, she sent the servants away.

"Take them forth now, Angus," Vashti commanded. "See that they all find lodging, and see to it that their treasures are put in safe keeping."

By this she referred to the fact that the poor women, unlearned in matters of investment, might abuse their endowments or, even worse, lose them to thieves within hours of leaving the grounds.

"I am your servant, Majesty," Angus replied, bowing as he led the ladies through the outer door.

Hadassah sat very still upon the balcony. The beauty of the women and the glory of the gifts had riveted her so that she could not pull away.

When Vashti had sent the slaves back down the hall she stood alone for a long moment, looking toward the door where the ladies had departed. Tears glimmered along her lashes, and the girl on the balcony held her breath, deeply moved by the queen's compassion.

What drew Vashti's gaze upward, toward the mezzanine, she would never know. But suddenly the sad eyes were upon Hadassah. The girl trembled, not knowing what punishment her eavesdropping might deserve.

Soon enough it was apparent, however, that the queen would dismiss the child's indiscretion. In her expression was only bemused surprise, as though she wondered how the young girl had come to be spying.

And then the expression turned to wonder. But Hadassah could not interpret this, for she did not fully appreciate her own charms.

Vashti did. The queen knew what loveliness was, seeing it every day about the courts and possessing it herself. The queen knew that, had this child been older, and a member of the harem, the king would have found it very hard to disown her.

8

Vashti observed the banquet preparations with mixed emotions. For a full three years Xerxes had been obsessed with plans to invade Greece. Once he had taken the throne, set his administration in order, and sent the harem away, he had turned his mind to the West with a vengeance that frightened his queen.

Now he was about to launch his expansionism, and to celebrate he had sent invitations to the 127 provinces under his rule, calling for the chief leaders and noblemen from throughout his empire to attend a six-month party in Susa.

Already thousands were arriving for the festivities, which would begin in a few days. 40,000 anticipated visitors would stay for varying lengths of time, arriving and departing throughout the festival.

Of course, the event would be honored by the entire city, as hostels and homes were opened to accommodate the influx. Local merchants rallied to prepare for the boost that such an event would be for the economy. People worked day and night to produce wares for purchase by the incoming tourists. From shoe merchants to jewelers, from bakers to perfumers, all made ready.

As for the palace itself, the inner court, or pavilion, would be the scene of the king's banquet. This open, colonnaded garden could be intensely hot in summer, but Xerxes planned to station a hundred slaves about the garden's numerous fountains, where they would fan the guests with imported ostrich plumes day and night.

Vashti stood upon the upper deck of the court, gazing across the sumptuous arboretum. Servants scurried amid flowering bushes and trees, arranging furniture and spreading pristine linens upon the tables. The colors decorating the extravaganza were of cool hues: Curtains of white, green, and blue were fastened to silver rings upon the marble pillars and were bound together by cords of royal violet. Chaises in the same fabrics were placed along the tables, their gold and silver frames resting upon decks of purple, blue, white, and gleaming black marble.

Xerxes had recently squelched insurrections in Egypt and Babylon. He had inflicted harsh penalties upon those states, leveling the Babylonian temple and melting to bullion their 1800-pound statue to Marduk.

These successes had piqued his appetite for further conquest, drawing his energies toward the West.

His wife, chief treasure of his heart, received less and less of his time as he pursued his dreams. It had begun in small things—tardiness to a rendezvous, the overlooking of an anniversary. Now their stolen moments were fewer and fewer, his attention span more fleeting.

Vashti had just come from the women's court, where her own banquet was being prepared. Only women of the palace, wives and daughters of the invited noblemen, would be attending her feast, which would likewise last for days. But it would be a tame, ladylike affair, unlike the boisterous and ribald merrymaking which would dominate the king's strictly male festivities.

As the headwaiter emerged from the palace's enormous pantry, leading a bevy of slaves, Vashti grew uneasy. Each slave hauled a small wheeled cart, piled high with gold drinking horns, every one of a different configuration, from winged griffins to strutting bears. This would be a drinking orgy unlike any held here before. And she hesitated to think of the excesses it would inspire.

Her husband had been busy all day with the governor of the feast, looking into the man's plans and adding to them. Vashti had not expected to see him this afternoon, and when he entered the court, across the way, she thought he might at last have a moment for her.

But it was not to be.

"Leave room along here," he was saying as the governor followed behind him. "Move in this row of tables so that my treasures may be paraded."

"Just so, Your Majesty," the governor agreed, clapping his hands and sending servants to reposition the furniture.

"The finest riches of the warehouse shall be brought forth for display, borne aloft upon silver trays or hauled in gilded barrows," Xerxes continued, his voice trailing down the hall.

Could he mean it? Vashti marveled, wondering at his compulsive pride. Such an exhibition could take weeks!

Once, she recalled, she had been considered his most precious possession. But today he had not even seen her standing alone, waiting for him.

Sadly she turned for her chamber, fearing another night without him.

9

Lights danced in the court of King Xerxes, potted candles on bobbing trays borne high on the shoulders of slaves, who dipped to serve as they wove between tables and couches.

It was the last week of Xerxes' feast, the evening of the seventh day. At least a thousand men had been served in the garden since morning, congregating in shifts to celebrate the culmination of half a year of merrymaking.

This was the final spate of excess, capping the previous six months of orgiastic feasting and drinking which had entertained notables from about the empire. And this week was reserved for the king's own, those who served his personal and state needs, from janitors to cabinet officials, in the palace itself.

As the candles spun a hypnotic web about the guests, the music of pipes and lutes and timbrels evoked enchanting delirium.

Of course, so did the wine. By pitchers and casks and buckets it flowed—into the golden chalices shaped in many shapes, down the mouths and throats of ten hundred laughing men.

"To Xerxes!" the toast rang, followed by clanking rims of tankard on tankard. "To Persia!" "To Mardonius!" "To Otanes!" "To War!" chased by clinks and gulps and cheers.

Jokes flowed too, and dares and taunts and jibes. From time to time, females imported from about the king's immense realm danced and teased and cavorted. They were not women of the palace, the king having removed his harem, and the ladies who now graced the ground of Vashti's banquet, wives and daughters of palace officials, would have been offended at such an invitation.

The fleshy bouquet of scantily clad dancers greeted an increasingly lusty crowd each time they were summoned, their presence stirring the room to ever-higher pitches of demand and appreciation.

Between the pageantry of the women appeared precisioned jugglers, hilarious clowns, and dexterous acrobats for the audience's pleasure. All the while, as the wine flowed and the delicacies of the king's kitchen were gorged upon, the treasures of the monarch were paraded in the background—furs never worn, cutlery and weaponry never brandished, diamonds and jewels never sported, fabulous works of art, and rare birds and animals from every corner of the empire.

For half a year these valuables had been displayed through the court, and now as the party was winding down, the king, besotted, gazed upon the end of their procession with heavy-lidded eyes.

He was deliciously relaxed as he lay back upon his chaise, high upon the uppermost deck of the court. But his closest valets, who knew him best, could see that he grew restless.

His plans to go against the West, hinted at numerous times in the previous six months, had finally been heralded privately before his own palace cohorts. Now he seemed anxious for action.

As clearly as he could think in his drunken condition, he tried to imagine some very spectacular way to climax this final evening of the most elaborate celebration which the world had ever seen.

His valets, middle-aged eunuchs with smooth faces and boyish voices, congregated at his back, sensing his regal agitation.

As the monarch rose upon one elbow, resting his pensive face upon his fist, he gestured for Mehuman, his chief valet, and the gaunt fellow hastened forward, bowing to the ground.

Xerxes, scarcely looking at him, stroked his head and patted him upon the cheek. "These are all my very best friends," he slurred, tears in his royal eyes as he scanned the loud revelers below.

"Yes, Your Majesty," Mehuman agreed.

"I have done so little for them," the king remorsed, weaving a bit upon his bed.

"But, sir," Mehuman objected, "you have reserved the finest for these folk. This week has been the highlight of the year."

"No, no," Xerxes insisted, flicking a long hand in the eunuch's peach-clean face. "They deserve more—something I have done for no one else, and shall never do again."

By now the other valets, nervous over the king's unhappiness, had gathered behind Mehuman. Biztha, Harbona, Bigtha, Abagtha, Zethar, and Carkas pressed close to the chief eunuch's bowed form, and each in turn received a stroke upon his bent head from the unusually affectionate emperor.

"What can we do for His Majesty?" they inquired, seeing that he was determined to have something.

"His Majesty desires to grace these revelers with some extraordinary benevolence," Mehuman explained. "He has shown them his treasures and bestowed upon them royal gifts, the finest wines and rarest delicacies from his larder. Yet he wishes to do more."

"Such is the nature of His Majesty's generous spirit," Harbona purred.

"Most Benevolent Lord," Zethar offered, "perhaps a tour of your grounds . . ."

"They have all seen the grounds!" Mehuman quickly corrected, seeing Xerxes' furrowed brow.

"Rings for their fingers," Carkas suggested.

"He has given fine jewelry to them all!" Mehuman replied, gesturing to a thousand braceleted arms and necklaced breasts.

In a huddle, the valets continued to confer but came up with nothing. At last Mehuman, frustrated, shrugged and said, "Your Highness, we can imagine nothing which you have not already given. You have bestowed food for their lips, wine for their hearts, song for their ears, women for their eyes . . ."

At this Xerxes lurched forward, his crimped beard quivering as his head shook. "No, no!" he cried. "I have been selfish! There is yet one thing I have withheld from my friends, from those who would give their life's blood for me!"

The king exaggerated, not about his generosity but about the loyalty of his companions. However, Mehuman dared not challenge his wine-dazzled estimation.

"All the women in the world would not be enough to honor my dearest allies," Xerxes enthused. "Had I given them my harem, it would not have been sufficient!"

Xerxes rode high on the excitement of six months, on the daring of future campaigns and on the praise of his plans for expansion. He soared on wings of wine and the sound of laughter swelling up from the court.

His multitude of comrades did not attend to him just now, for they were busy with the licentious freedom of the seven-day fling. Never would they or his valets dream that he was about to break one of the most stubborn taboos of his ancestors for their sake.

"Only one woman can do justice to the king's desire. Only Vashti herself, my chief treasure, is good enough for such friends!" Xerxes declared.

Mehuman drew a sharp breath.

"You cannot mean . . ."

"Bring her forth!" Xerxes commanded.

Suddenly a pall of silence overtook the eunuchs. The guests below, ignorant of the proposition, went on with their hilarity unimpeded. But the valets were appalled.

"Your Highness," Harbona dared to remind him, "it is the law that no man apart from the emperor himself is to look upon the queen."

Yes—this was the law. It was impossible that she would be spared the gazes of all men whatsoever, exposed as she was to life in the palace, but the spirit of the injunction applied against men looking upon her to lust after her.

Still, Xerxes darted a threatening glance at the disapproving Harbona.

"Am I a child, that my eunuchs are my counselors?" the emperor snarled. "I said, 'Bring her forth!' "

"Your Majesty, how shall we summon her? What shall we say?" Mehuman hedged.

"Say, 'Your husband desires your presence in the garden!' " Xerxes replied, his tone tinged with sarcasm. "What do you suppose you should say?"

"Do you simply wish for her to appear? And nothing more?" the valet hoped.

Xerxes, reading his apprehension, grew impatient. "What evil do you imagine of me?" he said with a glare. "Tell the queen to place the royal crown upon her head, so that all the men may gaze upon her beauty! She is a very beautiful woman!"

Mehuman bowed, agreeing utterly with his assessment, but still uneasy over the results of such an appearance before this disorderly mob.

"If you feel this is wisdom . . ."

"Are you questioning my sagacity or my sobriety?" Xerxes smirked, leaning cavalierly upon his pillow. "Go now!"

Mehuman glanced at his fellow eunuchs, his face full of doubt.

But, failing to dissuade the king, and knowing that he dare not try again, he bowed and left the chamber.

The other six eunuchs did likewise; following their master, they scrambled for the hall.

"Can he mean it?" Abagtha marveled.

"He means it," Mehuman sighed. "And we shall comply, though I fear going before the queen with this request more than I fear defying the king."

10

With nearly as much expense and finery, Vashti had entertained the ladies of the kingdom since the beginning of the year. This final week, she, like her husband, designated the celebration for the palace workers as well as for the wives, daughters, sisters, mothers, and grandmothers of the men who reveled in Xerxes' court.

But her banquet and her festivities were of a different sort than the wild abandon which characterized the men's party.

The ladies feasted on the daintiest of foods, the rarest of wines. But the temperament of the women's garden was marked with ladylike restraint.

The displays which the queen paraded for their viewing pleasure were not calculated to inflate their estimation of her own glory or wealth. She had scheduled dancers and musicians as well as jugglers and clowns and acrobats, just as had Xerxes, but their acts did not appeal to prurient interests and the occasional fashion show which edged the court was not a display of the queen's own garments and jewels but had been put together by experts who wished to show the latest in womanly attire for the interest and entertainment of the guests.

None of what Vashti presented was intended to arouse jealousy or to pique her own pride.

Nor would her guests dream of humiliating this sovereign lady by drinking to excess or by gormandizing on the delicacies she provided. Often she encouraged them to display their own talents, inviting this one to sing for the group or that one to tell a fetching story.

All in all, the scene in Vashti's court was a far cry in color and demeanor from that promulgated by her husband.

And the queen enjoyed it immensely. If any heavy thought tinged her pleasure, it was the realization that Xerxes had changed, the knowledge that what went on in his pavilion would have embarrassed herself and her guests had they been privy to it.

Just now she strolled with several of her companions along an arbor path, the scent of hyacinths and roses making a heady climax to a satisfying evening. Several hundred women lounged around the fountains of her retreat, listening to the entrancing notes of a flute and observing the fluid movements of a young dancer decked in trailing scarves. Surges of soft applause brought a smile to Vashti's lips as she conversed amiably with her closest friends, wives of prominent noblemen, daughters of the seven highest houses in the land, and sisters of her childhood.

When a slave came running, announcing the appearance at the garden door of Xerxes' eunuchs, Vashti was not a little surprised.

"They say they have a request for you, from His Highness, your husband," the messenger explained.

The queen's face lit with enthusiasm. It must be, she reasoned, that Xerxes wished to meet her after his grand celebration for a private rendezvous.

When she went to the door to receive the eunuchs, therefore, she was troubled to see their uneasy countenances.

"Your Majesty, live forever!" Mehuman cried, falling on his face before Vashti. The other valets, likewise bowed themselves to the floor, and when the queen asked them to rise, Mehuman's face was red.

"Queen Vashti," he stammered, "Our Lord Xerxes wishes us to convey an invitation . . ."

"Yes?" the woman spurred him.

"He wishes you to come before him . . ."

Aha, she had supposed right! He wished to have her private company this night.

". . . with the royal crown upon your head . . ."

The queen studied Mehuman in amazement. She never wore the heavy ornament except to make public appearances.

"Go on," she whispered.

". . . so that he might show you to his companions."

Vashti, scarcely believing her ears, surveyed the man with contempt.

"Say again," she commanded.

Mehuman summoned as much diplomacy as he could muster, and cleared his throat. "He wishes to bestow upon his friends the gift of your beauty, My Queen. He would have you appear before his servants and noblemen, that they may . . . gaze upon you."

The eunuch sighed. Try as he might, there was no graceful way to dispense with this duty. And when the royal lady evinced incredulity, her poise a poor covering for utter horror, he looked away shamefaced.

At this pronouncement Vashti's lady friends began to mutter among themselves, and quickly their astonishment caught the attention of others in the court, until the entire company of guests grew apprehensive.

The music ceased, the dancer stopped in her steps, and silence descended.

No queen of Persia had ever been placed in such a predicament. No matter how Vashti responded, her integrity was at stake.

It was beyond comprehension that a royal spouse would ever defy a king. Yet it was also inconceivable that a regal lady should expose herself to a crowd of drunken, leering males, be they friends of her husband or gutter vagabonds.

A queen was expected to be the epitome of wifely duty and purity. What she chose to do spoke to all women of the realm, and were she to disobey her lord and master, her actions could easily be misconstrued as condoning the undermining of male authority everywhere.

Indeed, Vashti was in a most uncomfortable and irresolvable dilemma.

The silence burned her ears as the scrutinizing gaze of a thousand eyes seared her back.

As she looked upon the man with the bowed head, time seemed to stand still. Her next words could mean life or death to her. Were she to actually refuse the king's invitation, she could lose everything.

Memories of Xerxes' coolness toward her, of his unthinking rejections over recent months, still haunted her. And she had no way of knowing just how cruel he might be if she were to resist his summons.

Yet it was a certainty that an appearance before the inebriated mob in his court would forever mar her own selfhood, stripping her of a dignity even more precious than Xerxes' esteem.

"Tell the king I shall *not* appear," she replied.

A rush of whispers and a rattle of shaking heads and conferring voices followed her words.

Some denied that she had said what she did. Others insisted that she had.

Mehuman himself, who had heard the words directly, trembled with wonder.

"Your Majesty?" he marveled.

"Tell the king I shall *not* appear," Vashti repeated.

Indeed, she *had* chosen disobedience! Like a flurry of chortling doves, a chorus of awe-filled commentary rose through the roofless air.

Gathering her silken robes in calm hands, Vashti departed the garden, her head held high, her back straight as an upright spear.

11

"She what?" Xerxes growled, leaping from his couch of pleasure and glowering at Mehuman.

Despite the loud partying which went on in the court below, guests turned in surprise at this sudden movement on the king's part.

Only the seven eunuchs knew the reason for his volcanic reaction. Only Mehuman and his cohorts knew of the ludicrous summons sent to Vashti.

"The queen refuses to appear," the chief valet repeated, cringing as though he himself might receive the full force of the king's anger.

Indeed, such a thing was not out of the question.

Messengers had been known to die at the whim of a dissatisfied monarch for bearing less sorry news than this.

Xerxes' fury pushed past his drunken lethargy, pulsating in clenched fists and throbbing temples. Face red, the emperor paced to and fro before his couch until every eye in the room was on him and not a sound of music, laughter, or even of breathing broke the air.

The eunuchs to Mehuman's back stood with bowed heads, cowering together like a pack of desert dogs, fearing that their fate, like Mehuman's, hung in the balance.

Meanwhile, seven other fellows, the king's legal counselors, began to draw near. Thinking that there must be some matter of politics, injustice, or threat against their master, they were eager to assist him.

"Your Majesty," their leader intervened, "what troubles you? May we help in any way?"

Xerxes, too flustered and wine-soaked to readily reply, only continued to pace his porch. At last Mehuman answered for him.

"Our Lord sent a summons to his queen, requesting that she appear at his party . . . so that all of the men might . . . gaze upon her."

Mehuman's own embarrassment was evident, though he tried to conceal it. And the attorney, Memucan, was caught in a hard place.

Not quite as inebriated as the emperor, he instantly understood the queen's reticence to comply. But at the same time he knew he dare not call the king's commandment into question.

Looking awkwardly at his fellow lawyers, he sought some suggestion, but they only shrugged, not wishing to touch the matter.

However, it was too late to withdraw an offer of assistance. And when Xerxes turned to them, his bloodshot eyes full of ire, it was their turn to cringe.

"So what shall we do about this situation?" the emperor demanded. "What penalty does the law provide for a queen who refuses to obey the king's orders, properly sent through his aides?"

Again Memucan looked to his fellow counselors. Did the emperor want an honest answer? In his drunken state, did he have any idea what he was asking?

The drama was now open to a thousand observers. What was decided here today would play heavily upon families throughout the empire. Most important to those present, it would play on the image of the king and the status of men throughout the realm.

Surely, were Xerxes in a more rational condition, matters would not have gone this far. Nevertheless, it was Memucan's responsibility to handle the king's legal affairs. Though this time he was not dealing in matters of criminal justice or interprovincial legislation, he had been asked a direct question. And it concerned issues perhaps equally as great as ones of imperial policy.

Shuffling uneasily, he fumbled for a reply. In truth, there was no specific injunction regarding this dilemma, and no precedent in Persian history, for no queen had ever thus defied her husband.

Naturally, uppermost in the counselors' minds was their own welfare. The advice they framed must appease the king's anger and bring them the best advantage.

Noting his retributive countenance, they knew that no soft action would suffice to save his pride. Vashti could be reprimanded and undergo some loss of privilege, but what if she were to disobey him in the future on some other matter? Surely the attorneys would pay dearly for not recommending a stiffer penalty. Furthermore, they were aware of the careful scrutiny which their advice would receive from other noblemen of the realm. If it were too gentle, it could appear to favor the undermining of men's authority in general.

Therefore, looking to their own futures, it was clear that their decision and their counsel must take a hard line.

They discussed this only briefly among themselves. All of them saw the implications of mercy all too well, and therefore their conference was brief.

While the emperor still paced his deck, wringing his hands and scowling at the courtiers who lined the walls, Memucan addressed his question adroitly.

"Your Majesty, live forever," he said, bowing before Xerxes. "My friends and I have considered the crime and have reached a conclusion."

"Speak!" the monarch bellowed, weary of delay.

"Queen Vashti has wronged not only the king, but every official and citizen of your empire. For women everywhere will begin to disobey their husbands when they learn what Queen Vashti has done."

At this a murmur of agreement arose from the besotted crowd, and so Memucan took courage.

"Before this day is out, the wife of every one of us will hear what the queen did and will begin to deal with her husband in like manner. There will be contempt throughout your realm."

Again a chorus of consensus rang from the court, and Memucan began to swagger with confidence.

"Therefore," he declared, "we suggest that, subject to your agreement, you issue a royal edict, a law of the Medes and Persians that can never be revoked, that Queen Vashti be forever banished from your presence and that you choose another queen more worthy than she! When this decree is published throughout your great kingdom, husbands everywhere, whatever their rank, will be respected by their wives!"

Because Memucan was more aware at this moment of the reaction of the crowd than of the king, he swelled with glory. He did not note the emperor's sudden halt, nor did the twinge of grief which passed over Xerxes' face reach his inflated spirit.

Few, in fact, heeded the monarch's mood, so taken were they with Memucan's daring.

Perhaps the valets, intimately acquainted as they were with their master, thought they read a less-than-enthusiastic expression on his face. But not one of them encouraged a rebuttal, fearing the authority of the counselors.

Of course, Memucan's advice was founded on the most bizarre logic. That every wife in the realm would begin to despise her husband based on Vashti's actions was pure paranoia, and that the crowd could embrace such an assumption was classic evidence of their alcohol-altered mentality.

But then, such was the mood of taverns late at night, the coveys of negligence and excess where men supported one another and where women were warned against. Such was the potential reasoning wherever wayward husbands gathered, and wherever families were scorned by guilt-ridden souls.

All of this might be clear in the light of day, when the haze of alcohol lifted and the clarity of sober thinking descended. But it was not clear now, and *now* was when the decision would be made.

Xerxes, though appalled by the advice, would never admit it under these circumstances. Though he could see its folly, even through besotted eyes, he could not speak against it before a thousand comrades.

He was a man, a man's man, a man of men. To soften now, even for the sake of Vashti, his "most treasured possession," was unthinkable.

As the company in the court looked to him for his reaction to the attorney's counsel, his face was a mask of unwavering strength. Behind it was the soul of a young boy, the one who had once stood with Vashti upon her father's balcony, who had promised always to cherish her, who had reveled in her love and thrilled to her caress. But the mask would win tonight, the love of men's approval, the insecurity which drove him always to conquest.

Hesitating only briefly, he looked at his valets, at the counselors, and at his many assistants. Not one gave argument against Memucan, and each, when pressed, colluded in the deception that he agreed, giving assent with a nod.

"Let it be," Xerxes said, his voice huskier than he wished.

And with this he turned for his private chamber for the comfort of another wine goblet and for the sanctuary of sleep.

12

As morning sun filtered past the heavy blinds of Xerxes' chamber, he rolled over with an ache in his chest. His head throbbed after days and nights of drinking. But the dull pain in his heart was more troubling than the hangover.

At first, as he struggled to sit erect, propping himself against his pillows, he could not recall why he should feel such heaviness. But as wakefulness replaced drugged stupor, recollection pierced him like a physician's scalpel.

"Vashti!" he groaned, staggering from his bed.

He was alone with the dim reality of what he had done the night before. As it settled over him in waves of irrefutable certainty, as the growing illumination that it was no dream, no nightmare, crashed in upon him, the ache in his breast brought tears to his eyes.

Limping to the window, he pulled back the curtain and stared into a high-noon desert. He had slept too long. His commandment would already have been fulfilled, and Vashti would have long ago been shunted from the palace.

Exiles of Persia could be sent to any number of wild and isolated places. In his besotted condition the night before he had made no formal selection of a site for her banishment, and he knew now that her fate had been left to the whim of whoever hauled her away.

"Almighty Ahura-Mazda!" he cried, falling to his knees. The bleak wilderness of the uncharted Zagros haunted him, beckoning with blunted fingers across miles of steamy mirage. "Where is she? Where is my beloved?"

But there was no retracting his judgment. There was no

reversing his command.

The one who had waited for his attentions night after night would wait no longer. For she could never be his again.

PART III

Descent of a Kingdom

13

Hadassah stood outside the village gate, gazing across the swaying grainfields. It neared sunset, and she knew that her cousin David would soon be returning from his daylong labor of scything ripe barley into sheaf-ready piles. She would wait here in the harvest gloaming, enveloped in twilight until he returned.

The sickles of a hundred workers had raised a fine dust through the evening air. The sun's setting was therefore a crimson blush, billows of coral clouds reflecting the same color that sailors see when they watch the golden orb descend through a veil of fog.

But there was no sea here—only endless miles of hot earth, fertile in the Zagros valley, but nevertheless a desert.

As Hadassah watched the returning laborers, their sweat-streaked bodies glistening in the pink light, many of them nodded to her, passing through the small town gate with words of greeting. No man among them failed to appreciate the fresh beauty of the teenaged girl, and it was safe to say that each bore a bit of envy for David, knowing that it was he who held her heart.

"He is not far behind," one elderly fellow acknowledged, smiling as she blushed and looked away. As soon as he was gone, however, she was on tiptoe, seeking the figure of her cousin in the suspended haze.

When at last she spied him, one of the very last to arrive, her heart stirred eagerly, though not without a twinge of sadness. Too often she read growing frustration in David's face. Eighteen he was, and bound forever, it seemed, to work the soil. His artist's soul had not died, though at times he surely wished it would so that he might find contentment with his lot and not continually wish for broader opportunities.

It had not escaped her, however, that when David was with her, the sadness lifted. Such was the case just now, as, coming upon her, his countenance lightened and a smile touched his lips.

Though Hadassah knew he resented his lot, she always considered him most beautiful when he returned from the fields. Always he was her golden boy, gold of hair and eyes, but never more than when he had put in a day beneath the sun, his skin bronzed and the fine chaffy silt of harvest clinging to his torso.

"Hello, Blossom," he greeted, lifting his heavy scythe higher on his shoulder, his free arm scooping her into a playful embrace. The term was one of endearment, playing with the meaning of her name, "Myrtle." As much as David was her goldpiece, she was his priceless flower. And though neither of them had ever revealed in words the depth of their caring, every action and every expression betrayed it.

"Cousin Leah says supper will be ready any moment," Hadassah said, laughing as he hugged her.

"We will be there in time," he replied. "Sit with me a while."

Drawing her aside, he guided her to a grove of gnarled palms which shaded a corner of the town wall and bade her rest with him in the little oasis.

"But aren't you very hungry?" she marveled, knowing that he usually rushed home for dinner like a starving prodigal.

"I am," he agreed, "and thirsty." At this he pulled from his belt a skin-bottle of warm wine and swigged it eagerly. Capping it, he sighed, "But I have not seen you for days. That is more important."

Hadassah had not visited the village for several weeks, for her papa was busy with the inventory of Vashti's abandoned possessions, stored in the queen's warehouse during this full year since her banishment.

It was a sad task, one put off all these months since her going, in deference to the king's wishes.

"I suppose the queen's inventory *could* take a while to count," David smirked, showing his disdain for the royal household.

"Yes," Hadassah nodded. "But Vashti was a good queen," she insisted. "A very good woman."

David noted the defensiveness that Hadassah always manifested when she spoke of the grand lady. Many times she had recounted the occasion when she observed Vashti's kindness firsthand. It had made a lasting impression upon her young mind, and David knew she admired the queen's refusal to accommodate the drunken king.

Mordecai had not been present at the banquet when Vashti was deposed, having attended during an earlier shift. But in his growing love of Judaism and skepticism of Persian politics he conceded that Jehovah would have honored Vashti's choice, and that her exile was a crime for which Xerxes would pay dearly.

"Where do you suppose she is?" Hadassah sighed, gazing wistfully across the desert.

David, sensitive to her tender feelings, knew the question reflected sincere concern for her heroine.

"I have heard there is a great highway," he replied, "running all the way to India—the silk route, plied by kingly caravans and fabled merchants. Have you heard this?"

"Yes," Hadassah answered, warming to the poetry in David's speech.

His eyes took on a faraway look, and she knew he pondered not just the queen's fate but also the many distant places which he could visit only in daydreams.

"She could have been taken that direction, to any of a hundred outposts along the way. Or," he continued, studying the bleak range which hemmed the valley, "it is said that years ago the royal house sent Greeks into the Zagros, captives taken by Darius when he passed into Europe. Perhaps the queen was sent to dwell with them."

Despite the heat Hadassah shivered, considering the irony of such a possibility. "But Xerxes plans war on the Greeks," she objected. "Surely he would not send his wife to live with the enemies."

David smiled fondly at the girl. "Can you think of a better punishment?" he asked.

Hadassah kicked absently at the dirt. "What a dreadful man the king must be!" she exclaimed, her face contorted with anger.

But David, wishing to lighten her mood, drew nearer, directing her to study the vast valley floor.

"On the other hand, "he offered, "perhaps she plays with the Quasqui."

"The Quasqui?" she repeated.

"Nomads of the plain," he said. "I saw them once when I was a small boy. My Papa took me on a trip to Ecbatana and we saw their encampment one evening, near the oasis where we slept."

His romantic soul surged at the memory, and he pulled Hadassah close as he recounted it.

"They live like kings in their own right, you know—summer homes and winter homes, mountains in the heat, valley in the cold. And they eat like kings, on roast wild partridge and grilled lamb livers, wafer-thin bread and fragrant tea, yogurt and skewered quail. They sleep on downy quilts and sing to guitars . . ."

Hadassah was breathless as he wove these images, entranced as much by his mesmerizing voice as by the word pictures he painted.

"I heard them sing a love song that night while they were camped about their fire. Beautiful it was!" he declared, taking Hadassah's hand in his.

" 'The tribe has left, the dust remains,' " he sang, his voice liquid and mellow. " 'The sun has gone, the yellow glow remains; I never kissed those dark eyes . . . the sorrow remains . . .' "

As he recited the last phrase, he gazed into the girl's open countenance with a strange sorrow, a sadness for which she could not account.

And her fingers trembled in his grip.

The sun was sinking fast, dark coming upon them all too quickly. Eyes closed, Hadassah tilted her head back. For a long moment David studied her supple lips, but then he suddenly stood, pulling her to him and bending over her with a hesitant sigh.

"We must be going now," he whispered, resisting the urge to kiss her. Turning, he led her back to the village.

After all, he told himself, she was a child of status and he was but a poor farmer. He thought it best not to love her.

14

Xerxes had spent four years preparing for his invasion of Greece. Shipbuilding alone had taken nearly a quarter of the imperial budget.

One thousand seaworthy vessels were launched from the eastern shore of the Mediterranean and the north shore of Africa when at last he went to war. His forces, the most numerous ever to traipse the earth, were led by his three brothers, the sons of Darius with whom he had dreamed his greatest dreams since childhood.

Arsames was placed in charge of an enormous Ethiopian contingent, and Achaemenes and Anatrigines shared the leadership of the navy. As for Xerxes himself, he took the admiralty of the Phoenician fleet, fulfilling an ambitious vision for a man reared in Persia's landlocked interior.

This afternoon a balmy breeze swelled the sails of his trireme as 600 oars pushed the sleek vessel across the Thracian Sea toward the Greek mainland. He had traveled by camelback up the royal Persian highway from Susa through the Taurus Range, and after entering the Cicilian Gates he had crossed the Hellespont by two bridges of boats. Awaiting Xerxes in the Greek towns of Asia Minor (which his father, Darius, had conquered a dozen years before) had been standing armies levied for his purposes against their European compatriots. He had enlisted some of them as sailors and had left the rest to his generals for invasion against the Hellespont's western shore.

Darius, more bent on reconstruction than revenge, had established democracies in the Ionian towns. Therefore it was with mixed feelings that the Greek forces met the emperor, some of them grateful to Persia for its fair treatment but others, especially the older ones, still full of resentment against their conquerors.

Xerxes had spent the winter at Sardis before advancing on Ionia. Ahead of him he had sent supplies, and now stores of corn for his infantry were accumulated at intervals leading all the way into Europe.

In all, nearly two million foot soldiers and sailors composed the force that Xerxes brought with him from Mesopotamia and points east. As they were joined by contingents from about the empire, he would be advancing upon Europe with over five million men, the most awesome horde ever to practice battle.

His dream this day as he stood at the helm of the warship, observing the pilot's dexterous work and listening to the chanting slap of the vessel's oars, was that all the West would be his. As the sleek bark passed island after island along the Dolopes chain, his pulse skipped.

This was, he reasoned, where a man's heart ought to be: in war and its implements, in power and command. Nothing short of this was worthy of attention, and surely not of grief.

Vashti should have come to him when he called for her. Did she not know that matters of marriage and love could not always be of grand importance? Not to a king, anyway.

In the cold heights of the Asian mountains, as he had slept in his guarded tent, he had often reminded himself of this. On desert nights when he slept beside his spear, and wondered where Vashti was, he had taken comfort in the conviction that such questions were beneath him.

As he had ridden high in his camel's swaying canopy, leading his millions toward the goal of glory, he had forced his queen from his mind, drugged by the call of destiny and the praise of his comrades.

In time, he told himself, she would cease to haunt him. When he owned Europe and held the entire world in his grip, she would fade forever from memory.

Just now, scanning the advancing shore, the coast which cradled Athens and Sparta, he girded his spirit for adventure— adventure craved by his forefathers but never tasted.

Where Xerxes set foot, Persia set foot. As Persia prospered, so would his soul.

This he told himself when Vashti's sweet face darted across his conscience. It worked to quell his guilt, to appease his yearning for her touch—sometimes.

15

For several months Xerxes' millions had been positioned at various sites throughout the Aegean and Thracian Seas. When 180,000 of them went against the Athens-Sparta alliance, they were met by only 10,000 Greeks and 300 ships.

On their way to Athens the Persians had encountered unprecedented victory at Thermopylae. When they easily overtook the Greek capital, besieging the acropolis and setting the temple of Athena aflame, the horrified Athenians bowed to eastern occupation with chagrin.

For the first time in history an Oriental power not only invaded the West but held its most prestigious city in a stranglehold. Xerxes had, therefore, fulfilled more of the Persian expansionist dream than any of his predecessors, and after sending word of victory to Susa he headed for Salamis, plotting to take over the entire Dorian sector of the Hellenistic world.

It was September 23, over a year into the emperor's European experience. What he had only imagined in fantasy was spread before him as he sat beneath a striped umbrella high atop a hill at the head of Piraeus Harbor. A soft southern breeze wafted up from the Myrtoum Sea, bringing the scent of clashing steel and the sound of bloody cries across Salamis Isle.

This was the gateway to all points west. If Xerxes won this round, nothing could stand in his way. Though the forces were fairly equal, the Persians, having demoralized the Greeks at Athens, were enjoying the advantage.

Xerxes straightened the silken folds of his lavender gown and rested his flared sleeves upon the arms of his portable throne. Sunshine glinted off his upturned face as his secretaries raced back and forth with word of his captains' exploits. Dozens of ships representing both sides of the fray expressed their differences in the narrow slit of water separating Salamis from the mainland. While presently the battle was quite balanced, the emperor was confident.

His Phoenician navy was an awesome contingent, not only for expertise but also for appearance. Its squat, flat-bottomed boats, propelled by two decks of oars, denoted divine retribution with their huge idols of the stocky god, Baal, leaning threateningly from each prow and with sharp-nosed battering rams pushing ominously through the water.

The Greeks' more curvaceous, streamlined vessels appeared fragile by comparison, and although the goddess Athena was often depicted as a warrior, in crested helmet and full armor, her likeness did not adorn her ships.

Despite the huskiness of the Phoenician craft, however, the Greek ships proved themselves a formidable force. About dusk the scales began to tip in favor of the Europeans, and Xerxes' secretaries hesitated to bear the discomforting tidings to their king.

Nevertheless, it was increasingly apparent that, while the Phoenicians were masters of the open seas, the more slender and maneuverable Greek barks were better able to cope with the restricting canal. The Hellenists, accustomed to the narrow shoals and treacherous conditions of island waterways, managed to lure the Phoenicians into straits beyond their ken.

Perhaps Xerxes need not be told the worst. He could surely see for himself the broken wreckage of several Persian vessels floating in the canal. And along the rocky shore wounded sailors swam, clambering up the beach toward the village of Psyttaleia.

Soon, from the vantage point of his sheltered throne, Xerxes could see that nearly the entire Persian garrison scrambled ashore, thousands upon thousands abandoning floundered ships and dragging wounded comrades across bloody sands.

Close on their heels followed the enemy, shooting down those who ran and falling upon the disabled as they hacked them to pieces with broadaxes.

Those still manning the faltering ships retreated now, trying to flee the scene of battle, the waters strewn with hulks and corpses and flailing swimmers. Few would escape, taking with them the memory of comrades clubbed to death by the enemy's oars or spitted like tunny on steamy lances.

The slaughter continued until nightfall. Two hundred Persian ships were lost in the Salamis strait to only 40 Greek vessels. While the emperor's fugitives fled to Phalerum, the chagrined monarch sat like a statue upon his regal chair.

As the sun dipped over the westland, which he still longed to possess, tears trickled down his cheeks. And a Mediterranean breeze, warm but not conciliatory, dried them.

* * *

Winter was approaching. Xerxes and his defeated troops limped back to Susa along the same route they had followed into Europe.

Though he was not utterly abandoning dreams of westward expansion, the emperor must give his demoralized and disorganized forces time to recuperate. Those who retreated with him would be sent home, most of them too badly wounded to fight again. The larger part of his army, that which had not seen action at Salamis, had been sent north to await spring. Under General Mardonius they would seek alliance with Athens, and though Xerxes had lost command of the sea, a fleet now guarded the Hellespont, plotting another foray into the hinterland.

The dream was tentative, however. As Xerxes withdrew into Asia, word came from other parts of Greece that his brothers, all three of them top commanders, had given their lives in his cause.

How swiftly ambition had turned to ashes, dreams to dust! Somewhere in the foothills of Cicilia, Xerxes laid his royal head upon a lonely pillow and remembered Persepolis, the ceremonial halls where he and his young brothers had been trained for war.

Little was left to him now of human love. Father, wife, and kin were gone. Only the adoration of his subjects remained, and unless he took the West, even that hollow consolation could fade away.

16

Xerxes, Emperor of the East, trembled as he knelt in his private chapel before the frieze of his god, Ahura-Mazda. In stone relief the winged deity hovered above him, its wheeled craft soaring, aloof, yet unmoving.

For weeks all of Susa had sat on edge as news from Greece fluctuated between victory and defeat.

Mardonius, left with the best of Xerxes' troops to complete the work begun in Attica, had failed to achieve an alliance with the trampled Athenians, and so had occupied the city since spring. Recent word was that the Greeks had at last taken the offensive, and so the general had burned the capital to the ground, thus procuring an empty retribution by destroying the greatest prize of the emperor's campaign and evacuating Attica itself.

While there was strong Persian fighting here and there throughout the Greek isles, just today a messenger had brought tidings that Mardonius and his troops were huddled behind a wall of felled trees at Plataea, and that their situation was very precarious.

Nearly a full year had passed since the battle of Salamis. In all this time Xerxes had slept little, eaten little, and fretted much, living only for the sporadic reports which filtered to his palace from the warfront.

The three battle points which counted most were at Plataea, Mycale, and Sestos. If Mardonius lost Plataea, one-third of Xerxes' remaining hope would die. And so he prayed today in the small sanctuary adjoining his bedchamber—pleading with his god to give his generals wisdom, his admirals craftiness, and his armed men strength.

Every day of his life he had practiced prayer, but the last time he had done so with such determination was when he begged

Ahura-Mazda to hasten his wedding to Vashti. The god had granted that request. Perhaps he would grant this one.

But as Xerxes knelt before the carving of his beloved deity, he doubted whether his petition would be honored. Fasting and agonizing until his face was gaunt and lined, he wondered if the god who had blessed him with the girl of his dreams could ever again look kindly upon him after he had sent her away.

Soon enough his doubts were confirmed. A rap upon the chapel door lifted him from his knees.

"Enter," he called hoarsely.

Pushing open the door, the chamberlain admitted three young boys, all dusty and windblown, having traveled hundreds of miles and each bearing word from the European forces.

Quickly the news was dispensed as the youngsters fawned and shivered before the mightiest man on earth. Mardonius and his troops had been slaughtered like sheep at Plataea, the fleet at Mycale had been destroyed, and the garrison at Sestos, being reduced to eating their bedstraps, had abandoned the town by night.

Xerxes, receiving the messages numbly, could have called for the execution of the three lads. Instead, after gazing upon them mutely, he dismissed them and turned again to his prayers.

"Mighty Ahura-Mazda, you who answer when I call, *so* you have answered," he wept.

Burying his nails in his scalp, he mourned—for himself as well as for those who had given everything for him.

17

The seven eunuchs—Mehuman, Biztha, Harbona, Bigtha, Abagtha, Zethar, and Carkas—stood outside the king's council chamber, peering past his guards and consulting among themselves.

"For days he has sat thus," Mehuman whispered, his face furrowed with concern. "He mutters to himself a great deal, and whispers Vashti's name too often."

The eunuchs studied the king's slumped form as he rested upon his throne, and they shook their heads sadly.

"It is not only his defeat in Europe which haunts him," Biztha surmised.

"I think it is less that than anything," Mehuman agreed. "He shall rally from that in time, for there are always more lands to conquer. But Vashti he shall never forget."

"It is our responsibility to lift His Majesty's spirits," Zethar announced, his chin jutting in determination. "We must think of something!"

The others murmured agreement, and through a process of elimination they began to arrive at a plan.

"Riches are not the answer. We should make no suggestion which could inflate his coffers," Carkas reasoned.

"Right," nodded Abagtha, "nor would a round of parties or entertainers do the trick."

"I agree," said Harbona. "And we have already ruled out conquest."

Bigtha shrugged. "A *woman* has been his downfall; perhaps a woman can *save* him!"

All eyes were on Mehuman, awaiting his response to this astute observation.

For a long moment he contemplated the matter. Then a smile tugged at his lips.

"Very well," he assented. "I can see no other way. We must provide the king with a romance, something to surpass what he had with Vashti."

The others nodded enthusiastically. But then, one by one, their faces fell.

"How can such a thing be accomplished?" Carkas stammered. "His love for Vashti was a rare thing. And there are no women from among the seven royal families to compare with her."

Carkas' referred to the injunction that no queen was to be taken from outside the seven highest houses in Persia, a law established by Darius in order to honor the seven men who had been loyal to him during an insurrection.

"This is true," Mehuman conceded. "But our king's health is failing. Something must be done. And this law was made years ago. It is reversible under a new administration."

The eunuchs raised their eyebrows at this, but would not question Mehuman's interpretation of the edict. Indeed, there was no formal stipulation regarding an emperor's contradicting the decisions of a former ruler.

"Still," Carkas objected, "where are we to find a woman worthy of Xerxes?"

Biztha jumped on this. "Why, we should seek high and low for her. We should bring beauties from all about the king's empire, and let him choose for himself!"

At first the suggestion seemed so absurd that the others laughed—all except Mehuman. And when he seemed to be thinking upon it, the snickers subsided.

"You cannot actually take such a notion seriously!" Harbona cried. "Why, this is tantamount to calling for a new harem— something Xerxes would never condone. Did he not just recently divest himself of such pleasures, sending hundreds of women from the palace?"

Mehuman did not reply quickly, but peered in at the king, who sat lethargically in his solemn chamber, tipping a goblet of red wine back and forth and gazing upon its contents.

"A man in His Majesty's condition could consider almost anything," he concluded. "Give him a few more days, and then we shall approach him."

18

Hadassah sat up in bed and peered toward the dim yellow light glowing beneath her chamber door. In rooms down the hall her female cousins, Marta and Isha, breathed in contented sleep beside their husbands. But voices in the parlor had jolted her awake.

Anxiously she leaned over the edge of her low pallet and tried to make out the words of Mordecai, Leah, and Moshe in the room beyond.

At first she could not believe her ears when she heard Mordecai in the house. He had not intended to come to the village until later in the season, giving her several more weeks of her seventeenth autumn to spend with her dearest companions. Why he should be here now, and in the middle of the night, she could not imagine. But she was not eager to return home. As much as she loved her adopted father, she much preferred to be with her cousins . . . especially with David.

As she pieced together snatches of the conversation, however, it seemed that Mordecai had not come to fetch her home, but was instead enlisting his sister's aid to continue maintaining her here.

Past a sleepy haze now, she managed to pick up the idea that some news from the palace greatly troubled her papa. As she concentrated on fragments of his story, she realized that he feared for her safety.

"'Let there be fair young virgins sought for the king,'" she heard him expostulate, as though he quoted some royal edict. "Can you believe that Xerxes would stoop to such indulgence?"

Leah's voice followed this, with a heavy sigh. "Well, though he has been known in the past as a moral man, Brother, he *is* a pagan, after all. He does not worship Jehovah. And remember that even certain of Israel's own kings kept harems—David . . . Solomon . . ."

"Yes," Mordecai granted. Despite his growing love of Judaism, he could be embarrassed by certain aspects of its history. "Still, it is disillusioning."

"Only if you expected better things," Moshe shrugged.

"So, go on," Leah urged him. "Surely you have come here at such an hour with more than courtroom gossip."

"I have," Mordecai acknowledged, rubbing his hands together anxiously. "Word in the palace is that the king has appointed officers in all the provinces to seek out and bring to Susa hundreds of young damsels. From among them, Xerxes shall choose a queen to replace his lost Vashti."

His eyes were wide as he spoke, and when his relations only studied him impersonally, he shook his head in frustration.

"Can't you see what this could mean? Are you blind, or am I the only one who has noticed my daughter's beauty?"

Suddenly, with a pang of recognition, Leah's breath came sharply.

"Hadassah!" she groaned, glancing toward the girl's chamber.

Her motherly heart raced protectively. Though there were other lovely maidens in the village, she knew that Hadassah outshone them, and that any procurator sent here would snatch up the willowy lass with the raven curls.

Nor need Mordecai go into detail as to how the king would sort through the hundreds brought to him. Moshe, drawing his manly shoulders into an indignant square, imagined the sweet child herded into Xerxes' bedchamber, to be exploited and then tossed aside.

"What can we do?" he whispered, almost afraid that the sniffing hounds were in the street at this very moment.

Mordecai paced the floor of the tiny parlor. "You must try to keep her from daylight until this misery passes. She must remain with you, and you must keep her from view."

"But," Leah gasped, "how are we to explain this to Hadassah? Surely it would terrify her to know the truth."

"Indeed," Mordecai agreed. "She is very innocent about such things. A good girl, she is. You know?"

"Of course," Moshe assured him. "We know her as well as you do."

"Then," the guardian declared, "tell her whatever you must. But keep her secluded."

At this the voices tapered to a solemn whisper. Hadassah leaned back upon her pillow, her hands clutching at her blanket, and her whole body aquiver.

19

When the eunuchs had presented Xerxes with the proposed "solution" to his loneliness and depression, he had grasped at it. Of course, as at the party where he had deposed Vashti, his decision to seek a new queen had been made through a wine-soaked fog. There would be times throughout the ensuing months when he would feel the guilt of this choice, just as he felt remorse over the loss of his wife. But he would manage to push it aside as day after day lovelies were paraded before him.

It took only a few weeks, following his acceptance of the advice, for the harem quarters to be refurbished and for hand-picked virgins to begin arriving at the palace, first from points closest and then from provinces along the farthest reaches of the empire. Soon the king's manly blood was stirred by the presence of innocent beauty in his courts.

Access to the damsels would be postponed, however, for what became an excruciatingly long time as the girls were put through a routine of cleansing rituals and beautification, taking a full 12 months from the time of their arrival. The king's desire, piqued by this anticipation, began to alleviate his former depression, replacing it with energies he must release in creative ways.

Mehuman, the eunuch, had foreseen this. When Biztha had proposed the procurement of a new harem, he had quickly realized the effect that a bevy of women on the palace grounds would have upon the emperor. And as Xerxes began to take up administrative duties with a vengeance, channeling his aroused and unrequited passions into business, politics, and parties, the valet smiled with private gratification. "As good as a physician's prescription!" he reasoned. "Our king is himself again."

It was the month of Tebeth, "mud" month of midwinter, four

years after Vashti's deposition and more than a year since Xerxes' defeat at Salamis. Even in Susa, the weather was cold.

Hadassah worked in the smoky kitchen of Leah's little cottage, chatting gaily with her cousins. Her seclusion, which had begun three months before, did not seem so strange once the weather turned bad. Until the muddy time, Leah and Moshe had expected to be questioned often by their niece as to why they found so much for her to do inside and kept such close track of her whenever she went outdoors. But, to their surprise, she had accepted the peculiar isolation quietly, and had not once complained when Mordecai sent word that she should remain with them through the winter.

Though the guardians never suspected that the girl had overheard their midnight conversation with Mordecai, it was not long before news of the king's edict was public knowledge, and so Leah sought opportunity to caution the pretty girl.

Moshe, David, and the young husbands of Leah's two daughters were away from the house this evening, working beside the other men of the community to lay out fresh straw upon the empty grainfields, a duty required several times during the winter to prepare the muddy ground for spring planting.

The women labored over piles of onions and carrots in the dimly lit kitchen, peeling the vegetables for stews and soups. An aromatic broth simmered on the brick oven in the center of the room, and though it was chilly outside, the ladies wore light frocks in the steamy quarters.

Leah nervously broached the subject of the edict, addressing her daughters rather than Hadassah. "I hear there have been a good many coaches and carriages passing under the gates of Susa lately, bearing guests for the palace," she said.

"Guests?" Marta laughed. "Why, mother, you know all those young girls cannot be guests!"

Leah glanced at Hadassah, expecting her interest to be aroused. But the girl only kept her head bowed, intent upon the task of slicing cabbages.

"Well, then," the mother went on, "if we all know who the young ladies are, and why they have been taken to the palace . . ."

"Taken! Yes, Mother! They are *taken*, against their will, aren't they?" Isha cried. "How awful!"

"We are lucky we are married," Marta chimed in. "At least we needn't worry . . ." But then she caught herself, her hand flying to her mouth. "Oh, I am sorry," she groaned, gazing at Hadassah with round, sad eyes.

At this the girl at last looked up from her work, her own eyes moist with tears. Leah flew to Hadassah's side, throwing her arms about her.

"Dear child!" she wept, seeing unconcealed terror in the innocent face. "You have known all along, haven't you?"

The girl did not reply, but nestled her dark head upon her cousin's shoulder.

"Then I needn't warn you more strongly," Leah insisted, lifting Hadassah's chin and studying her perfect countenance. "You must be careful. Continue close to home. Do not go out in the daylight, or linger, as you often do, near the gate when David comes back from the fields. Do you hear me?"

"I hear you," Hadassah stammered, frightened all the more by Leah's curt tone.

Softening, the woman held her close and looked anxiously at her daughters. Drawing near, they embraced their cousin, and together the women stood in a huddle, listening to the wind outside and wishing their men would return.

20

The flame of the candle on the window ledge fluttered uneasily as a rainy breeze pushed through the half-open reed blind. Soon David, Moshe, and the other girls' husbands would be coming in from the fields. Surely, Hadassah reasoned, it could not hurt if she sat in the little hall of Leah's entryway and watched for them in the street outside.

This had always been a safe little hamlet. Folk did not cover their windows with grates or slats, as in the city. Only in inclement weather did they even lower flimsy shades like this one, which admitted the winter wind.

Feeling quite secure within the house, Hadassah rested her elbows upon the sill and leaned her chin on one hand. A slender moon glanced between heavy clouds, and she remembered the night that she and David had sat in the little oasis beyond the town wall.

She was of marriageable age, and had never met a man more to her liking than David. Having lived much of her life in the royal city, she had seen many a handsome and wealthy fellow. But David was a kindred soul.

A good man he was—committed to his family despite the fact that such service frustrated his desires to pursue his artistic leanings. Yet he did find ways, even in the village, to express the creative side of himself. Many a night he sat beside the parlor fire, spinning glorious yarns in song and poem, of mountains, bedouins, and distant kingdoms. When a spare moment granted the luxury, he painted or carved his imaginings upon small shards of pottery and hunks of cast-off alabaster.

From the parlor, the orange glow of Leah's little firepit blended with the flame of Hadassah's window candle. Trickles of gentle rain dashed against the sill, and her mind drifted out toward the fields, toward the one she loved.

A stir down the street seemed to say that the men were coming in from the evening's labors. Eager voices from many doorways called out greetings.

Hadassah leaned her head out the window, straining for the sight of David rounding the dark streetcorner.

The flash of torches verified that a company passed into town. Had she not been anticipating her cousin, she might have paid more attention to the accompanying sounds, for housewifely hellos were suddenly muffled, and cries and weeping followed.

Too soon for her preoccupied heart to heed this change, the approaching torchlight blazed rudely across the housefront. Before she could duck inside, the disconcerting glare revealed faces unfamiliar to her. As though made to seek her out especially, one of the flares was brandished in her direction, lighting up her countenance like a miner's torch.

"Aha!" someone laughed. "Here's a pretty one!"

And then other voices joined in as Hadassah shielded her eyes.

"Pretty, indeed! She's a beauty!"

Lurching backward, Hadassah grappled with the blind.

But it was too late.

Leah came running from the kitchen just as the front door was kicked open and strong men in hard leather armor forced their way inside.

"This is your daughter?" the leader asked, grasping Hadassah by the arm.

"Why, no . . . yes . . ." Leah fumbled.

"Whatever," the official shrugged. "She now belongs to King Xerxes."

Crazed, the girl shrieked, and Leah clung to her until the guards beat her away.

Into the street Hadassah was thrown, her lavender dress torn at the shoulder and her pale face spattered with muddy rain.

Marta and Isha shrieked with her, holding onto one another as their favorite childhood playmate was thrust upon a waiting horse, and the horse was whipped into a gallop.

As the throng of thieving soldiers raced back toward the town gate, they took with them half a dozen girls of the village.

But the leader of the pack kept a keen eye on Hadassah. She was the evening's prize—perhaps the prize of his career.

He had done himself proud tonight.

21

Morning sun gleamed through a dreary blanket of fog over the palace of Susa. Mordecai the Jew sat in the gate of the royal house, behind his accounting table, and tried to keep his mind on the business of figures and ledgers.

On most days such preoccupation came easily to him despite the traffic of executives and officers who came and went upon the spacious stairway from the avenue out front. He was accustomed to the klatches of conversing courtiers and servants in the shady recesses of the gate's multistoried complex. But lately concentration came hard.

More young women had been arriving today than ever before, being escorted toward the harem quarters in the palace's most private sanctum. Mordecai's nerves were kept on edge as cluster after cluster of girls passed by his station, and as he surveyed them carefully, praying that his daughter not be among them.

After months of this surveillance he was still unaccustomed to it. And though to this point he had been spared the horror of Hadassah's capture, concern never ceased to possess him.

More than fear haunted him today, however. Haman, the king's vizier, was doing business in the gate, his boastful voice and ostentatious presence goading the Jew since morning.

It was not that Haman meant especially to offend Mordecai. Rarely had he ever paid much mind to the slight accountant in all the years he had served this administration. Day in and day out the grand vizier passed by the unassuming fellow who sat at the inventory bench. Day in and day out he disregarded him, interacting with the Jew only on those infrequent occasions when their business overlapped.

The only times that Haman seemed to actually have focused on Mordecai were when he had worn his fringed mantle to work, the one which designated him a member of the Jewish race. During Mordecai's early months of duty at this post he had not worn the garment. But as he had become progressively more involved with his heritage, and as he had fallen more and more in love with the teachings of Israel (scorned and avoided though they were in his youth), he had become more comfortable with those symbols which identified him with the despised ones.

It did not surprise him that Haman took note of him when he was so distinguished. Instinctively he had known the vizier would do so. So perhaps he was goading Haman subtly and quietly as much as Haman inadvertently goaded him.

Indeed, Mordecai's antipathy toward the Agagite, the Amal-ekite, was deep and strong. Though Haman had no idea that the old man whom his underlings had assaulted in the streets long ago was Mordecai's adopted father, he was not blind to the coolness of the Jew's greetings or the edge of bitterness which tinged their dealings.

When the accountant wore his shawl, as he did today, the Jew's antipathy was more distinct, for Mordecai himself was more distinct.

Haman did not like Jews. Though many of the race held prominent positions in Persia, the vizier looked upon them with suspicion. He did not like the way they kept to themselves, the way they attended to their own laws and customs. Strange they were, to him and to others. And sometimes he wondered how loyal they could be to the empire when they served from a divided heart.

The fact that Jews were rarely disobedient to Persian author-ity served only to confuse people like Haman. They were no-toriously scrupulous citizens, and this in itself cast a question over them.

Be that as it may, Haman cared little what Mordecai thought of him. Jew or not, he was a fellow of small importance to the empire. As long as he did his job, Haman ignored him.

Mordecai observed the prime minister's pompous swagger as he strode here and there across the steps, giving his opinion on this matter and that, sending his valets flying on errands and commissioning his executives with various tasks. Accompanied by his closest consultants, Haman approached a broad banister which hemmed the stairs. Perched upon it was a huge stone lion, one of two which guarded either side of the entry. The Jew watched with a gimlet eye as the vizier cavalierly leaned against the royal statue. And he clenched his teeth in private disgust.

His disdainful revery was short-lived, however. Another bevy of young beauties was being brought for the king's scrutiny. As always, they were marched up the stairs, huddled and quiet. As always, they received the leering glances of a hundred onlookers. But, unlike times past, Mordecai's worst fear was realized.

He was certain he saw Hadassah. She could not be mistaken—there in the center of the little group, taller and more striking than the rest.

Anxiously she surveyed the gateway, doubtless knowing that her papa would be seated here. But before she could spy him he ducked his head, fumbling for some nonexistent object upon the floor.

Once she had been led away he rose up again, fighting back tears. Haman still reclined upon the banister, representing all that was alien. While Mordecai had publicly embraced Judaism, he felt it best for now to shield Hadassah from such a connection.

Until this calamity be past, she must not be called a Jew.

22

Hadassah walked with her dozen sister captives through the palace's echoing halls, forced along at spearpoint by a group of rigid guards. Like frightened does, the young women hung close together, fearfully eyeing their surroundings.

Soaring pillars, narrow of girth and widely spaced, lent an airiness to the enormous compound, which opened out onto vast gardens and sparkling pools. From every cornice and column top small bulls' heads stared down upon their passage, and friezes along broad staircases told tales of kings and conquerors, slaves and tribute, impressing all who traversed the grounds with the grandeur and power that belonged to rulers of this dynasty.

Crossing several colonades and entering vestibule after vestibule, the girls passed many an archway and closed door, each leading to some private sanctum of the king's courtiers and governors. Straight-backed soldiers protected every entryway, but their attire indicated that they were meant more for show than for combat. In blousy pantaloons and silken shoes, the toes upturned, they hardly looked threatening. Nonetheless, Hadassah and her companions avoided their cold gazes.

Across expansive porches the women's footsteps rang, and where they were muffled by thick Persian carpets—red and blue and gold, fringed and intricately patterned—the sound of cascading fountains, the cries of strutting peacocks, or the music of caged birds and minstrels' lyres filled the air.

It seemed a century of distance separated the queue of girls from the outside world. Ahead was a scalloped archway leading to three lobbies, each descending after the other toward a sunlit court. Soft-shoed fellows again stood bastioned alongside this portal, but by their smooth cheeks and shining chins it was clear that they were eunuchs, not warriors.

As the ladies were ushered into the first and largest of these lobbies, they were greeted by the aroma of a heavy, bulbous smoking pipe which sat upon a low table surrounded by laughing men. Propped upon embroidered pillows, they passed the pipe's hose from mouth to mouth, playing a game of dice without looking up until one of the escorts cleared his throat.

The host of the jolly party glared at the intruder.

"Another lot for the king's harem," the guide announced.

"You know where they go," the gambler sneered, flicking a hurried hand. As he surveyed the knot of girls, Hadassah took a sharp breath. She had never forgotten the angry countenance of Angus, the man who had so callously commandeered a group of harem wives the day she watched them being evicted from the palace. She had rarely thought of him during the intervening years, the memory of Vashti being the stronger image from that long-ago day. But one glimpse of his round, gloating face brought back the incident as though no time had elapsed.

Quickly the soldiers led the girls forth, through the little vestibules and toward the harem's sunstreaked court. The mocking aroma of the men's smoking pipe blended with the heady fragrance of perfumes and bath oils as the women proceeded through the last arch. Overcome with anxiety and fatigue, Hadassah doubled a fist against her stomach.

The final portico, opening on a sumptuous arboretum, framed an elegant scene. Bowers of roses and lilies, slaves with broad, feathered fans—all seemed calculated to inspire romance and a sense of luxury.

Across the pool, at the far side of the garden, the harem apartments rose in several tiers up from the court floor. They were a pretty sight at first glance, fronted by narrow catwalks and decorated with hanging plants, vines, and statuary. But on closer inspection they resembled the wall of a hive. In contrast to the open airiness of the palace compound, the quarters of the harem girls were so many claustrophobic boxes stacked atop one another.

As it dawned upon the klatch of newcomers that these were the living quarters which came with being "chosen" women, they were hushed with horror.

Hadassah wiped her palms upon her torn gown, recalling the annual village fairs she had attended with Leah's children. Just like the cattle stalls where farmers brought animals for breeding and for slaughter, so were the rooms of the harem girls.

Somewhere in the small huddle of virgins, soft weeping broke tense silence. Last night, after the girls had been led captive from several villages near Susa, they had been herded into an encampment outside the city walls. None had slept well. Certainly not Hadassah. And to face a night—endless nights—in the confines of these narrow cells was too much to contemplate.

Tears forced their way to her eyes and spilled over her flushed cheeks.

She wondered where her papa was, and why he had not been seated at the palace gate. The young Jewess sorely needed his prayers now, for he was a man of God, and he understood Jehovah's ways more than she.

23

Hadassah lay within her narrow cell, upon an even narrower cot, her head toward the back wall. It had been 24 hours since she was transported from the encampment outside Susa to this little chamber. Not once since she had arrived had any official greeted the newcomers or explained to them what was to come.

All night long she had dreamed of David, trembling into wakefulness over and over as he had turned from her in her shame. Barely could her conscious mind consider her purpose here without the most horrid fears enveloping her. Repeatedly she told herself that some salvation lay directly before her, that surely God could not mean for the king to touch her, for her life to be irrevocably sullied and her future dismissed.

Soon, she reasoned, her uncle would hear of her imprisonment. Perhaps he could bring some influence to bear . . . some plea for her release. But even as she hoped for this, her throat grew tight. She knew very well that Mordecai was no great man in the palace. Likely, the king did not even know his name.

As dawn filtered through the court's latticed ceiling, spilling past vines and laces of flowers, women up and down the hive stirred awake. Throughout the night's bleak hours, soft sobs had drifted through the thin wall of Hadassah's chamber from the adjacent room. They had quieted just before the first gray rays of morning, but now they resumed.

The neighbor was a girl of Leah's village. Close in age, Hadassah and Maryam had known each other since childhood, and the Jewess wondered how her friend would endure this misery. Maryam was a delicate child, diminutive of stature, unlike the long-legged females generally selected for the harem. Pretty as a field flower, she was painfully shy and the ordeal had already taken a murderous toll on her.

Hadassah sat up in bed and leaned around the front edge of the partition. Like a tortured convict, Maryam hunched against the wall of her room, her knees updrawn fetally, her face ravaged.

The cell to the other side of Maryam's was occupied by a Phoenician beauty. Dark and hearty, like the heathered hills of her seacoast nation, this young woman had been brought to Susa several weeks earlier. Familiarity with harem life, however, could not account for her indifferent attitude.

She sat upon the narrow walkway, her legs dangling casually between spindles of the balustrade.

Dressed in the briefest of garments, her shoulders covered only by a mass of black curls, she glanced toward the weeping newcomer with a callous sneer.

"I hope we can get some sleep tonight!" she said, loudly enough that several other girls, sporting in the pool below, responded with sly smiles.

These, like the Phoenician, evinced a careless air, and must have been her favorite companions.

"Yes—it would be nice," one replied, and the other swimmers laughed.

Hadassah bristled, creeping into the cubbyhole where her fellow villager sat.

Placing an arm about Maryam's shaking shoulders, she whispered, "Please stop crying. Everything will be all right."

"Certainly it will!" the Phoenician shrugged, poking her head into the little chamber. "Did you know that when you are at last sent before the king, you will be given your choice of dowries? Silks and jewels and precious ointments! A fortune will be yours!"

At this Maryam only wept louder, and Hadassah studied the intruder with amazement. Clearly, a passion for luxury had thus far sustained the foreigner. And perhaps such greed was what it took to endure this imprisonment.

But Hadassah had known luxury all her life. Though she was very young, she knew that such things ill served the heart.

"What of family?" she softly challenged. And then with a wistful sigh, "What of love?"

Again Maryam sobbed, and the Phoenician glanced away with a fleeting grimace. Just as quickly, however, her careless ambiance returned, and she stepped away.

"I cannot send my mother or my 12 brothers and sisters love in a bucket!" she sneered. "But they will be happy to buy food for their stomachs!"

Hadassah drew Maryam close and watched the Phoenician's determined retreat.

There were various ways to handle heartbreak, she deduced. Weeping and wailing was one, and haughtiness was another.

24

Mordecai paced the floor of his bedchamber, sleepless for the third night with thoughts of his poor Hadassah.

The house was very quiet, the servants having retired hours ago. The silence was almost oppressive as Mordecai slipped into the hall and drew near the room where his uncle, Abihail, had spent his dying days.

This room was Mordecai's study now. A large table occupied the place where Abihail's bed had been, and spread upon it were not only ledgers and accounting tables but scrolls of the Jewish Scriptures, his most prized possessions.

Softly he went to the broad desk and sat down where his servants so often found him. Since he spent more time in this place than in any other room of the house, the chambermaid knew that it was her foremost duty to keep the master's reading lamp always full of oil, his quill sharpened, and his ink bottle full.

With the passing years Mordecai had come to devote as much energy to meditating upon the Torah as to his bookkeeping. Mordecai was not an old man, but as he increasingly preferred the look of a Jew, his beard had grown patriarchally long. Streaked with silver, it gave him an appearance of age beyond his 42 years, and his shoulder-length hair lent another Hebrew touch. Yet he was still in touch with Persia, and as he walked the courts each day, he sensed more and more the disparity between the two cultures.

Tonight, restless and anxious, he tried to collect his thoughts and focus them on prayer, for he knew he was powerless to help his daughter by any human means. Yet every time he attempted to intercede for her, the image of Abihail, prone upon the bed which had sat in this very place, haunted him.

Never before had such a phenomenon interrupted his meditations. Night after night he had studied in this room, and never
had the memory of his uncle interfered.

"Strange . . ." he whispered, his brow knit. "What is it?"

It was only to himself that he asked this question, but as he did,
the memory of Abihail's warning, the ancient story of King Saul
and Agag the Amalekite, leapt to mind.

Despite Mordecai's increased love of Israel and her traditions,
Abihail's interpretation of this tale had remained gibberish to
him. Suddenly, as he pondered it afresh, his skin crawled and a
pervasive sense of dread enveloped him.

Rising, he stepped to the chamber window and gazed out
toward the acropolis, toward the palace gate where he sat each
day beneath the shadow of Haman and his cohorts.

The impression was very strong, as though imparted by the
night's dark silence, that Abihail had been right. Evil stalked the
royal house of Susa, evil alien to Persia as well as to Israel. Until
Jehovah's will was done, it would fester, bringing misery to both
cultures.

* * *

The instant dawn broke over the royal compound, Mordecai
made his way through the palace gate.

All night long he had meditated upon the meaning of Abihail's
warning. And though he did not yet understand just how it
might involve Hadassah, concern for her well-being obsessed
him.

Accountants, even of the highest stature, must have good
reason to venture past the treasury rooms of Xerxes' residence.
But Mordecai had a plan, one borne of the genius which darkness and solitude can generate.

"I would speak to the Keeper of the Dowries," he announced,
rousing the guard from his morning post outside the harem
court.

"To what purpose?" the sentry asked. "And who are you?"

"Mordecai, Chief Accountant of the Treasury. It is required
that an inventory be made of the harem storehouse."

"Who requires it?" the guard challenged, wondering at the odd timing.

"I do," Mordecai simply said. "It will take several days, and we will begin straightway."

"But . . ." the guard objected, "the keeper is asleep. Can't it wait?"

Feigning impatience, the Jew looked up at the gray sunlight and sighed. "Very well. We will not waken the keeper. Only lead me to the storehouse and I will begin without him."

"But . . ."

"He may join me as soon as he likes," Mordecai snapped, rushing past the guard's objection.

Befuddled, the sentry lowered his spear and looked over his shoulder.

"I suppose it will do no harm. . . ."

"Hurry, man," Mordecai spurred him. "I haven't all day!"

Doubtfully the guard led him down the back hall of the harem. "The women are all asleep," the guard said. "See to it that you are gone before they take their morning walk. No man is to intrude upon their privacy."

"Of course," Mordecai sniffed, seeing an opportunity here. "Uh, when did you say that would be?"

"Three hours past cock crow," the guard replied. "See to it that you are nowhere near their passage."

"Certainly," Mordecai said with a bow.

They stood before the storehouse door now. Nervously the guard worked the key in the lock and let Mordecai enter the dark room. Setting a flame to the single oil lamp upon the interior wall, he stepped back and cleared his throat.

"The keeper will be informed of your presence here as soon as he wakes," he announced.

"Don't worry," Mordecai said, facing him with a condescending smile. "I am his superior. You have done well."

Bowing away, the guard softly clicked his heels together and left Mordecai to himself. The Jew beamed with private victory and began the task of counting ointment jars, his ears attuned for the sound of girlish voices in the hall.

25

Well into his "inventory" of the storeroom, Mordecai found his patience rewarded.

Girls by the dozens were emerging from their harem cells, to be herded down the hall into the morning light. They would be led to the outside garden which hemmed the palace compound, where they would enjoy one of two daily constitutionals.

Eagerly Hadassah's adopted father peered through the crack of the door, which he had purposely left ajar. He knew that the regimen of court life would repeat this spectacle again tomorrow morning. Therefore he waited to spy his daughter and to follow her beyond the wall—only to know her routine, and not, this time, to contact her. If he were successful in tracing her steps, he would venture to do so again tomorrow, and would pray for the chance to speak with her.

When at last he identified Hadassah toward the end of the line, he stifled a little cry. How sad she looked! Though she carried herself well, after the manner of her upbringing, her youthful dignity was poor compensation for the sorrow in her eyes.

Keeping close in the corridor shadows, Mordecai trailed the throng, avoiding detection by the guards who marched behind the girls.

Just as the outer garden became visible through the hallway's last door, however, Mordecai was called to a halt.

"What are *you* after?" a voice arrested him.

Wheeling about, the Jew found himself confronted by a portly lady dressed in the simple gown of a servant and bearing a tea tray.

"I . . . I . . ." he stammered.

"Yes?" the woman demanded, trying to show disapproval despite the twinkle in her eye. "You had business in the cloisters, and you saw the girls go by. It has happened here before." Then, growing very serious, she leaned near. "While your appreciation of their beauty is understandable, you must know that it is against the law to hang so close."

Waving a chubby finger under his nose, she warned, "I could turn you in, you know." With that she bustled past him. "You'd best be gone straightaway!" she called over her shoulder.

Mordecai grimaced, but something in the servant's mercy encouraged him.

"Madam," he replied, his tone anxious, "please stay a moment. I must speak with you."

Bewildered, the woman glanced back at him.

"You are very kind," he asserted, joining her near the door. "I should be forever in your debt if you might indulge me further."

The servant said nothing, but curiosity shown on her face.

"I am not what I seem," Mordecai insisted. "I am not some lecherous fool, here to spy on the maidens."

"No?" the woman said, skeptical.

"No," the Jew asserted. "I am guardian to one of those lovelies—her adopted father. You must believe me, for this hardship is very great."

The servant, knowing that such a tale could have little purpose as a lie, listened with more sympathy.

"I must know how she fares, my lady," Mordecai pleaded. "It would be worth a great deal to me."

The emphasis placed on this last statement sparked warmer interest.

"Indeed?" the woman whispered. Peering through the garden portal, she sighed, "Very well. Which child is she? And how may I serve you?"

Mordecai smiled. All morning he had counted treasure, but none of it was so valuable as this encounter.

* * *

Hadassah sat upon a bench at the nearest end of the outer court.

The helpful servant who had met Mordecai in the hall, and whose name was Dorca, assured him that the girl often sat there alone, and that he could usually find her there when the women were led to the garden.

He had waited until the second day to venture down the hall again. Now he stood within fetching distance of his daughter, trying to work up courage to call her name.

She looked thinner than he liked to see her. Surely the king's harem was afforded the finest cuisine. Was Hadassah failing to eat?

Surveying the corridor, Mordecai saw that he was alone. Leaning his head out the garden door, he saw also that there were no keepers near his daughter.

"Child!" he whispered. But his voice was lost in the sound of breeze and splashing fountain.

"Child!" he tried again.

Hadassah turned about, not certain of what she heard. And when she saw her papa, her hand flew to her mouth. Tears welled in her wide eyes, and Mordecai hushed her with a gesture.

Then, beckoning, he pleaded that she join him in the hall.

Hadassah fearfully peered about, and finding that she could do so without notice, she slipped discreetly from the bench.

Falling into her papa's arms, she quietly wept upon his shoulder.

"My Dove," he sighed, "my Myrtle Blossom. You are so thin. Are you ill, my child?"

Hadassah shook her head but continued to tremble in his embrace.

Question after question followed this as he sought to know how she was treated, how she slept, what she knew of her future.

"Tomorrow we are being sent to Hegai, Keeper of the Women," the girl informed him. "Since we arrived, we have been kept in a lesser court until he could receive us. Others have gone in already, but tomorrow my sisters and I are to go before him."

"Your sisters?" Mordecai puzzled.

"The girls with whom I entered. Hegai receives each group in its own turn."

Mordecai nodded, but grew more concerned than ever. "You must eat, my daughter. It will not go well for you here if you do not care for yourself!"

Hadassah shook her head. "But, Papa, you have taught me that certain foods are not fit for a Jew to eat. Even Leah and Moshe taught me this. There is little among the king's delicacies which is lawful."

Amazed, the Israelite studied her sincere expression. "Dear girl," he marveled, "you have always been an obedient child. But this . . ."

Words failed him. She was right, of course. Although he had not been a rigid Jew himself when Hadassah was born, he had grown more scrupulous in his observance of kosher law as she had grown. Since she had been quite little, both he and her closest kin had taught her "clean" from "unclean."

Faltering, he continued. "You are in a Persian house now. As long as Jehovah has brought you to this place, it is your duty to live according to what is provided."

He could not look at her as he said this, uncomfortable with his own logic. When she suddenly pulled away, aghast, his face burned.

"Papa!" she cried. "How can you even suggest that Jehovah has brought this trouble upon me?"

Mordecai knew all too well the reasoning which must have been hers these long days since her abduction: that surely Jehovah would not willingly subject a daughter of Israel to such humiliation, nor expect her to cooperate in any way toward its consummation.

Never had his own faith in the oracles of Mosaic law been so tested. What counsel had he for this innocent one?

A dreadful moment followed as he fought for guidance. But it was Hadassah who at last broke the silence.

"Perhaps," she softly wept, "perhaps I have done something wrong and am being punished. Perhaps I have been an evil girl, and this is my reward!" Bitterly she stared into her papa's desperate countenance. "Yes, that is it! You have told me the stories of Jehovah's vengeance—how He recompenses evil with evil!"

Flushed, she buried her face in her hands, trying to contain her tears.

Grasping at her, Mordecai clutched her to his bosom.

"You have done nothing amiss, Hadassah!" he insisted. "Even

in the moment of your capture, you honored the law."

Bewildered, the girl looked up at him. "I did?" she asked.

"Indeed!" he asserted. "Leah told me so—how you cried out in the house and in the street as you were taken."

More puzzled than ever, Hadassah shrugged. "Any girl would have done so."

"Most likely, yes," Mordecai replied. "But do you not see? This is all the law of Moses requires. When a young woman is forced into disgrace, she is absolved before God and man if she cries out. This is all that is necessary, for it is all a girl can do. Beyond this, nothing is expected . . . except that she go on living!"

Trembling, Hadassah absorbed his confident assertion. As he reached up to wipe a tear from her cheek, she clasped his hand to her lips.

"I am not wicked, then?" she whispered.

Mordecai smiled broadly and shook his head. But just as quickly he hushed her.

"I must be going," he said. "But I shall walk near the harem each day. Though I may not see you for a time, I have ways of knowing how you are. And I shall pray for you constantly. Only . . ." Here he paused, looking about warily. 'One thing you must promise me."

"Yes?" she asked, picking up his careful tone.

"Have you let any of your keepers know you are a Jew?"

"I have not been asked," she said.

"Very well," he nodded. "You must keep your race a secret. Tell no one. Do you hear?"

"But, Papa, why . . ."

"It is not for shame that I say this, Daughter. It is to save your life, just as all my counsel is. Will you obey me in this?"

The girl did not understand, but complied. "I have always obeyed you, Papa," she answered.

Content now, Mordecai stepped back as though he would be going. But his daughter had fresh tears in her eyes, and reached for him pathetically.

"What is it child?" he inquired.

"David . . ." she stammered, the very word causing her to

quake. "What must he think of me now? Oh, Papa, will I ever see him again?"

Gazing upon his beloved with a heavy heart, Mordecai tried to address her gravest fear.

"Trust David to God," he said. "Trust everything to God."

PART IV
The Ascending Star

26

Otanes, father of Vashti, stood on the balcony once belonging to his daughter, from which she as a child had often watched the distant highway and the bustling city below.

For some months now he had known of her whereabouts, having received the information from Angus, guardian of the new harem.

Angus and Vashti had not always seen eye to eye. From the time she had been a little girl in the courts of Darius, she had resented his treatment of the king's women, and he had resented her interference, her constant suggestions and counterpoints. But the callous fellow had a soft spot for the princess in his brutish heart, and since her banishment and the reinstatement of the harem, he had turned his resentments toward Xerxes.

Otanes had been present at the banquet on the night that his son-in-law had, in besotted stupor, cast Vashti from the palace. Ever since, he had sought to know anything he could about her.

General Otanes had opted out of Xerxes' Greek campaigns, unwilling to serve Darius' successor once he had betrayed the queen. As head of one of the seven most privileged families in Persia, he had the right to bow out of military service, and he did so in spite of the fact that he had long lived and breathed to incorporate Greece into the empire.

From the night of the banquet, seething hatred of Xerxes had grown in him, festering into unrequited desire for vengeance. With the acquisition of the harem, and now talk of a new queen, he was bent fully on revenge.

Yes, he knew where Vashti was. And his skin crawled at the thought of her lonely, outcast existence in the wilds of Zagros, in the prison camp of Persia's enemies.

Since the time of Darius' forays into Europe, captured Greeks had been exiled in the stark and snowbound region east of the desert. Otanes had once seen their village, no more than a tract of wooden huts and mud houses. He had deposited a wagonload of prisoners there years before. It had been spring, and though the narrow valley was covered with cedar and mulberry trees, and wildflowers graced the rugged steeps, melting snows had left the rutted street a torrent. Sewage flowed down every path, and sickness stalked the doorways.

He could imagine his gracious Vashti, his aristocratic daughter, taunted every day, persecuted for her relation to Xerxes. He could imagine her sitting in some dark cabin, her once-royal garments long ago fallen into disrepair, and herself obliged to don the habit of strangers.

Greeks were a volatile race. He knew this, for he had observed them firsthand, both in war and as an occupying officer in their Ionian district. While they were also a merry lot, "descendants of Dionysus," god of wine, they were also captious and restive. He could imagine them dancing around his daughter, laughing and deriding as she sat unwilling beside their evening fire.

With their tight-braided hair, heavy black robes, and tattooed hands and faces, they would be leering at her. They would be swaying about her, arms raised, as pipe and drum echoed their hilarity. A thousand clacking cowrie shells, strewn upon their belts and dangling from their headdresses, would mimic their derision. And Vashti—hopeless, alien, exile of exiles—would endure the humiliation alone.

How Otanes hated Xerxes! The lad he had once loved like a son, who had grown up beside his daughter, whose alliance with her had been a coveted thing, was now the object of his fondest loathing. If he could but find a way to bring him down, to make him suffer the way Vashti surely suffered!

But he would need help. Though he was a man of influence, treachery against a king required careful planning and collusion.

Turning from the balcony, he raked his memory for faces and names of those in power who might feel antipathy toward Xerxes. It need not be antipathy of the same intensity he felt, nor for the same reasons. But if there was a seed of it anywhere, he could help it sprout and blossom.

Whether it was a good or an evil spirit which presented the suggestion to him, he knew not. Neither did he care. Indeed, it was genius which reminded him of Haman, the man currently closest to the king.

He recalled, as though it were yesterday, the little cabinet meeting held in Darius' chambers as that monarch plotted his ill-fated escapade into Greece. He recalled how Haman had disapproved the tax break given the citizens in celebration of Xerxes' upcoming marriage to Vashti.

How petty it had seemed that anyone could think a war venture required such stinginess as he proposed.

Otanes had hated Haman then. He had despised his casual disregard of Vashti and her happiness, of Prince Xerxes and his betrothed.

But now he saw Haman's resistance in a different light, in the light of his own loathing. Although Haman had risen high in the service of Xerxes, being one of his closest advisers, perhaps a shred of his former attitude remained. Perhaps Haman was not as devoted to the king as he seemed.

A smile lit Otanes' lips as he reclined upon his daughter's childhood bed. For a long time he stayed in her chamber, pondering possibilities.

27

The murals and frescoes lining the walls of the women's hall depicted a harem life unlike that which Hadassah experienced. Today, as she and her sisters were ushered away from the hive to meet Hegai, Keeper of the Women, the young Jewess wondered what artist had conceived such carefree scenes.

The pictures were from the era of Darius and his predecessors. They supposedly related to events and themes from a previous time. But Hadassah did not believe them. She did not believe that women of any harem spent most of their time laughing and dancing and sporting about. She did not believe that women who would never again see their families, women who would never have husbands of their own choice, women, who, unless the king especially delighted in them, might never twice be called by him, could be happy.

As the girls shuffled down the polished corridor, hesitantly obeying the voice of the guards, Hadassah could not imagine them ever joyous over being here. If some long-ago artist had come upon a scene of merriment and sisterly abandon, he perceived it wrongly. Perhaps he had seen girls frolicking in the pool, splashing one another and giggling, as girls will do. But he had not known their deepest hearts. Perhaps he had found them, from time to time, given to the rhythm of a pipe or tambourine. But he did not understand that they danced around heavy hearts, vainly trying to bury their misery in the moment.

If he saw the other side of their existence, he did not portray it. Such a thing would not have satisfied a king when he came to gaze upon his women. Such a thing would have cooled the ardor of a hungry monarch, passing this way to indulge his senses and select a beauty for the night.

Xerxes had not yet entered this hall, for the women were still in preparation for him. The year of his yearning for a bride was not yet over, and the selection process had not yet begun. But soon enough it would begin, as evidenced by several servants just now kneeling in the corridor with paintbrushes and putty, filling in chips, refurbishing faded colors, and updating the frescoes.

Tears threatened to spill over Hadassah's stony face as she plodded behind her sisters. She wondered if Hegai, Keeper of the Women, would interrogate her today, if he would ask her nationality or her family name. She prayed that he would not, for she did not know what she would say, and she was determined to honor Mordecai's request for secrecy.

They waited outside Hegai's door for what seemed a very long time before a portly woman came to fetch them.

Hadassah could not know that Dorca was Mordecai's "connection." But Dorca knew who Hadassah was, and she smiled especially kindly on her as she guided the virgins into the chamber.

The girls were all dressed alike, in simple cotton smocks, their street clothes having been taken from them—to be burned, they were told. Dorca understood, as they might not, that they were dressed simply and uniformly so that when Hegai looked upon them for the first time he would be able to judge them on fundamental beauty alone. No extravagant clothing, coiffure, or adornment must distract his eye from its discerning purpose.

For Hegai was seeking not just a quantity of women who would please the king, but that one special girl worthy to be queen.

Hadassah had expected Hegai to be another Angus. She was therefore very surprised when a little wisp of a man emerged from the office and came forth to greet the girls.

While Dorca introduced Hegai as the one who would manage them during their preparation, he circled the group, round and round, his hands rubbing together and his beardless chin studiously wagging this way and that.

"Uh-hmmm," he intoned, over and over, "Uh-hmmm."

Nervously, the virgins clung together as he surveyed them up and down, much as a housewife might inspect the meat hung out at market.

Yet there was much of the artist in his eye, the experienced critic. It was obvious that he knew beauty and imperfection, and could have turned away from the entwined huddle with a firm memory of each dimple, each freckle, each sweaty little hand.

Hadassah's heart pumped rapidly as he stopped near her elbow. Once more he circled the group, and then returned to her, observing her more pointedly than the others.

As he did so, his eyes brightened. And then he drew back, thoughtfully stroking his shiny chin.

"All right, all right, Dorca," he demanded in a boyish and impatient voice, "line them up."

His gaze was on Hadassah until she grew uneasy, but she followed Dorca's command and fell in line against the chamber wall, side by side with her sisters.

"Disrobe," Dorca ordered.

At this, indignant gasps arose from the little group, and the girls clung modestly to their smocks.

"It must be done," the servant insisted, trying to be callous.

Dorca had not been doing this long. She had not worked for the harem of Darius, and this routine was still uncomfortable for her. Her expression betrayed more sympathy than she liked.

As the girls shielded themselves, observing Hegai in horror, Dorca whispered, "He is a eunuch, after all. There is nothing to fear."

If the keeper heard this, he did not comment, only standing impatiently by and leafing through a sheaf of fabric samples.

When he glanced up, he again focused on Hadassah, who fumbled with her gown.

One by one the young ladies complied and cringed in shame under his scrutiny.

But it was all done quickly, and red-faced, they donned their clothes again.

Hadassah's cheeks burned and her fingers were palsied as she tugged her short tunic over her head, drew it down to her knees, and stood shaking against the wall.

"They will do," Hegai crooned.

Dorca nodded. Like so many humiliated sheep, the damsels were herded from the room until Hegai's voice stopped them.

"This one," he called to Dorca, "this one—speed her up!"

The servant followed his pointed finger and studied Hadassah with him.

Perhaps she too had seen what Hegai saw in the girl. It seemed not to surprise her when Hadassah was singled out.

"I shall," she agreed.

The young Jewess could not imagine what design they had in mind. She only crossed her arms and huddled against the back of the line.

As the virgins exited, led back to their hive, she was sure she would always feel naked. For the rest of her life.

28

Mordecai wrung his hands as he glanced between the pillars of the harem corridor. Dorca was late. Normally she met him in the hall, with word of his Hadassah, before the women's midday repast. But it was already early afternoon, and she had not come yet.

When the shuffle of her slippered feet caught his ear from behind, he wheeled about nervously.

"Madam," he greeted with a short bow, "the guard is growing suspicious. My 'inventory' work must terminate soon, and I will not be able to meet you here."

Dorca nodded. "I have expected that. But if you wish me to continue in your service, I can find a way."

The Jew smiled relief. "I do wish this," he asserted.

"Then meet me each evening in the entrance garden. I can arrange to be there after dinner," she offered.

Mordecai knew she referred to the large lobby just inside the main gate of the palace. This would be convenient to Mordecai as he sat all day upon the porch, doing his ledgers.

"Fine, fine!" he exclaimed. "The garden is open to officials of my rank. I will not attract undo notice."

Dorca's smile was reticent. "I have news today which would please most men of ambition. But in your case . . ."

"Yes," he spurred her. "It regards Hadassah?"

"She has been promoted."

Mordecai's eyes brightened reflexively. But just as fast the twinkle vanished.

"What does that mean?" he hesitated.

"Hegai sees something special in the child," the servant replied. "I just left her with the matrons where she is to enter

preparation immediately. Tradition requires a full year of puri-
fication and beautification, but your daughter's time will be
overseen with particular detail, as she is a rare find." Color fled
Mordecai's face. His middle-aged hands trembled.

"You are not proud," Dorca observed. "I feared this."

"I shall not see Hadassah after I leave this place," he sighed.
"So long as I have worked in the harem storeroom, I had the
chance to glimpse her."

The servant put forth a plump finger and stroked his sleeve.

"Perhaps the next time you see her she will be a woman in
regal splendor. My friend," she whispered, "try to see this as an
honor. Hegai is a connoisseur of beauty, and in Hadassah he has
found something rare and wonderful. The girl has been greatly
blessed."

But Mordecai only looked at the lady sadly.

"Blessed . . . or cursed?" he pondered. "I am not certain
which."

* * *

Hadassah sat upon a ledge of her private pool. Cooling fountains splashed into silent, lily-laden waters as her personal maids,
seven in all, bustled about to the commands of the head matron,
Dorca.

Here one young woman poured a flask of frankincense into
the girl's fragrant bath, and there another mixed a beautifying
paste of flour, mustard oil, turmeric, and saffron according to a
recipe recently received from India.

After Hadassah's third dip of the day into the perfumed
waters, the paste would be applied to her face and she would
sleep through one more aromatic night, still unused to the
pungent smells of her heady lair.

The evening before, a Bengalese mixture of sandalwood and
aloes had been administered, leaving her cheeks atingle, and
when it had been removed this morning, a stubborn flush had
remained part of her complexion for hours.

But all of this was supposed to perfect her—to make her more
beautiful than any other woman in the empire.

She wished that she might feel some enthusiasm for the project, which had already extended over three months. She knew that many of her harem sisters would have traded places with her at any opportunity.

The Phoenician was one of her handpicked helpers. Dorca had let Hadassah have some say in which girls were taken from the hive to assist in her personal preparation. She had selected the dark beauty from the coastland out of compassion, though the proud girl would have scorned the notion.

As for Maryam, her fellow villager, she envied Hadasssah not at all. Tender pity marked her attendance on the Jewess, for she knew Hadassah would never have chosen this "honor." She was only glad that Leah's young cousin had not forgotten her, once gone from the lower harem, and she was grateful to serve her.

Two other girls fumbled through a pile of silks and velvets, giggling and trying on today's collection of fashionable gowns, all made to complement Hadassah's natural glory to best advantage. "Oh, my lady," one exclaimed, "you will love these! Why, they are the best yet!"

Dorca, with a gesture, flicked the girls away from the rack. "The lady's linens must be changed," she barked, ordering them to the boudoir where Hadassah would recline for the night. Quickly they scurried away to change Hadassah's bedding for the second time since morning, since she had napped upon the couch, soiling it with the pastes and oils applied earlier to her skin.

Everything about this private chamber, the most indulgent in the harem, was pure luxury. Countless girls would have found life here beyond their wildest fantasies. But Hadassah had never longed for such attentions.

When Dorca set a tiny tray of stuffed prunes and iced apples before her, she only sighed. And when the matron turned away, a tear trickled down Hadassah's cheek, streaking the face cream spread upon it.

Maryam bent over her, stroking her dark curls.

"The king was seen from the harem wall today, riding with his attendants along the river," she whispered. "His royal parasol tipped back, Hadassah, and some of the girls saw his face . . ."

The Jewess did not respond.

"Oh, Hadassah, they say he is very handsome!" Maryam went on, trying to cheer her.

Still the favored one said nothing. Memories of David's golden eyes haunted her, and in her heart she walked beside him through the wheat fields.

29

Xerxes sat on the edge of his bed, staring through the twilight which crept with desert dawn through his chamber window. His huge feather pallet, elevated from the floor on golden ram's feet and enclosed with gauze draperies, cradled a young woman. Upon her face his regal gaze lingered.

He could not recall her name. He would forget her as soon as he sent her from the room. And he would never request her again.

For three months the king of the Eastern world had enjoyed the company of a new girl each evening. But he could remember only a handful. When he especially admired a certain female, he commanded her name and a brief description to be registered in his private chronicle so that he might summon her again.

Thus far the list in the royal book was quite short. And he had not bothered to request a girl a second time.

Upon dismissal from the king's chamber, each young lady was ushered to the house of the concubines, to live out her life on the chance that she might be useful in the future. Most would face years of loneliness and despair, their youthful beauty fading, their isolation prison-like despite its luxuries.

Most girls, however inexperienced, could tell after their first night whether or not they had pleased their "husband." For Xerxes was developing a volatile temper, and some of the women were thrust from the chamber before the moon had fully risen, their virginity still intact.

The sweet and simple child who now lay sleeping beside him would not encounter that side of the king. It ebbed and flowed unpredictably, and she had come to him when he was in a conciliatory mood. Nor did most of those who were rebuffed know what they had done to incur his wrath, being often among the loveliest and most charming of the "brides."

Beyond the bedroom door two guards stood, waiting on the emperor's emergence, waiting to escort the girl to the Keeper of the Concubines, the Shaashgaz, who was in charge of the second harem.

The guards had come by their work ironically. Having once served as Vashti's sentinels at the door of her private chamber, they were promoted to serve the king when she was sent away.

Their new station did not please them. They had loved the queen a long while, being her attendants when she was a child and having served her in Otanes' house. Sorely did they resent the lady's banishment, and it distressed them each time a new "bride" arrived to consort with the king.

When the door to Xerxes' chamber was at last drawn open, and the most recent "wife" stepped shakily into the corridor, they bowed rigidly toward the room's dark shadows.

They could not see the king, nor did he speak to them. Without a word he had dismissed the lady, and she stood now with the sentinels, wondering what was to come.

"You take her back," Teresh said, nodding to his companion. "I tire of this."

Bigthan, the other guard, sighed sympathetically, turning toward the errand with stooped shoulders.

Their brief interchange did not go unobserved. Otanes, father of Vashti, was rarely so near the king's chambers, especially this early in the morning. But family business had brought him at dawn to this sector of the palace, and as he passed by the emperor's quarters, he overheard the unhappy murmur.

Eager as he was for names to add to his ledger of malcontents, he registered their identity in his mental file.

These two fellows might be advantageous to him—a snare to the king.

30

Mordecai paced through the porch before the palace's garden gate, darting glances through the portal.

"Late again!" he muttered, wondering what could be detaining his contact, Dorca, this time.

The sky above the open porch was dark with thunderclouds. It was "mud month" again, a full year since Hadassah had been abducted to the harem. Anxiety had been growing in the girl's adopted father as the anniversary of her imprisonment drew near. Daily he raised earnest petitions to Jehovah, pleading for the child's release, for some miracle of intervention which would spare her from shame.

It was dinnertime throughout the palace. Most of the executives and hired help who lived outside the king's house had gone home for the evening. Mordecai would have been among them except that he had an arrangement to meet Dorca at this time each day. So far no one had questioned his lingering after hours. But he feared that sometime his "late work" might be suspect, should anyone find him pacing the open air of the garden.

The longer Dorca took, the more fidgety Mordecai became, until he heard her quick shuffle in the entry.

"I am sorry, sir," she apologized, coming upon him with her own anxieties, "I could not break away from Hegai. He kept me late tonight, preparing our dear lady for the morrow."

Though this announcement was given without hesitation, her face showed lines of regret.

"Hadassah . . ." Mordecai whispered.

"I fear so, my friend. But you must have known it was inevitable. Tomorrow is one year to the day since she was brought here. Hegai will not delay sending her to His Majesty."

"Tomorrow evening?" he said, his voice tremulous.

Dorca only nodded, and Mordecai stared at the floor through tear-filled eyes.

Hope lay in shattered shards at his feet, faith peeled itself from his heart. For 12 months he had prayed for Hadassah's salvation, finding it incredible that Jehovah could allow an innocent child to undergo such defilement.

Perhaps, he thought, perhaps he should have taught her to rebel, to risk her young life to escape the evil design. Perhaps he had been woefully remiss in suggesting to the girl that Jehovah could have brought her here. Perhaps he should have told her that she had the right to save herself regardless of the cost.

Suddenly reality clutched at him with cutting claws. Nothing he had assumed seemed apt to prove itself. Nothing he had dreamed would come true.

Dorca stood uneasily in his presence, waiting for her pittance of payment, the daily drachma of wage received for her secret service.

When Mordecai appeared to have forgotten her, she did not press him.

She said something about meeting him another day, but he did not hear her, and after she had departed he stood for a long while, staring blankly at the swirling floor.

It was not until another set of feet shuffled into the silent garden that Mordecai glanced up from his sad preoccupation. When his gaze fell upon Haman, his blood ran cold.

Stealthily he turned from the arboretum, and with a chill across his shoulders he hurried home.

Had he remained, he might have witnessed yet another rendezvous within the twilight court. For it was Otanes who had requested Haman's presence here, and moments after the prime minister's arrival, the general joined him.

The plot they discussed was private unto themselves. But in time the simple bookkeeper, the Jew who had long suspected Haman's capacity for treachery, would be their unwitting foil.

31

Hadassah stood before a long brass mirror in her private dressing room. Her seven personal maids surrounded her, their faces smitten with awe.

After four hours of helping their mistress to dress and undress, to try on one gown after another, it seemed that the most radiant combination of raiment, accessories, and hairstyle imaginable had been struck upon. Surely the keeper, Hegai, would be pleased this time when he came to inspect their handiwork. Had he not, after all, personally selected every piece of this ensemble? His temperamental taste had driven him to rage more than once this day when he had come to approve their choices. Nothing, nothing had pleased him. But surely this time there was no improving upon the lady's appearance.

Indeed, Hadassah herself was stricken speechless as she gazed upon her likeness in the mirror. Despite her fears and the dreaded ordeal which lay ahead, she could not repress a smile of surprise and delight as her reflection stared back at her.

Hardly did it seem possible that this was she! Hadassah had never been blind to her own beauty, but the regal glory of the female in the glass was beyond any she had ever witnessed before.

A lump caught in her slender throat as she turned slowly this way and that. Raising her hand to her mouth, she held back a little cry of joy.

Her keeper had chosen the most complimentary of colors for his favorite damsel. The gown, of purest linen, had been dyed a pale lavender and was cinched to her tiny waist by a broad cummerbund of royal scarlet. The scarlet, in fact, verged on magenta, with every tuck and hem piped in deep purple.

Upon her small feet were slippers of velvet, likewise of magenta hue, encrusted with gleaming rubies, violet sapphires, and amethysts. The slightly upturned toes sported tinkling bells, so teeny that they would be heard only when she walked upon the deep carpet of the king's silent chamber.

But even as she peered down at the silver ornaments where they glinted against the velvet, her heart quivered, and she could not retract the tear which gleamed upon her cheek.

David should be the first man to see this glory. Yes, David, her love—and not a Persian despot.

With numb fingers she brushed the betraying tear from her face and tried to smile again. However, when she looked once more into the glass, the image of her beloved had transposed itself over her own, with sad and hurt-filled countenance.

None of her companions saw the phantom in the mirror, and no one seemed to notice her sorrow. Save for Maryam.

As the other women laughed and giggled about her, holding the broad train of her dress to their own cheeks and dancing, her little friend came close and placed a sympathetic hand upon her shoulder.

But Maryam had no time to speak a comforting word, for suddenly the chamber door opened and Dorca bustled in, chatting excitement to Hegai, who followed with an anxious step.

"See," she exclaimed, "see! Is it not as I told you? How can she be better? She is the beauty of the world!"

The maids, who had worked so hard to achieve the effect which Hegai would now assess, held their breath as the eunuch drew into the lamplight and beheld Hadassah.

For a long while he said nothing, his face vacant. And the girls were more nervous by the minute.

Their lady was due to go before the king this very evening. If the keeper did not appreciate this work of art . . . they feared the consequences.

Slowly he circled the Jewess, uttering not a word, until even Dorca became apprehensive.

When the keeper suddenly fell to his knees, bowing over and over before Hadassah, everyone drew back in wonder.

Except for Dorca. Her expression, while one of amazement, was mixed with relief, and she nodded her head, smiling to herself.

As for Hadassah, she observed the eunuch fearfully, pondering the meaning of his strange behavior.

"My Lady!" he cried, lifting wet eyes to the Jewess, "surely you are Vashti! Surely you are the dear queen!"

Hadassah looked about her, more terrified yet, seeking an explanation.

Instantly Dorca was at her side, bowing from the waist.

"Hegai is right, my child," she agreed. "How you resemble our banished Lady!"

Recalling the one time that she had been privileged to look upon the queen, when as a child she had peered between the spindles of the garden balcony, Hadassah turned again to the mirror and with hesitation surveyed her reflection.

A chill passed down her spine and she grasped her skirt with a trembling hand. Long ago as it had been, the recollection of Vashti matched that in the glass, and Hadassah braced herself against vertigo.

But now Hegai was standing, and as the girl studied the mirror, Dorca handed the keeper the cape which he had designed for this ensemble.

Stepping behind the Jewess, the eunuch tenderly draped the stole around her shoulders and gazed with her into the glass.

"It is a miracle!" he cried.

And it was. The purple stole, embroidered with pink and lavender irises, drew the entire outfit together, lending Hadassah an unmistakable look of royalty.

Feeling faint now, the girl put forth a hand, and Hegai held her upright.

"It is fitting that you should have a new name," the eunuch pronounced. "A new name for a new life. You shall be called 'Esther,' for you are worthy of nothing less."

Hadassah clutched his hand more firmly, her breath coming anxiously. Esther? No more dreadful designation could be applied to a Jewess, for Esther, or Ishtar, was the most pagan of goddesses, the Astarte of the Canaanites, the Aphrodite and the

Venus of the Greeks. Goddess of fertility and sexuality, she was a demeaning label for any girl who loved Jehovah.

Shaking her head, Hadassah wished to cry aloud. But, remembering Mordecai's injunction to keep her race a secret, she choked back her horror.

And now Hegai was standing before her, placing a fresh orchid in her raven hair and weaving its short stem between the intricate waves.

Bidding her take his arm, he turned her about and led her forth from the chamber.

She would not remember the long walk down the palace's cold corridor. She would not notice the awe-filled faces of all who saw her, nor would she hear the gasps of wonder which followed her bleak passage.

She walked into a void, mystified that faith should have failed her.

32

Esther stood within the king's dimly lit chamber, the door having been closed behind her.

Xerxes, Emperor of the East, master of the greatest empire on earth, had not yet acknowledged her presence, but only sat brooding at his northern window. He had no reason to pay this new "bride" any more mind than he had paid the dozens brought before.

It was true that Hegai had personally escorted Esther to his door rather than sending her with a guard. It was true that the eunuch had, upon introducing her to the bridal suite, emphasized her new name. And if anything should have piqued the king's interest, it would have been this.

For though the emperor was a devout adherent of the one god Ahura-Mazda, the name "Ishtar" in any language had a way of thrilling the blood of most men.

It had troubled the keeper when Xerxes had ignored the introduction, receiving Esther with a flick of the hand and failing to even turn his head toward her. But Hegai had shut the door upon the couple, confident that when the king did glimpse the girl he would succumb to her humble charms.

And humble she was. This too might have troubled Hegai. He might have wondered just how adept the young virgin could be at seduction. But he passed off the concern. What need had such beauty of experience or of effort? The fact that any female so designed was flesh and blood, and not a statue conceived by wild fantasy, would be enough to secure her place in Xerxes' favor.

For no man could fail to love her. No man could ignore her, Hegai was certain. Even he, stripped of his masculinity, rendered impotent from birth that he might serve the palace with docile single-mindedness—even he was moved in his own way by this girl.

So Esther stood, unspeaking in the shadows, awaiting whatever lay ahead.

Never had she prayed so fervently as during these moments. If Jehovah intended to intervene, He must do so now. For weeks she had, in hours of fear, rehearsed the childhood lessons of Judaism learned upon Mordecai's lap, memorized at Leah's knee. Tonight, however, they eluded her, and she found herself cast helplessly upon blind trust.

Somehow, though it made no sense to her, she must accept whatever should happen here. Having done all she could to please Jehovah, she must abandon herself to any tyranny that God might permit.

With an empty sigh she looked down at the garment that Hegai had prepared for her. Each girl was allowed to choose the outfit she would wear upon her "wedding" night, heeding or disregarding Hegai's advice as she wished. But Esther had not quibbled, having determined ahead of time that she would accept the eunuch's advice. Truly his taste was impeccable, and he had done well by her.

The garment symbolized the end of life as she had known it. It was, in fact, all she had in this world. Every young woman, upon the day she went before the king, was allowed to take from the harem whatever she wished. Most girls had given this privilege much advance thought, gathering up enough jewels, gold, spices, and fine fabrics to secure their futures and the futures of their loved ones beyond the palace walls for years to come. But Esther had requested nothing but the clothes upon her slender frame.

This was all she needed. Material goods would never cheer a future without family . . . without David. . . .

It seemed she waited in the shadows for an eternity, though by the wintry glow of sunset beyond the king's window it had been only moments since she arrived.

Quivering, Esther surveyed her intended. Though he was in silhouette against the ruddy night, she could see that he was a tall man, and strong. His features, framed by the departing light, were regal; his hair, where it spilled in waves to his shoulders, was lustrous and dark.

Still, until she could see his eyes, she would know little about him save what rumor had imputed to him. And rumor had painted a fearful picture—one of capriciousness and cruelty.

Through the window's scalloped arch the famed Zagros mountains loomed, distant and austere.

Was the emperor at prayer? Esther wondered. The faraway mountains were sacred to the Persians, she knew, especially to those who followed the teachings of Zoroaster.

But, then, she reminded herself, Xerxes was the man who had sent his queen into exile. Could such a creature bear a bone of religious devotion in his body? Ahura-Mazda, she had heard, was very much like Jehovah—God of the universe, a kind and just deity. If it were possible that the Persians received some spiritual light from their worship, Xerxes had surely turned from it.

It must have been the descending dark which spurred the king to turn at last from the window. When he did, he did not immediately focus on the girl in the shadows. It seemed, in fact, that he had forgotten her very presence. And Esther was surprised to note that his eyes, now visible in the lamplight, bore a heavy sadness. Far from indicating a cold heart, they betrayed a wounded spirit, taking Hadassah aback.

"Well, let us see what we have here," the emperor suddenly commanded, gesturing her forward, though still not looking upon her.

Cautiously the virgin Jewess stepped into the lamp's exposing glow, and at last the king glanced up from whatever wistful thoughts had held him.

As he did, his expression grew from one of apathy to one of incredulity. Gripping the bedpost, he held himself steady and slowly sank to the mattress, sitting palefaced as one who witnessed an apparition.

"Lord Ahura-Mazda," he gasped, "can it be? Vashti, my bride!"

Esther, rigid with fright, dared not contradict the king.

Finding strength to rise, Xerxes approached her, his lips trembling.

"Thank you, Ahura," he was whispering over and over. "Thank you."

Reaching for Esther, he enfolded her in strong arms, repeating Vashti's name in her ear.

Terrified, the girl struggled in his embrace. But he allowed no resistance.

"My child," he groaned, "bless me. Do not deny your king . . . your husband. Let me believe in miracles."

Pressing his lips to her neck, he drew her cape from off her shoulders, stroking her bare arms with gentle hands.

Dizzy from his persistent caress, Esther closed her eyes, and the lamplight yielded to the night.

* * *

Somewhere deep in the Zagros, Vashti, deposed Queen of the East, lurched upright on her bed of animal skins.

Her face, still lovely despite the lines which loneliness and alienation had traced, peeked through the darkness toward her distant royal city.

Something had roused her from near slumber— some dread awareness.

She was alone in her wooden hut. Everyone else in the village was asleep. But there would have been no consolation even in brightest daylight. Had she spoken fluent Greek, none of her fellow exiles would have cared for her plight.

Lying down again, she listened to the beating of her solitary heart. Somehow she knew that Xerxes was not alone. Somehow she sensed the rising of another star.

PART V
For Such a Time as This

33

The sky over Susa was a rainbow of color. Phosphorescent greens, blues, and vermillion lit up the night in explosive auroras.

Xerxes had spared no expense in celebrating his marriage to Esther. Within a week of her coming to him a holiday had been declared, imperial gifts in the form of reduced taxes had been given the provinces, and people had exchanged lavish presents.

The wedding itself, held in Persepolis, was unparalleled in Persian history. And immediately following, the king announced a banquet in Susa's royal house. "Esther's banquet," he called it, a reception second in grandeur only to the many-month celebration at which he had banished Vashti.

Fireworks had been displayed each evening for a week, igniting the sky above the acropolis with symbolic splendor, because the emperor, after years of disappointment, misery, and futile endeavors to find happiness, was experiencing life once again.

Daily he called his new queen to dine with him in his private suite, and nightly he loved her with an ardor unknown since last he had lain with Vashti.

He assumed that Esther must be as happy as he was, though not once had he asked her. In fact, he knew nothing of Esther's heart, reading in her only what he wanted to read. And what he wanted to read was that she was the answer to prayer, the closest thing to Vashti returned to him.

There was another man, however, who wondered how Esther felt. She had never been out of his thoughts since the night she was abducted to the palace.

David stood at his village's western gate, watching the bursting aura across the desert.

Hope had died when Hadassah was taken to the king's chamber.

David had known what evening that was. He had counted the dawns and sunsets leading to it, 365 of them.

As he stood tonight at the low village wall, studying the celebrating flashes, each explosion sent a spear through his heart. He was no warrior. He had no weapon with which to fight back—only the farmer's hoe upon which he leaned. And the acropolis, bathed in azure and scarlet, mocked his poverty.

Should he wonder any longer how Hadassah felt? Was she not the owner of an emperor's embraces, pride of a sovereign's heart, wealthiest woman on earth?

David gripped the handle of his hoe in a stranglehold. Perhaps he should wrap the long tool in fancy paper and send it to the palace, he thought cynically. It was all he could offer as a wedding gift. It was all he possessed.

Glancing heavenward again, he shrugged and dropped the hoe against the wall. Downcast, he plodded home, pushing against the weight of a hollow heart.

34

Clouds of nearing spring swept over Susa's acropolis. Queen Esther, hastening through the inner court, glanced skyward but did not see the cottony tufts, her mind speeding higher, seeking Jehovah in earnest prayer.

She would be with her papa in a few moments. Using her regal position to advantage, she had arranged to "interview" the book-keeper for a position as her private accountant.

She had let no one know of her relationship to the Jew, in accordance with Mordecai's wishes. It was only under the guise of business that she could even properly be seen by any male other than her husband. But she had made certain that no one else would be present, sending all her maids off on errands and scheduling the "audience" in an unguarded alcove.

"Let nothing hinder this stolen moment," she pleaded as she hurried toward the rendezvous.

Passing through the final vestibule before the garden, she came to a frozen halt, a deep shadow having fallen across her path.

High above, upon a fluted pedestal, the enormous black stone head of a sacred bull stared down upon her. Fully as great in length as the lady's own height, and half as wide, it hovered over her like a disapproving giant. And across the broad aisle was its partner, equally brooding.

Though she was queen, she had not been trained for the part. She was still a humble Jewess, quiet daughter of a quiet man.

The bulls threatened her, doubting her ability, suspecting her.

For a long moment she hesitated beneath their austere gazes. Gleaming in the brilliant sun, they leveled dark questions at her, their cold, polished eyes and heavy brows deflecting all signs of weakness.

Quietly she eased past them, entering the garden and the alcove through a haze of self-castigation.

But when she saw Mordecai, her countenance brightened.

"Papa!" she cried, flinging her arms wide and flying to him. Mordecai drew back, shaking his head and bowing.

"My Queen," he hailed.

Horrified, Esther stared at him, hot tears rising to blind her. "Papa?" she returned. "It is I, your Hadassah."

But Mordecai could only gaze speechlessly upon her.

Did he disapprove as well, she wondered? Did he recoil from the stain upon her life?

In agonized silence the girl turned her face to the floor, and Mordecai, seeing her distress, at last found words.

"Hadassah . . ." he whispered. "It is only that you . . . you are royalty now. And a woman, a beautiful woman . . . not a girl. Hardly would I recognize you, did I not know you so well."

Though this acknowledgment bore a sting, a smile parted Esther's lips, and with a sigh she reached for him again.

"It has been so long . . ." Mordecai cried, returning the embrace. "Can you still care for this old man—this . . . commoner?"

"Papa!" Esther rebuked him. "Do not speak so!"

But it was Mordecai's turn to smile. And clinging, they wept together.

Just as quickly, however, the Jew held her at arm's length, his face etched with urgency.

"Child," he whispered, "bear with a bit of whimsy, if you will. There is something I must tell you."

Esther studied him quizzically, wondering at the anxious mystery in his tone.

"Of course, Papa," she nodded. "What troubles you?"

Casting a wary glance over his shoulder, he continued, "There is evil afoot in this place. I have felt it for months, and today, on my way here, I witnessed it firsthand." Then, bowing again, he seemed to beg her indulgence, and she spurred him.

"Papa, I am your Hadassah," she asserted. "Please go on."

"Perhaps it was my imagination . . ." he hesitated. "But as

I came down the main corridor, I passed by two men who consulted together, dressed like guards—royal guards. Both were tall, and very strong, as though . . .”

“The king's doorkeepers,” Esther guessed. “Dark and bearded?”

“Yes, yes!” Mordecai enthused. “You know them, then?”

Esther's mind flashed to the night she had first been introduced to the king's chamber, and she nodded with wistful sadness.

“Then I am not mistaken!” the Jew determined. “The king is in danger!”

Quickly reciting the conversation overheard in the hall, he warned the queen that this very evening Xerxes' life was at stake. “ ‘When he is asleep, after the chamberlain puts out his light . . .’ ” he quoted them. Then, rubbing his hands nervously together, Mordecai continued, “Oh, child, they thought they were alone, and when I suddenly rounded the corner, coming upon them, they covered their plot with idle chatter.”

Esther's face grew pale, and drawing close, she confirmed Mordecai's fears. “There are many who hate the emperor,” she agreed. “Many loved Vashti, and I have sensed jealously for that lady in the air since the day I took the throne. . . .”

“Then, my child,” Mordecai cringed, “you also could be in danger!”

Esther shivered, and placed a cold hand on her papa's arm.

“You shall be rewarded,” she commanded him. “I do not know the king well, but I know he honors his friends.”

Mordecai glanced at the tiled floor, an ironic smirk working at his lips. “I, a *friend* of Xerxes,” he laughed. “I dare say, I love him less than anyone could.”

Gazing into Hadassah's sympathetic eyes, he shook his head. “There is more . . . much more than I have told you,” he insisted. “There is more evil here than a plot between bedroom guards.”

The queen awaited an explanation, but he could give none. It was an intuition of the blood which told him—an insight of the spirit giving warning.

“In time we shall see it all,” he said. “For now I know nothing.”

Esther felt the pallor of his prophecy, and did not question it. Recalling the dark gazes of the garden bulls, the black gleam of their marbled eyes, she knew he spoke the truth.

The palace of Persia was a battlefield, and the opponents played a contest more profound than politics.

35

The incident with the king's guards was to be only the first skirmish in the supernatural battle staged in Persia's royal house. Of all the people in the land, only Mordecai the Jew saw it as something more than a human battle. And even he could not foresee the part it played in the greater drama.

Otanes and Haman certainly did not perceive the working out of a higher plan. To Otanes, the attempt to overthrow Xerxes was a justified act of retaliation. To Haman, whose assistance Otanes had promised to reward, the goal had been personal advancement.

When the general and the prime minister lost the first round, they determined even more sincerely to work for Xerxes' demise.

In the executive courtyard they met this afternoon, beneath the swaying shadows of two corpses, the bodies of Bigthan and Teresh, suspended from the gallows of Xerxes' wrath.

"Who revealed the plot?" Otanes snarled, disappointment heavy beneath his breath.

"A minor executive," Haman replied, "the Jew who now keeps the books for Queen Esther."

His loathing of the race readily surfaced, and Otanes shrugged. "The one who used to sit at the gate? Head of inventory?"

"The same," Haman smirked. "One can never be too careful."

"Careful?" Otanes sneered. "The fools must have heralded their plan upon the palace roof!"

"Well, it is done now," Haman sighed, glancing up at the dead men on the gallows.

Otanes said nothing, deep in thought. Then, having struck upon a new idea, he eagerly pursued a different tack.

"Haman, how would you like your reward *now* . . . before the deed is done?"

The prime minister studied the general, incredulous. Leaning forward eagerly, he dreamed of glory.

* * *

Trumpets blared in the gate of Susa's palace. Haman was entering, and everyone prepared to do him homage.

Xerxes, prey to the blindness common to the powerful which renders them insensible to dangers directly beneath their noses, saw Haman as a loyal adviser, a man of duty and accomplishment who had served his father well and who served his own administration admirably. When Otanes came before the king praising the prime minister and suggesting that some great honor be heaped upon him, Xerxes, wishing to appear magnanimous, elevated the Agagite, establishing his position as second in command of the empire. With this, he went so far as to require all servants and princes of the royal house to bow down whenever the man passed by. Refusal to do so would not only merit Haman's disapproval but would invoke the wrath of the emperor himself.

In reality, the "advancement" carried little political clout. Haman was already grand vizier. But this public commendation on the part of Xerxes raised his prominence in the eyes of all, forcing them to render obeisance, however begrudgingly.

Haman was not a popular figure. He had few admirers and fewer lovers. But since the king's edict had been enacted, it could be suicide to ignore him.

Therefore, it was with incredulous wonder that the palace servants, bowing as Haman entered the gate, observed Mordecai's rebellion.

The Jew would not bow. The Jew would not pay homage to an Agagite.

Stiff and austere, the gray-bearded Hebrew sat behind his accounting bench upon the public porch, unyielding as the prime minister passed his way.

Until Mordecai foiled the assassination attempt, Haman had brushed elbows with the Jew on numerous occasions but had paid him little mind. He was, as he had told Otanes, a "minor executive," and a Jew at that.

But this day, when Mordecai drew attention to himself through blatant disrespect, Haman had more reason than ever to notice him. In an instant the Jew leapt from obscurity to public prominence.

Haman, stopping directly before the bookkeeper's table, said nothing, waiting for his compliance. But Mordecai's behavior was not the product of oversight. Directly he stared back at the prime minister, refusing to bow, until Haman's face flushed crimson with anger, and amazed whispers fluttered about the court.

Had Haman only rebuked him, the Jew's position might not have seemed so precarious. But when the Agagite turned for the palace door, entering the royal house without a word, retribution was all the more imminent.

Once Haman was out of sight, the spectators gathered around the quiet Hebrew like astonished gossips.

"Why are you transgressing the king's command?" they queried.

Mordecai, a very private man, had never drawn so much notice. But an answer was ready on his tongue.

Stroking his frosted beard, he framed the reply with dignity. "Because," he said, "I am a Jew."

36

Haman paced the king's council chamber, counting the alabaster tiles with his toes, his face etched with feigned frustration.

"How your royal patience must have been strained all these years, Your Majesty! I do not know how you have endured it," he exclaimed.

Xerxes leaned forward upon his throne, his own expression one of bewildered scrutiny.

"Say again, Haman," he implored. "These folk to whom you refer—they have been party to sedition?"

"Indeed, Your Highness. But you must know it. Surely—oh, I see . . . How clever of you to test me, Sire. You wish a fuller disclosure of their activities?"

Xerxes, not wishing to appear unaware of the supposed dissension within his kingdom, only nodded.

Haman, with a sigh of deep concern, ceased his pacing and rubbed his hands together. "O King, live forever!" he intoned. "You know that there is a certain people . . ." And here he peered about him, as though concealing their identity was of critical importance to the safety of the realm, ". . . a certain people scattered abroad and dispersed among the folk of all the provinces of your kingdom. And their customs are different from everyone else's. Nor do they keep the king's laws," he lied. Then, with a quick and deliberate pronouncement, he concluded, "Therefore it is not for the king's profit to allow them to continue!"

The emperor sat back, studying Haman blankly. Dare he let on that he was less informed than his key adviser regarding such widespread subversion? And dare he question the very man whose reputation he had so recently secured, whom he had just publicly endorsed as second-in-command of his entire empire?

He knew not of whom Haman spoke. He did not know that this tax pirate had a personal vendetta against a single Jew, a modest bookkeeper. He did not know that Haman's wounded pride could prompt him to appeal for a pogrom against an entire race.

Xerxes had his own struggle with pride. Therefore, rather than admit to ignorance, he would affirm Haman's stand.

Swallowing hard, he considered the prime minister's intentions.

"What do you wish of me?" he asked at last.

A gleam flashed through Haman's eyes. "If it please the king," he said with a low bow, "let it be written that these people may be destroyed."

He hesitated to look upon Xerxes. Quickly he added, "I will pay 10,000 talents of silver to the mercenaries who carry out the business . . . for the king's treasuries, of course."

Haman, still in a bowed posture, remained that way for some seconds as the king surveyed him with a drumming heart. When Xerxes finally spoke, a thrill of certain vengeance shot through the Agagite.

Taking his royal ring from off his finger, the one with which he sealed all documents of law, the emperor handed it to Haman.

As the prime minister held forth a sweaty hand to receive it, Xerxes grasped at a show of power. "Keep the silver," he flaunted. "Go and do as seems good to you."

37

Xerxes ambled through the court of his harem, luxuriating in the fleshly beauty of half-clad women who, on cue, sported before him in their garden pool.

Never let it be implied by blushing cheek or hesitant gyration that any girl upon whom he gazed was obliged to tease him. The flirtatious cavorting must always be spirited, as though prompted by ardent love.

After all, were not his visits to this sanctum very rare? Especially since he had taken Esther to wife, he had seen little reason to grace this court with his regal presence.

As compared with previous Persian monarchs, Xerxes' attention to his concubines was becoming more and more casual. In fact, now that he had married the lovely Jewess, his lifestyle bordered on monogamy.

It was true that he still allowed his underlings to continue bringing beautiful young virgins to his palace, and that he had at his disposal an entirely new bevy of maidens ready for initiation into the house of wives. But he had virtually ignored them.

As he passed through the garden this evening, it was with only cursory interest that he lingered over them. He was headed for Esther's suite.

Usually he met with his bride in his own chamber. But he had tired of that, and now wished for new surroundings. What he did not anticipate was that meeting Esther upon her own ground would reveal a side to her that he had not yet seen.

Indeed, there was much about his wife which was unknown to him. For months now he had freely called her "Vashti," reveling in her embrace as though it were the embrace of his first love. Many times Esther would have addressed this fact; she would have challenged her "husband" regarding his illusions. But she had never found the strength, had never felt it her place to do so.

Tonight, as she waited in her room, in lonely anticipation of the king's arrival, some seed of self-assertion awoke within her. Perhaps it had cracked open days before, sending forth a shoot of courage when her papa had spoken of the evil in this place. But tonight it struggled for expression, and as she heeded its demands, she steeled herself against Xerxes' touch.

When he appeared in her doorway, however, he was his commanding self, the sovereign who had forced her obedience months before. His striking frame nearly filled the entry, his handsome bronze face irresistibly appealing.

Had his eyes not beseeched her, she could have been angry with him. But in his face she read his humanity—the vulnerability which allowed him to be wounded as much as he had wounded others.

As he approached across the room with admiration in his gaze, she could almost believe that he loved her—*herself*, Esther . . . Hadassah.

If, as it seemed, she was destined to remain forever with him, she must believe this. Life would be unending torment otherwise. And though she did not love him, she might be persuaded to try . . . if only . . .

But when Xerxes spoke, she knew again the truth.

"My Lady," he said, sighing a smile, "you are, of all women, worthy of this chamber. Only such great beauty as yours should enter here."

Esther had not risen from her seat beside the fireplace. Sadly she studied the shadows between the flames, the amber light betraying her heavy spirit.

"Sir," she whispered, "you often say such things, thinking they do me honor. And so they do. But they also prick my heart."

Xerxes had never heard her speak so. In fact, in all these months of marriage her heart had remained a closed scroll, nor had he attempted to read it.

Stepping close, he leaned over her, passing a gentle finger across her cheek.

"You are not yourself tonight, my dear," he crooned.

Esther pulled away and surveyed him quizzically.

"I suppose that depends upon who you think I am. If you refer to me, Esther, I am indeed myself," she asserted. "If you think of me as Vashti . . . I am not."

There. It had been said. Xerxes was incredulous—not at the revelation, for he knew he clung to illusion. But at the girl's newfound courage he was taken aback.

Still, Esther took a deep breath and added, "Is it not true, My Lord, that you did not admire *me* when you entered the room, but your memory of Vashti as she once graced this chamber? And is it not true that you still love her, and have never loved me?"

Xerxes did not readily answer. Lowering his eyes, he shunned her observation.

"By the faith of Ahura-Mazda," he swore, "I have loved you!"

At this Esther stood and faced him squarely.

"You claim the blessing of your god upon our union?" she challenged. "Do you not call him God of the Universe, King of Heaven?"

The emperor could have been offended by her tone, but instead he nodded solemn agreement.

"Then," the young Jewess declared, "he never countenanced the treachery which sent your first queen from you, and which brought me to your bed. He did, perhaps, allow all this for some cause unknown to us. But he did not ordain it. And he will not suffer the lie forever."

Esther's pulse quickened with the confrontation, and for a long moment Xerxes stood confounded by her discernment.

Longing to draw her to him, he at last turned for the door, leaving the room with stooped shoulders and wondering if he should ever hold her again.

38

The rackety clatter of large bone dice was muffled by the thick Persian carpet in Haman's council chamber.

Three young men, longtime servants of the prime minister, were huddled about a circle of goat hide upon which were mystical designs and a chart of the houses of the heavens. Over and over they rolled three "purim," the bone counters, against the leather map. As the pieces took their places upon the star chart, the men chanted out the weeks and months of the year.

For the chart was not only an astrological map but a calendar, and the bone dice chose not only certain celestial positions but their corresponding dates as well.

Night after night, the men had met to carry out the strange ceremony, and night after night Haman had watched them, pacing anxiously along the carpet and asking the interpretation of their findings.

He had chosen these fellows to perform this rite because they had always served him well. Having been his students years before in the accounting school, they had risen with him in imperial administration.

The sacred "purim," obtained by Haman from the palace priests, were used to determine the times and seasons of special events. Such dice had been rolled when Xerxes and Vashti awaited the pronouncement of their wedding date, and they were being rolled now to set the date of the pogrom against the Jews. Normally only the priests would have handled the "purim." But the case to be decided here was a matter of national security, Haman claimed, and government officials could be ordained to determine the times for such things.

As the servants tossed the counters again and again, brows

154

dotted with sweat from the hours-long ordeal and throats rasping from interminable chanting, they rocked to and fro upon
their heels, their knees sore with chafing against the woolly
carpet.

At last, however, one of the men gave a cry.

"We have a match!" he declared.

"A match?" Haman repeated, hesitant to enjoy the possibility.

"It is definite, Master!" another confirmed. "The number of
our throw corresponds perfectly with the number on the dice,
and it has fallen upon the same number upon the calendar."

"Yes . . . yes . . . what is it?" Haman demanded, weaving his
fingers together.

"The twelfth month, the month of Adar," the servant replied.

Haman was delighted to have an answer, but somewhat put off
by the fact that Adar was yet 11 months away. Nevertheless he
asserted, "Very well. And now, what of the day?"

"By tradition, sir," the third reminded him, "the day is always
one number larger than the month. We need not throw the
purim to decide this."

Haman's eyes brightened. Of course he remembered this.

"Then," he reckoned, "the annihilation of the king's enemies
is set for the thirteenth of Adar."

"Indeed," replied the first. "Now, sir, may we know against
which people we have been performing this duty? Who exactly
are these enemies of the king?"

Haman was not a very superstitious man, but he would not
risk the goodwill of the purim by prejudicing his servants in the
performance of their task. Therefore he had not told them just
whose lives were at stake in the coming purge. Now that the date
had been established, however, he could let them in on the
secret.

Drawing them to him in a tight circle, he whispered, "Do you
recall, years ago, how I spared you from judgment in the matter
of an old man's death—an old fellow you challenged in the
streets one New Year's Eve?"

Thinking back, the men did recall an incident in which they
had in youthful frolic done bodily injury to an elderly gentleman. Unfortunately, the old man had been too frail to survive
their exuberance, and had died shortly thereafter.

"We recall, Master," they acknowledged.

"Well, he was not the last of his race to receive a kick from you."

Haman's toothy grin sent chills down the servants' spines. Though they admired their master, something about him could chill the coldest heart.

"He was a Jew, was he not?" one asked.

"You have a keen memory, Drusal," Haman commended him. "A sneaking, money-grubbing Jew. The kingdom will be better off without his kind."

Drusal and his companions surveyed one another silently. Through each of their minds flashed the image of Abihail, the innocent one whom they had shamefully attacked.

He had not seemed a wealthy man. Had he not been dressed in a farmer's rags?

And he had not appeared bent on any treachery that long-ago night as he carried his wriggling bundle through the dark street.

But they would not correct Haman on these points. Their duty had been done. It was now left to them to deal with their consciences, to find ways to sleep each night for the next eleven months.

39

Mordecai the Jew sat in the public square outside the palace of Susa, sifting ashes through his fingers and pouring them over his head. The ashes mingled with the silver streaks of his already-gray beard and clung to his eyebrows. Ashes covered his shoulders and the pathetic garment of sackcloth which he had donned.

Upon the ground he sat, rocking to and fro, as all about him Jewish brothers and sisters from all parts of Susa—from the fine mansions lining the Shapur River to the filthy ghettos on the far side of town—chanted the horrid tale of Haman's hate.

This very day the edict, sealed with the king's own signet ring and declaring the destruction of their entire race, had been delivered by courier throughout the capital. Even now copies were being sent to every province of the empire, declaring the date for the annihilation of the Jews.

Confusion reigned, among Gentiles as well as Hebrews. For this pronouncement had not been preceded by any warning, and there had not been any escalation of bias against this group of people. For decades, Jew and Gentile had coexisted peacefully, with only occasional spates of racial tension coloring their interaction.

Certainly everyone knew that the Jews were an odd lot. They themselves were fond of acknowledging that they were a "peculiar people," having their own brand of history, their own slant on imperial politics, and even their own code of religious laws and traditions. However, they were known to be quiet folk, generally honest and reputable citizens of the kingdom. Few could think of any reason for this sudden turn of policy on the part of the emperor.

But Mordecai knew the reason, and there were others who suspected that it was due to his refusal to bow to the prime minister that Haman had set the king's heart against the Hebrews. Even those who suspected this, however, were amazed that Xerxes could so lightly be moved against such a large portion of the population.

Had they known that Xerxes had signed the edict without even inquiring as to the identity of the targeted group, they would have been even more chagrined at their sovereign's shallow nature.

Tapping into palace rumor, Mordecai had learned more than most about the details of the case. In fact, because he was so personally involved, friends brought him every word they heard from the interior. And so he knew even the amount of money that Haman had volunteered to pay for the extermination.

It had been noon when the edict was posted in Susa's square. By early evening, thousands of horrified Jews and their sympathizers had crowded into the square outside the palace.

No one was allowed inside the King's Gate while dressed in mourning, but the cries of protest and pleading which filled the dusky air had surely reached the ears of Xerxes, who, it was reported, sat at wine with Haman himself.

Of course, word of Mordecai's likely involvement in all that had come to pass had spread throughout the Jewish community. He could have been the most despised man among his brethren. But instead, his refusal to accommodate the pride of unpopular Haman had become a symbol of racial integrity, and Mordecai had in a few short hours been catapulted to the prominence of an ethnic hero.

As for Mordecai, there certainly had been moments since news of the edict when he had regretted his rebellion, wondering if Jehovah had been with him. It was true that the proposed move against the Jews was still nearly a year away, but no amount of time would save his people. Were they to gather together in force even now, they could not succeed against the entire empire of Persia.

However, in the presence of this reassuring company Mordecai found his faith uplifted, and felt hope in the midst of hopelessness.

As he sat, eyes closed and head tilted back, imploring heaven, he felt a tap on his shoulder. Peering above, he found a grandly attired fellow bending over him.

By his appearance he was a eunuch, bald and clean of face, decked in pure linen embroidered with gold. In strange attitude he bowed to the Jew, holding forth a bundle of even finer clothing in his arms.

"Mordecai?" he greeted.

"I am."

"Our Lady, the Queen, has sent me to you, pleading that you take these garments and cease your mourning."

Mordecai stared at him in mute consternation.

"You are Mordecai, the bookkeeper to the Queen, are you not?" the servant repeated.

"I am," he replied again.

The eunuch, maintaining his dignity despite uneasiness at the task he had been given, went on.

"Our Lady's maids brought her word of your condition, saying you were in this square. The queen begs you to take off your sackcloth and accept her gift."

Straightening his back, Mordecai insisted, "Does the queen not understand the reason for my grief? Has no one told her?"

The servant, unused to questioning a royal command, could only shrug. And Mordecai, clearing his throat, answered, "Tell Our Lady that her lowly employee appreciates her concern. But . . . I cannot accept her gracious gift."

Stunned, the eunuch stepped back, looking awkwardly at his bundle.

But seeing that Mordecai was intent upon his decision, he bowed slowly once more and retreated toward the palace.

All about the bookkeeper a huzzah of astonishment rose as folk observed Mordecai's daring. His status as hero grew on the instant, his name becoming a chant which filled the sky above the court.

"Mordecai, Mordecai," it rang, the syllables exciting the twilight. As dark descended, the name continued to mark the moments until the Jew, sitting calmly in an attitude of prayer, was again roused by someone's hand.

Looking up once more, he found yet another eunuch standing above him, this one even grander than the last.

"I am Hathach," the servant announced, a hush coming over the crowd, "one of the king's eunuchs, appointed to Her Majesty."

This man's demeanor was more challenging than that of the last. Had Mordecai not learned the confidence of faith, he might have trembled before him.

"Her Majesty, Queen Esther, wishes to know the meaning of your behavior this day, and the purpose of this . . . gathering."

This last word, preceded by an aloof glance about the court, was said with a sneer.

But Mordecai cared not for Hathach's assessment. Gathering his dusty garment to his chest, he looked upon the eunuch with equal condescension.

"Can it be, sir," he inquired, "that Our Lady is not privy to the news of Persia? Does the palace so insulate her that she has not heard of the king's edict? And is it possible that such a notable as yourself can likewise be ignorant of affairs affecting thousands across the world?"

Hathach, taken aback, had no ready answer, and was about to repeat the queen's command when Mordecai rose to his feet and grasped him by the arm.

Hundreds watched in silent admiration as their hero guided Hathach across the court, talking all the while about what had transpired between himself and Haman, and the exact amount of money offered by the treacherous prime minister in return for the lives of the Jews. Leading the bewildered fellow through the crowd until they stood before a public notice board, he turned him about to face the masses.

Then, reaching for the hideous parchment which had been posted that noon, he ripped it from the billboard and waved it beneath the eunuch's aquiline nose.

"Here!" he shouted. "Take this to the queen, and read it to her. Plead her forgiveness for the embarrassment heaped upon her, for the hypocrisy which expects her to rule without knowledge!"

Hathach, face red, tried to stammer some defense, but Mordecai would hear none.

"When you are done explaining this horror to the queen," the Jew demanded, "charge her to go to the king, to entreat Xerxes on behalf of these folk and to supplicate for their lives!"

Charge the queen? Such a notion was unthinkable.

But Mordecai, seeing Hathach's hesitation, shouted again as he walked away, "Our blood be upon you, and upon Our Lady, if you do not what I say!"

Stumbling across the congested pavement, Hathach scurried toward the palace, eager to be free of the mocking throng.

In his hand was the parchment, tightly crimped and awaiting the queen's scrutiny. As he disappeared behind the golden doors, the crowd's laughter turned once more to chanting, the name of Mordecai heralding the emergence of the moon.

40

Esther stood upon her balcony, listening to the chants which rose from the distant courtyard. She could not see the people who by blood were her kindred and who wrestled with the fate mapped for them. But she shared their agony, for she too faced the possibility of death.

Tears glimmered along her lashes as she turned a small parchment over and over in her fingers. It was a letter from Mordecai, and its contents bore the gravest challenge of her young life—a prospect even more frightening than eternal imprisonment within these palace walls.

To Mordecai's plea that she entreat the king on behalf of the Jews, she had sent word reminding him that no one could go into the king's court without his personal summons. Not even she, his queen, could do so without risking execution. Only if he were to extend his golden scepter to her might she be received. And though most would expect that she, of all people, would be welcomed into his presence, she had neither seen nor been requested by her husband for 30 days.

All this she had told Mordecai. But perhaps he had not believed her. Who could believe, having not heard her last conversation with Xerxes? The royal couple's most intimate servants had doubtless noted the distance between the king and his bride. But likely they assumed he had simply tired of her, that the growing harem was of more interest these days.

Esther, however, knew the true reason for her husband's aloofness. She knew he had been pained by her rejection, and that the rebuff merited his regal indignation. Indeed, it was a wonder he had borne the humiliation so calmly.

In her brief reply to Mordecai she had revealed none of this.

But as she surveyed his response, she knew it would have made no difference.

"Think not that just because you are in the king's palace you will escape," was his unwavering directive. "If you keep silent, deliverance will rise for the Jews from another place, but you and your father's house will perish."

The warning stung her, forbidding all complacency. *Had* she come to trust in her newfound privileges? *Had* the station into which she had been thrust become less than loathsome to her?

Gazing about at the fine furnishings of her boudoir, she shook herself. Mordecai's injunction had drawn the knife of conscience, making her cringe beneath its exposing gleam.

"No," she asserted. "I am *Hadassah*."

The name still felt at home upon her tongue, and she knew she still loved her heritage. Always she had been Israel's child. Why, even her challenge to Xerxes had come from a heart miserably entrapped within these Persian walls.

To others she was Queen of the East. To herself she was yet Hadassah.

Still, fear was her companion. Her defense to Mordecai had been fitly framed. She *would* be taking her life in her hands to step unbidden into the emperor's stateroom.

Trembling, she listened to the chants pushing up from the courtyard. Fumbling once again with the parchment, she contemplated its closing words.

"Who knows," it said, "but what you have come to the kingdom for such a time as this?"

For such a time as this . . .

The phrase beckoned, repeating itself over and over.

As though it were yesterday, she recalled her conversation with her papa when he had first met her in the harem hall.

"Jehovah has brought you to this place," he had deduced. "Trust everything to God."

How she had hated those words at the time! But now, telescoping into the present, all the unthinkable events which had led to this moment seemed suddenly capable of interpretation.

Perhaps, after all, she had been drawn into Persia's royal life for a high purpose—a purpose far greater than that of being queen. Perhaps she could be a servant—savior of her people.

A quiver of awe thrilled through her. Hardly did she feel worthy of such an assignment.

But as the chants outside grew more insistent, she suddenly raised her chin. Wheeling about, she clapped for a maid, sending her off to find a scribe.

And when the scribe arrived, she gave quick instruction. "Draft a note to Mordecai the Jew," she commanded. "Tell him to gather together all the Jews of Susa, that they may fast for me. They must neither eat nor drink for three days and nights. I and my maids will also fast. Then I will go in unto the king, which is against the law. And if I perish . . . I perish."

PART VI
The Triumph

41

Esther the Queen left her chamber in the strength of prayer. Robed in purple, her royal crown upon her head, she stepped into the hallway for the first time in three days.

Early she had risen, calling for her maids to prepare her bath, and eagerly they had complied, having been denied access to Her Majesty and having done her no service since her meditations had begun. Bewildered, the maids had filled their time in trivial employments during the queen's self-imposed isolation. They did not understand her ordeal of private prayer, or her command that they fast for three days along with her. They knew she prayed for the Jews, who still chanted in the public square. But her seemingly inordinate concern for their welfare was a mystery.

Esther had kept her devotions private, just as she kept her race and her faith a secret. Her servants did not know the God to whom she prayed, and so she had faced this test alone.

Now, however, as she emerged from her cloister decked in regal attire, her face barely showing the strain of hunger and fatigue, folk gathered about her in amazement.

Dorca was there, as well as Hegai, waiting in the hall and worrying. Her seven chambermaids, her devoted friend Maryam, and countless palace servants clustered in the corridor, gazing upon her and restraining the questions which hammered to be spoken.

"Your Highness," Dorca said with a bow, "we are so pleased to see you! We have been gravely concerned, My Lady, for your welfare."

"I am fine," the queen replied, smiling, her chin lifted in a determined angle. "I have been upheld by the prayers of many people."

The plump servant studied her vaguely, wondering at the statement. Whispers passed among those gathered.

"But I have one request of you," Esther added.

"Anything, Your Majesty!" Dorca replied, her face radiant.

"Prepare a table in my dining room. Three wine goblets and a carafe of fine wine."

"Yes, Your Majesty," the servant said, squelching her curiosity.

No one asked the reason for this assignment, nor for the queen's monastic behavior during the past days. It was not proper to question royalty. But when Esther lifted her skirts and turned toward the king's stateroom, a murmur of fascination, and then of fear, filled the onlookers.

"His Majesty is in his receiving hall, is he not?" she inquired.

At this Hegai drew near, his face white.

"He is, My Lady," he answered furtively. "Always on the third day of the week . . ."

"Very well," Esther nodded. And with a placid countenance she continued on her way.

"But, My Queen . . ." the eunuch objected.

"I am well," Esther assured him.

Passing through vestibule and lobby, she attracted a train of awed followers, but offered no further consolation.

* * *

Esther stood outside the emperor's audience hall, the elegant Apadana, whose princely columns, though 36 in number, were so narrow of girth that they barely intruded upon the vast space.

As the airy lightness of the stateroom collided with the shadow of the outer court, the queen's tamed fears clawed to assert themselves. At her back a dozen personal aides pleaded that she reconsider.

"Your Highness," they reminded her, "you know the penalty . . ."

"I know," she insisted. Walking up to the guards at the stateroom door, she stood silently, peering between their spears.

Beyond, she could see her husband seated upon his throne, a ledger of appointments in his hand, and his seven aides at his side.

"Our Lady," one of the guards whispered, his spear quivering in a sweaty hand as he recognized her intentions. "Do you mean to enter here?"

For a long moment Esther said nothing, only studying Xerxes as he casually chatted with his valets.

"I do," she replied at last, taking a deep breath.

Glancing at his fellow guard, the sentinel hesitated, feeling that to raise his long weapon and admit the queen was tantamount to decreeing her death.

But his partner, nervously complying, warned him with a look that they must obey their lady's wishes.

Ever so slowly they turned their spears upright, allowing Esther to step into the stateroom light. Fearing for their lady's safety, they could not bring themselves to announce her, but only stood aside like impotent shadows.

Silent as a statue she stood, waiting for the emperor to look upon her. Her pulse counted the minutes with a stammer, as her life hung on the king's response.

It was Mehuman, the chief eunuch, who at last spied the queen standing at the edge of the court. Eyes wide, he turned to his master and whispered in his ear.

Lurching erect, the emperor stared across the room, puzzled at the sight of his wife.

The instant Xerxes saw her, Esther lowered her head and bowed in a deep curtsy, her knees nearly touching the floor, a gesture befitting a queen only in deference to her husband. And for a long while she held this position, not daring to glance up, her heart drumming.

As the eunuchs conferred together, wondering at the woman's motives, the king only leaned forward in amazement, studying his daring bride.

Beautiful she was, in her courage, in her humility—as beautiful as ever he had seen her. How she reminded him, again, of Vashti—not only in appearance but in spirit!

His hand tightened upon the arm of his chair as he recalled, as though it were yesterday, the night his first queen had challenged him. Her self-assertion had exiled her as he in his pride had retaliated.

Once again, a lovely woman was laying her very life at his feet. But this time he could not imagine the purpose.

As he pondered the mystery, however, an explanation much to his liking suddenly dawned upon him. Perhaps, his fond heart told him, perhaps Esther, heartsick at his monthlong rejection of her, had come to plead for his husbandly attentions. Yes, he counseled himself, the love she had experienced in his kingly arms must have been a treasure sorely missed. Indeed, she regretted her unkind words when last they met. Life had lost all meaning without him, and therefore was worth risking, if only he might be hers again.

As he considered the countless females whom he had spurned, the harem wenches and concubines who had lain with him only once, forever after to live in solitary widowhood, a glib smile pricked his lips.

Lifting a hand, he reached for his scepter, and Mehuman, who had witnessed his abuse of Vashti, handed it to him fearfully. The eunuch knew that whatever Xerxes did with the royal wand would decide Esther's fate. If the emperor thumped the floor with the scepter's foot, the queen would die. If he extended it, she would live. Not having a clue to the king's heart, Mehuman quietly joined his brethren behind the throne.

Whether it was compassion for this lady, or guilt at the remembrance of Vashti, not even Xerxes could have said. But something softened his despotic nature as he gazed upon the queen. Her loveliness alone could have worked the miracle. But more than physical winsomeness worked for her this day.

When the monarch raised the golden shaft, a hush thrilled through the court. And when he extended it, pointing the glistening head toward his queen, a great sigh of relief ascended.

Scarcely believing what her ears told her, Esther found strength to lift her head. Tears nudged at her lashes as she saw the beckoning orb. Rising, she crossed the room, bowing again when she reached the throne, and touched the scepter's top with careful fingers.

"What is it, Queen Esther?" Xerxes said, his heart pounding now as the gentle woman stood before him. A quaver of manly emotion colored his tone as he proclaimed, "What is your request? It shall be given you, even to half of my kingdom."

Standing, Esther smiled. But though he tried desperately, Xerxes could not interpret her feelings.

"If it please the king," she replied, her voice sweet and supple, "let the king and Haman come this day to a dinner that I have prepared."

Quizzically, Xerxes sank back upon his throne. Haman? Why Haman?

But of course, he reasoned, she was being coy. She would win him cautiously, in the presence of another.

Not taking his eyes off her, he gave a condescending nod. Flicking a careless hand toward Mehuman, he commanded, "Fetch Haman quickly, that we may do as Esther desires."

At this the queen curtsied again and backed away from the king's platform. Turning, she hastened toward the door.

Smitten by the woman's self-possession, the emperor watched her departure. When she disappeared from sight, he shook his head, chuckling with delight.

42

Haman doffed his leather skullcap to every servant, every chambermaid, every doorman as he sidled through the palace halls, his head light with wine and his heart merry. Smugly smiling to himself, he reveled in the irony of the honor just heaped upon him.

How Otanes would laugh with him when Haman told him he had just come from dinner in the queen's hall! He, Haman, coconspirator for the death of Xerxes, had just sat at private banquet with the emperor and his lady. He who had only recently been publicly elevated, obliging obeisance from all who saw him, had now been received by the queen—an award only rarely bestowed. In fact, he could not recall such an honor ever being given a palace official during Darius' reign or since.

Not only this, but he had been invited to dine with the royal couple again tomorrow evening! The prestige was almost more than he could bear.

He could not imagine what he had done to deserve either invitation. He could accept the thought that he was a stunning fellow, brilliant and charming. Perhaps this was enough. And perhaps, he snickered, not even his plan to overthrow the king could be thwarted.

His step lively, he ambled through the court on his way home, recalling with fond satisfaction the luxuries of Esther's hall. How lovely the queen had been! Reclined upon her dinner couch, her linen gown the same lavender as the lounge's linen upholstery, her hair and eyes black as the marble tiles bordering her porch—she was a memorable sight.

The conversation had been airy and carefree. Matters of state did not intrude as the empress spoke of the weather and asked caring questions about his wife and family.

Proudly he had told her of his ten sons, and if her eyes darkened at this, he knew not why, nor did he notice.

Toward Xerxes she had shown the same casual ease. Haman had not attempted to interpret her feelings toward her husband. Her gracious hospitality toward himself was all he absorbed.

His blood glowed with the wine's caress as he headed toward the palace door, eager to share his good fortune with plump and comely Zeresh, his wife of a quarter-century.

But just as he entered the outer porch, near the king's gate, the chanting of the Jews in the public square reached his ears, and a chill ran through his veins.

Ahead sat Mordecai. Having removed his sackcloth and having washed himself, he had taken his station behind his accounting desk. Though it was night, he had perched himself there, awaiting Haman's emergence. And the instant the prime minister saw him, Mordecai's eyes locked on his with a knowing twinkle.

When the Jew neither rose nor trembled before him, Haman seethed with indignation.

Restraining himself, he passed by without a word. But his glorious day had been ruined. Utterly ruined.

* * *

Haman entered his house with a bowed head. Zeresh, who had eagerly anticipated his homecoming all evening, rushed to him with open arms. But seeing the dark cloud upon his face, she faltered.

"My Lord," she fawned, stroking him on the shoulder and removing his cape with solicitous hands, "I trust it went well—your dinner with the queen."

"Call Otanes," was all he could say. "Call my friends, my confidants."

Bewildered, Zeresh would have inquired more deeply, but knowing her husband's determined personality, she hastened to comply. Sending her servants through the neighborhood, she saw to it that all her husband's associates were summoned, and then she sat with him by the fire to await their arrival.

"It did not go well?" she managed.

"I will tell the tale when I have an audience," he curtly corrected, though Zeresh probed his expression for further clues.

Shortly the house filled with Haman's executives, who gathered doubtfully, wondering why they were required to leave home and hearth at so late an hour.

When at last Otanes arrived, seating himself across from Haman's ten sons, the grand vizier began to pace the floor.

"You are all aware of the honor I received this day . . . that I did dine with the emperor and his wife in the queen's hall," he said.

Murmurs and nodding heads confirmed this.

Then, with dramatic tears in his eyes, he recounted the trophies of his life.

"You all know that I am a wealthy man, that no one in the kingdom surpasses me for financial security."

Again, everyone agreed, though not without resentment.

"I have fathered ten sons!" he cried, throwing his arms wide, and caressing his heirs with proud scrutiny.

Zeresh beamed, and Haman's friends condoled that this was indeed true. The fact that they did not feel as much warmth for their superior as he imagined would not trouble him.

"Furthermore," he went on, "everyone knows how I have been honored by His Majesty . . . his public endorsements of me . . . the promotions I have received in sight of all the empire!"

Heedless of his associates' growing uneasiness, he did not consider the affront which Otanes might feel at this self-aggrandizement. Nor did the memory of Otanes' personal involvement in his "promotion" faze him.

"Why," he boasted, "I have been advanced above all the princes and servants of the king! Even Queen Esther let no one come with the king to the banquet but me!"

Any applause now elicited was given only out of duty. But Haman accepted it with condescension.

"And tomorrow also I am invited to dine with the queen and king! Yet . . ."

Here he paused, his voice cracking and his face falling.

"Yet . . . all this does me no good as long as I see Mordecai the Jew sitting at the king's gate!"

At this Zeresh stood and rushed to his side, begging him to seat himself, to calm his heart lest it break.

After a hesitant moment, one by one the advisers began to console him.

"Truly, Master," they sympathized, "this monster, Mordecai, would be a thorn in any man's side. Such patience you have shown in enduring his insults!"

Haman kept his head bowed, gazing into the fire with contorted countenance. But how he loved their forced support!

For a long while Otanes studied his partner in crime. He had no great love for Haman. In fact, he despised the pompous braggart. But Haman was the most useful pawn to the general's vendetta against Xerxes. The prime minister's recent intimacies with the royal family could only hasten the fulfillment of Otanes' plot. If Mordecai were dampening Haman's spirit, he must be done away with.

A cold-blooded warrior, one who enjoyed the sport of power, Otanes would just as soon kill a man as put up with any inconvenience he might pose.

His voice smooth as honey, he called Haman's name and crossed the room, embracing Zeresh as though he treasured her. "Dear friends," he began, "I cannot express the sorrow I have at the sight of your discomfort. I think we all agree that this is a serious matter, calling for immediate action. For you, Haman, are our brother as well as our superior."

No one dared deny this as syrupy smiles graced each conciliatory face.

"Therefore, after due consideration, I have a plan which, with your indulgence, Prime Minister, I will address."

Haman glanced sideways at Otanes. Feigning deference, he bowed.

"Let a gallows 50 cubits high be built," Otanes coolly suggested. "And in the morning, tell the king to have Mordecai hanged upon it. Then go merrily with Xerxes to the dinner."

How simply the matter had been resolved! How easily death became the answer!

Here and there a face went white, but no one spoke contrary to Otanes.

176

Zeresh, her lips wet, planted a firm kiss on Haman's wan cheek.

"Oh, my husband!" she cried. "Heed our beloved Otanes! Free yourself of this plague, of the cloud which hangs over you, and be our merry Haman once again!"

Nothing but endorsement issued from the little gathering. Haman had his answer—an answer which set well with his callous spirit.

"Thank you, friends," he smiled, a polished tear reflecting firelight on his face. "It shall be done."

43

That night Xerxes found sleep impossible to achieve. Each time he came near dozing, the sight of Esther, gracefully reclined upon her dinner bed, invaded his masculine heart.

He had never thought of her as a seductress. She had not needed to play such games with him. But he was certain that today's invitation to the dinner, given at peril of her own life, was an attempt to woo him. Even buffering the encounter with the presence of a third party, Haman, was doubtless part of her strategy.

How coolly she had handled things during the rendezvous, focusing more on Haman than on himself—asking all those idle questions about the vizier's career and family, chitchatting about the weather and the delicacies of the table!

Certainly her tactics were effective. She had captivated him, and his thoughts had been on her alone all evening.

Wide awake, he paced his room, glancing out at the desert moon over and over. Thoughts of Vashti and thoughts of Esther blended into one, as always they had done since the girl had come to him. Deep inside he knew that Esther's accusation of him had been valid—that he saw his first wife in her more than he saw herself. But perhaps today's encounter had been her way of telling him that she could live with the fact. That she would take him—indeed, craved him—regardless.

As he stepped onto his balcony with the dawn, having paced and tossed and turned all night, a strange sound, intermittent and persistent, intruded upon his reveries. It seemed to be a hammering of some kind, as though a construction job were underway upon the acropolis.

Generally Susa was quiet at such an early hour. Though the labyrinth of palace corridors and walls could deflect vibrations at misleading angles, he was sure the pounding came from the direction of Haman's house. As he cocked his head to listen, he noticed that the odd chanting which had filled the public square for days and nights had ceased, as though the hammering had replaced it.

Persians could be a hot-blooded race, and the many diverse nationalities comprising Susa were a volatile combination. Protests or sit-ins were not a rare sight in the public market. Xerxes had not bothered to ask just what the most recent discontent regarded. If it concerned his edict against Haman's alleged foes of the state, he knew it would pass. After all, he was certain the accused people must be only a minute fraction of the population, having done nothing to attract his attention before Haman clued him to their subversion.

Glad he was that his prime minister was so in touch with the citizens. Surely no king could have a more efficient adviser.

But glad he would also be to sleep.

In times past he would have called for one of his harem girls to distract him, to soothe his body and tire him enough for slumber. Now, however, he would have been content with no one but Esther. And he knew the timing was not right to have her. She must play out her winsome plan, and he must indulge her scheme.

Meanwhile, as his heart drummed to thoughts of her, and as the mysterious hammers chattered through the twilight, he grew irritable.

Clapping his hands, he called for Mehuman, who appeared the instant the guards opened the king's door.

"Mehuman!" Xerxes snapped. "What is that infernal pounding?"

"Hammers, Your Highness," the eunuch said with a bow.

"Of course it is!" the emperor growled. "I know it is hammers! But why—why at this hour?"

"Some project of Haman's, Your Majesty," Mehuman replied. "A gallows of immense proportions. I am certain he will inform you . . ."

"Yes, yes. Very well," Xerxes nodded, raising a limp hand to his throbbing temple. "I have not slept all night."

Mehuman, whose duty it was to anticipate the emperor's every need, quickly offered to send word commanding quiet in the acropolis. But Xerxes only quipped, "It would do no good now, since the night is already gone. My spirit is restless."

"Perhaps, Your Highness, if someone read to you . . ."

Xerxes had suffered often from insomnia, especially since sending Vashti away, and sometimes his troubled mind was calmed if someone lulled him with a reading.

His tired eyes brightening, the king grasped at the idea.

"Send for the Book of Memorable Deeds," he cried. "Yes, yes . . . I do enjoy that!"

He referred, as Mehuman knew, to the royal chronicles, a scrupulously maintained record of all the valorous and complimentary things done in the empire by folk of all stations. If a general pulled off an amazing feat in battle, if a commoner performed some especially heroic act, if an inventor notably contributed to the empire's technology, or if a physician advanced the cause of medicine by discovering some valued cure—any such achievement would be noted in the chronicle.

Of particular honor were acts of benevolence directed toward the king's personal welfare. And periodically Xerxes enjoyed being updated as to the contents.

Two scribes appeared quickly with the priceless volume, bowing through the door. To the monarch's delight, they began to recount the story of how a certain Jew had once saved the emperor's life.

"Mordecai, you say?" Xerxes mused. "Of course, I remember. He revealed the plot of my treacherous guards, Bigthan and Teresh!"

"Yes, Sire," the readers confirmed. "It says here that he reported the scheme to your queen, and she to you."

Xerxes' eyes again brightened at the thought of his wife. And fondly he contemplated the tale of Mordecai.

"He is a palace accountant?"

"Head of inventory," the scribes reminded him.

"And what honor or dignity has been bestowed on Mordecai for this kindness?"

The readers scanned the pages, their fingers tracing the scroll line by line.

At last, shrugging, they replied, "Nothing has been done for him."

* * *

Somewhere beyond the palace wall a morning cock crowed.

And with the twilight, hastening footsteps rang through the king's receiving hall.

"Who is in the court?" Xerxes asked as he sat upon his state-room throne. To his right, on a low table, sat the Book of Memorable Deeds, and upon his lap was a roster of items to be considered this day, judgments to be made, and visitors to be entertained.

"Haman is here, Your Majesty, asking to see you," Mehuman replied.

"Good, good," Xerxes smiled. "Let him come in." Then, glancing at the book of deeds, he enthused, "I could use his advice!"

Promptly Haman entered, eager to speak to the king regarding his planned execution of Mordecai, and ready for the quick consent which was always given his wishes. When the emperor interrupted him with a spirited inquiry, he was caught off guard.

"Good morning, friend," Xerxes called as Haman approached. "What shall be done to the man whom the king delights to honor?"

Assuming that this was a mere pleasantry, Haman only bowed. But when the king repeated the question, the vizier gave it more thought. Of course Xerxes must be referring to the prime minister himself. Whom, after all, would the emperor delight to honor more than himself? Had not Xerxes already heaped acclaim and dignity upon him? It seemed there was no limit to the king's generosity toward those he loved.

Haman cleared his throat. "Why, Sire," he chuckled, feigning embarrassment, "for such a man let royal robes be brought, which the king has worn, and the horse which the king has ridden, on whose head a royal crown is set." Gaining more boldness with each selfish syllable, he continued, "And let the robes and the horse be handed over to one of the king's most noble princes. Let him array the man whom the king delights to honor, and let him conduct the man on horseback through the open square of the city, proclaiming before him, 'Thus shall it be done to the man whom the king delights to honor!' "

Leaning back on his throne, Xerxes laughed with Haman. "Ah-hah!" he cried. "Marvelous! Make haste, my friend. Take the robes and the horse, as you have said, and do so to Mordecai the Jew who sits at the king's gate. Leave out nothing that you have mentioned."

44

There was no parade in the Susa streets, but folk from all quarters lined the viaduct before the king's palace. There was no military processional or train of acrobats and actors to draw a crowd. But thousands had turned out to observe two men's passage down the royal avenue.

The rumor of the king's command to Haman had spread through the palace court like wildfire, and by the time Mordecai had been summoned, an amazed throng awaited him.

When he appeared upon a white, prancing charger, upon whose noble head was set a shining tiara, the crowd was delighted. Mordecai himself was dressed in a blue gown of purest silk, his silver beard lying gloriously against it. Not only did Jews line the avenue, but supportive Susaites of all sorts. And when it was seen that *Haman* had been commissioned to parade the bookkeeper through town, hilarity was the order of the day.

In fact, the hilarity had begun at court, when Haman set about to fulfill the king's commission. Calling for Mordecai, he was obliged to deck the Jew, firsthand, in the royal apparel. Then, leading the regal horse to his enemy, he bowed in chagrin as the accountant mounted the beast.

Now, of course, his humiliation was unbounded as the thousands who had chanted hatred for him watched, hissing and spitting, while he conducted their hero through the streets.

Mortified, he kept his eyes to the ground as Mordecai was lauded, wondering how this irony had come to be, and how the man he had planned to execute on this very day could be his sudden superior.

When he reached the public square, he was obliged to make the pronouncement which he himself had ordained: "Thus shall it be done to the man whom the king delights to honor," he cried, his voice a rasping croak.

Over and over he shouted the words, until he thought his tongue would bleed for shame.

And all the while Mordecai said nothing, only reveling in the victory of Jehovah.

* * *

Zeresh swabbed her husband's perspiring brow with a damp cloth. Red-faced and close to weeping, he had come home with his head covered, not needing to tell his sorry tale, for his wife, along with all Suṣa, knew of his humiliation.

Nevertheless, the grisly details spilled forth in a torrent of shame and self-pity as he recounted to her, to his household servants, and to the advisers who lived on his estate the horrid events of the day.

"With my own hands I was obliged to drape the royal cloak about that scoundrel's shoulders!" he wailed. "With my own hand I was forced to lead him forth through the streets! Oh, my friends," he bellowed, "how shall I ever live it down?"

Zeresh tried to calm him, but it was no use. One by one his counselors, who had themselves encouraged him to take vengeance against the Jew, offered worthless comfort.

"Lord," they reasoned, "surely Xerxes was unaware of your hatred for this man. Perhaps he did not even know Mordecai is a Jew. Had he known," they insisted, "he would never have elevated him."

Haman sank into his chair, shaking his head. He could not admit to his friends that Xerxes was unaware of more than this—that Xerxes did not even know that the edict so recently published against the "subversives" was against the entire Jewish race.

But as the counselors considered their master's unhappy state, another concern formed in their minds.

Whispering together, they contemplated a new side to the dilemma, and Haman, observing their knit brows, leaned forward anxiously.

"What is it?" he demanded.

"Uh, sir," one spoke, clearing his throat, "it occurs to us that your humiliation may only be beginning."

"How so?" he inquired.

"Why," the adviser said softly, "if Mordecai, before whom you have begun to fall, is of the Jewish people, and if Xerxes knows this, the king may begin to side with the Jews. And you will not prevail against Mordecai, but will surely fall utterly."

The possibilities were too horrible to contemplate. Loss of influence, perhaps even of position . . . or of life . . .

When Xerxes began to put all the facts together, seeing that Haman had no just cause for the edict, there would be no salvation!

Quaking, Zeresh drew close to her husband and cried, "They are right, of course! How can you stand before the king?"

But there was no time for answers. At that instant messengers from the palace arrived at the mansion, summoning Haman to the feast prepared in Esther's hall.

Turning helplessly to his wife, Haman stood on shaky legs as Zeresh handed him his cloak and studied him with mournful eyes.

Feeling as though he were headed for his own execution, the man who had just last night commissioned a gallows left the house.

45

Today's banquet was even more festive than yesterday's, confounding Haman.

If he had been confused by Xerxes' commission to heap honor upon Mordecai, he now began to suspect that the king and Esther were playing games with him.

Yet if it was a game he had no choice but to play along—to hope that his past status as the king's favorite would carry him above the mixed messages he was receiving. He must not mention the morning's humiliation. He must draw no further attention to Mordecai, in conversation or in attitude, lest the king pursue the issue.

Perhaps, after all, Haman was still the emperor's most esteemed prince. Perhaps the incident with Mordecai was a fluke, and his own fears were unfounded.

Stretching his lips into a smile, he followed the messengers into the queen's hall. He tried not to register surprise at the sumptuous array upon the long table, or at the elegant decor which had been lavished on the place. Yet it was evident that Esther had spared no expense in making the room and the meal even more luxurious than yesterday's feast, surrounding the little gathering with immense bouquets and calling all her servants to serve.

As he bowed to the royal couple—the king, who sat upon a high pile of ornate pillows, and the queen, who reclined majestically upon her couch—his chest ached with anxiety. When he took his own seat, he hesitated to study their faces.

What he saw when he did so gave no clue to their view of him. Xerxes, after a cheery greeting, seemed to focus all attention on his queen, so that Haman began to wonder if his presence were a hindrance to their bliss. Esther, on the other hand, attended to Haman with a persistence which made him equally uneasy.

Not once did she allow his cup to run dry or his plate to go bare. Not once did the conversation lag, though he sensed a peculiar scrutiny in her eyes and an ironic lilt to her voice.

Just as he was thinking he might enjoy her attentions, however, Xerxes drew her away.

Hoisting a fluted goblet, the king toasted his lady's beauty. Then, almost groaning, he suddenly declared, "What is your petition, Queen Esther? It shall be granted you! And what is your request? It shall be given you, even to half of my kingdom!"

Servants ceased their serving, slaves lowered pitcher-laden trays from their shoulders, and the men who guarded the chamber stood rigid with surprise.

Such a statement made by a king was not unheard of. Xerxes had spoken this very thing to Esther yesterday. It was usually reserved for those who had performed some great feat in service to the empire, and it was never to be taken literally. Still, it was an incomparable honor, and to be spoken twice in two days to a woman, even to a queen, made it even more noteworthy.

If the offer were amazing, however, so would be the queen's response. No one anticipated that she would so boldly pursue Xerxes' generosity—not the king himself nor any of the onlookers.

Esther felt a flush rise to her cheeks, and every fiber of her being tingled with the opportunity afforded.

Hammered and honed by palace life into a female of power and prestige, Esther was no longer the meek Jewess who had been dragged into the harem. A few weeks earlier she had boldly confronted her "husband" with his unfair use of herself and Vashti. Then, wielding the weapon of faith, she had risked her life to enter his stateroom, seeking help (unbeknownst to him) for her people.

Now in a compulsive moment he had fulfilled her deepest longing, unwittingly granting her the chance to attain salvation for the Jews.

As she studied the floor, framing in her mind just how to speak her wish, Xerxes wondered at the interlude.

Indeed, he had opened the world to Esther with a few words. But surely she must not make so much of it! Was she so unschooled in Persian protocol that she knew not the typical response? Would she not simply smile and calmly thank his lordship, fawning over the treasures of her chamber and the glories of his love? Would she not simply say that she had everything a woman could ask, and that to receive more would overwhelm her?

Still, she pondered her answer until even the servants grew embarrassed. Then, as she turned scalding eyes on Haman, boring through him with a vengeful stare, whispers filled the room.

At last, tears trickling down her hot cheeks, she slid from her couch and fell to her knees, burying her face in her hands.

"Oh, My Lord!" she cried. "If I have found favor in your sight, O King, and if it please the king, let my life be given me at my petition, and my people at my request! For we are sold, I and my people, to be destroyed, to be slain, and to perish. If we had been sold into slavery, I would have kept silent, for such a thing would not be worthy of the king's attention."

Unprepared for this strange turn of events, Xerxes beheld his lady with amazement. "Of what do you speak, my dear?" he marveled.

The queen, rocking back on her heels, at last revealed her long-kept secret. "I am a Jewess," she declared, "the daughter of Mordecai, whom you have honored this day. But I and all my people live in fear for their lives!"

"Who would do such a thing?" the king demanded, scowling about the room. "Where is he?"

Esther leaped to her feet, abandoned now to the liberty of the moment, and pointed a revenging finger at their guest. "A foe and an enemy!" she cried. "This wicked Haman!"

Utterly bewildered, Xerxes digested the accusation, his volatile nature seething with indignation. So, Haman had pressed an edict against an entire race, even to the life of his own queen!

Rising from his bolsters, the emperor glowered down upon the cringing vizier. No word escaped his lips, but his countenance was livid. With a clenched fist he stalked from the banquet hall, exiting into the adjacent garden.

Mortified, Haman turned to the queen, his own face now covered with tears. Esther, having returned to her couch, scorned to look upon him until he, a crazed fool, threw himself at her feet.

"Oh, Your Majesty," he wailed, "Take mercy upon me. Speak unto the king on my behalf, My Lady, I beg of you! For my life surely is in your hands!"

When Esther only recoiled, drawing her skirts up from the floor, he grew even more desperate. In an attitude of utmost despair he scrambled toward her, flinging himself across her dinner bed and weeping like one of the damned.

"Will he even assault the queen before my very eyes?" Xerxes shouted, reentering from the garden. At this the eunuchs scurried forth, draping Haman's head with a cloth for shame, and dragging him into the center of the room.

There he sat, rocking to and fro, wailing like a skewered hog, until Harbona, one of the king's attendants, reminded Xerxes of the gallows which Haman had built only the previous night.

" . . . made for Mordecai, who saved the king's life!" he revealed.

"No, you cannot mean it!" Xerxes spat.

"Indeed, it is so," Harbona declared. "This fiend would have killed the Jew for no matter greater than his own pride."

Even in his escapades against the Greeks, when he would have taken the Western world, Xerxes had never felt a desire for revenge more strongly than he did this moment.

Pointing a spasmed finger at the cowering Haman, he roared vindictive judgment.

"Hang him on it!" he commanded.

With this the guards hurried forth, jolting Haman to his feet and carrying him from the room. Xerxes, his face contorted with bombarding emotions, took Esther's hand, lifting her to his bosom and holding her close to his heart.

46

"Oh, Papa! How wonderful you look!" Esther declared, studying her adopted father's reflection in her hallway mirror. "A more distinguished fellow has never come before the king's throne!"

Mordecai gazed upon his dapper likeness, not concealing a broad smile. For his daughter had just draped about his shoulders a robe once belonging to the king. And his tunic, given him only yesterday by Haman, was the one he had worn as the prime minister led him through the Susa streets.

"Are you not splendid?" Esther laughed. "I am proud of you, Papa!"

Mordecai turned about, grasping the queen's hands. "Why has the king called for me?" he wondered. "Has he not already honored me?"

Esther perceived his anxiety at the notion of standing before the despot. Trying to reassure him, she nodded, "Xerxes has his gentle side, Papa. And he is very generous, once he takes a liking to someone."

"And swift to retribution when someone crosses him," he added, remembering the vizier's quick demise.

Hung on the gallows prepared for Mordecai, Haman had met his death only last evening. And just as quickly, at the king's command, the dead man's house and all his wealth had passed to Queen Esther.

"But in his eyes, Papa, you are a hero. You once saved his life. Remember?"

"I have sometimes questioned the wisdom . . ." he grinned.

"Hush, Papa," Esther giggled, glancing warily down the hall. "Now, come! He waits for you!"

As the bookkeeper entered the lobby, the king's eunuchs stood ready to receive him. Hastening, they took the queen and her adopted father to the stateroom.

The reception would be quiet this time, but very dignified. When Xerxes, seated upon his throne, had extended his scepter to the couple in the presence of all his princes and advisers, he stretched forth his open palm, upon which was perched his signet ring.

"This I took from the hand of your enemy, Haman," Xerxes explained. "It is my own ring of law, by which your enemy did seal the death of your people. So now receive this, my friend, as a token of apology, and in honor of your kindness to me."

Mordecai stared mutely at the gift, hardly daring to consider the implications. Glancing at his daughter, who only nodded enthusiastically, he at last reached out and took it.

"Behold, my new prime minister!" Xerxes announced, gesturing toward the humble Jew with a dramatic sweep of the hand.

Trumpets blared and applause rang through the court. But scarcely could Mordecai believe his ears until Esther herself bowed before him.

Rising, she took from one of the king's aides a small pillow upon which was the key to Haman's house.

"With the emperor's approval, Father, I pass the wealth of your enemy into your keeping," she declared, placing the cushion on his hesitant hands.

Again celebration filled the air.

Wonderful as all this was, however, the queen's heart was not wholly joyous. She must speak again, and that without delay.

Turning to her master, she appealed to his generous mood, falling to her knees and releasing all the pent-up stress of past days.

"O My Lord," she cried, "surely the good you have done this day is only the beginning of your kindnesses. My people still fear for their lives due to the edict of Haman!"

Xerxes had known she would address this matter. He was learning to anticipate her bravery.

Extending to her his scepter once again, he bade her rise and speak her mind.

Smoothing her linen gown, she phrased her words with care, words rehearsed in the night.

"If it please the king, and if I have found favor in his sight, and if the thing seem right before the king, and I be pleasing in his eyes," she began, "let an order be written to revoke the letters devised by Haman the Agagite, the son of Hammedatha, which he wrote to destroy the Jews who are in all the provinces of the king. For how can I endure to see the destruction of my kindred?"

Her concentration on this little speech was so deliberate that she dare not contemplate the emperor's face until she was done. But when she at last allowed reflection, she found his countenance soft toward her.

In his eyes was the warmth of love, and she cared not now how genuine.

"Behold," he addressed both Esther and her father, his own voice husky with feeling, "I have given Esther the house of Haman, and have hanged him on the gallows, because he would lay hands on the Jews. And you may write as you please with regard to the Jews, in the name of the king, and sealed with the king's ring. For an edict written in the name of the king and sealed with the king's ring cannot be revoked."

47

Esther stood once again at her chamber window, where so much agonized prayer for her people had been lifted. She turned over in her hands a piece of parchment similar to the one on which Mordecai had challenged her to go before the king.

This paper, like that one, bore the handwriting of her papa, but these words were not for her eyes alone. They would be duplicated by countless scribes and sent to all parts of the empire, for they were the first edict of the new prime minister.

Persians were fond of saying that the laws of their kings, sealed with the royal signet ring, were irrevocable. But no dynastic ruler who reigned over half the world could truly be subject to such a restriction. While no subordinate official nor any uprising of the people could revoke an emperor's command, the emperor could not be his own slave.

Out of deference to his image, however, Esther and Mordecai had worded the new edict to accommodate the original. They would not do away with the planned day of assault against the Jews, but would instead send word throughout the empire telling the Jews to arm themselves.

Of course, there was more behind their decision to do this than honor for the king.

Esther felt a chill crawl up her arms as she dwelt on Mordecai's reasoning. All her life he had raised her in the ways of Israel. But tonight, for the first time, he had shared with her the tale told by Abihail, her departed father—the story of King Saul and the wicked foe, Agag.

"I thought Abihail was a foolish old man when first he spoke of the ancient tale," Mordecai had said. "But now that we have seen the wickedness which Haman devised against our people, I know that Saul was remiss in not stamping out the Amalekites."

Amazed, Esther had listened to the story, overwhelmed with the personal involvement of God in her own life. "So," she had replied carefully, "are you saying that Jehovah is using us now to right that wrong done so many years ago?"

At this Mordecai had risen from the queen's desk, where he had been penning the edict, and had gazed out the night window. Far away his mind was carried to the land of Israel and the distant time of King Saul his own ancestor.

"God never lets His purposes go unfulfilled," he answered softly. "All the world is hallowed ground, and years are of small consequence to Him. In His good time and in His chosen way He always brings about His will. Only we poor humans are bound by the frustrations of how and when."

"But why *me*?" Esther marveled. "Why has God chosen me, an orphan and a commoner, to perform this thing?"

Mordecai gazed lovingly into her awe-filled face.

"Why did He choose Rahab? Why Ruth? The women who mothered king David were of humble birth," he asserted. "Often God has raised up salvation for His people from the most unlikely places. Why," he mused, "who knows but what the mother of Messiah Himself shall be a girl of low station?"

Esther raised her hand to her mouth, stifling a giggle. And her papa, drawing her close, whispered, "Did I not tell you when you first came here to be anxious for nothing? Trust God, my dear Hadassah."

The last word had infused the young woman with zeal.

" 'Hadassah,' " she repeated. "I am still Hadassah, aren't I, Papa?"

"You never were anyone else," he assured her, bowing low and bidding good night.

That had been two hours ago. The queen should have been asleep long since. But, her heart still full of wakeful contemplation, she found sleep impossible.

The new edict, as Mordecai and she had agreed, would not only honor the king but would help to establish the people of God. While a simple revoking of Haman's command would have saved countless lives, the call to defense would secure the peace of the Jews by revealing who their enemies were, and who their friends. Like Saul should have done generations before, the Hebrews would now be able to stamp out their foes.

If the Jews were allowed to arm themselves, so would be their sympathizers. It had become quite obvious during the growing unrest over Haman's edict that there were many more who would side with Israel than not, given the opportunity. Mordecai's order would free them to aid their Jewish neighbors, and so the tables would be turned, resulting in a purge against the anti-Semites.

It seemed to Esther that she was being carried through these events on a supernatural wave—by a force outside herself. Never had she become accustomed to her role as queen. Perhaps, she thought, even that role was only a garment which she had donned for higher purposes. Inside, where her spirit dwelt, she was still a young girl standing at the village gate, tripping through the wheat fields, watching for her beloved David. And such memories lifted her above the present distress.

A knock at her door roused her from poignant reveries, and brushing a tear from her cheek, she went to answer it. In the hall's shadow stood her master, Xerxes, his ruddy face flushed with long-suppressed feeling.

"My Lady . . ." he whispered, bowing his head.

Esther's throat tightened. "It has been a long time, My Lord," she softly replied.

"Too long," Xerxes sighed. "May I come in?"

It occurred to Esther that this man could do as he pleased, entering and exiting at will through any door on earth. That he should humble himself in this way touched her.

Stepping away from the portal, she assented, but as he walked to her couch, removing his cloak and draping it over the foot, she hesitated to follow.

His gaze passed over the room, and she knew that, as always he thought of Vashti, who had once dwelt here. But his eyes fell on the parchment which Esther had set upon her desk, and for a moment she expected he might ask about the new edict.

Instead, however, he seemed to study her sadly, and she hoped he would not speak of love.

When he did begin to talk, she was surprised at the direction the conversation took.

"So," he said patting the seat beside him and bidding her draw near, "I have taken a Jewess to wife."

Esther nodded, sitting down. "Does this please or displease you?" she inquired.

"Nothing about you displeases me," he replied with a smile. "You are only a source of continual delight."

Esther blushed and looked away. It was not the blush of a virgin, for she was that no longer. Rather, it was the result of unvoiced longings, unmet needs.

"No," he went on, barely sensing her frustration, "I have nothing against the Jews. They are an odd lot, no doubt, but good people. And Mordecai is a popular man."

Then, reaching out, he touched her hand. "But I have not come for this, My Lady," he asserted tenderly. "Haven't you missed me all these weeks?"

Part of him still hoped that her recent advances toward him indicated more than a yearning to save her people, and he still dreamed she might crave his embrace.

Yet she was unyielding.

"You know, My King, that I have never belonged to you," she insisted, looking bravely into his face. "Since you know that I am a Jew, you must understand this now more than ever."

Something like a shudder passed through Xerxes as the long-avoided reality was addressed.

"And you have never truly been mine," she went on.

"This is not so," he objected. Then, more uncertainly, "Not so . . ."

Esther rose from the couch and stepped to the archway. For the first time he saw in her the attitude of the caged doe, of the wild thing in captivity, as she watched the distant fields and the dim-lit burgs of the peasants far beyond.

Xerxes was capable of sympathy. He was not an utterly heartless man. And he also knew, as he had known in Salamis, when he had lost and when to retreat.

"I could demand your love," he sighed, joining her at the window.

"No one can demand another's heart," Esther countered. "You have not even been able to force *yourself* to love *me*. Don't you see? It has all been a wicked game, My Lord, one which Jehovah has miraculously turned to His own ends."

Her tone was rising with her courage, but she caught herself short of disrespect. "My soul belongs to the God of Israel," she softened, "and my heart to yet another."

Xerxes bristled at these last words, his fists clenching. "Another? Do I know him?"

"He is a poor man, My King. Not mighty, not monied. But a prince nonetheless."

Xerxes would hear no more.

"What can I do?" he sighed. "I would give you anything . . . unto half my kingdom . . ."

For a long while their eyes locked on one another. Rigid body confronted rigid body until Esther dared reply.

"Let me go, then, My Lord. And restore Vashti to her rightful place."

Dumbfounded, Xerxes could say nothing. Was this child, this humble orphan girl, suggesting once more that he should reverse himself?

"You have the power, O King," she insisted. "Nothing is too hard for the Monarch of the World."

Possibilities swirled through Xerxes' head. But he resisted them. Had he not rejected Vashti? Had he not commanded a harem and slept with countless women since? Never could he bow to such humiliation as this slip of a female suggested.

Yet . . .

"If you reversed Haman's edict, sealed by your own signet ring, why cannot you do this?" Esther continued.

"Stop!" the king suddenly shouted. "How dare you . . ."

Gently, Esther drew near and took him by the hand.

"Follow your heart, Majesty. What is it you wish? You may have it with a word," she reminded him. "Or you may concede again, to pride, and lose all hope forever."

Staring at the floor, Xerxes stood with stooped shoulders. But gradually a smile conquered his downturned lips.

"Are all Jews as headstrong as you, my dear?" he asked.

"We are a stiff-necked people," she laughed. "A peculiar people."

Dawn was creeping over the Zagros. The king glanced toward the hazy realm of the East, and his heart seemed suddenly to drop its fetters.

"A glorious people!" he cried, sweeping the girl into his arms. "May your God be blessed, as you have blessed me, dear child!"

48

It was a time of fulfillment.

Such liberty and grace had not been experienced by the exiled Jews since their taking away into captivity, more than 200 years before. In a matter of two days, the thirteenth and fourteenth of Adar, the twelfth month of the year, the Jews had overcome their enemies.

Throughout Persia's vast empire, governors and deputies had risen to the aid of the "peculiar people," and those who had dared come out against them had been slain.

In Susa 800 enemies had been killed, testimony to the slim number who took such a stand and to the vindication of the Hebrew race. Elsewhere, over 75,000 met their deaths at the hands of the Jews and their sympathizers.

Even the ten sons of Haman had been destroyed, run through with Jewish swords, and then, at Esther's suggestion, hanged from the very gallows upon which their father had died.

"Let it be a testimony to the fulfillment of God's will," the queen had said. "Agag and his descendants are gone forever!"

Only the Jews could fully appreciate the meaning of this. And only they understood why, in observance of Jehovah's counsel to King Saul, they were allowed to take no spoil from their enemies.

Yes, it was a time of fulfillment—and it was a time of returning. All along the roads of the empire, Jewish warriors traveled to their homes from scenes of victorious battle. Having gone wherever the need was greatest, they had fought in town after town in every province across the map. In two short days they met the centuries-old command of their God to obliterate the Amalekites, and now they would celebrate.

Esther drew her lavender shawl across her shoulders and peered into the eastern sunset. Tonight, in Leah's village, as in all cities and villages of the empire, there would be great merry-making, and she would be with her family, for the first time since her abduction, to join the party.

She passed beneath the gate of the royal palace riding in a queenly carriage. This would be her last time to enjoy the luxury of such a conveyance, and the last day she would ever be called "Queen Esther." Granting her fondest request, Xerxes had agreed to return her to her people, once the "Day of the Jews," as he called it, had passed.

And such a time it was, of victory in war over the Israelites' foes. On the thirteenth and fourteenth of Adar the Jews of Susa were allowed 'to fight, and on the thirteenth the Jews of the smaller villages prevailed over their enemies.

Just this morning Esther had stood with her papa, Prime Minister Mordecai, upon the king's porch before all the people of Susa. There, together, they had proclaimed their blessing upon the ensuing holiday, enjoining all their brothers and sisters to remember the Hebrew glory from that generation forward in annual celebration of "Purim." For the dice, the purim, cast by wicked Haman to determine the date of the Jews' annihilation, had selected the very date on which Jehovah gave His people victory over their enemies and established them as citizens of the world.

Such happiness there would be in the old hometown tonight!

Hadassah, humble daughter of Abihail and beloved of Mordecai (whose name was now great in the earth), turned her dark eyes one last time toward the palace as it retreated behind the gated wall.

To her delight, Xerxes had stepped onto his chamber balcony, watching her departure with a sad smile.

Lifting a hand, she waved goodbye to him, and he, feeling many things, returned the gesture.

But then it seemed his gaze was caught away. And when Hadassah scanned the roadway, wondering what attracted him, she felt her heart leap to her throat.

Another noble carriage, this one heading toward the city, was just now passing hers on the highway. As it drew within the torchlight of the sunset wall, it favored Hadassah with a view of the interior.

There, barely concealed by a gauze curtain, was the unmistakable face of Vashti, a bit older than the girl remembered her, but beautiful as ever.

The returning queen was riveted by the sight of her beloved at his high balustrade. And her heart was full, it was clear, of love and forgiveness. In the king's embrace she would revel this night, and he in hers.

Vashti did not see Hadassah as she passed by. For this the younger woman was glad. She would rather not be known.

But if the lady had glimpsed the Jewess, she might have remembered the lovely child who had peered down on her from the garden rail so long ago. She would have seen the image of herself, and would have understood her husband's clumsy attempt to love another.

ESTHER

EPILOGUE

Better is the little of the righteous
Than the abundance of many wicked.

The Lord knows the days of the blameless;
And their inheritance will be forever.

Psalm 37:16,18 NASB

The lights of Leah's village square warmed the dark night as Hadassah wound her way through the merrymakers.

No one had yet recognized her as she passed through the dancing townsfolk and through the musicians who frolicked the night away.

She had slipped from her cab quietly, bidding sad goodbyes to Dorca and Maryam, who had ridden out with her. And she had privately entered the town gate.

She sought among the laughing villagers the faces of Leah and Moshe, and her cousins, Marta and Isha. But most especially she sought David. Her ears were atuned for his voice amidst the sounds of celebration, and her eyes focused for the hue of his hair and the angle of his chin.

But her cousins saw her before she identified anyone. And their squeals of delight drew the crowd's full attention to the newcomer.

Hadassah had always been a star to these folk. Since she was a child, she had captivated old and young alike. Now she was a regal celebrity.

No one had anticipated her homecoming. Vashti's resumption of the throne was news not yet delivered to the empire, and no one had looked for Queen Esther to be leaving the palace. That she should appear unannounced in this little place upon this festive occasion was a fantasy hardly credible.

As the reality of her presence dawned upon the locals, silence overcame the crowd, the music ceased, and awe marked every face. Leah, upheld by Moshe's strong arm, advanced toward the long-lost girl, tears spilling over her cheeks.

"My child!" she cried. "Can it be you?" the woman stammered, afraid to touch her, and bowing reverently before Her Majesty.

"Stand up, Cousin," the star smiled. "Call me not Esther. I am your Hadassah."

Leah turned hesitantly to Moshe, who could only shake his head. "We do not understand," he marveled.

"All in good time," Hadassah laughed, her dark eyes sparkling. "God's time is always perfect."

Nobody questioned her further, but Leah studied Hadassah's furtive glance about the square, and knew what occupied her heart.

"You seek David?" she guessed, drawing close.

"I do," was the simple answer.

The newcomer could see from her cousin's somber expression that all was not well.

"He went off days ago to fight at Ecbatana."

"Yes—yes," the girl replied, recalling how David had once spoken of the fabled city, and of the nomads who sang in the desert.

"We have not heard from him since," Moshe stepped in.

Hadassah's pulse quivered, as she feared to contemplate the meaning.

"Have others returned from that battle?" she spurred him. "Is David the only one missing?"

"Most have come back, but not our son," Leah sighed.

The younger Jewess hesitated, but then bravely insisted, "Of course not!" Then, trying to calm the quaver in her own voice, "He would have seen matters through to the end."

"We hope so . . ." Moshe agreed.

"How can you doubt?" Hadassah cried. "He is coming! He must come!"

With this she tore herself away from her friends, heading for the town's northern gate. Leah would have restrained her, but Moshe held his wife in check.

"Let the girl go," he soothed. "God is her strength."

* * *

Hadassah stood on tiptoe outside the low village wall, straining her vision up the highway which led to Ecbatana.

Overcome by memories, she trembled, gripping the rough slats of the gate and pulling herself as tall as she could stretch. How often she had done this very thing as she waited for David to come home from the fields! But tonight there were no homecoming workers to greet her, no friendly winks or nodding heads.

For long hours she stood, watching as darkness deepened, and as the villagers in the square danced and sang. She stood vigil until her legs ached and her eyes burned, and until the heat off the moonlit desert cast a shadowy mirage across her gaze.

Sometime past midnight her weary eyes were caught by a movement near a plot of palms which marked a bend in the highway.

Thinking perhaps she had dreamed it, she shook herself alert and focused on the spot. The more she concentrated, however, the more she was certain someone traveled toward her.

David, her soul pleaded.

But this man did not have David's walk. This man had a strange, limping gait—as one who had been . . . wounded.

Suddenly, as she absorbed the implication, she grew rigid. *Lord, could it be?* Before her intellect received the word, her heart knew. And when the moonlight reflected off his golden hair, she was charged with certainty.

Flying across the fields and the dry plateau beyond, she hastened after him.

The bone-tired soldier, the plowboy who had traded a hoe for a sword, fearfully studied the oncoming phantom. Something in the grace of the form was familiar, but not until he heard her call his name would he ever have dreamed it was Hadassah.

Even when she was upon him, flinging her slender arms about his neck, he could not accept what his eyes told him.

"My lady?" he marveled. "Are you a desert angel? Or have I passed on to Abraham's bosom?"

"Neither, my dear, dear David," she replied, laughing and crying at once. "It is I—your Hadassah. Like you, I have come home this night."

"Home?" he sighed. "To me?"

"Yes," she insisted, still clinging to him.

Suddenly he could bear no more, and thrusting her from him, he glared at her in torment.

"You mock me!" he groaned. "What have you to do any longer with a peasant?"

At this he staggered on toward the village, leaving her alone.

"You are hurt," she cried, seeing plainly now his bandaged leg and twisted foot. "Let me help you."

Rushing to his side, she pulled him closer, drawing one of his strong arms across her shoulders.

"Why have you left your palace, my queen?" he quipped. "Have you come out to play with the poor folk?"

"Enough, David," she returned, stopping still in her tracks. "You have not seen me for years. Is this how you greet me?"

The young veteran studied her quizzically, his pride more badly wounded than his leg.

"I will have a hero's welcome when I reach home," he said. "I need no greeting from the acropolis."

"And you shall have none," she answered. "I no longer live there."

The wounded warrior feared to contemplate her fevered eyes. Barely could he tolerate the hope her words instilled.

"Tell me no lies," he pleaded.

"Call me not your queen, then," she sighed, "unless I am queen of your heart. For I am no longer Queen of Persia. I am not Esther, but Hadassah. And I love you."

David's mind raced with questions.

"I am a poor man," he objected. "You have possessed a king's caress, you have owned an emperor's embrace . . ."

"I was his prisoner, David, not his lover."

"You have had everything . . ."

"Nothing—nothing without you," she insisted.

Tears quivered along the young man's lashes. The moon set fire in his golden eyes.

"Hadassah?" he whispered.

"Say you love me," she pleaded. "You have never said it."

Bending over her, he drew her to his bosom and breathed into her hair. His sigh said it all, and his lips met hers, to the soft sound of dancing beyond the village wall.

Joseph

DREAMER OF DREAMS

ELLEN GUNDERSON TRAYLOR

HARVEST HOUSE PUBLISHERS
Eugene, Oregon 97402

JOSEPH—DREAMER OF DREAMS

ISBN 1-56865-138-4

For My Sons
Who have taught me about Brotherhood.

Contents

Behold, how good and how pleasant it is for brothers to dwell together in unity!
Psalm 133:1 NASB

PROLOGUE

The boy crept between the tents of the dark caravan, avoiding the glow of a dozen campfires. The spine of mountains running south from Bethel to Ephrath was capped with frost tonight, and the boy's feet crunched against an icy powder as he sought his mother's tent.

His father, Jacob, had ordered him to spend the night with Bilhah, his mother's maid. "She will care for you," Jacob had insisted. "Your mother cannot do so just now."

Young Joseph had not needed to ask the reason. He understood that Rachel would give birth this very evening. He understood that he could not be with her.

Still, he had awaited this event for years. It had been only a few months since his mother had told him she would have another child. But he had longed for a brother of his very own for as long as he could remember. Even a sister would be better than nothing, he reasoned.

His half brothers, Dan and Naphtali, were no fun. Though they were his father's children by his mother's maid, they looked down on him, considering themselves better than him because they were older.

It mattered not that Rachel was Jacob's beloved and that Bilhah was only a servant. Joseph was scorned because he was the baby and, he knew, because he was Jacob's favorite.

But tonight there would be *another* baby, and another favorite! Joseph would no longer be alone.

When Bilhah had bedded him down in her tent at sunset, Joseph pretended to sleep. He knew she would leave as soon as he did so, for she would be needed in the birthing tent.

Dan and Naphtali snored contentedly outside as Joseph sneaked away. He was glad for this. They surely would have reported his escape, not caring that he fretted over his mother's welfare, or that he yearned to glimpse the newborn.

If he could only make it past the shelters of Leah, Rachel's sister and Jacob's eldest wife, and her handmaid, he might be safe. Once near his mother's tent, he knew no one would turn him away.

As he inched through camp, he considered how often he had known fear. Too many of his ten years had been spent on the run as he and his father's people fled from one threat after another.

Even among the folk of his tribe, Joseph sensed that his safety was often in jeopardy. No one had ever demonstrated that this was true. But he was the eleventh son born to Jacob, and because he was Rachel's, Leah hated him.

So did her children—at least most of them.

The goatshair birthing tent was now visible, pitched at the center of the tribal circle. As he came upon it, he heard cries of anguish from within.

He had heard women in travail before. In a tribe the size of Jacob's, the drama of birth was commonplace. Joseph remembered the bustle of the midwives and the tense expectation in the air whenever a baby was due.

But the sounds coming from his mother's tent tonight were frightening. Her pain was greater than it should be.

Joseph's boyish heart sped as he drew within the tent's shadow. Anxiously he peered through the curl of smoke wafting from the fire outside, but as he leaned around a support pole, studying the fretful scurry of the midwives, he was suddenly pushed face first to the ground.

Rising up on scraped knuckles, he stared into the leering countenance of Simeon, Leah's second son. He was a grown man, eight years older than Joseph and as vicious as a mountain cat.

Joseph crawled to his knees and brushed his dark curls from his forehead. His large black eyes snapping, he challenged: "Leave me be, Simeon! My father is in that tent. He will come after you!"

"*Your* father?" the bully spat, the red of his bushy beard catching firelight. "Always *your* father! Who do you suppose sired *me*? Some *field hand*?"

Tears rose hot in Joseph's eyes, but he restrained them as he stumbled to his feet and, fists clenched, glared brazenly up at his muscular opponent. Even stretched to his fullest height, he came only to Simeon's chest, and the athletic fellow sneered down upon him with gritted teeth.

"Shouldn't you be asleep, Little One?" Simeon laughed. "It is a full hour since sunset."

"My mother needs me!" the lad cried, trying to push past the human bulwark.

But it was no use. Immediately another enemy emerged from the darkness, Simeon's younger brother Levi, and a scuffle ensued, the two big fellows passing Joseph back and forth between them like a sack of barley chaff.

Such a disturbance was not long ignored, as folk left their fires and their shelters to gather around the tussling trio.

It was Reuben, Leah's eldest, who at last intervened.

His commanding voice parting the crowd, he came upon Simeon and Levi like an avenging angel.

"Leave the boy alone!" he commanded—and grasping both of his brothers by the necks, he cast them aside.

Joseph, who lay sprawled like a discarded doll, awkwardly lifted himself from the ground and reached for Reuben's hand.

The rescuer gently raised him up and, with friendly pats, brushed the dust from the lad's tunic.

Joseph studied him with grateful amazement. Reuben could just as easily have joined the tormentors. Though he was not the cruel sort, he could be impetuous. Joseph counted himself fortunate that the volatile young man had taken his side tonight.

"This is what comes of sneaking out at bedtime, Small One," Reuben warned.

The statement was a rebuke, but the tone was kind. Joseph took courage.

"This is what comes of having lions for brothers!" he countered. "Why must they hate me?"

Tears flecked his cheeks, now that he had a sympathizer. But Joseph knew the answer to the question, and Reuben need not reply.

As Simeon and Levi stalked away, uneasy silence descended until Joseph's attention was drawn again to the tent.

"Mother!" he called, responding to another cry of pain issuing on the night air. Darting past Reuben, he forced the crowd aside and pushed through the tent flap.

His sudden entrance jolted Jacob's focus away from his ailing wife, and Joseph confronted a full view of the tent's dark interior.

Never had Rachel looked as she did tonight. Drawn and white, her face was etched with distress. Cold sweat poured from her forehead.

Horrified, Joseph knelt beside the birthing chair, where his mother sat propped against Bilhah's open lap.

The maid was about to chide the boy, but Jacob hushed her.

"Perhaps it is best he is here," the father sighed.

Joseph could have been relieved to hear this. But he did not like the resigned quality in Jacob's voice.

Gazing upon his mother, the boy took her crabbed hand in his and lifted it to his lips.

How often throughout his life had that hand reached for him in tender caress! Now it was unable to reassure him.

And what countless times had he marveled at his mother's ageless face, at the beauty of her violet eyes and golden skin! Now the face was contorted, aged beyond its years in an evening's time.

No word of comfort rose above the panting and the tears from that voice which had sung him to sleep since his earliest memory.

Cradling his head against her swollen belly, Joseph wept. Nor would he be moved until a sudden lurch threw him backward.

Rachel had wrenched with the final throe of travail. For a brief instant, silence filled the room. Then, the shuddering wail of the newborn replaced it.

Joseph's eyes flashed to the baby where it wriggled, wet and red, in the midwife's outstretched hands.

It was a boy! He had a baby brother! He could barely refrain from reaching out to touch it.

But that honor would first be Rachel's, then Jacob's.

As the midwife placed the child on its mother's lap, however, Joseph could see that Rachel was still in anguish.

A fleeting smile touched her lips as the babe nuzzled against her. But just as quickly, the smile vanished, and Rachel pressed herself back against Bilhah, looking as though a searing iron had passed through her.

"Ben Oni!" Rachel cried. "Ben Oni!"

She was naming the child, and the name was not pleasant. "Child of my pain," the words meant. And Rachel clutched the little one to her breast, weeping.

"Mother!" Joseph implored. "What is it?"

But now the woman was still, her head limp against Bilhah's chest, her hands loosening their grip on the squalling infant.

Suddenly Jacob was on his knees, rubbing Rachel's hands and arms, pleading with her to respond.

As Bilhah caught the babe, who moved too freely in its mother's loose embrace, Joseph's heart surged.

"Mother!" he cried again.

But the woman did not reply.

Joseph leapt to his feet, refusing to face the truth. Pushing past his father, he entered the night, tears scalding his cheeks.

Heedless of those who tried to halt him, he raced through camp, toward the frosty fields beyond.

Running blindly into the dark, the boy wept aloud, calling out Jehovah's name.

The oppressive loneliness of his life was suddenly overwhelming. That which he daily endured was now suffocating him.

Where was his father's God when Joseph needed him? Why did he appear to Jacob and not to his young son?

As he reached the top of the ridge, he could hear Jacob calling, pleading for him to return. Yet in mad haste Joseph continued to flee until he was far from the lights of camp, far from the reach of human hands.

Falling to his face, he clutched at the icy ground, and for a long while he lay there, his tears melting the frost in little puddles.

Gradually, memories of a long-ago night pressed through his melancholy—memories of a night when his father had felt equally lonely and afraid.

As he sprawled against the earth's cold bosom, he resisted the demanding recollection. It seemed to offer hope—a hope he feared to embrace.

But the memory was persistent, invading his rebellion, piercing his spirit and his soul....

PART I
The Wrestler with God

1

Though Joseph was only six years old, it was a night he would clearly remember, a night he would never forget.

It was the night his father wrestled with an angel.

Little Joseph never saw the angel. He never saw Jacob struggle with the great being whose hold was stronger than iron, and who would, before the night was over, permanently cripple the man.

But Joseph saw the difference in Jacob. He saw the limping gait which would forever after be his. And though Joseph was very young, he sensed the maturing of his father's character from that night on.

Joseph had every reason to believe in angels. He had heard of them in stories passed down by Jacob from his father Isaac, and from *his* father Abraham before him. He had never seen one himself. But he knew they were as real as the wind that licked over the Gilead hills or the water which tumbled through the Jordan chasm.

Even before the angel moved against his father, however, the night was marked for memory.

For several days Jacob's caravan had been on the road from Padan-Aram toward Canaan. Joseph was too young to understand all that had transpired in Padan-Aram, the land of his birth. He knew that Jacob and Rachel had not been happy there. He knew that Jacob had not gotten on well with Grandfather Laban, Rachel's father. But this was all he understood.

Much clearer to him was the fear toward which the

caravan traveled as it inched out of Mesopotamia and entered the borders east of Jordan River.

He had heard all his life of Esau, Jacob's notorious elder brother. And he knew that Esau lay in wait to kill his father, once the tribe entered Canaan.

Sometimes he wondered why the family must go to Canaan, if danger lurked there. The country of Grandfather Laban had been a safe place. No one had feared for life or welfare in Padan-Aram.

But just as he had always heard of the red and hairy villain, Esau, so he had always heard of Canaan.

"Promised Land," it was called. Land vouchsafed to Great-grandfather Abraham, Grandfather Isaac, and Father Jacob, by the One True God.

Indeed, more than Esau or Canaan or Jordan River or the breezes of Gilead, Joseph had heard of the One True God.

Every morning of his life, Joseph had witnessed Jacob's early-rising prayers, his burning of sweet incense upon piles of rocks outside their tent home, and his monthly offering of a slaughtered lamb for the sins of the tribe.

He knew that there were other people dwelling nearby who did not believe in the One True God, and who had many other gods besides. But he had been assured since infancy that Jehovah was the only God and that he alone was worthy of honor.

Also, Joseph had been told, this God belonged especially to Abraham, Isaac, and Jacob, for they were his chosen people.

Now this night, when the angel wrestled with Jacob, settled over the caravan like a black shroud. Five days earlier, the enormous tribe had entered Gilead. And five days earlier, Jacob had begun to plot his inevitable meeting with Esau.

Full of trepidation, Jacob sent messengers ahead to scout for his enemy, to tell him he wanted peace. When the messengers returned, saying that Esau was headed north with four hundred men, terrible fear gripped the tribe.

Tension rose with each step the caravan took through Gilead. According to Jacob, it must break up once it reached the southern edge of the region, and the people must travel in two divisions as they approached Edom, the land where Esau lived.

Earlier that day, before he wrestled with the angel, Jacob sent droves of sheep, cattle, and goats down the road toward Edom, each drove numbering several dozen animals and manned by half-a-dozen shepherds. Seven droves he sent on before the caravan, and the family camped at sunset beside the ford Jabbok at Gilead's southern border.

When night had fully fallen, the great tribe, composed of Jacob's two wives and two concubines, as well as their many children, servants, and servants' families, settled down to sleep. Joseph would never forget watching as Jacob crept away to his tent, looking distressed indeed, the fear of Esau heavy upon him.

It was the middle of the night, the encampment quiet and dark, when suddenly Jacob reappeared. He threw back the flap to Rachel's shelter, rousing the woman and young Joseph, who slept beside her.

In the light of the smoking lamp suspended from the tent roof, the boy say his father's distraught countenance, and his heart raced fearfully. As he pulled close to Rachel, she took his hand and caressed it reassuringly.

But Papa was evidently afraid—how could Joseph not be?

The boy, eyes wide, listened as Jacob gave instructions.

"Wife," he began, "I have not been sleeping tonight. The power of God is in this place. Do you feel it?"

Rachel replied nothing, always awed by her husband's intimacy with the Almighty. Shaking her head, she admitted she had no such sense of things.

"I did not tell you," he went on, pacing the room, "but a few days ago I saw the hosts of the Lord encamped about us. The hills were full of them! Bright as sun! Did you not see them?"

Joseph knew "the hosts of the Lord" was another term for angels, and he listened intently.

"No, husband," Rachel answered. "I saw nothing."

"They met me on the road. Surely you saw!"

But Rachel only lowered her eyes.

"So be it," Jacob muttered, obviously disappointed. "But I know the Lord is in this place. I must seek him! Help me rouse the camp. All of you are to cross Jabbok while it is yet dark."

Rachel did not understand. "Why, my lord?" she implored. "Can we not wait with you?"

Jacob could not explain. He only knew that he must be alone, for the Lord would not come to him while he was in company.

Urgently he pressed his command. "Up, Rachel! Take the lad and help me wake the others. We have only a short while before morning."

Certain things about Jacob's character had already been imprinted upon Joseph's young mind. His father was very changeable: sometimes, like now, forceful and commanding; other times, betraying cowardice and uncertainty.

Had Joseph been older, these discrepancies might have caused him to question what Jacob said. He might have doubted the man's visions; he might have doubted the reality of angels altogether.

But the child loved his father passionately. If Jacob said they must be going, Joseph would cooperate.

Jumping up, he ran to a corner of the tent where a satchel was kept, his satchel for carrying toys and valuables dear to his heart. It was full, as he had picked up his possessions before bedtime, and he proudly set it beside the door.

"So, Little One is ready!" Jacob observed, smiling broadly.

Preoccupied, Jacob had barely noticed the child when he had entered the tent. But he beamed now with pride at the handsome lad who so resembled himself.

Calling Joseph, he reached for him, and the boy eagerly rushed into his strong arms.

"Help your mother," Jacob said fondly, his dark eyes mirroring his son's.

With that, the man left, summoning his servants to load the wagons.

Rachel, who was never prepared for her husband's swift alterations, tried not to reveal, by expression or word, the weariness she felt.

Brushing her long black tresses back from a too-pale face, she sighed.

She would much prefer to sleep until morning.

2

Joseph huddled between rough sacks of winnowed grain in the back of Leah's jolting wagon. Rachel had prevailed upon her sister to keep the lad in the cart where Leah's daughter, Dinah, was hidden, while she and her handmaid loaded their own supplies. Now he peered out from the protective tarp, watching as Gilead retreated in the night.

Haughty Leah had, in her typical manner, scorned Rachel's request, taking opportunity to gloat over the pleasures of having many children.

"Too bad Joseph has no brothers or sisters of his own to cozy up with," she huffed. "You would do Jacob a service to give him another son."

Rachel's face burned, showing more color than it had in recent weeks. But, nodding, she indulged her jealous sister. For she knew it *was* only jealousy that prompted the cruel remark.

Leah hated Rachel. She hated her because Jacob loved her. And because she knew that Jacob never would have been her own husband, had Father Laban not insisted on it.

It seemed to make no difference that Leah had given Jacob six sons and a daughter, or that her handmaid, Zilpah, had blessed him with two sons more. Though Jacob was justly proud of all his children, Rachel, who had borne him only one heir, held his heart in an unyielding knot of love.

Could Leah help it that she was not as beautiful as her younger sister? Mousy-haired and wan, she had never been smooth-complected or ruby-lipped like Rachel. Could she help it that her vision was weak, so that she could not do the fine needlework for which Rachel was renowned, or that her dull brown eyes did not dance with lavender lights like Rachel's?

Leah was at least a good cook. One did not need perfect vision for that. And Leah was the elder. Surely she deserved preference for that reason, if no other.

Besides, of late Rachel was pale-skinned, the blossom gone from her cheeks. Could not Jacob see the alteration? Was not Leah the stronger of the two?

She would never understand Jacob. From the moment he had shown up in Laban's camp, on the run from Canaan and the threats of Esau, she had been smitten with him. Though her sight had been poor since childhood, she was not completely blind to the lithe and strapping handsomeness of her cousin from the west.

He, on the other hand, had not given Leah a second look.

Jacob had first laid eyes on Rachel, and from that instant his soul belonged to the younger sister.

Over and over, Leah had chided herself for not being in the field the day Jacob arrived. Rachel was tending sheep that afternoon, something the elder girl scorned. Smelly, despicable creatures they were, and whenever possible, she passed the task to Rachel.

But Leah should have been with the sheep the day Jacob came. Perhaps if he had seen her first he would have fallen in love with her, and Rachel would not have moved him as she did.

Thus did Leah comfort herself. Thus did she lie to herself.

Year in and year out she dreamed that the next son she bore would win Jacob's heart from Rachel's grip. To this day, it had not happened. But, in time...

As Joseph hid this night in the covered grain-cart, his half sister, Dinah, nestled close. Dinah was nearest to him in age of all Jacob's children, and despite her mother's objections, she loved the boy dearly.

His sole playmate, she was only two years his senior. But since she was his only female sibling, she enjoyed mothering him at every opportunity.

The wagon rocked against the brook's bottom as the caravan forded the Jabbok River in the dark. Father Jacob was somewhere in the night beyond, shouting commands as loudly as he dared, trying to hasten the train to a safe stopping place.

No one but he understood why the caravan could not wait to pass over in the morning. Only Jacob knew with certainty that he must be alone in Gilead with the Lord.

Dinah pulled Joseph's head to her shoulder, crooning a soft lullaby in his ear. But the child was too old for this, and asserting his masculinity, he pulled away.

Joseph wanted to see where they were going. He wanted to be riding with his father, upon his father's horse.

Reaching for the wagon's back rail, he peered again from beneath the tarp at the long caravan behind.

Just as he did so, two of his half brothers rode up, their horses splashing effortlessly through the cold stream. Though the riders were only teenagers, they were larger than life to Joseph, who held them in high esteem. For Reuben and Judah were generally kind to the youngster.

When the two horsemen caught sight of Joseph's round face and rounder eyes gleaming beneath the moonlit tarp, they laughed, nodding to him. And when Reuben winked congenially, the boy blushed with admiration.

"Where is Papa?" he called. "Have you seen my Papa?"

But already the brothers had passed, their powerful steeds leaving a glistening wake. The only reply Joseph would receive came from two others, following on their trail.

"This son of a second wife calls for his Papa!" a mocking voice announced.

And another scoffed, "You don't suppose he means Jacob? Why I thought Jacob was *your* Papa, Simeon."

"And *yours*, Levi!" the first replied.

Joseph sensed their sarcasm and felt the rejection keenly.

Dinah yanked on the boy's tunic, but he refused to rejoin her, staring after Simeon and Levi with sad eyes.

Reading his dejection, the girl tried to console him. "They are fools!" she whispered, still clutching at his garment. "Never mind those two."

The lad's lower lip jutted in an offended pout. Soon a salty tear slipped down his cheek.

"Let me go!" he cried. "I want Papa!"

At last the caravan reached the south shore and soon a silty dust rose from the damp wheels. Somehow through hazy starlight, the boy spied his father.

Jacob had seen the caravan safely over and waited now on a knoll of the brook's border. Tall and dark against the sky, he sat astride his horse, and Joseph wondered why he did not join them.

When Rachel came looking for her child amidst the grain sacks, Joseph climbed out eagerly. "I want to go to Papa!" he called, directing her attention to the distant figure on the rise.

"Hush, son," Rachel soothed. "He cannot come just now."

"Why?" the lad pleaded. "Is he afraid?"

Flashes of the legendary Esau gripped his imagination, conjuring visions of monsters and assassins.

"Your Papa is never afraid," Rachel whispered.

But Joseph knew better.

"He runs from fighting Esau," the youngster muttered.

Rachel studied her perceptive boy with wonder. Shaking her head, she spoke a mystery.

"It is not Esau whom your Papa must fight tonight. It is the Lord."

The boy absorbed the words in quiet awe. Clutching his mother's skirt, he shivered, still entranced by the figure on the hill.

Suddenly Jacob turned to leave, guiding his mount back into the water. A sheen of moonlight glinted across the waves where the horse's strong legs broke the eddies, and the man sat erect in the saddle.

That moment, Joseph was prouder of his father than he had ever been. For whatever it was that called him back to Gilead, Jacob dared to face it.

3

Like the glint off a giant's spear, morning burst upon the caravan.

Joseph, having rested fitfully all night, crawled out from his mother's tent and rubbed his bleary eyes in the glaring sun.

The great train had set up camp close to the brook, but because Rachel's and Leah's tents were at the center of the encircling tribe, Joseph could not see the place where his father had departed.

Somehow he knew Jacob would be returning early from whatever had faced him in Gilead. Scrambling between the wagons, he found the edge of camp before any adult awoke to find him gone, and when he gained the brook's shore, he peered across the undulating hills on the far side.

Within moments his eager expectation was rewarded. The sight of his father emerging from a crease of the northern slopes provoked a cry of delight.

But presently his enthusiasm was dampened as Jacob appeared to slump in his horse's saddle.

"Papa! Papa!" the boy called until the caravan was roused, and men and women joined him on shore.

The closer the rider came, the more evident was his sorry condition. In the blaring sunlight, sweat streaked his body. Beneath a layer of dirt, the scrapes and bruises on his torso, arms, and legs throbbed.

Horrified, Joseph stood dangerously close to the water's edge, trying to reach across. In an instant he was grasped from behind, hoisted to someone's shoulders and scolded without mercy.

It was Reuben who held him, Reuben who scolded him. But Joseph kicked his heels into the tall fellow's breast.

"Enough, Little One!" the elder snarled, grasping his ankles. "See what a good view you have from up there! Jacob is nearly here now."

Leah, her eyes snapping, came near to Reuben, ready to reprimand him for associating so closely with the lad. But with a look, he silenced her.

Jacob had reached the southern shore and, dismounting, he staggered, holding onto the saddle for support.

A gasp went up from the crowd, and those nearest rushed to help him.

But soon they were pushed aside as Rachel forced her way through to her husband.

"Jacob, what is it?" she cried, seeing how he limped upon one leg. "What has happened to you?"

Bending over, she probed his leg with deft hands, seeking a broken or disjointed bone.

"Not there!" he grimaced as she reached toward the backside of his thigh. "Do not touch me there! And do not call me 'Jacob,' for the Almighty has called me 'Israel.' "

This was spoken with such authority that the woman jolted upright, staring into the man's face as into the face of a stranger.

Israel. "Wrestler with God," the name implied. Joseph remembered how his mother had said Papa must fight with the Lord, and clutching Reuben closer, he studied Jacob with wonder.

The patriarch gave no further explanation, only passing through the crowd until he came to the center of the caravan.

Snapping his fingers, he called for a bucket of water and began washing himself in the presence of the people.

Gingerly he cleansed his own wounds, all the while avoiding the tender spot beneath his hip.

His tunic, which hung in shreds upon his naked body, must be removed, and Jacob, disregarding public exposure, lifted it over his head, cast it aside, and stood for all to see covered only by his loincloth.

When he called for a clean garment, Leah ran to her supply cart, unfurled a freshly laundered tunic, and brought it to him.

Almost in ritual did Jacob don the spotless garb. When he pulled it over his tall form, he raised his eyes toward heaven in private communion.

The crowd, riveted by his strange behavior and by the mystery of his struggle in the wilderness, watched in breathless suspense.

For a long time he stood thus, head back, eyes closed, until the quiet of the hills was broken. Somewhere beyond the valley of the Jabbok, from across the southland, the sound of a tramping horde invaded the tranquil moment.

On the instant, Jacob ceased his prayers. With a stalwart stride, he passed toward the highlands hemming the caravan's southern rim.

Every heart in the company surged with fear. They knew it was Esau who advanced upon them—Esau with his army of four hundred.

Before the dust-raising horsemen appeared on the barren hills, Jacob began shouting orders.

"Each man to arms!" he cried. "Advance to the front, but keep your weapons in their sheaths!"

The order was, on the surface, contradictory. But to this point Jacob had let Esau know that he intended peace. The sight of bared swords and poised arrows would indicate the contrary.

Louder and louder came the sound of the troops, billows of fine silt wafting skyward from their marching feet, lingering on the warm currents above the rise and signaling the company's ascent toward the Jabbok.

Sweat streaked the faces of Jacob's servants and shepherds, who, though they had been trained for battle, had no experience with it. In awkward bands they arranged themselves along the edge of the caravan, ready to kneel behind the carts, ready to draw their primitive staves and heavy knives.

With amazing coolness, Jacob called to his womenfolk, ordering his maids and their children to stay nearest the caravan, while his wives and concubines gathered near the brook.

"Bilhah and Zilpah!" he shouted. "Leave room for Leah and her children behind you!"

Readily the women complied, trying to keep their anxieties under control.

As they arranged themselves according to his instruction, he turned his attention to Rachel and Joseph. In that moment he revealed, as never before, the exact priorities of his heart.

"Wife," he called, "take the final station! And keep Little One with you at all times!"

Leah did not notice this interchange. She was distracted by her four eldest sons, who bitterly resented Jacob's restraint, and who desired to be in the forefront with the men.

But Dinah frantically tugged on her mother's skirts, pointing to Joseph.

"May I stay with my brother?" she pleaded. "It is safest where he and his mother are."

The elder woman flashed angry eyes on Rachel and on her husband. Never had she hated her sister as she did just now, and never had she felt such antipathy for the man she craved.

Scooping Dinah into her arms, she ran for the privacy of her canopied wagon, where she would stay, hidden and heartsick, until the crisis was over.

As for the rest of the company, all eyes were on the patriarch as he faced the southern hills.

Emerging along the horizon were the four hundred soldiers, and leading them, a ruddy commander. Esau, whose thick red beard and heavy turban lent him a fearsome aspect, rode a big-boned mount. Black and glistening, the horse's studded saddle and burnished harnesswork befitted the legendary image of its master.

Jacob's men flinched at the sight. For weeks, they had dreaded this moment, their imaginations piqued by the tales that had long circulated in Padan-Aram of this son of Isaac and his vendetta against the younger brother.

Wet palms slipped against the handles of their swords and coveted the feel of the bow. How the men longed to break with Jacob's order, to draw their weapons and fell Esau where he stood!

But it was Jacob who would make the first move. And his move would be peaceable.

Confronting the man who watched from the mountain, the patriarch began a slow advance up the rise that hemmed Jabbok Vale.

As he did so, his would-be soldiers poised their hands to grasp their weapons. But their commander would not indulge them.

It was with the attitude of a servant that Jacob approached his brother, his limping gait evincing pain with each step. To the amazement of his troops, he began to bow, over and over, as he walked up the hill toward Esau. Nor was this a cursory gesture. Six times he performed the obeisance—stopping in his tracks, falling to his knees, and with arms outstretched along the ground, touching his black-bearded face to the earth.

That scene would be indelibly imprinted upon the mind of Joseph. He had long sensed Jacob's fear of this very encounter; he had witnessed his restless nights and the growing agitation of his spirit as they had come near the land of Esau. But Jacob's behavior this day, though

self-effacing, bore no hint of cowardice or helpless sur-
render. The patriarch manifested strength of purpose,
steadfastly pursuing the meeting even as he declared his
humility.

The boy, staying close to Rachel, observed the drama
with wonder. He did not comprehend why Esau wished
to kill Jacob, nor why his father had run from the land of
Canaan years ago. But he did know that Uncle Esau could
take Jacob's life at any moment.

For the younger brother was no longer running. Jacob
had come home, and he hid behind no army, no weapon
of his own. He was offering himself as a sacrifice, appealing to whatever goodwill Esau might possess, and ready
to die rather than run again.

As he approached the enemy, the crowd's attention
shifted to Esau, who sat unmoving, watching his brother
with stormy eyes.

Not only were years of Jacob's personal history about
to be resolved, but the fate of the entire tribe hinged on
Esau's response—the fate of innocent hundreds who had
followed the younger patriarch out from Padan-Aram.

To this point, the company from the east had been
awed by their leader's bravery. However, the seventh time
Jacob bowed himself to the ground, he was nearly within
the shadow of Esau's horse. The elder brother had the
right, at that juncture, to climb down from his steed,
placing his foot directly upon Jacob's neck. Should he
choose to do so, he would in fact be conqueror of Jacob
and all his people—a conqueror without a war.

Never had the Jacobites dreamed their patriarch would
stoop so low! Had he brought them out from their homeland only to hand them into slavery? Incredulous, they
witnessed his symbolic submission, and a rush of angry
whispers filled the vale.

For a long, anxious moment, Esau studied his prostrate brother. It seemed a lifetime since he had last laid

eyes on the prodigal—a lifetime of festering hatred and desire for revenge.

When Jacob had slunk away from Canaan, he had been a desperate character, poor as an alms seeker, possessing nothing but his guilt and the clothes on his back. Now here he came, returning from his hideaway, chieftain of a mighty tribe, leader of a fabulous caravan.

When the first bevy of cattle and presents had arrived on the southbound highway, brought by peace-seeking messengers, Esau had been amazed at his brother's apparent success in the land of Uncle Laban. But he despised the placating gesture, and his longing for vengeance had only been piqued by Jacob's show of wealth, his belated attempt at appeasement.

Now as he gazed down upon the penitent, his heart was a muddle of conflict. Part of him yearned to squash the fellow into the dirt. It would be so easy to do so. Another part seethed with resentment at the ease of such conquest, for Jacob had effectively taken the luxury of violence from his sword-hungry hand.

There was a nobler motivation, however, which was stirred by Jacob's humble homecoming. It was brotherhood, the kind that had resisted all attempts to kill itself.

For Jacob was bone of his bone, flesh of his flesh—his twin, born at the same hour, born in tandem with him, grasping his heel (so the legend went) as Esau declared his supremacy, his right to primogeniture.

From that moment, the secondborn was called Jacob, "the supplanter," and so he had proven himself to be—fighting and scratching for equality, and ultimately, by connivery and deceit, winning the birthright itself.

But at this instant, as Esau observed Jacob's willingness to make amends, none of that seemed to matter.

Suddenly, in a breath, the heart of the elder melted, and the past was absolved. Barely understanding his own actions, Esau leapt to the ground and ran the short distance between them, bending over and grasping Jacob by the shoulders.

The runaway lifted his head, staring into Esau's face in bewildered amazement. What he saw there astonished him: tears streamed down Esau's cheeks, trickling into his crimson beard as he lifted his brother from the dirt. Embracing Jacob, Esau fell on his neck and kissed him, and together the men wept.

Drawing back, Esau looked his long-lost brother up and down, and grasped him close again and again, letting the tears flow.

After this catharsis of revelry, Esau studied the great multitude waiting on the plain below.

"Who are these with you?" he inquired.

Jacob could hardly speak, absorbed as he was in the incredible turnabout.

"The children whom God has graciously given me," he at last replied, beaming with pride.

Wheeling around he motioned to the throng and called for his wives and young ones to come forward.

Bilhah and Zilpah, nearest the front, complied first, trailed by their reticent sons: Dan, Naphtali, Gad, and Asher. Lingering at the foot of the hill, they bowed themselves.

Next came Leah, who by now had seen the necessity of emerging from her cart, obeying her husband in begrudging silence.

Her sons were no more willing to condescend than she. Hotheaded and strong-willed, all six of them resisted this twist of events, but one by one they fell in line behind their mother in order of their age: Reuben, Simeon, Levi, Judah, Issachar, and Zebulun.

Stiffnecked, the lads bowed before their uncle, wishing his heart had not changed before them, wishing he had chosen war.

Dinah, clinging to Leah's skirts, peered back at Joseph, wondering what he thought. But he paid her no mind.

Alone among his brothers, Joseph was eager to meet the amazing Esau.

At last, Jacob called for Rachel, his expression soft, his voice full of love.

"This is my wife," he introduced her, "and this is Joseph, my youngest."

Esau could not have missed the tenderness in his brother's tone. Obviously Rachel held his heart, and Joseph, though least of the brethren, was foremost in his father's estimation.

Nor could the other people in Jacob's company miss the intimation. Even Reuben, who loved the boy, felt the prick of jealousy, and his body grew rigid. With mixed emotions, he watched as his young brother strode boldly up to Esau, bowing to the ground just as Jacob had done.

Esau, a lump in his throat, gazed on the lad, and Joseph lifted his round face to the "villain" whose very name had always filled the child with horror.

Leaning down, Esau held out his hairy arms, and without hesitating, Joseph ran to him. Raised up on the man's broad shoulders, he saw the great tribe from the "enemy's" perspective.

Though Jacob had every right to be proud of his company, it did not compare to the trained army at Esau's back. Joseph knew that Esau could have wiped out his people, and he keenly perceived the man's merciful kindness.

"Brother," Esau was speaking again, "what was the meaning of all the gifts you sent before you?"

Jacob looked at the ground. "They were to find grace in the sight of my lord," he replied.

"But I have enough, my brother," Esau said, smiling. "Keep your possessions."

Jacob shook his head. "No, I beg of you; if I have found grace in your sight, receive my gift. For I have seen your face, and it is like the face of God. You have forgiven me.

Now please take my gift, for it is the gift of the Lord unto your servant."

Joseph, who clung to Esau's neck, felt him tremble as he at last relented, accepting Jacob's love and loving him in return.

In that instant the lad knew that not only had Jacob changed during the struggle of the night, but that change had also altered the heart of Esau.

Whatever had transpired in the hills of Gilead had indeed been supernatural. Joseph would always wish he had seen the encounter firsthand.

4

For four years Jacob and his people dwelt on the east side of the Jordan River. And for four years, Joseph pondered the mystery of his father's fight in Gilead.

Not once in all that time did he speak with Jacob about the incident. Perhaps he felt the topic too holy to pursue. Perhaps he feared it.

When he was ten years old, the great tribe moved across the Jordan into the legendary region of Canaan, into the Promised Land where Abraham and Isaac had dwelt. With that move, Joseph hungered even more after spiritual things. He longed to understand the mystery of his people and the tales of the elders.

Indeed, Grandfather Isaac still lived there. Though his dwelling place was at the Oaks of Mamre, in Hebron—much farther to the south than the place where Jacob settled—Joseph hoped to one day meet the venerable fellow. As the boy grew toward manhood, so did his curiosity regarding Isaac's God.

After the tribe made its entrance into Canaan, Jacob selected a site near Shalem to pitch his tent.

Shalem, nestled in the pleasant hill country twenty miles west of the Jordan, was the headquarters of Hamor, a Hivite, and his eldest son. In fact, the region around Shalem was named for the son, Shechem, who was considered prince of the region.

The Hivites were a violent brood, lovers of war and jealous territorialists. But then so were most Canaanites, and Jacob knew that diplomacy would be required wherever his tribe settled.

Joseph sat one noon in the sunny patch outside his mother's tent. Across the narrow common that ran between the dwellings of Jacob's wives he watched as Leah brushed out his sister Dinah's auburn hair.

The girl had persuaded her mother to let her go into town to sell some of their honey cakes at market.

Leah had come upon an abandoned hive in a hollow tree trunk the day before, and Dinah had helped her knead and bake the succulent yeast dough which was sweetened to a mouth-watering confection. All morning the aroma of rising dough and browning loaves had filled the vale where the caravan rested. One by one Dinah had glazed the rolls with cinnamon and honey and had carefully wrapped them in oilcloth. They were stacked now in a satchel at her feet, waiting to be carried to Shalem's bazaar.

Joseph was not too young to realize how pretty his sister was. Eagerly he waited while she stood and turned about for her mother's inspection, her flowing gown conforming to her willowy legs as she twirled.

He would be very proud to accompany Dinah to Shalem. And he was thrilled that the girl had persuaded Leah to let him do so. No one else was available to be her escort, as all the older brothers were off in the high fields, tending Jacob's herds.

For days, Dinah had fretted over the desire to go to market, to meet the girls of the town and make some friends. Hers was a lonely existence, sole daughter among eleven sons. Since Jacob had rented Hamor's campsite for the entire season, she knew she would have time, for once, to form relationships.

Joseph, likewise, was lonely. Though there were playmates among the servants' children, he, like Dinah, was the child of the tribal elder. Neither of them was very free to mingle with the lower class.

For Joseph, however, loneliness went beyond this. This morning his elder brothers had brushed him off when he requested to go with them into the hills.

Always he was "Little One." More than this, he was "Rachel's son," and he sensed increasingly that he had inherited the same jealous treatment his mother had always endured at Leah's hands.

The sons of Bilhah, Rachel's maid, were less resentful of Joseph than were the others. But even these, Dan and Naphtali, often snubbed him, knowing that he was Jacob's favorite.

Perhaps, Joseph thought, he would meet some youths of his own age and class in Shalem. Anticipating a delightful afternoon, he was impatient for Dinah to be ready.

Although Joseph related to his sister's isolation, one thing lately gave him great enthusiasm for the future. No one had told him, but he knew that his mother was pregnant. And he trusted with all his heart that she would present him with a brother.

Just now, Rachel emerged from her tent and passed before him in the sunlight. With boyish curiosity Joseph observed how her long tunic stretched more snugly than usual over her abdomen. And he noticed that her lap string was riding higher on her belly.

He also knew, based on his observations of other ladies in the tribe, that it would yet be several months before she bore the child. Eagerly he contemplated the event, running his tongue over his lips as the idea tantalized him.

At last Dinah joined him, her beauty session at an end. Following his gaze across the courtyard, she softly rebuked him. "It isn't nice to stare. You could embarrass your mother."

Joseph jolted, and receiving the correction, blushed violently. "I . . . I didn't mean . . ." he stammered.

"Come," the girl laughed, tossing her red-brown curls as she turned on her heel. "Time to go."

Joseph leapt to his feet and ran to catch up with her. Offering to carry Dinah's satchel, he gloated, "Mama is going to have a baby!"

Dinah giggled. "Hush," she warned. "Such things should not be spoken until your mother says so."

But Joseph was heedless. Matching Dinah's stride, he beamed proudly, as though he could somehow take credit for his good fortune.

* * *

The marketplace of Shalem was crowded with afternoon shoppers when Joseph and Dinah arrived.

With a light step, the daughter of Jacob sauntered through the aisles, admiring the produce, the pottery, and the dry goods arrayed in colorful rows all about.

Only moments after entering the bazaar, Dinah sold her honey loaves. Though she was certain she must be a natural hawker after striking an ample deal on her first try, Joseph was not so sure it was business savvy that had brought her price.

It had not escaped his notice that the old codger she dealt with seemed to be swayed as much by her endearing charms as by the quality of her wares. Nodding his head enthusiastically, his little goatee bobbing and his pea-black eyes twinkling, he had purchased her entire satchel-load with hardly a quibble.

In fact, Joseph found his protective hackles rising as he accompanied his sister through the market's narrow walkways. For all about were men, old and young, observing the maiden with undisguised admiration.

Dinah, who seemed oblivious to the onlookers' unabashed stares, had but one thing in mind now that she had sold her baked goods: She had come to market to meet girls her own age. She searched the booths and the klatches of customers, hoping to find companions.

At last she spotted a group of young ladies gathered about the stall of a fabric vendor, and she eagerly turned to Joseph.

"Now, you are my escort," she reminded him. "You must introduce me."

"Me?" Joseph objected. "Not for a bag of silver! I'll not join any gaggle of girls! Let go!" he barked, jerking his sleeve from her grasp.

"Hush!" she ordered, her face scarlet. "They'll hear you."

But it seemed they had already heard, and they watched the awkward interchange with muted laughter.

"Now you've done it!" Dinah sighed, her lip jutted in a pout. "I'll never make friends here!"

Putting her hands to her tear-streaked face, she headed for a quiet alcove behind the town fountain. Joseph, unprepared for this reaction, stood dejected in the midst of the bustling market.

When he saw that the girls at the fabric stall twittered hilariously, he turned with humiliation to join his sister.

By the time he reached her, however, someone else had come to her rescue. Joseph stopped in his tracks as a strapping fellow, dressed in princely finery, approached Dinah upon a tall white steed.

The son of Jacob was not the only one to be amazed at the sudden appearance of this character. Young ladies throughout the marketplace turned to gaze upon the stately fellow, whispering his name and pointing. For Prince Shechem, son of Hamor, lord of the region, did not often mingle with commoners.

As Joseph came upon his sister, cloistered behind the fountain, the man had already dismounted and bent over the maiden as though he knew her.

Stunned, Joseph did not know how to approach the prince.

For royalty he was—tall and handsome, his glistening black beard set off against a tunic of rose-colored satin.

Upon his head was a sequined turban, and draped about his broad shoulders was a velvet cloak, wine-hued and embroidered in silver.

Nevertheless, Joseph did not appreciate the man's familiar gesture. Standing at the corner of the alcove, he listened to the fellow's smooth talk and tender words as he tried to comfort the girl.

"Sir," Joseph interrupted, clearing his throat, "that is *my* sister. You would do well to leave her alone!"

Dinah, who by now had turned to face the stranger, seemed highly impressed by the man. Glaring at Joseph, she warned him with a look to keep his peace.

Joseph, however, would not be dissuaded. Young though he was, and small, he was still her escort, and he would not be deterred from his protective duty.

The prince greeted the interruption with a smile, his white teeth shining in his moustached face.

"This is *my* city," he countered, as though speaking to the lad took more condescension than he was used to. "I do not like to see a maiden weeping within these gates."

Joseph, put off by his silky manner, his costly raiment, and perfectly crimped coiffure, was momentarily struck dumb. But lifting his chin, he argued, "We are children of Jacob the Hebrew, who rents land from your father. You would do well to keep our goodwill!"

Shechem rolled his eyes, looking to the hills as though they bored him. He was about to fling out an epithet regarding the bedouin lifestyle, but caught himself as he considered Dinah's feelings. Not wishing to offend the object of his desire, he recast his approach.

"Please give your father my regards," he said, bowing to Joseph. Then, turning to Dinah, he took her hand and kissed it softly. "You and I, dear lady, shall meet again."

With this he remounted his horse, and hailing the girl, exited through the market gate.

Dinah stood mute with wondering adoration.

But her brother's skin crawled. He suspected the man meant just what he said: He and Dinah would meet again. The prospect did not sit well with Joseph.

5

Joseph lurched awake. It was the middle of the night, he knew, by the slant of the moon's rays entering his mother's tent.

Someone stood silhouetted in the doorway, and as his pulse raced, he realized it was Dinah.

He sat up in bed, ready to call her name, but she hushed him. "You'll wake Rachel," she said. "Come out here."

Dinah's voice was strained and urgent. When Joseph joined her on the common, he saw that she stood hunched and shaking in the shadows.

"What is it?" he whispered. "Are you all right?"

The girl shuddered. "Tell no one," she implored as she pulled him toward the grove of oak trees that sheltered the camp. "You must promise to tell no one."

"Tell what?" the boy puzzled.

"I left Leah's tent this evening. I could not sleep for thinking of Prince Shechem."

Joseph rolled his eyes, but Dinah shook her head. "This is important, Little One," she insisted. Then, studying her own quivering hands, she groaned, "I have been defiled. Do not hate me."

The lad had heard the term before. He knew what "defiled" meant. But he could not couple the idea with his sister.

"I do not understand," he sighed.

Dinah, surveying his innocent face, began to sob, and she led him to a fallen log, where they sat together.

"I wandered out from camp tonight," she confessed, her chest heaving. "Farther out than I should have gone. Everyone was asleep. The prince must have been waiting for me. I do not know how he knew . . . but he found me in the vale. And . . ."

Her voice broke, and she choked back the longing to cry aloud.

Quickly the scenario flashed through Joseph's mind. "The swine!" he spat, leaping to his feet. "I shall kill him!"

His fist clenched, he looked about frantically, as if seeking a weapon with which to wreak revenge. Bending down, he ripped one of the dry roots off the fallen tree and lunged through the darkness, wielding it like a bat-tle-ax.

"I will tell Jacob!" he declared. "You return to your mother!"

With this, he was off.

"I begged you not to tell! You mustn't tell, Joseph!" Dinah called.

Running after him, she caught him about the waist, pulling him to the ground.

Though the girl had been badly shaken, she was still stronger than her little brother. Staring him full in the face as she wrestled him into submission, she pleaded, "Hear me. Shechem says he loves me. He says he wishes to marry me. Perhaps he is not so evil!"

Incredulous, Joseph lay stone still, his thoughts a blur.

"Are you lunatic?" he muttered, his teeth gritted. Then with an accusing tone, he asked, "*Did* he force you, or didn't he?"

Dinah drew back, appalled at the intimation. "Why . . . why . . ." she faltered, "what do you take me for?"

"*Did* he force you," Joseph challenged, "or did you . . ."

At this, Dinah's eyes flashed, and slapping her brother across the cheek, she rose, running deep into the woods.

"Of course he forced you!" Joseph shouted after her.

Scrambling to his feet he leapt like a deer through the oak vale, disappearing toward Jacob's tent.

Once Joseph was out of sight, Dinah fell to her knees, alone and desolate. Suddenly she knew not who she was. She could not be certain of her role in what had transpired. Was she a victim, or had she invited Shechem's advances?

Impressions and distortions from the interlude tormented her: the fear, the guilt, the pleasure.

And now a searing pain shot up from her groin, and she rocked to and fro, her heart and body in conflict.

She knew not whether to love Shechem or hate him. She knew nothing about life whatsoever.

* * *

Father Jacob sat in the shadow of the oaks outside his tent door. Between the fingers of his right hand he twirled a foxtail reed, twisting it in hypnotic circles as he gazed across the plain of the Hivites.

He had not spoken to anyone all morning. He had not pursued his daily chores, nor even communed with Rachel.

Joseph, who milked one of his mother's cows, observed Jacob from across the common, wondering what ran through his mind.

Ever since he had relayed the news of Dinah's defilement, he had been amazed at Jacob's composure. When he had entered the man's tent before dawn, waking him with the story, the patriarch had only drawn up rigid on his sleeping mat, and after a long moment, had replied, "You have done well, Joseph. Go to bed."

All day the man had sat alone outside his door, obviously deep in thought, watching the plain as though he expected someone. Joseph might have concluded that he awaited the arrival of the ten elder sons, who had been away in the shepherd fields. But the fields they worked

were behind the camp, in the hills, and not down in Shalem Vale, which Jacob faced.

Now and then Joseph noticed a smug look cross Jacob's features. What he could be plotting, or how he could take any pleasure from his daughter's pain, the lad could not imagine.

But mostly the man just sat there, unmoving, silent; his countenance brooding and sullen.

When, upon a rare occasion, his eyes left the plain, they traveled to the great stone altar he had erected upon first arriving here. As though he sought guidance, he would linger over the pedestal, communing with his God.

Joseph rested his head against the cow's warm flank, his heart aching for both Dinah and Jacob. So long had the patriarch held his peace that it came as a great surprise when he suddenly spoke aloud.

"Does she love him?" he asked.

The boy, not certain his father addressed him, rose and wiped his milk-stained hands upon his cloak.

"What, sir?" he said.

"Your sister—does she love this man?"

"How should I know?" Joseph shrugged, tracing his toe through the dirt.

"You should know because she came to you in her hour of need," Jacob reasoned, disliking the lad's insolent tone.

Joseph looked up sheepishly. "I suppose she thinks she loves him," he admitted. "But . . . what can *she* know?"

At this, Jacob rebuked him sharply. "A man of God will respect his ladies!" he commanded. "Do not speak disparagingly of your sister!"

The lad received this like a cold slap. "Yes, sir," he whispered.

Jacob now returned to his silence, twirling the reed around and around. At last he inquired, "Did she say how he treated her? Did he speak his heart to Dinah?"

Joseph, increasingly uneasy with the topic, wished his father would ask these things of the girl, and not of himself. But Dinah had hidden all day in Leah's tent, and Jacob, taking pity, had let her do so.

"She says he spoke tenderly to her—that he was kind—and that he..."

"Yes?" Jacob prodded.

"...that he wishes to marry her."

This last, Joseph hated to acknowledge. As he feared, it seemed to please Jacob.

"I have heard good things of Shechem," the patriarch recalled. "Better things of him than of his father..."

"Papa, you cannot think... But Papa, Shechem defiled my sister!"

Jacob heard this objection, but made no reply. He knew that Joseph saw no redeeming potential in the evil wrought against the girl. But the patriarch would not expound the possibilities just now.

The elder brothers, returning from the fields, could be heard descending the hill behind. Jacob must turn his attention to them and must break the news of their sister's shame.

6

Jacob's elder sons paced the slope before his tent, breathing out vendettas against Shechem and Hamor.

Back and forth they stalked, Simeon raving, Levi pounding his fist against his thigh, Reuben and Judah plotting revenge.

Gad and Asher sat muttering together, while Issachar and Zebulun, Dinah's closest brothers, seethed to avenge the girl's honor.

Over and over Jacob sought to temper their impetuous spirits.

"Consider Dinah's feelings as well as her reputation!" he warned. "Do you know her heart or the heart of this Shechem?"

"We know an evil deed when we hear of one!" Simeon declared. "Surely you do not defend the Canaanite! Such a thing as he has done ought not to be done!"

Jacob shook his head and stood up from his shady seat. "Such a thing is indeed very wrong. But even the worst evils can fall out for good. Hear me, now. If this Shechem wishes to marry your sister—and I understand that *is* his wish—then we will take advantage of that desire!"

Joseph, who sat outside Dinah's tent, could not comprehend his father's view of things.

Caught away in possibilities, Jacob began to expound his vision.

"This will be our bride price," he asserted. "We will exact trade relations with the Hivites whereby our taxes will be lower. We will insist on a surtax on the goods we sell, so that they bring in extra revenue. Since we will be relatives, we will demand an unlimited lease on this property, so that Hamor can never evict us, or raise our rent.

"Furthermore," he enthused, his eyes sparkling, "when Dinah bears Shechem a son, ours will be a royal family, for the lad will be in line for the Hivite throne!"

Joseph was incredulous. So this was the side of his father which had made him notorious, which had exacted Esau's birthright for a bowl of porridge, which had taken the upper hand over Grandfather Laban's flocks by finding a way to make his own sheep and goats proliferate. Yes, this was the Jacob who had even deceived his own father, posing as Esau to win the patriarchal blessing!

To the boy's amazement, Jacob's reasoning appeared to please Reuben and Judah, who listened intently, their expressions eager.

But Joseph could see that Simeon and Levi were dissatisfied. Jacob did not seem concerned when the two of them leaned together, consulting privately. So confident was the patriarch in his own judgment that he assumed all the brothers saw the wisdom of his plan.

There would be no time for discussion, however. Across the Hivite plain, arising from the direction of Shalem, a great host approached. It appeared that every male of the city was in that throng, led by two men on white, prancing horses.

Joseph instantly recognized one as the Hivite prince, and his skin bristled.

Tall, dark, and grand, he rode ahead of the others, his chin held high, as though he had not within the last few hours committed a great crime.

To Jacob's youngest son he was a monster, and the lad clenched his fists. How he wished the elder brothers would take vengeance here and now! He would join them. He would fight beside them like a soldier.

Jacob saw things differently, however. All day long he had awaited this very moment. He had known Hamor and Shechem would not long delay in asking Dinah's hand.

But the clever elder would play his own hand craftily.

At the sound of the horde, the Jacobite tribe gathered on the rise, wondering what transpired. To this point, no one but Dinah, Jacob, and Jacob's sons knew the situation.

Among the uninformed tribespeople, the first thought was that the Hivites were on the attack. But when they saw that their leaders were unarmed, and that the advancing throng carried no weapons, they watched the drama in murmuring fascination.

Determined to appear nonchalant, Jacob returned to his seat and resumed twirling the foxtail reed in his fingers.

He did not see Dinah emerge from her mother's tent, fearful and wondering. But Joseph saw, and he noted the look of conflicted love she gave the dashing Shechem.

As soon as the girl appeared in the tent's distant shadow, Shechem likewise saw her. And the expression on his face could only be called adoration.

Joseph's stomach tensed. Protectiveness, anger, and jealousy struggled within him. But he had no right, being the youngest, to express them.

Hamor, reining his mount a courteous distance from Jacob, stepped down and bowed. Though this was his tenant and not his superior, he had come to ask something of him and must show respect.

The patriarch, knowing he had the upper hand, nodded to him coolly.

"Jacob, called Israel," Hamor began, "my people are neighbors with your people. I come as your friend."

The Hebrew, raising a skeptical eyebrow, made no reply.

Standing up, Hamor surveyed the angry faces of the eleven sons, their tense postures and clenched fists. "I shall not mince words," he said, clearing his throat. "I am sure you know why I have come."

Casting a wary glance at the brothers, he proceeded. "The soul of my son, Shechem, longs for your daughter," he declared, bowing again. "I pray you, give her to him as his wife."

At this, Dinah blushed with joy, her eyes locking on Shechem's with girlish ardor.

But Hamor was not finished. "Furthermore," he suggested, "let us be allies in this wild land. Many are our enemies all about, who desire to take what we have. Let us make marriages among ourselves. Give us your daughters, and take our daughters for your sons.

"You shall dwell equally with us," he went on. "The land shall be yours to live in, conduct business in, and prosper in."

Jacob, stunned, sat white faced before the man. So far beyond his wild scheme was this offer that his incredulous ears tingled.

Judah and Reuben, likewise, scarcely concealed their astonishment. And when Shechem dismounted, falling reverently before the Hebrew, Jacob was mute with shock.

"Let me find grace in your eyes," the prince pleaded. "Whatever you shall ask of me, I shall give."

The young man's apparent sincerity was intensely appealing. Women in the tribe gasped, whispering together. And Dinah's cheeks were moist with tears.

"Ask anything at all, but please," he begged, "give me the maiden as my wife."

Jacob was speechless. At last, leaning down from his seat, he tapped the prostrate fellow on the shoulder and bade him arise.

Tenderly he studied the fervent countenance, and a smile stretched his lips.

But just as he would make reply, Simeon and Levi, who had been privately leaning together, hastened forward.

Crooked grins worked on their faces, and quickly they intercepted the dealings, as though they had the right.

"We cannot do this thing," Levi objected, trying to appear disappointed. "After all, you, being a Canaanite, are...uncircumcised!"

Jacob shot a quizzical glance at the two intruders. But, again, before he could speak, Simeon interrupted.

"Yes, yes. It is against our tradition...a reproach, actually, against our people."

"What?" Jacob tried to intervene. But Simeon talked over his head, and over the murmuring tribe.

"However," he suggested, rubbing his hands together, and playing at condescension, "we will consent if you will all be circumcised, every one of you. Then we will give you our young women, we will take your ladies for ourselves, and we will be your allies."

"Indeed," Levi added, seeing that Jacob stood angrily to his feet, "if you will *not* do this, we will take our sister and be gone!"

The patriarch, confounded, held his peace. He could not imagine why his sons insisted on imposing this bloody ordeal on the Canaanites. There was no regulation such as they described for the marriage of young Hebrew women. Yet to confront Simeon and Levi with their deception could only cast doubt on the integrity of his whole tribe. When Hamor looked at him suspiciously, Jacob only shrugged.

Dubious, the Hivites conferred among themselves. But when Hamor stepped again before Jacob, agreeing to the stipulation, the patriarch could do nothing but accept.

Shakily he called for Dinah.

The girl, seeing no one but her beloved, hastened from her mother's tent. In simple ceremony, Jacob placed her little hand in Shechem's, and the prince, mounting his horse, lifted her up behind him.

Dinah was thereby married, and Joseph watched her ride away, his eyes misting.

7

Three nights later, flames raged through the town of Shalem, leaping tall and orange against the black sky.

Whether it was the ominous glow of the pyre-like city or the frantic cries preceding it that roused Jacob's camp, within moments the entire tribe was alert.

Jacob scrambled out from Rachel's tent, his loincloth still loose upon his body, and Rachel peered out from her bed, grasping her blanket close to her chest.

Joseph, who did not share his mother's tent so often as he had when he was younger, had slept beneath the stars tonight. He, along with the shepherds of the hills, had been the first to hear the cries and see the fiery flashes lick the dark.

Flinging back the flap of his bedsack, he joined his father on the rise. Following close were the others: Reuben, Judah, Gad, Asher, Dan, Naphtali, Issachar, and Zebulun.

But where was Simeon, and where was Levi?

Quickly Jacob assayed the situation, and as the crafty plot of the missing sons dawned upon him, his face was a contortion of rage and shame.

"What have they done!" he cried, throwing his arms wide. Falling to the earth, he scraped up handfuls of dirt and poured them through his hair. "Jehovah!" he wept. "God Almighty, save us! What have they done!"

Reuben and Judah glanced at Joseph, who did not comprehend what evil had been perpetrated upon the Hivites. Drawing near the lad, Reuben bent close and whispered, "Simeon and Levi have dishonored our father. They have fallen on the Shechemites, who trusted us, and have taken them in their weakest hour."

Joseph's face clouded. He knew that "weakest hour" meant the time of debilitation which followed a man's circumcision.

Always the people of his tribe performed the rite when a baby was only eight days old. Something about that timing produced the least pain for the male. This they had learned through generations of experience. But the Shechemites had endured the surgery in the prime of life. The third day after circumcision was always the hardest.

Barely had Reuben spoken when their eyes were drawn to the gate of the city. Two figures emerged on horseback, followed by a contingency of Jacobites, all on foot. The onlookers recognized them instantly as Simeon, Levi, and their personal menservants, nearly fifty in all.

In their hands they brandished bloody swords and dripping scabbards, and upon their faces were gleaming grins. Shouting and laughing, they raced toward camp, Simeon carrying Dinah like a bag of barley, slung across the back of his saddle.

Flailing and kicking, the girl cried out for her beloved—for Shechem, who would never be hers or anyone else's again.

Joseph, too, cried out, matching her pain with his horror.

Racing down the hill, he was suddenly caught by Reuben's outstretched arm.

Frantically he looked into the man's kind face, and burying his head on his broad shoulder, he wept aloud.

"It is all my fault!" Joseph sobbed, imagining the city's helpless men, easy prey for the ruthless hunters and unable to defend their families. "It is my fault!"

"How is that, Little One?" Reuben queried.

"I should not have told Father about Shechem's crime," he replied, his chest heaving. "Dinah begged me not to. No one would have known...no one would have died...."

"Enough," Reuben insisted, holding him close. "You were right to defend your sister's honor."

The lad's thoughts were a blur. As he saw Simeon and Levi draw near with their agonized sister, and as he observed his father, weeping and scraping upon the ground, he suddenly knew hatred as he had never known it.

Always Simeon and Levi had been his tormentors. Always they had been wild men. But never had he hated them.

Until now.

8

The fields of Hamor retreated in the night behind Jacob's fleeing caravan.

Joseph rode in the back of his mother's wagon, watching over the woman whose pale face reflected sadly in the moonlight.

Although the lad looked forward to the formal announcement of Rachel's pregnancy, he did worry over her health. Other women, he had observed, glowed like rubies when they were with child. But Rachel seemed frail, and rather than gaining the fleshly plumpness typical of others, she was thinner than ever.

Jacob was on the run again. For four years he had dwelt peaceably in the Jordan region, his struggle with Esau at an end and his hopes high for the future.

Now, under cover of dark he must once more play the part of the refugee. The Jacobites, or "Israelites" as they were becoming known, would not be welcome in Canaan once the many tribes and cities of the country learned of the havoc wreaked at Shalem.

It was autumn. Fields of charred stubble passed by, and Joseph could smell the ashes of the turned earth where farmers had burned their depleted plots in preparation for next year's crop. As the wheels of Rachel's wagon crunched over the rutted fields, Joseph knew his father avoided the main highway.

The only word Jacob had given his frightened tribe was that the Lord had told him to flee for Bethel, the place of his first encounter with the Almighty years before.

There he had first sought guidance after fleeing Esau's threats. There the angels of the Lord had appeared to him in a dream, coming and going upon a ladder stretched between earth and heaven.

And there, he hoped, his people would find sanctuary.

But more than tribal safety was at risk in this crisis. As Joseph observed his mother's wan countenance—the way her hands folded across her swollen belly, the way her despairing eyes wandered over the moonstruck fields—he wondered if this journey would require too much of her.

He knew that if it did, he would never forgive Simeon and Levi. He would never overlook their selfish need for power, and he would have even more reason to hate them.

INTERLUDE

Joseph lay face down on the ridge of the Bethel-Ephrath mountains. The frigid earth with its unyielding frost was no comfort to the lad whose mother had just died in childbirth.

From somewhere overhead the haunting cry of a nighthawk, shrill and accusing, thrilled through the icy air.

Rachel was dead, and Joseph felt responsible.

Yes, his tormented heart insisted, if he had obeyed Dinah, if he had not betrayed her secret to his father, Simeon and Levi would not have invaded Shalem. The Israelites would still dwell at peace in Shechem Vale, and his mother would never have been forced to endure the harsh escape.

For a long while he lay prostrate, until the guilty thoughts were interrupted. At first he resisted the overriding refrain, the comfort which sprang from beyond himself, reminding him of the Hope of Israel, of the night his father had wrestled with the angel and had come out victor.

Sitting up, he put his hands to his ears as if to block the hope-filled impression.

Joseph had never seen an angel. *Joseph* had not been blessed with visions, as had his father.

And now that he was faced with the gravest loss of his young life, he disbelieved in them utterly.

As he sat fending off the persistent chords of promise, however, another voice invaded his solitude. Jacob had come to find him, putting his own fresh grief aside to quest after his heartbroken son.

Scrambling to his feet, Joseph stood numb and quivering in the blackness.

Surely he would die if his father found him. Surely any human touch would kill him.

Fleeing, he bounded across the ice-locked hills, slipping and sliding until his body lost contact with the earth.

Suddenly, unexplicably, Joseph was at the mouth of a cave. As his head whirled with a sense of the supernatural, he was stunned to see a fire within the rock room, and an ethereal figure silhouetted before it.

"Joseph, son of Jacob, behold," the figure addressed him.

Following the stranger's gesture, which directed him to gaze deep within the cave, Joseph stood up and rubbed his eyes.

Against the back wall, where the shadows and lights of the fire played, he perceived a scene drawn by some invisible finger—drawn for him alone. It seemed he and his brothers were binding sheaves in a field, and Joseph's sheaf, suddenly leaping to life, stood up. The other sheaves likewise arose, and turning to face Joseph's, bowed before it.

The lad, quaking, observed the image fade, and with it the mysterious stranger.

Bracing himself against the opening, he felt his knees buckle.

Whether the fire went out, or he only closed his eyes, Joseph knew not. But darkness, like a dream, caressed him.

* * *

Strong hands lifted Joseph from the sun-streaked earth. Upon his body was the crisp dew of a winter morning, and where he had lain curled up at the cavern door, a thawed patch traced his outline.

Struggling for consciousness, he saw his father's face brooding above him.

As Joseph shook himself alert, he stared into the empty cave at the place where a fire had burned just hours before and a phantom figure had communed with him.

"Father," he stammered, "in there...a man..."

Jacob studied the hollow room, wondering what his son alluded to.

"A fire, Papa!" Joseph explained. "There was a fire in this very place."

But there was nothing in the cave save a few charred remains of some long-deserted camp.

"No one has been here for many years," Jacob insisted.

Suddenly struck by his father's grief-etched countenance, Joseph realized how much the bereft man needed him.

Together the two upheld each other as they ascended the ravine down which Joseph had skidded in the dark.

Only once did the boy look back, marking forever in his memory the place of his own Bethel.

PART II
The Dreamer

9

Jacob would not suffer his wife to be buried in the icy winter mountains. Instead, he led his people down the west side of the hills to the lovely hamlet of Bethlehem, and there he erected the pillar which would forever mark her grave.

Joseph stood, this morning, outside the village walls, watching as Jacob laid stone upon stone until the little monument was chest high.

Bilhah, Rachel's maid, also watched, the wriggling babe whom Rachel had named Ben Oni clutched to her breast. Tears streaked her face, but she was typically quiet, and Joseph wondered how she had felt living in Rachel's shadow.

All the women with whom Jacob was intimate—Leah, Zilpah, and Bilhah—had endured secondary status. Joseph had always taken it for granted that this was as it should be. His fair mother was the natural favorite.

But now, as he observed Bilhah apart from Rachel, it occurred to him that such a situation might not be a happy one for the lesser wives.

For an agonizing moment, his father studied the pillar. Then with a groan of resignation, he lifted the last stone into place.

Joseph saw Bilhah's chest heave, as though she had performed the task, and not her master.

In that instant the baby began to cry, and Jacob turned to the concubine, calling for the child.

Quickly the woman came forward, placing the tiny infant in his father's hands.

Turning his gaze heavenward, Jacob faced the pillar and raised the baby aloft.

"His name shall no more be Ben Oni, 'son of my sorrow,' " the patriarch announced. "Ben Jamin shall his name be, 'son of my right hand.' "

The infant, his feet kicking the sky, received his new calling without a whimper.

Though Benjamin would never know Rachel's touch or the sweet sound of her voice, he seemed content to be Jacob's child.

And though he could not know it now, young Joseph, who watched his christening with quiet pride, would love him as ardently as any mother.

* * *

Joseph's heart was full that evening when he found his father meditating in the shade of a sycamore tree. Many emotions wrestled inside the lad—grief at the loss of his mother, joy at the gift of Benjamin, and wonder at the meaning of the encounter in the cave.

After a long day of setting up camp in Bethlehem's shepherd hills, a sense of urgency drove him to seek out Jacob. He had waited four years to ask about his father's struggle in the Gilead wilderness. He could wait no longer.

The boughs of the sycamore, beneath which Jacob sat, waved toward the fertile valley where Bethlehem nestled clean and white. A gentle breeze moved the branches in beckoning gestures.

Oblivious to Joseph's approach, the patriarch was caught away in private devotion. The lad, drawing near, lingered over the sight of his prayerful father, sure that he could never love Jacob more than he did at this moment.

Despite the trials of his life, Jacob was still a young man. His athletic body was lank and trim. His hair was black as night, and his beard was tinged with the same raging red that predominated in Esau's coloring. But as he sat with his face turned heavenward, afternoon sunlight spilled in patches through the leaves above, and Joseph noted fine streaks of silver at his temples.

Reverently the boy stepped forward, his shadow falling across Jacob's face. The elder jolted from his wistful meditation and smiled.

"Son," he said, "you startled me."

Joseph, fearing himself an intruder, stammered, "If you would rather be alone..."

"No, no," Jacob insisted. "I would have been coming home soon. Sit with me awhile."

The lad could see salty lines of dried tears upon his father's cheeks. He knew Jacob had been mourning Rachel, and the realization brought a tightness to his chest.

Joseph himself would be a long time grieving, although somehow the episode in the cave had helped ease his pain. But how he longed to discuss the mysterious encounter!

Leaning aside, Jacob bade Joseph sit with him, and as he did, the boy saw his father grimace from the pain of his bad hip.

"Papa," Joseph began, taking opportunity from what he observed, "I remember when your leg first began to trouble you."

This was said with much care. Jacob, unprepared for the topic, stared at Joseph in surprise.

"You do?" he marveled. "How is that possible? You were a mere baby!"

"I was six years old!" Joseph objected.

Jacob shook his head, chuckling. "Tell me, then... what do you remember?"

To Joseph the recollection was as clear as though it had happened yesterday, and not four years before.

"I remember that you disappeared into the wilderness on the day before you met Uncle Esau. And I remember that you were limping on that leg when you returned."

Jacob, seeing that his son's memory was correct, listened more seriously.

"I also remember that you took the name 'Israel' from that moment. And I know you fought with something... or someone...very powerful, as your new name implies."

For a long while the patriarch was silent, his thoughts far away.

"Papa, why have you never spoken of that night?" Joseph pressed him.

"Who would have believed me?" the man sighed. "Your mother, dear as she was, was confounded by too much of the supernatural. And your brothers..." Jacob only shrugged.

The first admission was made tenderly. As for the second, Jacob did not need to explain. Joseph knew the elder brothers would have responded with bewilderment, if not outright scoffing.

"It *was* an angel then!" Joseph deduced, his eyes wide at the long-kept secret.

"It was," Jacob replied.

The patriarch's gaze traced the treetops as he relived the distant evening.

"I had been running from the Lord a very long time," he recounted. "My brother desired to kill me. But it was not Esau alone who pursued me. It was God Almighty."

His voice dropped as he confessed, "I did evil to Esau, and he had a right to avenge himself. The Lord was not pleased with me."

Gaining courage from the admission, the elder lifted his chin and carefully recounted the tale of how he had usurped Esau's birthright—how he had taken advantage of the man's ravenous hunger upon his return from an unsuccessful hunting expedition and had traded him a bowl of stew for his inheritance.

As he spoke, his eyes misted. Yet he told all: how he and his own mother, Rebekah, had plotted the deception of Father Isaac; how he had posed as Esau before the blind elder; and how he had fraudulently secured the patriarchal blessing—a blessing that could not be revoked.

"What I did was unpardonable," Jacob concluded, "but Esau has forgiven me."

Joseph, who had heard these talks from others, barely breathed. "But, Father, you wrestled with an angel!" he whispered.

Jacob knew the notion was intriguing. He knew his son must have exercised great self-restraint, keeping his curiosity in check all these years.

"I had lived so long with fear," Jacob softly explained, "that when the Lord appeared unto me, I could not let him...I *would* not let him go until he blessed me!"

"Yes?" Joseph marveled, urging his father on.

Jacob placed a hand on the lad's knee.

"You wish to know more," he surmised, a twinkle in his eye. "You want to know what he looked like, how strong he was, and how tall. You want to understand how a mortal man could fight with an angel of the Lord."

Joseph did not deny this, eagerly nodding his head.

Leaning back, the elder pulled his knees to his chest and thought such a great while that Joseph grew uneasy.

"How does one describe light brighter than light?" he began. "He came upon me like the wind, and he encompassed me on every side. He was a man, yet not a man. When he laid hands on me, and I on him, it was as though the universe spun about my head!"

Joseph thrilled to the conviction in his father's voice. "Did you struggle with him a long time?" he asked.

"All night, until dawn broke in the east," Jacob recalled.

"But surely..."

"I know what you are thinking," Jacob mused, patting him on the shoulder. "You consider that any angel of the Lord Almighty should have easily prevailed against me."

"Why ... yes, sir," Joseph admitted, hoping he did not offend.

"Well," Jacob laughed, "that certainly occurred to me that night—and many times since. All I can conclude is that the Lord restricts himself from time to time, that he might reach into our lives."

"And he did that, Father!" Joseph enthused. "He gave you your blessing!"

Jacob clapped him on the back. "You are an able student, my child! You have a heart for things divine, and so you shall prosper."

Suddenly, with this encouragement, Joseph felt free to speak of the cave. He was about to declare the vision he had received, to revel openly in the notion that one day he would be blessed, that one day he would prevail over his brothers. But Jacob was not finished. As he gave his conclusion, Joseph was chagrined.

"Truly," he said, "the Lord did bless me. The memory alone of that encounter is precious, but the outcome more valuable than gold. He gave me a new name and a second chance," he testified. "But most precious of all, he restored love between me and my brother."

The patriarch paused, his throat tight with feeling. And Joseph listened, red faced.

"If you learn nothing else in this life," Jacob asserted, "learn this: brotherhood is a gift of God, and loss of goodwill between friends is a dagger to the soul. But God is a friend who sticks closer than a brother."

"Brotherhood..." Joseph recoiled at the term. Images of Simeon and Levi returning from the destruction of Shalem burned within him. He would far rather they bowed before him, like the sheaves on the cave wall, than that they be his friends. He would far rather that Gad and Asher and all the others groveled at his feet.

As his father continued to expound his philosophy, Joseph had leaden ears.

"The reward did not come easily," Jacob asserted. "The angel of God did not restore my brother to me without exacting a price. Every time I limp upon my sorry leg, I am reminded of my dependence on the Lord."

The son was silent, wishing now that he had not pursued this discussion.

Jacob, seeing his downcast expression, sensed the contents of his heart, the lifetime of hurt which had shriveled his soul. Drawing the lad to his bosom, he went on, "I asked the angel his name that night. He refused to tell me. But I myself gave a name to the place of my struggle."

Joseph avoided his father's somber gaze.

" 'Peniel,' I called it," Jacob said, " 'the face of God.' For I had seen the Lord face to face, and my life was preserved."

Sunset was coming upon them, and a cool breeze filled the mountainside with the smell of early spring. Joseph, resisting his father's embrace, leaned rigidly against him, listening to the rhythm of his heart.

"If you seek God's face," the elder exhorted, "he is able to make all men to be at peace with you. Remember this, my son, and you will do well."

10

The Oaks of Mamre! Joseph had heard of them all his life. Today, the last day of his twelfth year, he was privileged to see them.

From high atop his father's finest camel, he spied their lush greenery miles before the caravan reached the destination. Billowy, almost black against Canaan's yellow grass and rolling hills, they rose. He thrilled to the sight.

For it was here that Grandfather Abraham had settled, nearly two centuries ago, after entering this land.

Tomorrow would be Joseph's thirteenth birthday, the day of his initiation into Hebrew manhood. A full week ago, Jacob had announced that his tribe must move south, for he would have Rachel's firstborn meet Grandfather Isaac on the day he became a man.

Little Benjamin, who was nearly three years old, rode with Joseph, propped between his legs on the camel's swaying saddle.

"See there!" Joseph directed, pointing to the forested hills. "That is where our Grandpa lives. He is a very old man, and very wise."

Benjamin, whose luminous lavender eyes followed Joseph's finger, sat up straight. "Will he know me?" he asked.

"Papa has told him about you," Joseph replied. "Papa's messengers are always carrying word of Benjamin."

Pleased with that answer, the little boy settled back against Joseph's chest, and the older brother studied his raven curls, so like Rachel's.

As the caravan wound down the fertile slopes toward Mamre, a shout of greeting met them from across the valley. To everyone's amazement, another train could be seen approaching the Oaks from the east, and no one could have mistaken the leader of the vast host.

It was Esau who cried the greeting—Esau upon his black mount—Esau with his crimson beard.

Jacob, who walked alongside Leah's wagon, took off at a full run. Leaping across gullies and hills he tore jubilantly toward his elder brother.

Esau likewise jumped to the ground and ran to join him.

Racing across the valley, they met before Isaac's tent.

There would surely be a party in Mamre tonight!

* * *

Grandfather Isaac had dwelt so long at Mamre, that he was no longer a nomad. In fact, he had some years ago built a riverstone meetinghouse on the property where his great tribe held councils and worshiped Jehovah.

When Joseph first laid eyes on him, it was in that meetinghouse.

All evening the three tribes—Jacob's, Esau's and Isaac's—partied outside together, hundreds of merrymakers celebrating the family reunion and anticipating Joseph's bar mitzvah. Music and wine flowed freely, girls danced and men sang, until the forest's living rafters trembled.

And all evening, Joseph shot glances toward the council hall, wondering when he would see his grandfather, the elder, who had not emerged.

Isaac was seated at the council fire when Joseph, Jacob and Esau at last entered the building. It was midnight, and breaking into the first day of Joseph's thirteenth year. The lad's eleven brothers and Esau's sons joined them, waiting along the back wall as Joseph was ushered forth for formal introduction to the patriarch.

Through the dim and smoky interior he was led, past rows of smiling faces. Men all about reached out to greet his father and uncle, men who had known Jacob and Esau from birth and who now waited to receive Joseph into their fraternity.

Enthusiastically they hailed the youngster. At first he could hardly conceive that these people honored him. But ahead sat his grandfather, and when he saw him, the warmth of acceptance flooded over him.

In the orange fireglow, the old man was beautiful, his noble face translucent but smooth as a youth's. His patriarchal beard reached nearly to his lap, shining with silver and with the sheen of affectionate grooming. Though his filmy eyes were nearly sightless, he could make out his two sons and the beloved boy in the firelight, and his expression seemed to say he had awaited this moment for a lifetime.

To Rachel's firstborn, the firstborn of Jacob's heart, this was a hallowed hour. As long as he could remember, he had dreamed of meeting Isaac. He trembled as he came before him, as though he entered the sanctuary of God Almighty.

Indeed, Isaac was a living chronicle, the closest man to Abraham, Shem, Noah, or Adam, who walked the earth.

As Jacob and Esau reached down to embrace their father, the old man quaked terribly. The last time he had seen either son, the two had been at war. Jacob had stolen Esau's birthright, had deceived his father, and had fled. Esau, bent on killing him, had pursued him nearly to Padan-Aram.

Now the entire nation was reunited, the feud no longer separating tribe from tribe.

As Jacob and Esau sat down on either side of the patriarch, Isaac reached out his arms to receive Joseph. Falling into his grandfather's embrace, the lad felt the old man's tears upon his neck.

"Bone of my bone, flesh of my flesh!" Isaac cried. "How my soul has yearned for you!"

Releasing him, he held him at arm's length.

"My eyesight is very dim," he admitted, "but my hands see for me."

With this, he traced Joseph's youthful face with his fingertips, reading it like a scroll.

"Your features are beautiful, as Rachel's must have been. And your shoulders," he exclaimed, grasping him firmly, "they are broad as Jacob's!" Then leaning back, he proclaimed, "So they should be! For today you are a man!"

As if on cue, a small group of musicians, seated in a corner, began to play—timbrels thumping, lutes strumming, and pipes whistling.

Isaac clapped his hands, and as he did so, the crowd began to sing:

"O Lord, our Lord, how excellent is your name in all the earth! You have set your glory above the heavens. Out of the mouths of young ones you have ordained strength."

Emerging from other smoky corners, young girls came forth, strewing garlands up the aisle, dancing and twirling about Joseph.

As the music at last subsided, Isaac called for a cup of wine.

"This is the hour of your manhood," he announced. Joseph humbly took the cup and drank it.

Again, as soon as he was done, music began and the scene was repeated.

This time, as Joseph was traded from hand to hand among the dancing maidens, he was a little lightheaded. But now his father stood, and the crowd grew quiet once more.

"A man should look the part of a man!" Jacob cried, commanding everyone's attention. "A prince should look the part of a prince! Therefore," he said, reaching into a fold of his long cloak, "I present you with your royal coat!"

Suddenly unfurled before the audience was a magnificent garment—a long, striped tunic of many colors.

Joseph, dazzled, stepped forward and caressed the fabric. He recognized it immediately as his mother's handiwork, a project she must have spent years secretly pursuing.

Between each stripe, separately woven, was intricate stitchery of gold and silver. And upon each stripe, broad as a man's hand, were emblems of the nomad life: tiny sheep and goats, camels and tents and shepherd staffs.

Never had there been such a coat—a bar mitzvah coat befitting a tribal prince!

"Turn around," Jacob said proudly.

Before the onlookers, the father draped the tunic over Joseph's back. And the crowd applauded.

Little Benjamin, who had been watching from the rear of the room, from the height of Reuben's shoulders, squirmed to join his brother. Lowered to the floor, he ran forward, leaping proudly into Joseph's arms.

But the ceremony was not complete.

Isaac had yet to give the patriarchal blessing. Silence filled the long chamber as Isaac lifted his arms.

"Son of Jacob, son of Israel," he began, "the least shall become greatest, the last shall be first!" His words ringing with prophetic conviction, he declared: "Joseph, you shall be a savior to your people, the rescuer of your brothers and their strong deliverer. Have faith in God. You shall rise above all your enemies, and having the power of life and death, shall turn to save them."

An awesome hush thrilled through the congregation, and Jacob's ten elder sons stared mutely at their younger brother.

Was Joseph not merely the son of a second wife? Was he not inferior to the sons of Leah, and younger than the sons of Bilhah and Zilpah?

Levi and Simeon cast sideways smirks at each other, while Reuben and Judah murmured uneasily.

But now the musicians played again, indicating it was time to exit the council chamber.

Joseph, heady with the prophecy, the night, and the wine, carried his chin high, and Benjamin, riding in his arms, nestled proudly against him.

The honored Bar Mitzvah, Son of Israel, passed by his elder brothers in his princely robe, heedless of their anger.

He knew they resented him. But then, they always had.

11

Stars, like fiery prisms, studded the black sky. Joseph lay upon his back, his arms folded under his head as he studied the depths of the ebony night.

His priceless tunic was his pillow, carefully rolled and held beneath his neck as though he would defend it with his life.

Over and over he relived the evening. Isaac's ageless face dominated his reverie, and his amazing words resounded through Joseph's mind.

"You shall be a savior to your people...a savior...a savior..."

Contemplating possible interpretations, Joseph was filled with wonder. Just how could the tribe of Israel ever be so needy? And how could he alone save them?

He was too young and too unwise to be humbled by the prophecy. Throughout his entire life he had bowed to the shadows of his ten elder brothers. Isaac's words filled him with more eager pride than was becoming.

He sensed that the prediction paralleled his experience in the cave. Closing his eyes, he reconstructed the scene on the cave wall: the sheaves of his brothers bowing to his sheaf.

Of course they would bow! he reasoned. If he were to someday be their savior, they would surely make obeisance!

Opening his eyes again, he was captivated by an eerie movement in the summer sky. Whereas before, the stars, the moon, and the planets were in their natural positions, they were now strangely altered. Several stars, eleven to be exact, had formed a row in front of a twelfth, which seemed much brighter than they.

The moon also joined the lesser stars, and as Joseph watched, the sky was filled with light like the light of day. For the sun appeared as well, standing beside the moon.

Joseph blinked and shielded his eyes from the glare.

Despite the fact that the sun had appeared, the stars were still clearly visible. And to his amazement, the twelfth star shone as brightly as ever.

As the celestial bodies held these new positions, Joseph sensed that the eleven lesser stars, the sun, and the moon were honoring the twelfth and solitary star.

His skin was gooseflesh. Shaking himself, he sat up, trying to clear his head. But the peculiar phenomenon— the night turned to day, the day within the dark—did not depart.

It was not until Joseph was distracted from the amazing witness by a disturbance in camp that the sky returned to normal.

A sound of weeping and mourning had arisen from the vicinity of Isaac's tent.

Joining the other people who emerged from their shelters and their beds to investigate the matter, Joseph went hastily to the common.

In the still of the night, Isaac had passed away. The venerable elder, the one who had known Abraham, had been gathered to his fathers, 180 years old and full of joy at the reunion of his children.

As Joseph heard this, he suddenly cared little for the stars. He would have preferred more time in Isaac's presence to a thousand inscrutable visions.

12

The autumn fields beyond the Oaks of Mamre were wet with dew. Pink sunlight traced a halo across the valley, just breaking through the clinging mist that cloaked the verdant earth.

Seventeen-year-old Joseph hoisted his knapsack higher on his back and breathed deeply of the moist air. So fine a morning he had not seen in a long time.

The dew quickly seeped through his sandals and absorbed into the thick stockings that bound his feet. But he did not mind. He was off to find Dan and Naphtali, Gad and Asher, the sons of his father's concubines.

All summer he had served as a groom in the tribal corral, caring for the white and speckled horses which were Jacob's special pride. Shepherding suited him much better. To be out in the fields, beneath the stars, was to Joseph the closest thing to heaven. And to share in his brothers' manly conversation, the closest thing to complete fulfillment he had ever known.

Of all his brothers, he was most comfortable with the sons of Bilhah and Zilpah. True, there were times of tension between them. He noted this especially when he wore the parti-colored cloak that Jacob had presented at his bar mitzvah.

He would be sure to take it off and conceal it in his pack before he reached the shepherd camp. But for now, as he passed along the stream that watered the Oaks, he wore the garment proudly.

Perhaps it was inexperience, perhaps it was his pre-occupation with the glorious morning, but Joseph was oblivious to the admiring whispers of the maidens who knelt beside the stream doing the day's laundry. He was no longer the slight boy who had entered manhood in Isaac's council hall. He was no longer the awkward youngster who had danced with the girls the night of his bar mitzvah. But neither was he very moved by the beguiling glances that followed him when he walked through camp.

Taking after Great-grandfather Abraham, Grandfather Isaac and Father Jacob, the lad was striking in appearance. Tall as a young poplar, he stood out easily in a crowd, and he hoped that someday he might match Reuben for stature or Simeon for strength.

But most of all, he cradled in his satchel of dreams the mystery of the visions he had seen. And he wondered how they would be fulfilled.

Running his hand down the front of his princely coat, he smiled to himself as he reached the borders of Mamre, and trekked toward the pastures of fellowship. Passing coolly beyond the gazes of the maidens, he went in quest of the shepherds.

It was a fine thing to be a man, life stretching before him as fertile as the Hebron Valley.

* * *

The high shepherd fields where Joseph's brothers would be found were a half-day's journey from Mamre. It was nearly sunset when he located the glowing campfire marking their site.

Though a nippy fall wind spilled over the hills, he removed his striped tunic and donned a simpler one, rolling his fine garment into a ball and concealing it in his knapsack.

As he came upon the four brothers and their servants, gathered for the evening about a simmering stewpot, the sound of lively music warmed him. Someone played a small harp and someone else accompanied him on a flute.

"Joseph!" Asher cried, slurring the word over his wine-soaked tongue. "Join us! Join us! What brings you here?"

The youngster entered the circle of flickering light, and Gad, slapping him on the back and giving a besotted smile, made room for him upon the felled log that served as a seat.

"Father sent me," Joseph replied. Merrily he took the crescent-shaped wineskin that was thrust into his hands.

"Father... good old Father!" Naphtali laughed, hoisting another skin and declaring a toast. "To Father!"

A round of inarticulate cheers followed this, and fellows all about the circle directed the spouts of their bottles toward their open mouths, catching the maroon liquid on their tongues.

"To Father, and to Great-grandfather Abraham!" Dan added.

Again the skins were turned bottoms up, and the gang laughingly imbibed.

"To Father, and to Great-grandfather Abraham, and don't forget Grandfather Isaac!" Asher bellowed.

Hilarity ensued, and Joseph found himself swept up in the mood.

This was what he had come out for—not for the shepherding alone, but for the companionship.

Gad, who seemed most affected by the evening's frivolity, sat uncomfortably close to Joseph. His vinegar breath was hot against the youngster's neck, and he seemed to study him too closely with his bloodshot eyes.

Joseph pulled away and focused on the others, until Gad's merry spirit turned sullen.

"Yes," Gad slobbered, "dear old Isaac. Of course, he never welcomed the rest of us into his fraternity as he welcomed you, Joseph. But he was a good man. He never gave us a bar mitzvah like the one he gave you. But he was a good man."

Joseph cringed as Gad leered in his face. He did not like the man's tone. All too quickly the boundary had been crossed between wine-warmed fondness and surly belligerence.

As others about the fire began to pick up on Gad's resentment, Joseph grew even more uneasy.

"Of course," Asher joined in, "Father Jacob never gave any of us a royal coat like the coat he gave our little brother. But he's a good man, too."

"Yes, yes," shouted Dan and Naphtali, and the servants howled with them.

"But, Little One is not wearing his coat tonight!" Dan noted. "Maybe it's not good enough for him any longer."

Suddenly, Naphtali leaned forward, snatching Joseph's satchel and rummaging through it.

"Aha!" he cried, pulling out the striped coat and waving it in the air. "I knew he wouldn't go anywhere without this!"

Instantly, the rowdy group turned on the youngster, slinging irrational accusations.

"So, we weren't fit company for your royal robe!" Asher spat. "You'd wear it for the sheep, but not for us!"

"No, you don't understand ..." Joseph tried to defend himself.

But his brothers' hostility only escalated.

He would never be able to recount the next few moments. In a blur of movement and thrashing, he was tackled from the log and thrown to the ground. All about him were scuffling feet and pounding fists.

Somehow he managed to regain himself, and stood shaking in their midst as they gritted their teeth and hurled epithets at him.

Fists clenched, he rallied and began flailing, revealing to his brothers the prophecies which he had so long harbored.

"You will all be sorry!" he shouted, his feet kicking and his fists flying. "Someday all of you will cry out to me for mercy! Then see how I shall avenge myself!"

Asher was on top of Joseph, his meaty hand forcing Joseph's head against the earth. "What's that, Little One?" he laughed. "Have you been dreaming?"

Gad, whose besotted brain managed amazed curiosity, tried to intervene.

"Come, Asher! Off of him! Let us hear what this dreamer has to say!"

With that, Asher drew back, but still sat on top of Joseph and would not let him go.

"So, we shall beg for mercy?" he scowled. "You, young mongrel, son of a second wife, should be pleading right now for your life!"

Again, Gad tugged on Asher, and the other two brothers assisted him.

"Let him speak!" they implored. "This should be good for a laugh."

At last, Asher stood up, glaring down on the lad who lay sprawled in the dust. Joseph, climbing out from between Asher's legs, brazenly pointed a finger in his face.

"Indeed, I have dreams. The same dreams that Isaac must have had when he foretold that I would one day have the power of life and death over you!"

Murmuring together, the crowd was pricked by the memory. Still enraged, they snarled at him to expound his point.

"Twice have I seen visions!" Joseph declared. "Twice has Jehovah shown me that you will one day bow to me!"

As they glared hatefully at him, he related the dreams of the sheaves and the stars. And the men, despising him as never before, kept their distance, silent as stilled lions.

A breeze off Hebron rose over the hill, cold and frightening. The flames of the dying fire jerked like spasmodic fingers.

It was Asher who broke the ominous pall, his voice as low as a stalking bear's.

"Will you indeed reign over us! Will you indeed have dominion over us!" With this, he threw a piercing kick to Joseph's side.

Naphtali, more troubled by the prophecy than he cared to admit, grasped Asher about the waist and held him tight.

Joseph, scrambling to his feet, scurried toward his satchel, stuffed his offcast coat into the bag and headed for the dark whence he had come.

"I shall tell Father how you have treated me!" he warned, disappearing into the night.

The brothers, nervously eyeing one another, began to laugh again and swagger about the fire, pretending masculine indifference. But their careless mood would not be easily recaptured.

13

Dinah knelt before Joseph, washing and dressing the scrapes upon his shins and arms in the low light of Jacob's tent. Fussing over him like a mother, the girl who had never married again after losing Prince Shechem was in her element.

"How could you let them do this to you?" she complained. "You know better than to make your elder brothers angry."

Joseph, who had tolerated her fretful nursing, pulled away. "You speak to me as though I were a child!" he growled.

"And so perhaps you are," Jacob countered, pacing the tent floor in frustration. "Can't I send you out to the fields without worrying for your safety?"

Young Benjamin, who sat in a corner holding Joseph's striped coat upon his lap, observed the interchange in tense silence. He knew what it was to be one of the lesser brothers, what it was to be rejected by the elder ten. And he understood how easily Joseph must have fallen prey to their vindictiveness.

But he said nothing, sensing that Father Jacob was in no mood for explanations.

"They were drunk," Joseph protested. "They were spoiling for a fight!"

"You needn't have given them one," Jacob argued. "What did you do to inflame them, anyway?"

At this, Joseph looked away, wishing to avoid the issue. But his father grew more persistent.

"They made fun of my coat and scorned the blessing Isaac bestowed on me," Joseph revealed.

Jacob stopped his pacing and placed a hand on Joseph's knee. His eyes evinced sympathy, and he would have let the matter go, had Leah not appeared in the doorway.

Entering her husband's tent with an armload of clean laundry, she deposited it on Jacob's bed. When she saw that Joseph had returned, she scrutinized his sorry condition in the lamplight.

"What happened to you?" she snapped, her hands on her hips.

With Rachel's death, Leah had attained full matriarchal position in the tribe. By the law of the nomad, she had always been the "first wife," but so long as her sister had lived, that status had been a legal one only. Though Jacob would never love her as he had loved Rachel, she now had no competitor, and wielded her rights like a sword.

"It is nothing, Mother," Jacob intervened, calling her by the term that made Joseph's skin bristle. "The boy ran into some trouble in the hills. He will be fine."

Of course, he avoided reference to the elder brothers. Though they were the sons of his concubines, he knew Leah would eagerly take their side against Joseph.

Leah hastily surveyed the youngster's scrapes and bruises, and shrugged indifferently.

"Best keep him at home," she said. "He is apparently not ready for men's work."

Joseph looked at the floor, and Benjamin started angrily, but the elder brother silenced him with a glance.

When the woman had left the tent, Jacob wiped his hands nervously on his cloak. "Dinah, Benjamin, leave us now," he commanded. "I would be alone with your brother."

Hesitant, the girl rose, taking her bowl of water and the rag with which she had cleansed Joseph's wounds. Benjamin, tenderly placing the royal coat about Joseph's shoulders, followed his sister into the yard, and Jacob pulled the tent flap closed behind them.

Carefully studying his son again, he knelt before him, gazing into his pensive face.

"We cannot have dissension in our tribe," the father said.

"I know," Joseph agreed, feeling quite hopeless.

"Have you told me everything?" Jacob probed. "I must know everything that happened."

Taking a deep breath, Joseph braced himself. "There is more," he confessed. "But...they pushed me to it!"

When Jacob only eyed him insistently, he shook his head in dejection.

"I told them a prophecy, Father. Something I had never told a soul...not even you."

"A prophecy?" Jacob marveled.

"Do you remember how you found me in the hills after Rachel's death? How you found me at the mouth of a cave, and how I told you I had seen a man inside that cave?"

"I do," Jacob recalled. "You had been dreaming."

"Perhaps," Joseph said. "But what is a dream? I have had other impressions since, whether awake or asleep. And I never told a soul until I told my brothers."

With this he unveiled the secrets of his heart, the visions so long withheld from his father.

As he described the images on the cave wall, the sheaves that obviously represented his brethren, and their act of obeisance, Jacob listened patiently.

When he related the vision of the eleven stars, however, the man grew tense.

"The sun and the moon, as well, bowed down before me," Joseph concluded, barely speaking above a whisper.

At this, Jacob lurched away, standing to his feet and pounding his fists into his thighs.

"So this is what you told them! What sort of dream is

this? Will I and your mother and your brothers indeed bow ourselves to the ground before you?"

Angrily the patriarch resumed his pacing, a scowl of wounded pride etched deep into his face.

Joseph had hesitated to mention the sun and the moon. The fact that Jacob interpreted them to represent Leah and himself came as no surprise.

The youngster had no idea how to assuage the hurt this inflicted. And as Jacob castigated him, tears flowed down Joseph's cheeks.

"You are lucky they did not kill you!" the elder cried. "Wars have been sparked by less than this."

Indeed, in their culture dreams and prophecies were not taken lightly. Whether or not folks agreed with the dreamer was of little consequence. Dreams exposed the heart, and the products of Joseph's heart bespoke a haughty spirit.

"Father...I..." he stammered.

People were gathering outside Jacob's tent, guessing at the reason for the shouting. And Jacob hushed his son.

"I cannot help what I dream," the lad objected, his voice low and cautious. "What would you have me do? Cut off my head?"

Anxious, he twisted the edge of his coat in his sweaty hands. "You have never told anyone but me about your fight with the angel," he asserted. "You knew you could trust me to honor you. Why, don't you honor *my* visions, *my* struggle?"

Jacob stared in amazement at his daring son. For a long while he said nothing, but when he did at last open his mouth, it was in command.

"You were to serve in the fields," he declared. "I shall not let you shirk your duty. Gad, Asher, Dan, and Naphtali were due to leave for Shechem today, where your other brothers are pasturing their flocks. If you had not stirred up this trouble, you would have been on your way with them. Come," he ordered. "I will send you to them."

"Yes, sir," Joseph obeyed, following Jacob into the yard.

Shame filled the lad. Never had he questioned his father. If Jacob said he was to blame, perhaps he was.

The people outside the tent moved out of the way and the elder called for a satchel of fresh food and a skin of wine. Placing the satchel on Joseph's back, he tightened the straps and then slapped the boy on the shoulder.

"Go now," he insisted, his voice cracking. "See if it is well with your brothers and with the flock, and bring me word again."

Sunset was settling over the camp. Joseph must find his way through the wilderness in the dark. And he must not look back.

As Jacob watched him depart, a chill passed through the patriarch. Remembering Isaac's words, that one day Joseph would save them all, that one day they would prostrate themselves before the lad, the elder trembled.

His stomach tight as a knot, Jacob passed back through the bewildered crowd and sought the sanctuary of his tent.

But he would not shake the message of Joseph's dreams any more easily than he had shaken the angel's grip upon his thigh.

14

Cold sunlight, traveling with the wind down the slopes of Shechem and warning of winter, smarted Joseph's eyes.

Five days ago he had left Mamre, his limbs still stinging from his fight in the Hebron hills. The past two days he had wandered through the high fields to which Jacob had commissioned him, seeking his brothers, intruding upon the camps of strangers, and inquiring vainly after the sons of Jacob.

As always, the hills of Shechem were choice grazing ground, better than any Jacob had found since he and his tribe had dwelt here.

Seven years had passed since Simeon and Levi had devastated the city of Shalem, surely long enough for the memory to fade and for Israelites to traffic safely among the itinerants of the region. Among the dozens of tribes who wandered annually through the area, the men of Mamre should not draw special censure.

Still, no one seemed to have seen them or heard of their whereabouts among the many shepherd camps where Joseph inquired.

On this, his fifth day of travel, Joseph numbly woke to daylight's call and drew his cloak tight. Beneath the heavy outer garment was his striped coat. He was determined to wear it this time. He would bear the mark of his calling when he came upon his kin. And he would be as warm as possible in the meanwhile.

As of last night, when chilling dark had descended, he still had not despaired of finding the elder ten. But the hope that should have been nurtured by the wakening day was shriveling.

His stiff joints resisted the sun's freezing fingers. Another hour of bleak questing would surely defeat him.

Painfully he rose to his knees, rolling his bed into a ball and stuffing it into his bag.

Scraping crystallized dew from bent fronds of field grass, Joseph let it melt in his hand and swiped it across his face. He did not know which way to go. He had searched all of the common sanctuaries of the shepherds. He wondered, now, if his brothers had ever been here.

Trying to feel determined, he struck out once again across the fields until he came to a westward swale. Down to the left lay the Vale of Shalem. Black ruins still marked the site where Prince Shechem's lovely city once stood.

Viewing the evidence of his brothers' wickedness, his imagination suddenly ran wild.

Suppose, he thought, suppose someone, coming on his brothers' camp, had recognized them. Suppose their dress or their speech had betrayed them as Israelites to one who was an enemy.

Joseph's preoccupation with his own troubles was pushed aside as thoughts of his brothers' welfare consumed him. Running through the fields, heart drumming, he cried out, "Reuben! Judah! Simeon!"

Anxiously he scanned the hills, fearing that any moment he would lay eyes on a bloodsoaked field, fearing he would find torn bodies and ransacked tents.

At night it had been easy to mark the sites of the various shepherd camps, for each had its own campfire showing its position in the hills. But during the day, when the shepherds followed their flocks, there was no telling where they might be found, no telling which bend in the path might bring Joseph upon an enemy's fold.

As he rounded a low bluff, against which puffs of dark heather were pressed by the wind, he was greeted by the aroma of roasting meat.

Assuming that he was approaching another group of strangers, and that they would not welcome his intrusion at breakfast time, he climbed the bluff, and lying on his stomach, tentatively peered over the edge.

Indeed he had come upon a camp. But it was a very small one, occupied by only one man.

Sitting beside his little fire, the shepherd huddled beneath a hooded cloak and held a long stick over the flames, upon which was skewered a succulent piece of partridge.

Joseph's mouth watered as he watched the morsel sizzle above the fire.

Though the shepherd's face was concealed by his hood, a whispy white beard, reaching nearly to his lap, showed that he was an elderly fellow. His hand, also, turning the stick, was veined and wizened, and Joseph wondered what he was doing all alone in this wild country.

Mostly, however, Joseph contemplated the food, knowing for the first time how Esau must have felt when he came upon Jacob and his fragrant stew after days without a decent meal. "Almost would *I* sell *my* birthright for a taste of that partridge!" he thought, recalling Esau's foolish bargain.

Lying close to the earth, the young man gazed longingly upon the browning meat.

"Why don't you join me?" the old man called.

Joseph's heart leaped. He had made no sound, having learned at an early age how to be quiet in the hills. Nor had the old fellow so much as lifted his eyes to the bluff. How he had discerned Joseph's presence, the young spy could not imagine.

Still, the shepherd seemed friendly enough. Scrambling down from the hiding place, Joseph accepted his offer and within seconds was rubbing his cold hands over the welcoming fire.

Ravenous, he devoured the roasted partridge which was generously portioned out to him, and it was not until he was satisfied that he took a keener interest in his host.

When he did, it was with some uneasiness for the old man studied him with a penetrating gaze.

"What are you looking for out in these hills?" the fellow asked.

It was a reasonable question, but something in the way it was put implied the stranger already knew the answer.

Joseph could not tell by the man's accent what tribe or what country he was of. Nor did his woolen mantle bear any distinctive design or emblem. In fact, if anything distinguished the man, it was the directness of his manner and the stark simplicity of his garb.

"I . . . I seek my brothers," Joseph answered. "Can you tell me where they are grazing their flocks?"

Somehow he sensed this was all he need reply. Somehow he felt the elder needed no further detail.

"They have moved on from here," the man replied. "I heard them say, 'Let's go to Dothan.'"

The fact that the shepherd seemed to know exactly who Joseph's brothers were, and where they were headed, did not strike the youngster as strange. Perhaps later it would seem peculiar, but for now, as he sat in his presence, warm and secure, it was perfectly plausible.

"Dothan?" Joseph marveled. "They told no one they were heading further north. They must have been afraid to stay in Shechem."

Joseph spoke to himself, but he felt that the old man knew exactly what he meant.

"I must find them," he insisted, standing up from the fire.

Bowing low, he thanked the man for his kindness and picked up his knapsack to be going.

Something in the old fellow's expression, however, gave him pause. Sadness, longing... feelings which mystified the youngster.

"I will be all right," Joseph heard himself saying.

The shepherd nodded, a knowing gleam in his eye. "Jehovah is with you," he said.

With this, Joseph smiled and turned to go. As he walked into the morning wilderness, he glanced back once to wave goodbye.

But the old man was gone, and the place where the fire had burned was merely a cold circle, charred upon the winter ground.

15

Reuben sat upon the edge of a great cistern, a heavy saddle slung across his lap. His hands, slathered with mutton grease, hastily worked the surface of the saddle, forcing the tallow into the leather.

But his mind was not on his work.

Nervously he watched the highway which passed nearby. He and his brothers had come upon the oasis early in the day. If no one challenged their right to the site by nightfall, they would be able to camp here and pasture their flocks in the choice fields that ran along the road for a month or even more.

Such a location was enviable. Because caravans traveling from Syria to Egypt made this their regular route, shepherds fortunate enough to dwell here could live comfortably for extended periods of time, buying their needed food and supplies from the merchants who passed by.

To be in such a situation in the wintertime was highly desirable. Abiding in the hills at this time of year was especially dangerous, with prowling beasts finding prey hard to come by. Not only were shepherds' flocks in greater peril, but all too often had men themselves lost their lives to ice-bound wolves and lions.

Of course, part of what had convinced the brothers to move north from Shechem was fear of the local tribes. They had encountered no trouble during their brief stay near Shalem Vale, but Dothan was a safer place.

Beside the cistern where Reuben sat was another well of the same size, its steep sides sloping a full ten feet toward a dry bottom. In the spring, torrents of rain and groundwater would nearly fill the little reservoirs, making this oasis a stopping place for every caravan going by. For now, however, it would be possible for a family such as Reuben's to abide here unhindered.

Still, until night fell, by the law of the nomad, the Jacobites' right to stay here could be challenged. If the challenger had a larger flock and more men in company, he would win the site.

The likelihood of such a thing happening was remote. The ten brothers and all their helpers were a formidable group. But Reuben would not rest until the sun fell toward the great sea hidden in the west.

Beyond the cisterns, his brothers were already setting up the huge camp that would serve them for several weeks. Reuben's horse, tethered to the well, nudged him with its speckled nose.

"Supper will be soon," the master laughed. Pointing to the orange sun, which was veiled by a winter fog, he reckoned the time. "Supper for the two of us, in one hour."

As twilight descended, so did a cold wind off the range to the east. Apparently no strangers would be challenging Reuben's men tonight. Given the nature of the season, any shepherd clans in the region would have already begun bedding down their flocks for the night.

Reuben was pleased with himself for having decided to move on to Dothan. Only one thing disturbed his peace of mind as he gathered up his heavy saddle and his grease pot and prepared to join his brothers in the field beyond.

When the sons of Bilhah and Zilpah had joined with the others in Shechem, they had boasted of their encounter with Joseph. Scoffing about the lad's prophecies, they revealed how they had repaid the braggart, and they

104 Ellen Gunderson Traylor

were applauded by all but himself and Judah, who kept very quiet.

Reuben may have been hesitant to show it at times, but he loved Joseph dearly and was glad that at least the youngster was now safe at home with Jacob and Benjamin. Anger boiled in him at the callousness and unending hatred which his brethren had always manifested toward the lad.

It therefore caused him great consternation when he learned that Joseph was not, in fact, staying at Mamre.

Night had nearly fallen when Reuben's laborious trek toward camp was interrupted by Gad. Racing up from the field that ran toward the south, Gad hailed him, waving his arms and shouting.

"Asher and I were just bedding down our flocks," he cried as he came upon him. "From the rise we could see the highway, and coming this way a traveler!"

Panting and holding his sides, he caught up with Reuben, who anxiously inquired, "Does he have a large company? We will not give up our place lightly."

"No, no," Gad went on. "That was our concern as well. But when he came closer, we could see that no company followed, and... he is not a stranger!"

"I have no time for riddles!" Reuben snapped, and hastening on, headed for camp, supper, and bed.

"You do not understand," Gad replied, grasping him by the sleeve. "It is our brother. It is Joseph who approaches!"

Stopping in his tracks, Reuben studied Gad dubiously. As he absorbed the news, he also noted the scheming gleam in the man's eye.

Before he could question him further, Gad was off, himself heading for camp to break the word to the others.

On his trail came Asher, passing Reuben with an eager stride. The elder brother did not like his expression any better than Gad's.

Whatever the two were up to, he was certain they intended Joseph no good.

* * *

Encumbered with his bulky saddle, which needed to cure after its rubdown, Reuben slowly led his hungry horse toward camp. By the time he reached the others, they had already begun to contrive their wicked plot against Joseph.

"The dreamer is coming!" Gad and Asher had announced.

Quickly the hate-filled minds of the nine brothers colluded and conspired.

As Reuben came upon them, frightening words hissed from their drawn lips, and their bent heads nodded together. Judah stood a little way from the others, but Reuben noted that even he was not objecting to their plans.

"Let's kill him!" someone said. "He will not reach camp until it is fully dark. Even if someone passes on the road, we will never be seen!"

Had it gone so far, their jealousy? Had resentment blossomed into murder? With sweating hands Reuben set his saddle beside his tent and tethered his horse. Carefully he listened to the voices circling the campfire, and his flesh prickled.

Fidgeting with his brown beard, Reuben darted a glance over his shoulder. Vainly he hoped to see Joseph approaching, that he might warn him, that he might rush him away from the would-be assassins.

In fact, he would have turned away to find him, to divert him from the danger, but the brothers had already seen Reuben in the shadows and hailed him.

Quickly he considered his options. He could pretend not to hear them, he could say he left something at the cistern and go in quest of Joseph. But when Joseph did not arrive, they would likely suspect Reuben and come after them both.

No, he had no choice. He must join the jesters at the fire, the laughers with toothy grins and evil designs.

"Lord Jehovah," he whispered. Reuben must handle this very discretely.

Pulling his shoulders back, he pretended nonchalance.

"So, Little One is on his way," he said, approaching his companions with an easy swagger.

"You know?" Naphtali enthused.

"Yes, yes, we told him," Gad announced. "Have you seen him, Reuben?"

"Not yet," the elder laughed, taking a seat. "What's the plan?"

Eagerly they filled his ears. "We've had enough of his bragging!" Dan cried. "He plots to overthrow us, Reuben! Don't you know?"

The elder replied nothing, pretending neither agreement nor surprise at this aberration.

"Next year, when he turns eighteen, he will have menservants of his own," Asher projected, "and after that an army, if he wishes. How shall he force us to bow to him, as he says, without a war!"

"Indeed!" Zebulun joined in. "Shall we sit still while our enemy rises over us? You know he is Jacob's favorite. Anything he asks—soldiers, weapons, even war machines —all will be his!"

Reuben studied his brothers' crazed expressions in the firelight. They had not yet drunk much wine. It was not wine that inspired their maniacal imaginings. It was hate, and the imaginings excused their hatred.

"Let's kill him!" Gad suddenly reasserted, pounding his fist into his thigh and jumping up. His voice, momentarily stunning the others, was followed by cheers and the unsheathing of knives.

"We can cover the deed. No one need know!" he shouted. "We shall cast him into one of the cisterns by the road. We can tell Father a wild beast devoured him!"

"Yes," Asher raved, "then let's see what becomes of his dreams!"

Reuben rose up rigid on his seat. "Brothers, brothers!" he cried, raising his hands. When he had their attention he tempered his tone. "Are you sure this is what you want? Think! Jehovah watches!"

The group, silenced by the rebuke, squirmed angrily.

"Jehovah! Jehovah!" someone objected. "Indeed, he watches. Would he have us hide our heads while Joseph supplants us?"

At this everyone rallied, and cheers rose again.

Losing ground, Reuben turned to Judah. "Brother," he said, trying not to sound desperate, "do you agree with this?"

Uneasy at being singled out, Judah glanced nervously around the group. He was about to reply, but caught by Asher's warning look, he gave a weak smile and only shrugged.

"Of course he agrees!" Gad insisted. "He is a son of the first wife, like you, Reuben! Judah has much to lose!"

At this, Asher leaned close to Gad, whispering in his ear and eyeing Reuben suspiciously. The eldest brother must reconsider his position, and quickly.

Fearing now for his own safety, and knowing that if something happened to him no one could save Joseph, Reuben tried a different tack.

Standing up, he placed a faggot on the fire and casually wiped his hands on his cloak.

"I can see that Father and I have taught you well," he conceded. "You do right to put the interests of your property and your welfare above all else. After all, the protection of your inheritance is a sacred trust."

The brothers, mollified, listened with more respect, muttering to one another and nodding their heads.

Looking over his shoulder again, Reuben still did not see Joseph. Quickly he added, "It is a good idea to throw him into one of the cisterns. But, I say, let us not take his life."

When Gad and Asher started angrily, he repeated, "Shed no blood. Throw him into the pit, but do not lay hands on him, for how do you know but that his blood will be required of you? Then what will all your wise intentions have accomplished?"

If there was one thing on which all the cultures of Canaan and Mesopotamia were agreed, it was that reaping always followed sowing, not only in the natural world, but in the spiritual. Appealing to his brothers' fears of retribution, Reuben had them cornered.

Silence filled the firelit circle for a long moment. Then, at last, Asher rallied.

Hoisting a wineskin, he suddenly declared, "Well said, Reuben! Let the pit pass the judgment! What chance is there that Joseph can survive in a desert pit?"

Encouraged by this reasoning, the others applauded.

"What chance, especially after we are done with him?" Gad hooted.

Raucous laughter resounded through camp, and the wineskin was tippled from hand to hand.

With apprehensive eyes, Reuben gazed across the darkness toward the road. As he had feared, Joseph was coming, drawn like a pathetic moth toward the camp's beckoning fire.

His heart rending, Reuben would have called out to him in warning. But then he observed his brothers' knotted fists and their conspiring faces, and he resisted.

He only hoped he had bought a chance for Joseph, and that he could live with himself if he had failed.

PART III
The Castaway

16

Sun, like a fist, smote the bottom of the pit.

Joseph could not be sure he was awake. He was not certain he was alive.

The face of the old man, the shepherd of Shechem, came with the sun, not smiting him but passing in and out of his head like a windblown cloud. At first the face hovered above him, then it entered him, through his sealed and swollen eyes.

Somehow, Joseph managed to turn himself from his stomach to his back and lay for a long time face up, the sides of the tall pit enclosing him like a womb.

As consciousness replaced the swoon, so did throbbing pain replace its anesthesia.

Once, when with great effort he opened an eye, he thought the old shepherd sat on the lip of the cistern, his legs dangling over the edge toward him, his face somber but reassuring. When Joseph tried to reach forth a hand, however, the old man vanished—and with him, the hope he inspired.

Crushing pain enveloped the youngster just as the walls enveloped him, but searing him and coursing through him with each laborious pulse of his heart.

His body, which had not yet recovered from his fight in the Hebron hills, and which had endured the hard journey from Mamre to Dothan, had sustained further serious injuries. Could he have seen himself, his churning stomach would have revolted.

Several kicks to the torso had left him with bruised ribs and organs. His head, wounded when he was cast like a barley bag over the cistern's ledge, was distended, a large lump protruding from his brow.

It must be noontime, he considered. It was his first fully alert thought. The sun was directly above the cistern, and though it was wintertime, the pit captured the rays and held them against the dry bottom, wringing from them all the warmth they could provide.

Fever tormented Joseph, and he hated the sun. Vainly he tried to shield his face, but he could not raise a hand to do so.

Resigned, insofar as resignation or any act of will was possible, Joseph accepted that he would die here.

The swoon was about to reclaim him when a dull rumble reached his ears.

At first he felt that his head would burst—that the phantom sound was the rush of angels' wings, and that it heralded the coming of the end. But as reality again imposed itself upon him, he interpreted the roar more clearly.

Through the haze of growing consciousness he remembered that the pit was beside a highway and that it was a stopping place for caravans. Still unable to move, he let the sound of horses' hooves and churning wheels sweep over him.

As the company, enormous by the sound of it, came to a halt, and the rumble tapered to shouts and commands, Joseph vaguely recognized that the voices spoke an Arabian tongue. He cared not who they were or what nation they were of. He only hoped someone might glance into the dry cistern and see him, for no worse evil could befall him than he had already endured.

He must have groaned. Somehow, through his pain and his need, his soul found its voice, and he moaned loudly enough to be heard.

Momentarily, faces peered over the side of the pit—

brown faces, covered by desert dust or concealed by dingy white veils. Turbaned heads shook and nodded as the amazed caravaneers spied the source of the peculiar sound.

Then the men disappeared, and Joseph wondered if they were a vision, like the shepherd of Shechem.

But he could hear them now, conferring beyond the pit, rattling in their strange tongue.

Then another rumbling, as of a second caravan, could be discerned. Joseph could not tell north from south, trapped as he was. But it was apparent that this new train would converge upon the first from the opposite direction.

Suddenly the Arabians were more vocal, trading ideas back and forth and staring into the pit at Joseph as though he were a commodity and not a man.

Finding a remnant of strength, the son of Jacob managed to lift a hand, pleading for help. But the faces above were not sympathetic.

Were he capable of terror in his weakened state he would have been terrified as he caught a few familiar fragments of their conversation. "Ishmaelites," he heard them say, "Egypt." These words were universal to all languages of the area. And for a Jacobite, these words were cause for fear. For the Ishmaelites had long been enemies of the Jacobites, ever since Great-grandfather Abraham had blessed Isaac over his firstborn, Ishmael. And Egypt was an alien land, its thirteenth and fourteenth dynasties fond of taking Hebrew slaves.

He did not know what the men above the cistern had in mind for him as the second caravan approached. But he was alert enough to be apprehensive.

As the Arabians lowered a rope into the pit, sending one of their strongest after him, Joseph retreated to the sanctuary of unconsciousness.

Like a tabernacle it enveloped him, giving dark at noonday, and quiet oblivion to his fevered soul.

17

The flying hooves of Reuben's horse left an angry wake across the desert. Rising like a cumulous cloud, the dust raged, following his eastward trail.

From the fields of the Jacobites Reuben fled, seeking the cisterns and his younger brother, seeking one last chance to save him.

Just this morning, the nine conspirators, who had frolicked the night away in celebration of their victory, had laid yet another design against Joseph. From the site of their breakfast fire, which faced north, they had spied the caravan of the Ishmaelites, the second caravan to approach Joseph's pit. They had not seen the first, the one from the south, which was manned by Midianite Arabs. But the second had sparked their greed.

To Reuben's horror, it was Judah who contrived the plot. He could scarcely believe that his closest brother should stoop so low.

"What profit is it to us to let Joseph die in the pit?" Judah had asked, studying the great train that descended from Gilead. "What do we gain by slaying Joseph and trying to hide the fact? Come, let us sell him to the Ishmaelites."

At first, Asher had rankled at the idea. Murder, or at least the chance that the pit would claim Joseph, was his foremost desire. But as Judah continued his smooth talk the possibility of turning a profit became more attractive.

"As Reuben says, we should not kill our brother," Judah craftily reasoned. "We should spare him. After all, he *is* our own flesh and blood."

That Judah should use Reuben's own words to this end was unpardonable.

At the foot of the firepit lay Joseph's coat, an object of mocking hilarity all through the evening. Before roughing up the lad, the brothers had stripped him of his prize possession, the symbol of his heritage. They had kept it for themselves, passing it back and forth, wearing it and sporting in it all night.

Suddenly, Reuben could conceal his love for Joseph no longer. Caring not what risk it entailed, he leapt to his feet, grasping the coat to himself and racing from the camp.

Across the desert he sped, hoping to reach the cistern before the Ishmaelites did. He knew the brothers would be on his heels. He knew they would be hastening to intervene. But nothing mattered any longer except Joseph's life.

At the sight of the oasis, as he came over the rise on his stamping horse, Reuben's heart raced with hope. The Ishmaelites were already past the place, heading south, and the other caravan, which he had not expected to see, was done with its stop and was moving north.

By the time the brothers arrived, there would be no one to whom they might sell Joseph.

Eagerly he headed toward the pit—the one which only last night had been the scene of the grisly thrashing, the site of the horrible casting away.

In his hand he clasped Joseph's coat, ready to wrap him in it, ready to tenderly return him to his rightful station.

But as he drew near, the sound of his brothers' horses even now echoing from behind, a new fear filled him. What if the caravaneers had found Joseph? What if they had, for some reason, looked into the pit, and seeing him, had stolen him away?

Dread, like a noose, strangled him as he leapt from his mount and ran the last way to the cistern.

Leaning over, he found that the floor was indeed vacant. Little pools of dried blood were the only evidence of the lad's suffering.

Madly he surveyed the road and the retreating clouds of the dust-raising trains. And like a drunkard, he staggered across the desert.

Judah, coming upon him, was followed close by Gad and Asher. Snarling, they glared down at him. But he had no heart for their disappointment.

Defeated, he fell to his face before them, before his failure, before Jehovah.

And holding his hands to the sky, he wept, "The lad is gone! And I... where shall I go?"

18

The crunch and jolt of wagon wheels awakened Joseph. For a long while he lay dazed and still, wondering where he was.

Above him spread an opaque tarp, so heavy that no light and little air were admitted. Beneath him were bags of grain, as comfortable a bed as he had known since leaving Mamre.

It seemed he was a child again, six years old, and that he was hidden away in Leah's wagon. Any moment he would hear Dinah's voice beside him and feel her tugging on his arm.

Were he to rise up and peek from beneath the tarp, he would surely see the retreating hills of Gilead and his brothers' horses splashing through Jabbok ford.

Jacob would find him in the morning and would speak to him of the angel and the pain in his thigh.

But as he snuggled against the barley bags, he was himself in pain. Gradually the memory of his brothers' fists and kicking blows replaced his dream.

Also, he remembered the fearsome words spoken by his Arabian captors. He knew, now, that he was the unwilling property of whomever had placed him in this wagon.

He found he was able, this time, to move his hand. He was about to raise the tarp where daylight etched a bright line along the wagon rail, but just as his palsied fingers grasped the edge of the heavy fabric, the wagon came to a halt and the voices of the caravaneers filled the morning.

Lowering his hand, he lay very still and listened intently to their unintelligible tongue, hoping to catch a phrase here and there that would tell him more about them.

He did not expect the dramatic way in which his hope would be fulfilled.

Suddenly the tarp was flung back, and crisp sunlight spilled over him. As he turned his head from the glare a shadow fell across him, and he stared into the dark features of a leering Arabian.

"Allah be praised!" the man laughed. "He is still alive!"

The word "Allah," alone, was familiar to Joseph. But it was sufficient to answer many of his questions.

He knew now that his first captors had sold him to the Ishmaelite caravan which met them at the cistern. He also knew that his new owners could have nothing good in mind for him, probably intending to sell him as a slave when they reached Egypt. Such a fate had befallen many Hebrews separated from their tribes.

He also knew that if these men learned he was Jacobite, he might not live to see the borders of Egypt.

It was not so long before, in the scheme of history, that Great-grandfather Abraham had preferred Isaac to his firstborn, Ishmael, bestowing upon Isaac the patriarchal blessing and the greater part of the inheritance. For the Ishmaelite Arabs, the memory of that affront would never die, and any descendant of Isaac was considered an enemy.

Therefore, although Joseph's head was still foggy with delirium, he was wise enough to keep silent.

Reaching into the wagon, the big fellow who stared in at him poked and prodded him as a woman pokes a piece of meat at market.

With a wince, Joseph pulled away, and the man grinned, calling out some crudity to his friends. Hollow laughter met the remark, and soon the wagon was surrounded by other mocking faces.

In a round of gibberish, the men began to question their captive. But Joseph could not answer them, for he did not know the language. As they persisted, however, the big man pointed to his companions, calling out their names one by one and indicating that Joseph was to introduce himself.

Refusing to cooperate, he replied, "Call me Hebrew."

"Hebrew?" the man snarled. "Habiru!" he laughed, turning to his friends, and repeating the word in their tongue. Everyone laughed again, but as Joseph continued to deny a name, claiming his lifestyle as his only identity, they grew sullen.

Suddenly the leering fellow grasped at Joseph's tunic and pulled him to a sitting position. Patting him on the cheek, he bared his yellow teeth and breathed warm garlic into Joseph's face.

Directing him to look over the wagon's edge, he pointed an angry finger toward the horizon.

"Egypt!" he growled.

How long Joseph had lain semiconscious in the wagon, he did not know, but it was at least a month by caravan from Dothan to the borders of Egypt. To the youngster's amazement, the distant line of earth against sky was marked with a jagged wall, enormous, snakelike, designating the boundary of the greatest nation under heaven.

The Land of the Nile lay straight ahead—the sanctuary of the shepherds, the sons of Isaac, having faded with the desert far behind.

As the lad sat stunned on the barley bags, his captor, who appeared to be the train's yeoman, began shouting commands. Soon men were scattering, running for water, rags, and fresh clothes.

Placing his large hands under Joseph's arms, the yeoman lifted him from the wagon and stood him on his feet. Like a newborn calf, Joseph buckled, his legs weak as butter. But the Arab began to walk him about, forcing him to use his atrophied limbs.

At last, he took him to the shade of a small tent, and clapping his hands, called for a servant girl.

Deftly, the young woman began to wash the dirt and encrusted blood from Joseph's arms and legs. He would have resisted when she pulled his tunic over his head, leaving him in his loincloth. But the Arab was close by, and Joseph must submit.

He must submit likewise as she attended to his blood-matted hair. The lustrous dark locks must be cut, and soon a razor worked even at his disheveled beard.

Between the tentflaps Joseph could see the wall of Egypt, formidable, irresistible. As he studied it, his heart shivering, the razor sheared him like a sheep.

It was a shame to be shaven, the mark of a slave.

But freedom was his no longer. He had lost it at Dothan to the will of his brothers, to the will of his brothers' God.

19

Like a bloody finger, the red granite obelisk of On pierced the afternoon sky. Flies buzzed through the busy marketplace, tormenting the queue of naked captives who stood in the obelisk's shadow.

It was never wintertime in Egypt. Here, except for morning and afternoon thunderstorms, the season was hot. Joseph, who stood with his hands bound behind him, inched forward with the queue, his eyes locked upon the auction block where soon he would be standing. Sweat poured in rivulets down his bare torso, soaking his striped loincloth, the only garment allowed him.

He would have given an arm to just once swat at the pestering flies diving at his head. But he had no right over his own body.

His scalp burned, exposed to the sun for the first time since infancy. Shorn of his heavy hair and of his lustrous beard, the tender skin was readily inflamed. As he moved out of the obelisk's shadow, he cringed.

On was the first major city to which the Ishmaelite caravan had come upon entering Egypt. The capital of Egyptian science and knowledge, the magnificent city was also the religious center of the empire, devoted to the chief god, Ra, god of the sun.

Joseph had often heard of the great monolith whose shadow stretched the length of the central avenue. The obelisk represented all that was Egyptian, from worship to government. In effect its shadow reached from end to end of the Nile Valley.

For Joseph, however, as for any Israelite, the monolith was a repugnant sight, a symbol of the bewildering paganism which characterized this mightiest of nations.

The auction tent, spread through the middle of On's central square, was the chief attraction of the marketplace. Its enormous striped awning sheltered countless bales, casks, bolts, cartons, and barrels of goods.

The Arabian caravan that had brought Joseph to this land had been laden with flasks of balm, myrrh, and gum resin, all procured in Gilead. The costly products would sell for a high price in this bazaar.

Joseph wearily surveyed the marketplace. Visions of Mamre, of the verdant oaks and the clean stream that fed them, drifted through his mind, weighing him with sadness. Against a wall across the plaza stood the yeoman of the caravan, his hefty arms crossed over his chest as he waited for his most valuable possession to be auctioned.

The young Hebrew was a rare find, and though the Arab had paid dearly for him, giving the Midianites a full week's wages, the strong young man would bring a handsome price today.

True, Joseph was not in the finest shape. Bruised and debilitated, he did not make as good a showing as he might. But the reserve price placed on his head took this into account, and anyone considering the purchase could see by Joseph's physique and well-turned muscles that he was a good risk.

Throughout the trip to Egypt, the yeoman had seen to it that the captive was kept alive, fed, and nursed, at last, to consciousness.

Joseph had been bathed and his worst wounds were anointed with healing balm. Already the lad was reviving beneath the warming sun, color overcoming the deadly pallor that had been his. The yeoman eagerly licked his lips, savoring the scent of money.

As for Joseph himself, he felt anything but strong. His

knees were wobbly, he sweltered beneath the sun's caress, and each forward step required increasing effort.

"Lord Jehovah," he whispered under his breath, "God of Abraham, Isaac, and Jacob..."

The auction platform was now directly before him. He would be the next one called forth.

Shame filled him and he kept his naked head bowed even as one of the auction assistants bent over to un-shackle his ankles. But when yet another assistant grasped Joseph rudely by the arm, leading him to the block, rebellion suddenly surged through him, flooding him with adrenaline. Wrenching free, he wheeled about, striking the man with his two bound fists and throwing him off balance.

Stunned, the man fell back against the platform, and his partner, racing to help him, left Joseph standing free in front of the onlooking crowd.

Pandemonium broke loose in the marketplace, as Joseph's fellow captives took his lead, and rising up in kind, began to push through the throng, kicking their shackled feet and winding like a formidable chain toward the avenue.

With instant camaraderie, the captives—black Nubians from Ethiopia, pale-skinned barbarians from Europe, and olive-complected Semites of many tribes—forged ahead, upsetting business and terrifying those who stood in their way.

In ripple effect, the disturbance at the auction tent spread through the bazaar. Joseph, although the instiga-tor, found attention distracted from himself and within moments was mingling anonymously with the frenzied crowd.

Working his way toward the back wall of the mar-ketplace, he thought to find an exit, and once free, would seek escape. The fact that his hands were bound behind him was an inconvenience he could not correct just now.

Sidling through the press he found that the market ended only yards from the monoliths' broad base. Behind the obelisk was the gate to the Temple of Ra, portal to the city's acropolis and to the sanctuaries of government.

The Gate of On, main entrance to the city, lay a short distance beyond, and like an arrow he aimed for it.

Just as he did so, however, he was grabbed from behind and thrown to the ground, his face scraping the pavement.

Two hundred pounds of human flesh held him down, the Arabian caravaneer having once again captured him, and sitting now upon his back.

"So, you thought to rob me!" the Ishmaelite snarled, his words lost on Joseph. "Come!"

Grasping the youngster by the wrists, he wrenched him up from the ground, sending shooting pains through the captive's shoulders. Then turning Joseph to face him, he began to slap him, holding him by one hand and buffeting him with the other.

The people near the gate were joined by the crowd from the marketplace, which, unruly and loud, spurred the yeoman's vengeance. And when the human chain of shackled prisoners, so far unrestrained, approached the gate, they found their hero in sorrier condition than ever.

The caravaneer would likely have beaten his slave to death, had a new character not entered the scene.

The bloodthirsty crowd was reveling in revenge when suddenly a hush came over it. Those people closest to the temple were the first to grow quiet, and as they quieted, they bowed themselves to the ground.

Row upon row, the reverence spread, as a dignitary of some importance descended the temple steps. Soon his name was passing from whisper to whisper.

"Potiphera..." some said, while others used the nickname, "Potiphar..." The word obviously evoked awe, and soon everyone about the caravaneer and the captive was prostrate upon the ground.

The yeoman, recognizing that this newcomer merited obeisance, likewise bowed down, still holding Joseph firmly by the wrists.

Trumpets blared from the temple steps and one of the dignitary's numerous attendants announced his entrance.

"Potiphera, Priest of On, High Priest of Ra, Captain of the Sacred Bodyguard! All bow! Humble yourselves before His Reverence!"

Over and over the announcement was heralded as Potiphera made his way to the street.

Joseph, standing in the middle of the avenue, dusty and sweat-streaked, momentarily forgot his struggle as the auspicious gentleman drew near. Flanked on each side by attendants—scribes, valets, accountants, and counselors—and followed by spear-bearing guards, Potiphera was a striking figure. Joseph was head and shoulders taller than many of the men in the crowd, but Potiphera equaled him for stature. And the fine strands of silver that wound through his banded goatee added grace and dignity to his appearance.

Garbed in a tight body tunic which reached to his knees, Potiphera was royally attired. His headdress was a helmet, reserved for nobility of the highest class, and upon his neck and descending toward his breast was a broad collar of lacquered plates, edged in gold.

The most outstanding feature of his garb was the emblem that adorned both his headdress and his collar, a wide ornament shaped like falcon wings spreading out from a golden circle. From each side of the circle two snakeheads protruded, likewise of lacquer and gold. This ornament Joseph recognized as the winged sun-disk, symbol of the sun-god, Ra.

His wrists still gripped tight in the yeoman's hand, Joseph studied the priest with wide eyes. Like the rest of the onlookers, he was riveted by Potiphera's quiet glory, but unlike them, he did not bow.

Perhaps it was this that drew Potiphera's attention. Perhaps it was the fact that the priest had observed the scuffle in the street only moments before.

Whatever it was that captured his focus, Potiphera paused before the lad, surveying him with a bemused expression.

Up and down he eyed him, saying nothing, while the crowd grew restless and the yeoman apprehensive.

When at last the Ishmaelite got courage to peer up at the priest, he met with disapproval. Without a word, Potiphera persuaded him to release his grip on the youngster.

"Unbind him!" Potiphera commanded.

The yeoman stammered and stuttered, but Potiphera did not repeat himself.

At last, the Ishmaelite complied and, chagrined, he stepped aside.

Now the priest drew closer to Joseph. "Who are you?" he asked, using the Egyptian dialect which was the language of commerce familiar to all but the most ignorant of foreigners.

Joseph pulled himself up straight and tall, rubbing his throbbing wrists. "I am Hebrew," he answered.

The yeoman laughed nervously. "Yes, yes ... this is all he will tell you," he said, fearing the captive would offend the priest and call down further disfavor on both their heads.

But the priest, ignoring the yeoman, continued to study Joseph.

"Are you the source of disquiet in my city this day?" he inquired.

Of course he must have known the answer to that question, having been informed of the upset in the marketplace and of the upstart slave who had instigated it.

Joseph did not reply, refusing to accommodate the Egyptian.

The yeoman, fidgeting uneasily, was ready to intercede, but Potiphera silenced him with a glance.

Standing back, the priest walked around Joseph, and as he did, a smile worked at his face.

Then, turning to his attendants, he nodded. "We must deal with this rebel. He must be taught compliance."

"Yes, sir," one of the soldiers agreed, snapping to attention. Coming toward Joseph, he intended to haul him off to prison, but Potiphera shook his head.

"No, no," he sighed. "Handle him gently, and pay the auctioneer a fair price. The best way to keep an eye on this Hebrew is to take him home."

Bewildered, the soldier shrugged. "Your Highness, you mean..."

"Yes," Potiphera replied, and looking down at the Ishmaelite, "he is still for sale, is he not?"

The yeoman shot a quick glance at the slave. "Why, of course, Your Lordship. And a good price I will give you!"

"Very well," the priest said, and leaving the details to his accountants, he passed down the avenue without a second thought.

20

Glorious sunset, mauve and tangerine, lit the servants' court of Potiphera's house. It spilled in deepening shades through the open ceiling, reflecting off the scrubbed white of the limestone walls and strangely affecting Joseph's spirit.

He should have been miserable. He had just been hauled to the auction block of a slave market, had failed in his courageous attempt to save himself, and had been purchased, like chattel, by a pagan priest.

He was another man's property—the property of a heathen foreigner—and he had no rights, being less than a dog in Egyptian society. Indeed, among the pantheon of this bewildering empire, the dog was worshiped, as was most every animal that walked, crawled, or slithered across the earth.

Men and women, captured and enslaved, were less than human, less than the dogs or snakes or vermin to whom temples were erected and sacrifices offered.

Despite his situation, Joseph was strangely satisfied by the violet and vermilion of the night.

Little had been expected of him since he had been introduced to the house. He had in fact been allowed to recline in the servants' quarters upon the couch where he now sat, until his sorely depleted strength returned.

And he had already been fed more than once on fare both nutritious and exotic.

Potiphera had seen to it that he was treated kindly.

Joseph did not know why he was thus dealt with, but he did not question it, having little strength for deep thinking.

He did sense, when he pondered anything, that Jehovah was with him. And he sensed that this strange Potiphera, pagan though he was, could somehow be the instrument of God Almighty.

He shivered, drawing up his shoulders as he considered his powerless condition. Though the reality of it would take a long time dawning, the very thought of enslavement horrified him.

But then the russet light soothed him, calling to him from beyond the wall like the whisper of the Lord, caressing him like Rachel's hand, and upholding him like the voice of Jacob.

How long he sat upon the couch, silently observing the bustle of the kitchen hands and listening to the soft chatter of the maids, he did not know. The workers who went about their business in the court were of various classes. Those in charge were hired servants. Under them were indentured servants, each one designated by a silver post placed in a small hole bored through the left earlobe. Then there were the slaves, marked by brands upon their necks. But what struck Joseph was that, despite these outward emblems, everyone worked peaceably together. Even the slaves were accorded unusual respect.

Joseph's attention was attracted to one fellow in particular, who was apparently the kitchen manager. The Hebrew was intrigued by him, not only because he ran his affairs as chief baker with efficiency and authority, but also because his left ear bore the mark of the awl. Although he no longer wore a small silver post through the lobe, which all of the other indentured workers wore, there was a hole—a sure sign that this man had once owed his life to the master.

Why he would have continued in service to Potiphera, once having earned his freedom, Joseph could not imagine. But with dexterity and joy he ran the kitchen, and now and then, as he bent over the breadboard and joined his underlings in their mundane activities, a song or a merry whistle spilled from his throat.

Bald as a desert dune he was, round as a pumpkin; and his cheeks were like pomegranates, red and full. His servants and slaves called him by name, Phineas. But though the name was Egyptian, he did not have the lank body and narrow nose of the race.

Joseph studied him for a long while, cheered by his presence just as the others were, and he wondered about him.

Dark was coming on. As it did, the pace of the kitchen work increased. The grand meal of the day in Egyptian society was reserved for late evening. Several times Phineas clapped his hands, spurring his workers. It was time to serve the food. Trays of copper and silver, containing roast partridge, enormous honey rolls, and piles of succulent figs and olives, were carried into the dining room.

Joseph could not see this room as it lay beyond a narrow, curtain-covered portal. He could, however, imagine the activity of the chamber, as couches were arranged about low tables and golden goblets were filled with the first round of wine.

No one had yet arrived for the feast, but anticipation was in the air. Every night was banquet night in Potiphera's house, as the evening meal was a time of entertaining the endless stream of dignitaries who came to call.

None of the grand folk who frequented the residence could have impressed the young Hebrew slave more than Phineas, however. As he observed him, the plump fellow suddenly wheeled about, surveying the kitchen for any forgotten details. When he did, his eyes fell upon the newcomer, and his expression, already jovial, softened warmly.

"Hebrew?" he called across the room.

"Yes, sir," the slave replied, straightening his weary shoulders.

"You will help serve tonight," he commanded. "Look sharp now!"

Joseph stood up from the couch and cleared his throat. "Serve, sir?" he marveled. "But, I do not know..."

"You will learn quickly enough. Stay at my elbow and follow my instructions."

With this, Phineas motioned him forward and folded a pristine linen towel over his left arm. As he looked him over, turning him about, he shook his head and sighed.

"Madam arrives tonight...any moment I'm sure. She will be bringing a gaggle of fine ladies. Keep quiet and you will do well."

With that, he directed Joseph to follow him through the portal, where he would explain the details of the feast.

When Joseph entered the chamber, he was surprised by the feminine decor of the tables. Pink lilies from the Nile mixed in profusion with purple irises and red garden roses, all arranged like glorious bushes in ornate vases about the room. Muscular Nubian menservants, their dark skin oiled until it glistened, held ostrich-feather fans in each corner, adding a visual accent which would have pleased any woman's eye.

In this setting, Phineas, who had commandeered the kitchen, took a secondary role, deferring instantly to a tall thin man who bore himself with austere pride.

His eyes cold as spearpoints, the haughty one approached Phineas and scrutinized his charge.

"Is this the Hebrew?" he snapped.

"Yes," Phineas replied. "Is he not pleasing?"

The man, who was governor of the feast, walked

around Joseph two or three times, and at last sniffed disdainfully.

"Madam will be pleased," he conceded. "That is what matters."

21

Potiphera had one weakness. In all other matters he was a man of dignity: clearheaded, devoutly spiritual and keen witted. But in this one area, he could be as addle-pated as a schoolboy.

His single blindspot was his ravishing wife, Natira.

After 20 years of marriage, he was as smitten by her as the day his father, the previous high priest, had brought her before him.

Potiphera indulged Natira at every opportunity. No wish she might have was too great for him to grant, no whim too frivolous. He even anticipated her desires, seeking to fulfill them before she asked.

Thus it was that the priest had purchased the young Hebrew slave.

Natira had a penchant for handsome young men. She surrounded herself with them, possessing so many male valets and personal servants that her husband might have questioned her motivation.

But Potiphera never questioned; his trust of Natira was nearly childlike.

Tonight he stood in the entryway of his home, awaiting his wife's arrival. She had been in the imperial capital of Memphis for three weeks, visiting in Pharaoh's palace. This evening she would be returning and would be bringing with her a host of royal ladies who would guest in the priest's home.

Their visit would culminate in the arrival of Pharaoh

himself, and his queen, who would take up residence in the king's winter palace for his annual stay in On.

Situated somewhat inland from the Nile, On was less humid and less chilly than Memphis this time of year. For royalty pampered by the mildest of climates, slight variation in temperature was cause for relocation, and the priest's house had become a haven.

In fact, so connected was Potiphera's estate with the royal compound of On that the two were considered by the general populace as one property.

The priest leaned through the large door of his estate, looking eagerly down the cobbled boulevard. Rewarded by the sound of carriage wheels, he stepped onto the porch, smoothing his lavender tunic and stroking his crimped beard.

Ascending the main avenue to the acropolis was a stunning parade of horsedrawn cabs, glittering with gold and burnished by the rosy twilight. Within moments they lined the drive of Potiphera's mansion, and an even more stunning array of ladies emerged.

Perfumed and perfected by cosmetics, decked in a profusion of silks and jewels, the women formed a fluttery processional, descending upon Potiphera and his home like a flock of exotic birds.

The ladies were more alike than individual. Devoted to fashion, these high-society females strove for the thin look, denying themselves rich foods until they conformed to the body-hugging designs dictated for their gowns.

Paper-thin sandals adorned their feet, designed more for appearance than for practicality. Slender laces crisscrossed up their calves to emphasize the length of their legs.

The dresses they wore were simple but elegant— sarong-like and gathered at one shoulder, leaving the other bare. Whites and pastels dominated, allowing each woman's personal expression to radiate in her jewels.

Gaudy gold and silver ornaments were layered about the women's necks, and spectacular arm bands, anklets, and bracelets balanced the effect.

Delicate scarves trailed from waists, wrists, and necks; or were held lightly in the fingers and dragged carelessly upon the pavement as though they had not cost their husbands' budgets dearly.

But in each case the crowning touch was the coiffure.

Most of the women wore wigs, all in the perfectly black color so admired by their class. Any female blessed with naturally straight hair could forego a wig, though she must use dye to match the ebony she craved.

The hairstyle of the day was starkly streamlined, bluntly cut but meticulously woven here and there with jeweled braids or crimped curls.

Cosmetics were used liberally, porcelain complexions accented by ruby lips and heavily lined eyes. Mascara and charcoal were applied unsparingly, drawn along the eyelids and brought out toward the temples in winglike streaks.

Potiphera watched the parade with masculine appreciation, but his eyes favored Natira, leader of the flock.

Though this grand lady possessed an enviably thin waist and narrow hips, she was buxom as a Nile barge and did not quite fit the twig-like figure stipulated by the fashion powers. If she was proud of her well-endowed torso, it was because she knew what men liked, and what men liked did not always conform to trend.

Whenever Potiphera watched Natira walk, he was swept up on her movements, his heart helplessly carried like a leaf on a graceful wave. After 20 years he was still so affected, still so in love.

As she approached him this evening, her companions laughing and gossiping through the door, she paused. Lightly she stroked his face, running her scented fingers through his beard.

She said not a word, however, focusing on him only briefly and then hurrying off to attend to her guests.

Behind her trailed a younger woman, tall like Natira, but more slender. Quietly, she too paused before Potiphera, awaiting his attention.

With a sigh, the man at last entered the house, his eyes following his wife as she disappeared down the hall. He did not immediately acknowledge the younger lady's presence.

"Papa," the girl whispered, touching him lightly on the sleeve.

"Asenath!" he exclaimed. "I did not see you!"

The girl shook her head, laughing gently. "Surely you know by now," she teased, "I am never far from Mother's shadow."

Potiphera embraced the girl fondly, pressing his cheek to her silky hair.

"No, no," the priest corrected. "You are a child of the Sun. Shadow does not become you."

22

From the kitchen door, Phineas, the chief baker, watched his new slave fulfill his duties at the banquet. The young Hebrew was proving himself surprisingly adequate for the task, and the baker, knowing the striking lad had spent his life as a nomad, wondered how he could circulate so capably in this setting.

Proceeding from table to table, Joseph filled wine goblets and saw to it that the platters and bowls of food were kept hot and fresh. If he now and then showed a sign of nervousness, or forgot to serve from a guest's right side, the diners were not offended, charmed as they were by his quiet manner and his ruddy good looks.

For this was a women's banquet. Potiphera had turned the dining room over to Natira for the evening, and all of the ladies were enthralled by the handsome youngster with the night-dark eyes.

The chief baker did not know that Joseph had much experience as a servant. Despite the fact that he was a tribal prince, Joseph had often filled his father's cup at dinner, and had learned early how to fetch and carry for his elder brothers.

Then too, the chief baker could not know that Jacob had instilled in his son an abiding respect for women, never allowing a superior attitude toward Dinah, Leah, Rachel, or the concubines.

If Joseph appeared to move easily in this setting, however, it was not due to confidence on his part, or to lack of anxiety. The baker did not see that Joseph's hands sweated, or that he sometimes stammered when addressed.

Natira, of course, basked in the reception her new slave evoked. "Where did you get him?" her friends marveled. "Isn't he adorable!"

The hostess knew he was a favor from Potiphera, a homecoming gift, and she proudly told her guests so.

The notion shamed Joseph, who understood enough of the language they spoke to be appalled. But he did not show his feelings and kept his head bowed when he came to Natira's table.

Natira's table. The long, low ebony piece dominated the chamber, its crisp linen cover contrasting starkly with the gleaming veneer. The mistress, her skin as white as the linen, her hair as black as the ebony, reclined behind it like a peacock at rest.

When Joseph drew near to fill her cup, she nodded her head, the plume of azure feathers which adorned her coiffure waving to him solicitously.

The young man's heart surged, but not with admiration. In Natira's presence he felt only fear, as though she were very powerful and very dangerous.

In vain did he keep his eyes lowered. She bored through him with her gaze, her slender arm serpentine as she held forth her goblet.

Ascending from her wrist, up the curve of her forearm, was a golden snake, inset with rubies and emeralds. Like a beckoning finger it compelled his eyes to travel toward her face.

Studying the pitcher in his hand, he resisted, and moved on to the next lady.

"Thank you," a soft voice said as he finished pouring the neighbor's cup.

Struck by the kind tone, Joseph turned toward the voice and stood in stunned silence. Reclined upon the couch beside Natira's was another beauty, the image of the grand lady, only younger, more innocent.

Joseph was motionless, his pitcher poised upright in his hand. While he stared into this lady's eyes, a twitter of giggles passed about the hall. He did not hear them, focusing only on the Egyptian girl.

It was not until his mistress, Natira, called out to him that he lurched alert.

"Hebrew!" she barked. "You have not told us your name." Then, demurring, she recast her approach. "Please honor us with your name."

Natira was leaning toward him, her painted face insistent. Joseph knew it was not customary to introduce a slave to one's guests. Nor could he imagine the woman's purpose.

He would have kept the secret forever, never revealing a single thing about himself. But the younger woman was watching him.

"Joseph," he said before he knew it. "My name is Joseph."

It was to the younger lady that he spoke, as though she and not his owner had inquired.

This affront would not go unnoticed. Rising up on her couch, Natira studied the insolent slave with dagger eyes.

The giggle which had a moment ago filled the room, turned to disapproving murmurs. Joseph had crossed the sacred line of Natira's disfavor, and he would not readily be forgiven.

23

Joseph entered the kitchen, his pitcher still clutched in his hand and his throat dry. The Egyptian girl filled his mind, so that he hardly noticed his manager, Phineas, hunched in the corner.

Bent over the chubby fellow was the governor of the feast, the chief butler, his long, angular face contorted viciously. Joseph did not catch a syllable that passed between the two, but when the butler turned on him, he knew he was the cause of their conflict.

"Fetch him!" the man snarled, pointing Phineas toward the Hebrew.

With this, the plump baker hastened to Joseph, leading him across the room, shaking his head and clucking his tongue.

"Not good. Not good," he sighed. "Tophet is very angry. Madam is very angry. Master Potiphera would be angry if he knew."

"What is it, sir?" Joseph asked. "Have I offended?"

"You have insulted our lady!" Tophet replied, grabbing Joseph from Phineas and pushing him into the corner. "Who are you to ignore the mistress when she addresses you?"

"I...I did not mean..." Joseph stammered.

"You did not mean," Tophet mocked. "Phineas will see to it that you think more clearly in the future. Right, Phineas?"

The baker's eyes were wide in his round face. But the butler was insistent. "Yes, Phineas, he is your charge. You must put the brand upon his neck. Perhaps it will burn through to the cobwebs in his brain!"

The butler's hands were like narrow vises on Joseph's arms. The young Hebrew could have shaken himself free, but there was nowhere to run.

He knew what Tophet meant by "the brand." He had seen the ugly scars upon the throats of the kitchen slaves. Already he could feel the searing poker on his flesh and smell the burning of his skin.

Fear surged through him and he wrenched in the butler's grip. Phineas darted a compassionate glance at his fevered face and shook his head in warning.

"Steady, lad," he whispered. "You make matters worse..."

"Quiet!" Tophet growled. "Always you have too much compassion. Save your sympathy for yourself. You must soon answer to Madam for this Hebrew's behavior!"

* * *

Phineas gently wiped a yellow salve upon Joseph's branded neck, tears streaming down his cheeks as he did so. "I am sorry, so sorry," he wept, his voice husky and soft. "I had no choice, you must understand."

Joseph cringed with pain, wanting to shield the wound upon his throat, but Phineas pulled his hand away. "Let the salve do its work," he cautioned. "If you touch the brand it will become festered."

On the floor, the poker with the burning brand smoked and sizzled. Joseph studied it in horror.

"It is the sign of the sun!" he rasped, referring to the rayed symbol which throbbed red hot on its tip. "I do not worship the sun!"

Phineas knelt before the chair where Joseph sat, his expression full of feeling. "Does it really matter? You are Potiphera's slave now."

"It matters!" Joseph cried.

Phineas looked over his shoulder, as if to be sure they were alone on the kitchen veranda. It was very late, and the household servants had retired.

"I know it matters," he sighed, speaking freely. "I know who you are."

Joseph's eyes swam with tears, the brand pulsing mercilessly in his flesh. "You know my name," he groaned. "That is all."

"I know that you are a son of Jacob, the Israelite. Need I know more?"

The slave winced. "How have you learned this?" he marveled.

"I have been with Potiphera only a few years," the baker explained. "I have mastered the Egyptian tongue and have received a new name. But I am Hebrew like you."

Joseph surveyed him through bleary eyes. "Hebrew?" he whispered.

"A servant of Edom," Phineas confessed.

"Edomite?" the lad cried. "A member of Esau's tribe!"

The baker hushed him quickly, looking about again. "This shall be our secret, yours and mine," he cautioned. "It shall be our secret that we both worship Jehovah."

24

Joseph stood on the mezzanine of Potiphera's mansion, watching the rearranging of furniture on the court floor. At Tophet's insistence, he had worked for days in close quarters with Phineas, and had not been allowed to leave the kitchen except to sleep in his corner of the servants' chamber. It was refreshing to observe the activity of the larger world.

Strewn about the patio were recent market purchases. The young Hebrew was dazzled by the array of luxurious goods: bolts of colorful silks and tapestries, stashes of fancy baskets and copper vessels, casks of incense and vases of ornamental plumes. Amidst this profusion the furniture was being pushed and shoved as the housekeepers quibbled over the best arrangement.

"Well, what do you think?" Phineas laughed, joining Joseph on the balcony. "All this so that Madam may entertain in style! Every year it is this way. Just before Pharaoh arrives, she stocks the larders, hangs new curtains, reupholsters every couch, and replaces every dish in the house."

"Pharaoh Timaeus is coming here?" Joseph asked in amazement.

"As he does annually," Phineas replied. Then, smirking, he nodded toward the doorway across the court. Tophet had just emerged from the dining hall, gesturing nervously to the servants who scooted tables and lounges across the floor. "Over here, no over there," he commanded, directing a dozen people in a dozen different directions. "Oh, do be careful!"

But Joseph was still in awe of the baker's news.

"Pharaoh, here?" he marveled. "Have you ever seen him? What is he like?"

"He is Theban," Phineas answered cryptically, as though the term should say it all.

When the baker saw that it did not, he took the youngster by the arm and led him to the back of the mezzanine.

"He, like all his predecessors, allows Semites like you and me to be enslaved. Don't you know that the Hyksos would not permit this?"

Joseph had heard tales of the Hyksos, the "Shepherd Kings," a revolutionary tribe of nomads who had made inroads into the Nile economy, and who had learned to circulate capably within the society of citified Egyptians. They were a controversial people, looked on with suspicion by their Hebrew brothers and considered a threat by many of Pharaoh's advisers.

Nevertheless, their influence continued to grow, and those who advocated more humanitarian politics wished they might rise to power.

"I know something about them" Joseph replied. "Is not such talk dangerous, Phineas?"

"Dangerous, and necessary," Phineas whispered, leaning close to Joseph's ear. "I see you have much to learn."

Then, smirking again, he watched the chief butler go about his work. Tophet would not side with the Hyksos. He was a great lover of King Timaeus, proud of his pure Egyptian lineage, and a hater of Semites. Had Phineas not been such a capable servant, Tophet would not have tolerated his filling such a responsible position in the household.

But Phineas was clever and crafty. He had made a way for himself within the confines of captivity, and once regaining his independence, stayed on because it served himself best to do so.

"Tophet is far more dangerous than all the talking I might do," the baker warned. "He loves Pharaoh, and would as soon have you or me hung as allow us to breathe upon the king."

* * *

Pharaoh Timaeus would be here in two days. Anticipation was feverish in the high priest's house.

Joseph walked this afternoon with his overseer through the bazaar of On, watching carefully as Phineas bargained and haggled with the merchants.

"As a son of Israel, you are clever at market," the baker had guessed, assuming that no prince of a tribe the size of Jacob's could be less. "If you learn as quickly as I think you can, I will let you be my buyer."

Joseph knew Phineas had singled him out for this special opportunity because of their mutual heritage. He knew the baker was coming to think of him as kin, almost as a son.

"How did you happen to join Esau's tribe?" the young Hebrew asked as they wound their way between the market stalls.

"Many years ago," Phineas explained, "I was living in Edom, a Keturahite by birth."

Joseph smiled proudly. "A descendent of Abraham!" he enthused, knowing that Keturah had been Abraham's second wife. "Then we *are* brothers!"

"Thank you," Phineas said. "I should like to think so. My family and I had been hit hard by famine when I met your uncle. My elderly parents were very ill, and I, being a baker with no access to wheat, could not provide for them. It was then that I met Esau."

The man's tone was tender as he spoke the patriarch's name. Joseph recalled the fear which that word had once inspired in those of Jacob's tribe. But he had come to love Esau just as Phineas had.

"He took us in," the baker explained. "He gave us lodging and food and saved our lives. For this I devoted myself to him, and he let me be his servant."

To serve out of choice, and not compulsion, would be a fine thing, Joseph considered. Across the market square was the auction block where only weeks before he had entered into slavery.

"How did you come to be in Egypt?" the youngster inquired.

"I was abducted, just as you were," Phineas replied. "And just as thousands of our people have been, century after century. I was fortunate enough to be able to buy my freedom and become indentured. But I may as well have been a slave."

Joseph watched the ground as they walked, remembering the fields and tents of Jacob, for whom he longed with all his heart.

There was no love in Egypt, he concluded. It was a cold, unfeeling land, and hope eluded him.

Just then a disturbance at the head of the avenue drew his attention toward the temple. Descending from the acropolis, from the house of Potiphera, was a grand carriage, and the shoppers in the bazaar watched its approach with eager eyes.

Recognizing it as the carriage of the high priest's wife, they hoped to glimpse her as she rode through town. The curtains of the cab were drawn. It was unlikely that she would show her haughty face, but the chance that she might held them in worshipful suspense.

"Natira," Phineas explained. "See how these fools drool to see her!"

For Joseph, the very thought of the woman was unsettling. When a slender hand reached through the cab window, pulling one of the curtains aside, he dreaded the sight of her.

But the face which peered forth was neither haughty nor cold. It was soft and kind—the face of the young woman who had captivated him the day of Natira's banquet.

Her gaze, as she looked upon the crowd, seemed strangely compassionate, as though she saw them as individuals and not rabble.

In that instant, her eyes met Joseph's, and for a fleeting second he could have sworn she remembered him.

But just as quickly, the hand of another passenger reached over the girl's shoulder, grabbing the curtain from her light grip and closing it firmly.

"Natira," Joseph thought. "What hold do you have on my lady?"

25

Asenath. Her name was Asenath.

The baker had told him so. And ever since Joseph had heard the name, it had haunted him like sweet music.

He resisted its allure, believing it wrong to love an Egyptian. And he resisted the thought of her because he knew she was unattainable. She was, the baker told him, the daughter of Natira and Potiphera. Furthermore, as daughter of the high priest, she had been dedicated to the gods of Egypt from birth.

In fact, her name meant "daughter of Nath," the goddess of wisdom. Joseph thought it less than wisdom to love her.

Nevertheless, her porcelain face and winsome smile confounded him, and he knew she had been pleased to see him today when she looked out from her carriage.

Would she acknowledge him now, he wondered, were she to find him in the kitchen? He was glad that the fine ladies of the house rarely entered his workplace.

Standing in the pantry, he arranged small tins of spice and bags of yeast upon the shelves. With chagrin he thought of Jacob, grateful that his father did not witness his shame, the woman's work, the work of a slave, which was his occupation. And how he wished that Asenath might have known him in his princely role.

His face red, he gingerly touched the brand upon his neck. She could never love a slave, he knew. Yet a tribal chieftain, firstborn of Israel's favorite wife, heir to the promises of Isaac—this Asenath might have found desirable.

As he went about his mundane tasks, heaviness consumed him. Where *were* the promises of Isaac? Had Joseph's dreams been nothing but mockery?

His brothers would have said so. Perhaps they were right.

Still, he knew the old shepherd of Shechem had been real, as real as the man in the cave on the night of Rachel's death.

It seemed, now, that the old fellow must have known the future, that he must have known the sorrow which lay ahead.

Downcast, Joseph turned from the pantry, overwhelmed with the misery of his existence. What worse fate could befall him, he could not imagine. For he could conceive of nothing more shameful than to live out his life as a kitchen slave to a pagan priest.

Memories of the old shepherd still filled his head as he approached the pantry arch. Beyond lay the workroom where Phineas would have yet another meaningless job for him.

But someone blocked the passageway, and the workroom was quiet and empty.

At first Joseph could scarcely believe his eyes. Natira stood in the doorway, leaning, long and slender, against the frame.

"Madam," Joseph said, bowing from the waist, "how may I serve you?"

Natira surveyed him, a catlike smile pulling at her lips.

"I shall not dine with the guests tonight," she said.

Joseph would have asked why, but he knew personal inquiries were inappropriate.

"I tire of the politics and prattle of my husband's guests," she sighed. "Timaeus arrives tomorrow and I must be rested. I shall dine in my chamber this evening. And you shall serve me."

26

Joseph stood at the foot of Natira's couch, his face burning. The sense of discomfort he always had in her presence was stronger tonight than ever.

Bending over, he placed a large food-laden tray upon her table, and waited while she straightened her gown and positioned herself against her pillows. "Kalat!" she snapped, calling for her chambermaid. "These cushions are stiff!"

Instantly, a young servant rushed to her mistress's aid. Gently lifting pillow after pillow from Natira's lounge, she fluffed them and replaced them carefully for her comfort.

"Enough, enough!" Natira sighed, motioning the girl away.

Every corner of the room was occupied by a servant. And there were several corners, as the room had many alcoves and arches. Most of the servants were young men, of various races, all bearing the brand upon their necks.

Joseph wondered about them, how they had come to be slaves and whether they were as uneasy in Natira's presence as he was.

When Phineas had learned that Joseph would serve the mistress this evening, he had been unusually quiet. But just as the youngster had left for the duty, the baker had taken him aside. Looking up into Joseph's face, he had whispered, "Be careful, my son."

"Phineas speaks highly of you," Natira said, as Joseph

held forth her napkin. Taking the linen, she gazed into his face and smiled.

Surprised that the subject was in context with his own thoughts, he nodded.

"I have never had a Hebrew slave," she went on. "They are a wild race, are they not? Lovers of freedom."

Across Joseph's mind flashed the desert and the mountains of Palestine, and something like anger filled his heart.

"They are, Madam," he replied.

Straightening, he eyed her with cool detachment.

"Well," she offered, "I am sure that in time you will come to like it here."

With this, she reached out a solicitous hand and stroked his wrist. "There are advantages to being my slave," she purred.

Joseph recoiled.

Silence filled the chamber as the servants looked on.

"If Madam is finished with me, Phineas needs me in the kitchen," he managed.

Natira's face reddened, and her eyes flashed.

"Certainly," she said, dismissing him with a growl. "No one needs you here."

* * *

Shaking, Joseph stood in the shadows outside Natira's door. Moonlight beckoned from a balcony at the end of the hall, and seeing that no one was there, the Hebrew headed for it.

His heart drumming, he steadied himself against the balcony rail and surveyed the sprawling luxury of the acropolis. So grand a neighborhood was nowhere else on earth, but Joseph despised the streets and the walls, yearning for the wilderness of the nomads.

For a long while he stood there, taking in the music of the distant court as it wound through the mansion's twisting corridors. But he longed for the pipes and lutes of his tribal musicians and for the sight of wild-haired Israelite girls twirling and spinning in long, vivid skirts.

Joseph ran a hand over his bare head, shame coloring his face. Whenever his black hair had shown signs of growth, Tophet had seen to it that he was freshly shaven. He feared he would never again feel the comfort of curls against his neck or the warmth of his raven beard upon his cheeks.

As he brooded in solitude, the music of the court was joined by the distant laughter of women. Bracing himself, he cocked his head and listened. It seemed to be coming his way, growing louder and echoing down the hall.

Some group of females approached, and he had nowhere to run. Were he to exit through the corridor he would have to pass directly by them, and he would have to account for his presence here.

Pressing himself against the wall, he hoped the women would turn into some chamber down the way.

But he would not be so fortunate. Within moments they were entering the balcony, gathering along the rail and admiring the view.

At first no one saw Joseph. But he would not elude them for long.

"See here, what's this?" someone cried. "A man on the women's veranda!"

"Asenath, Asenath!" another called. "It is your mother's slave!"

Joseph took a sharp breath. Parting the company and standing before him was the lady of his dreams, daughter of his mistress, forbidden child of his master.

Wide-eyed, she studied him. "Leave us," she said, turning to her friends. "Let me question him."

The women, Asenath's favorite companions, obediently complied. But not without question. Shaking their heads and whispering together, they recalled the

Hebrew's insolent behavior the night of Natira's banquet, and they eyed him with suspicion.

When they had departed, Asenath tried to be firm. "You should not be here," she asserted.

"I know, my lady," Joseph managed, his throat dry.

"This place is off limits to men."

"I understand that, now," he replied. "It will not happen again."

Bowing, he backed toward the arch, ready to be sent from her presence. But she would not release him so quickly.

"How do you happen to be here?" she inquired.

Slaves were not often encouraged to explain themselves. Lifting his eyes, he found her expression warm, as it had been this afternoon in the market.

"I... I was summoned to serve your mother," he said.

Asenath stiffened. "I see," she replied. "And have you fulfilled your duty?"

Joseph shuffled awkwardly. "I have my lady." Asenath's face reddened, and Joseph wondered what she thought.

"I brought the mistress her meal, and I departed," he said. "I fulfilled my duty."

This seemed to relieve her. "Very well," she sighed. "Then you should return to the kitchen."

Bowing again, Joseph was about to comply, when the girl stopped him once more.

"Do you like the view from our balcony?" she asked, smiling a little.

The slave did not readily answer, and Asenath marveled. "Surely you have never seen any place more beautiful!"

"There are places more to my liking," he dared.

The girl drew back. "You? A Hebrew?" she laughed. "Whatever could you have seen to equal our city?"

Joseph took a risk in challenging her. But he cared not for his present well-being. Mountains and hills called him, and he would as soon die as be removed forever from them.

"I have seen places without walls," he answered, "places where the wind is the very breath of God. I have heard the desert sing and have possessed the stars at night. My Lady, you should be so wealthy as to own what I have owned."

27

Joseph waited along the back wall of On's most sacred chamber, the inner sanctum of the Temple of Ra. He, as well as all the other slaves of Potiphera's house, must be present at the reception of Pharaoh, which would take place here within moments.

Every year, Phineas had explained, King Timaeus came to this room, directly upon arriving in On. Here he would receive the blessing of the high priest and be ordained for yet another twelve months as ruler of the realm.

Of all the shames heaped upon the son of Jacob, this experience brought him lowest. For one who carried Jehovah in his heart, to witness the rites of pagan worship was unthinkable.

The stone walls of the chamber were cold to his back. His bare head, likewise, was cold, and he rubbed his hands together behind him.

Tall temple slaves with long slender beards, the only slaves allowed to go unshaven, stepped through the door at the back of the hall. In their hands they carried elegant tapers, the tips flickering with flame. Toward the platform at the front of the room they marched, followed close by beardless eunuchs in white robes. These eunuchs pounded small hand drums and rattled tambourines in cadence with the candlebearers' step.

Earlier in the day a grand parade, replete with flashing chariots, stamping stallions, and dancing girls, had brought Pharaoh into town. This evening's processional was shorter and simpler, in keeping with its hallowed purpose. On the heels of the eunuchs were more slaves, these bearing trumpets and heralding the entrance of the king.

When Joseph saw Timaeus, a chill passed through him. A giant of a man, his stature suited his position as emperor of the world. A broad, striped headdress fell to broader shoulders, and the sun-disk glistened on his bare torso.

His face, cold as iron, revealed a merciless heart, and he had apparently well-earned his reputation as a ruthless, unrelenting ruler.

Ceremoniously he walked toward the platform, flanked on each side by attendants. Normally Pharaoh would have been carried on slaves' shoulders, in a handsome cab borne atop horizontal poles. But in the Temple of Ra, he walked like any commoner.

The king looked straight ahead, not allowing his eyes to wander from the altar at the center of the platform. As he approached, Potiphera emerged from a curtained alcove.

Rarely since coming to dwell here had Joseph seen Potiphera. As he observed him now, he saw the same quiet dignity, the same kindness that had reached out to save him in the marketplace.

The ordination ceremony would be brief. To the rhythm of the soft drums, Pharaoh bowed before his priest. And the slaves with the long candles lit a fire upon the altar.

Holding forth a golden chalice, Potiphera poured the blood of some freshly slain beast through the flames, and it sent an acrid smoke toward the ceiling.

Countless times Joseph had watched as his own father performed a similar rite on the wilderness altars of his tribe. But as he had done so, he had sung hymns to Jehovah. Today, Potiphera invoked the blessings of Ra upon the king, chanting a theogony in ancient Egyptian.

Though Joseph could not understand the words, he was repelled by them.

He might have witnessed all this with less resentment, however, had Asenath not entered on the scene.

Apparently taking a cue from her father's words, she emerged from the same alcove and joined the priest on stage.

Speaking now in common Egyptian, the priest introduced her as the goddess of wisdom, "daughter of Nath," and holder of the secrets of life.

The young Hebrew was appalled at her appearance. Though she was still lovely and innocent of face, she was garbed in gaudy gold from head to toe, and her fluid gown was embellished with pagan emblems. Her eyes, painted darker than usual, held fast to the king, and as she stepped forth, she placed her hands upon his head.

Wisdom was to be the hallmark of a Pharaoh—for Pharaoh was the god of light incarnate.

Thus, in symbolic ceremony, he and the goddess were joined, light and wisdom energizing one another.

The ritual complete, Timaeus was asked to stand, and the procession led him forth to a new year of power.

As Joseph watched the king pass by, he wondered how he—an enslaver of men, a worshiper of false gods—could be considered wise.

And he wondered if gentle Asenath were beyond redemption.

28

Pharaoh and his entourage had been vacationing at Potiphera's mansion for two months. With their stay, Joseph's responsibilities had expanded.

Phineas's assessment of Joseph's abilities, his assumption that as prince of a Hebrew tribe the youngster was highly capable, was not unfounded. And though Tophet, the chief butler, had resisted his swift advancement, even he had come to admit that Joseph was an asset to the workroom.

Gradually Joseph was called upon to oversee the tasks of slaves and servants who had worked for Potiphera for years. Already he served as the baker's chief buyer, as first assistant at all banquets, and as manager of Tophet's waiters.

One of the privileges of the Hebrew's increased authority was that it brought him into more frequent contact with Potiphera. Although he had been purchased for Natira, he was, from time to time, called upon to run personal errands for the high priest or to make purchases directly related to his chamber. As their daily interaction developed, he sensed that the high priest enjoyed his company.

This evening he accompanied Tophet to serve at a select gathering of Pharaoh's officials. Often, when Timaeus was present in On, the chief butler served as royal cupbearer, and he must focus full attention on the task of keeping the king's cup filled. Therefore, he must pass his regular duties as governor of the dinner to another. It was Joseph who would fill that capacity this day.

Although servants and slaves were supposed to be deaf to the conversations of their masters during such engagements, the gossip of the court always fell readily on their ears. Tonight Pharaoh and Potiphera, along with all their aides, discussed economic matters, and Joseph listened with ardent interest as he oversaw the smooth running of the meal.

It seemed a minor famine in Goshen had produced a setback in the wheat crop, and Pharaoh and those around him collaborated on the matter of making up for the dearth with imports.

They could not agree upon where to find the cheapest prices. And Joseph itched to share an opinion.

They considered Gilead, where gentle rains and winds produced the finest crops. But the cost of Gilead wheat could be prohibitive. They wondered about Phoenicia, but while the seafoods from that land were excellent, the farm produce was never of the highest quality.

At last Joseph could restrain himself no longer.

"Shechem," he muttered.

Potiphera, attuned to Joseph's voice, asked him to speak up.

"Shechem wheat will be fine this spring," Joseph offered.

"Do tell," the priest marveled. "How do you know this?"

The advisers whispered around the table, wondering at the slave's boldness and at Potiphera's indulgence.

"Winter was hard in the Vale of Shalem last year," he explained, recalling his days of miserable wandering in quest of his brothers. "The seeds that manage to survive in the ground will come up hardy and rich in that part of Palestine."

Timaeus leaned over, conferring with Potiphera, and as he did, one of his advisers smirked. "Palestine was hit hard from border to border that season. What is so special about Shechem?"

Joseph did not remind them that the little city had been burned to the ground a few years before. Nor would he reveal the part his own family had played in that devastation.

"The economy of the vale is very poor." he simply said. "The locals would settle for a bargain price."

The counselors looked at one another in amazement, but the first challenger was still not convinced.

"The lad is Hebrew," Potiphera reminded them. "He speaks of things he knows."

"Very well, sir," the adviser conceded. "Then perhaps the Hebrew can shed light on the matter of the wool we imported last year. Did it not come from heather-fed sheep along his country's coast? It was some of the poorest we have received."

"Do not go to the coast for your wool," Joseph responded. "You will receive a good price, but only because the seacoast is not shepherd country. Rather, go east, even east of my people. The region of Zoar has ash in the soil, and the grass is as lush as a Lebanon forest. The sheep there grow fat and their coats are like blankets. You will pay more, but you will not regret it."

The men were dumbfounded, never having considered the plain where Sodom and Gomorrah once stood to be worth much of anything.

"Also, sirs," Joseph went on, his voice picking up courage, "you will find a treasure in the sands of that region. Dig down and there are carpets of green glass, glass superior to anything the Phoenicians produce, hidden to all but the bedouins who know the source."

Pharaoh was quizzical. "Indeed," he laughed. "And what is the source?"

"The God of my people destroyed the cities of the plain years ago," the youngster said matter-of-factly. "He destroyed them with brimstone, which accounts for the ash in the ground. And he destroyed them with unearthly fire, which melted the very sands of the wilderness."

At this, the company hooted. "Just who is this god of whom you speak?" Timaeus sneered, pressing him like an offended deity.

"My God is the God of the desert and the sea, the winds and the cities. He is God over all the earth, though its people do not remember him."

Potiphera, stunned by the lad's daring, gripped the arms of his chair. When Pharaoh started angrily, he reached out a hand to console him.

"Let the lad speak," he counseled. "Surely Your Majesty is not troubled by the ravings of a shepherd boy."

The king, confounded, kept a seething silence. But the ministers were not appeased.

Jeering, they challenged him again. "What other advice does this upstart have?" they mocked. "Perhaps he can save the land of Egypt!"

Joseph knew they referred to more than economics. Had he been careless of his life, he would have counseled them, then and there, to evict their emperor and bring in the Hyksos.

"If you are purchasing your horses from the Midianites, you could do better," he suggested, trying to be respectful.

Again, they laughed. "We have *always* purchased our mounts from the Arabs! The whole world knows they are the finest stock on earth!"

"Not so fine as the horses of the Edomites," Joseph offered, remembering Esau's beautiful herds. "The horses of Jordan are bred on wind and wild wheat. They are restive, but tamable. And when they obey the rein, they are the gentlest creatures under heaven."

A hush filled the chamber as the young Hebrew shared his knowledge on yet other topics.

Tophet, who stood at Pharaoh's elbow, was incredulous.

What manner of fellow was this who had come to serve in his kitchen? He feared, now, for his own position. And with good reason.

In time, should the youngster's advice prove worthy, he could take over management of the entire house.

PART IV
The Accused

29

Potiphera walked with Joseph through the grain fields beyond the wall of On. The property, which belonged to the high priest, had not yielded as well as he wished for several years, and he watched today with his Hebrew slave as his farmers tilled ash into the soil.

This practice was new to the priest, and he tried it as an experiment at Joseph's suggestion.

Potiphera's face glowed with anticipation as he dreamed of the crops he might harvest in the fall.

Joseph had served Potiphera four years, working for him now as much as for Natira. Every idea he had shared with Potiphera and his advisers had borne fruit. The purchase of Shechem wheat had been a boon to Egypt's economy and had seen it through a hard year. The wool of Zoar was exceptionally fine, just as the Hebrew had said. And Pharaoh had begun to outfit his stables with the horses of Edom.

This last suggestion Joseph had made with secret motive, knowing that as Esau prospered, so would his brother Jacob. For the two tribes were interdependent, and what good befell one was sure to bear on the good of the other.

Joseph had never told Potiphera about his family. He still spoke of himself as a Hebrew, with no reference to his tribe. And respecting his privacy, his master had never pressed him.

As they passed this day through the grain fields, Potiphera placed an arm about Joseph's shoulders. "You have been a blessing to me," the priest said. "Have I ever told you so?"

"Many times, sir," Joseph replied with a smile.

For a quiet moment, Potiphera was deep in thought. "Almost would I think you the son I never had," he confessed. "It seems everything I place in your hand prospers."

Joseph was flattered, but his heart was pricked with memories of his true father, Jacob, and of the sonship he had with him.

"It is truly amazing how successful you are," Potiphera continued. "Sometimes I believe this god of yours must be as great as the Sun."

The Hebrew knew the priest was being facetious, but he took his comment seriously.

"With all respect, sir, my God is greater. He made the sun and all the stars."

With this, Joseph privately recalled the vision he had had the night of his bar mitzvah, the waking dream of the humbled stars, the bowing sun and moon. Longing and sadness, which he had managed to suppress with his busy schedule, rose up from a dark place within.

But his master did not read his feelings.

"I should be angry with you when you speak so," Potiphera sighed. "But so long as your beliefs do not interfere with your work, I cannot be."

Such was the liberality of the Egyptian religious system, a system which accepted all worship and had, in fact, made all creatures sacred. Joseph might have admired the priest's indulgence, but knew it was based on a loose theology.

"What I really wish to address is your future with me," the master explained. "Do you see all this?" he said, gesturing to the fields which stretched for miles in every direction. "All of this I place within your keeping, along with my whole house. As of this day, you shall be my chief steward, overseeing all my affairs so that I may devote myself to study and contemplation, which is my rightful duty. No one shall be over you in my house, and everyone who serves me shall serve you. Are you pleased?"

Was he pleased? Joseph stared at Potiphera as though he were not real, as though the words he had just spoken could not be part of any language.

"Master!" he marveled. "How can this be? I am but a slave, a thing of purchase..."

"Stop, Joseph!" Potiphera commanded. "Never speak so of yourself. From this day, you are no longer my slave, but my chief overseer."

They had come to the highway which ran through the fields. Potiphera's carriage awaited them, and taking their seats inside, they headed for the acropolis.

The young Hebrew's head still spun with the announcement as they approached the gate of Potiphera's mansion.

"See here?" the priest added, indicating the gracious residence and its many outbuildings. "All of this is in your hands. Nothing you ask shall be withheld from you."

Suddenly, however, the man's eyes were caught away to the sight of his wife, who was sitting upon her balcony high above. Her hairdresser brushed her dark hair in the afternoon sun, making it shine like polished onyx.

"Nothing shall be withheld from you," he repeated, "save Natira."

Joseph could scarcely believe his ears. That the master could even consider the possibility of such betrayal was appalling.

But the Hebrew said nothing, noting the man's love-struck gaze as he observed the mistress.

"She is my life, Joseph," he whispered. "My very life."

30

Nearly seven more years had passed in gratifying peace as Joseph fulfilled his service to Potiphera. The high priest's prosperity doubled under the Hebrew's administration, and everyone came to view Joseph as chief overseer of the house.

Even Tophet bowed to the Hebrew, although his resentments were never mollified.

Early on Potiphera had encouraged Joseph to let his hair and beard grow. "Wear them in the manner of an Egyptian," he suggested, "but do not shave them again."

In robes of wealth was Joseph attired, his luxurious beard crimped stylishly and his dark locks loosely fettered by laces of pure gold. His garments, though never as much to his liking as the long-lost coat which his father had given him, were of the finest linen, edged in lavender, his master's color.

Tonight a sweet breeze off the river of On wafted through the mansion's rooftop garden. Joseph never ceased to remember the wilderness of Israel and the freedom of his nomad existence. But he always found a measure of solace in the quiet bowers of this place.

Across the parapet that enclosed the roof was a magnificent view to the north, and often in private meditation the Hebrew would study the distant desert, dreaming of the day when he might return to his father's people.

He was a free man now, not a slave. He could demand

his right to leave the country. But he had come to love Potiphera and to believe his service here was of value.

Furthermore, he sensed that the timing was not right for his departure, that if his God planned for him to go home, it was not to be just yet.

His father surely thought him long dead. His brothers likely wished to believe so themselves, and had never told Jacob of their cruelty toward him.

Whatever the case with his family, every time he thought to return, something restrained him.

Tonight, the week before his seventh anniversary as Potiphera's steward, he contemplated upcoming events. The high priest had planned a great banquet in his honor and had told him to consider his future well. For he would be giving him a reward, and Joseph must be prepared to ask whatever he wished of his master.

Years ago, when the priest had first told him of his new position, he had said he would withhold nothing from Joseph. All that he had was at the Hebrew's disposal, save Natira.

There really was nothing he lacked, Joseph thought as he pondered the offer, nothing but the fellowship of close kin. He knew not what to request and was concerned lest he disappoint his generous lord.

As Joseph studied the sunset desert, a light footfall roused him from his thoughts. Turning about, he saw that Asenath had entered the garden. After all these years, the sight of her still never failed to stir his heart.

Always he had steeled himself against his feelings for the young lady. Yet as he had become an intimate part of the priest's household, he had found himself falling more and more in love with her.

Though they were rarely alone, their few private conversations were always rich with wonder and sharing.

Asenath was no longer a girl. Tonight, more than ever, Joseph could see this. Tall and willowy, she had reached full-flowered womanhood, her arms soft and supple beneath her shawl, her breasts high and round beneath her clinging gown. Yet never had she married, unwilling to settle for any of her many courtiers.

However, her face always seemed to light when she saw Joseph, and her voice was laced with music.

Such was the case just now as she discovered his vigil in the garden.

"Joseph," she called, hurrying toward him through the twilight. "I thought I might find you here."

Joining him at the railing, she laughed gaily. "Father says there will be a dinner in your honor next week. How proud you must be!"

The Hebrew smiled down upon her. "Your father is very kind."

"It is not kindness!" Asenath objected. "It is duty. No one deserves recognition more than you. Father would be remiss to overlook your loyal service."

Bowing, Joseph conceded. "Never has he overlooked me, my lady. But I am pleased that you are pleased."

Asenath quietly followed his gaze as he turned again to the rail. The northern folds of wilderness, as it stretched toward the great unseen sea, were purple and gold.

"Father will have you say a few words that evening, to all the company. Will you speak of your God?"

Surprised at the introduction of this topic, Joseph considered the idea. "If it is appropriate," he said. "Why do you ask?"

"You speak of him often. Many here would like to know more about him."

Joseph read a peculiar longing in her tone, a longing that had manifested itself many times.

"Are you among them?" he asked, trying not to show his eager hope.

"I was taught by my father to represent wisdom," she said. Nervously she ran a slender finger along the marble balustrade. "I have studied beside him in the libraries of

On, and I was raised on prayers to the goddess of understanding."

Joseph listened with respect. "There is much to know about divine things," he agreed. "But there is no god or goddess who can teach you. Only the One True God, the Maker of all, is capable of that."

Asenath could have been offended. But to his amazement, she was not. Gently she touched his sleeve, sending a charge of sweet energy through him.

"What is the name of this God?" she inquired. "You have never told me."

Joseph sighed, shaking his head. "I do not know," he confessed. "We call him 'Jehovah,' 'the Lord.' But to my knowledge, there is no man or woman on earth who has heard his name."

He knew this seemed very strange and might make his testimony implausible.

"I only know that my father, grandfather and great-grandfather—and I myself—have encountered him," he went on. "He is a mover of the heart. And he is moving yours just now. Is he not, Asenath?"

The woman was captivated by his witness. Unable to deny her longings, she nodded.

Bending over her, Joseph steadfastly studied her face. He knew now what he would ask of his master, what his request would be.

This woman was a kindred spirit, and he longed to make her his own.

With a daring borne of unfettered love, he caressed her bare shoulder, and she, yielding, entered his embrace.

For the first time in Joseph's life, he felt the ache of passion, and pressing his lips to hers, he dreamed of its fulfillment.

31

There was only one drawback to the Hebrew's privileged station in the house of Potiphera. His elevated position brought him into daily contact with Natira.

Though she had not touched him since the long-ago evening when she had called him to serve dinner in her chamber, her attraction to him had never been veiled. Often she had let him know, by innuendo and direct statement, that she desired his company.

Generally, however, Joseph's spirits were high as he went about his work.

Especially this day was his heart merry, as he anticipated the banquet and his planned request for Asenath's hand in marriage. The kiss they had shared the evening before told him the lady was willing, but he must first secure the approval of her father.

When Phineas knocked on the door of his office, where Joseph was tabulating stacks of accounting tablets, the baker's crestfallen face clashed with the Hebrew's joyful mood.

"What is it, friend?" he asked. "This is too grand a day for unhappiness."

"Indeed, it should be, Master," Phineas agreed, calling him by his rightful title. "I hope my news means no trouble for you."

"What could trouble me today?" he laughed. "It is a bright future which spreads before us. Yes, Phineas, I plan not only to ask my own reward at the banquet, but to request honors for you and Tophet as well."

"You are too kind," the baker said, bowing. But his brow was still furrowed. "It seems that Potiphera is not the only one dispensing awards. Our lady, Natira, requests your company in her chamber, that she may... honor you, as well."

Joseph rolled his eyes, something he would have done in no one else's presence. "Well," he sighed, placing the accounting tablets in a neat pile, "what is the worst that can happen? It is only an inconvenience."

Phineas tried to agree. "Of course, sir," he said through a strained smile. "But do be careful."

* * *

Joseph had never grown accustomed to seeing Natira reclined upon her couch. She was gifted at it, like a lounging snake upon a limb.

He had learned how to handle her advances, her seductive smiles and suggestive comments. As long as she did not touch him, he could work around her, ignoring her beguiling devices and deflecting her attempts with kind detachment.

Today, however, Natira was at her best, her vampish skills finely honed, her beauty most insistent. And when he entered her room, he cringed. For they were alone.

Not one slave, valet, or chambermaid occupied her chamber. Every station was vacant where an attendant usually stood. Every alcove was silent.

Perhaps Natira presumed that since the subtler approach had never worked, straightforward eagerness would. Her intentions had never been so blatant.

"Sit with me," she hissed, moving over on her bed and patting the mattress. "You are an honored servant. Let me reward you."

Joseph's cheeks colored. "Surely Madam has some service... something I may do for her..." he stammered.

This only evoked a gleaming smile and Joseph reconsidered.

"May I fetch something..." he choked.

"You fear Potiphera," she cooed. "The master is away. He will not be back until evening. Here," she beckoned, pulling her legs toward the back of the couch, "lie with me."

Joseph's face burned. But he maintained his dignity.

"Madam," he argued, "Potiphera is my friend as well as my master. With me in charge, my master does not concern himself with anything in the house, and he has put all that he owns in my hands. There is no one greater in this house than I, and he has withheld nothing from me except you, because you are his wife. How then could I do this great evil and sin against God?"

With this, he clenched his fists and headed for the door. His heart pounding, he hastened toward the safety of the busy household.

Never would he tell a soul of Natira's plot. And never again would he go near her chamber alone.

32

Only two days remained before the banquet. Although the event was in honor of Joseph, it required much extra work on his part.

As overseer of the house, preparation for any such affair demanded his attention.

Since morning, he had been in every corner of the mansion, seeing to it that the chambermaids had made up the guest rooms and that all things were in order for the meal and the entertainment.

Though Pharaoh was not due for his annual vacation in On, he would be coming early from Memphis for the feast. His arrival alone had required days of planning.

All this busy work helped to take Joseph's mind off the encounter with Natira. And it helped him avoid being near her.

The few times they passed in the hallway or were obliged to consult together, he was in company, and she must settle for giving him cutting looks instead of words.

He hoped there would be no further incident before the banquet. Once Potiphera promised Asenath's hand in marriage, Natira would surely keep her distance.

The day was exceptionally hot for early spring. Joseph had just seen to the unloading of supplies in the gate outside and hastened now to other work in the main portion of the house.

Potiphera and his officials were in a cabinet meeting this afternoon. The baker and butler were with the women servants in the kitchen wing, and the menservants were working in the fields.

The house was very quiet, a relief to Joseph's overtaxed mind. As he passed down the empty corridor leading toward his office, he halted at the sound of his name.

It was more a lisp than a real word—more an evocative challenge than a name.

Wheeling about, he saw the woman in the shadows, her chest rising and falling as though her pulse pounded madly.

Against her breast she held a long-legged cat, one of the family pets, and she stroked its dense ebony fur as though she were herself feline.

"Joseph," she purred again.

Natira was fingering the slack at the neck of her gown. Gently she lowered the cat to the floor and pulled the silky fabric of her dress downward, revealing the cleft of her bosom.

Dumbfounded, Joseph tried to inch past her so he might head back outside.

Then he felt it. Her touch. Her grasping hands upon his garment.

"Lie with me!" she commanded.

"Lord Jehovah!" he cried, tearing free and rushing blindly for the door.

In Natira's clutches he left his cloak, ripped from his shoulders as he fled.

And as he hastened outside, he heard her cries, her hateful revenge.

"Rape! Rape!" shrieked the scorned Natira. "Oh, help me! Guards!"

33

In a swoon-like sleep Joseph dreamed he was in the wilderness cistern, cast off by his brothers and left to die. No sun pounded down upon him, but life seeped from him like the sweat of a fever.

In his torment, his dreaming eyes scanned the cistern's lip, longing to see the old shepherd. The sight of him might inspire hope, but he was nowhere to be found.

Across the desert, the sound of caravans approached, and he relived the fear of capture. Jolting awake, he found that the rumbling was not of wagon wheels, but the tramping of feet, guards outside his prison cell.

Straightening his cramped body, he leaned against the mossy wall of Potiphera's dungeon, and he winced at the pain in his shackled ankles.

As the guards passed his door, he called out to them. "Send for Master Potiphera!" he cried. "Surely he will hear my defense. Send for Phineas. He will vouch for my character!"

But no one heeded his plea. "So the chief Hebrew has come to this!" the guards mocked, reveling in his overthrow. "You would be better off a sandflea once again!"

Voluptuous Natira filled Joseph's head, her steamy smile and slick accusation stripping him of hope. He knew she must have spun a convincing lie, one which could lock him away forever.

He could imagine it now. She would have waved his cloak like a banner. "See here," she must have said, "he left his garment in my hand as he fled. Is this not proof that he tried to take me? Is it not proof that I struggled against him?"

And he could imagine his dear master, disillusioned, heartsick, filled with wrath at the supposed betrayal.

Huddling against the cold floor, he fought tears. Tomorrow there would be a banquet in the mansion, the banquet which should have been his own. With Pharaoh and a host of guests due to arrive, it was too late for the affair to be canceled.

And so Potiphera would find other reasons to make merry. Light and laughter would fill the dining hall while Joseph sat in lonely darkness, the vacuum of despair his only cellmate.

The Hebrew would be asked after. Guests would wonder why he was not there, and when they heard Natira's tale, they would hate him as though eleven years of faithful service were not evidence of his character.

Better would it be to die, he believed, than to dwell in this netherland of outcasts. Better would it be if he had never been taught that Jehovah cared.

For faith had departed, and perpetual night was Joseph's lot.

* * *

When the evening of Joseph's feast arrived, Tophet fretfully bustled about the kitchen, trying to do two jobs at once.

He was, as usual, governor of the dining hall. But tonight he was also filling Phineas's shoes, managing the mundane tasks of the workroom.

Exasperated, he glanced toward a corner of the pantry. Phineas was slumped upon a chair, a wine bottle in his hand.

When Tophet had found him in this drunken state, it had been time to prepare the main course. Propping him in the storeroom, he had left him there and told the servants to start cooking without him.

Now, however, Phineas was becoming rowdy, calling attention to himself with loud talk.

"We must keep him quiet!" the butler growled, grabbing the bottle from his hand. "Brew up the strongest tea you can find!"

As guests began to file into the dining room, servant after servant attempted to force the potent liquid down the baker's throat. But all efforts to sober him up were of no avail.

Tophet should have resigned any hope of having his coworker's help tonight. He should have sent him to his room as soon as he began to rave.

For Phineas was beyond self-pity, beyond quiet slobber. He was beyond calling out for Joseph and blaming himself for not warning him more strongly.

Phineas was becoming belligerent, his slurred words growing in volume. As they reached past the kitchen walls, they put Tophet and his entire crew in danger.

"Potiphera is a fool!" he ranted. "Natira is a whore! Pharaoh is a king of whores and fools!"

Suddenly the merrymaking in the banquet hall tapered to shocked silence. Potiphera rose up on his dinner couch, clutching at his napkin. Darting a startled glance at Pharaoh, he saw that his own neck was at stake and instantly sent to see who was responsible for the insults.

When word returned that the baker was drunk, Potiphera called for his dismissal. As guards were sent for Phineas, his raving continued to spill forth from the workroom.

"Tophet is the baker's overseer, is he not?" Timaeus recalled, his face livid.

"He is," Potiphera stammered.

"They must *both* be dismissed!" the king shouted. "Both of them to the darkest cell of your prison!"

34

A flash of torchlight filled Joseph's cell, waking him from fitful slumber. The scuffle of feet and the creaking of hinges told him someone was being thrust through the door.

The light revealed several men, two guards and two captives. As the Hebrew's eyes adjusted, he recognized Tophet and Phineas.

Scrambling to his feet, he watched in amazement as the door was slammed in the butler's face. Tophet clung to the bars of the door's small window, shouting epithets at the departing guards, and Phineas hung his wine-soaked head in bewildered horror.

"You can't do this!" Tophet yelled. "I have always been loyal to Pharaoh! The most loyal servant in the house!"

He was answered by the sound of fading footsteps.

What little light filtered through the doorgrate revealed Joseph in the corner, and when Tophet wheeled about, finding him there, he snarled like a dog.

"This is what comes of giving a Hebrew authority!" he swore. "I never trusted you from the day you came here! Seducing our lady! Upsetting the entire house! It is a wonder Pharaoh did not have our necks!"

Of course, Joseph knew nothing of what had led to their incarceration. Seeking an explanation, he turned to Phineas, who still held his head and moaned.

"Have some respect, Tophet!" the baker managed. "You know Joseph is innocent!"

"And what of *you*? the butler growled. "It was your traitorous ranting that brought this fate upon us! You have always wanted Timaeus overthrown, haven't you! I almost suspect you would side with the Hyksos, given a chance!"

"Oh..." Phineas groaned, rubbing his throbbing temples. "Joseph, come to me. Let me see you."

"So, I have brought you with me, old friend," Joseph sighed, dragging his ankle chain and creeping toward him. Receiving his embrace, he gently chastised him. "You are too loyal to me, Phineas. See where it has gotten you."

But Phineas paid him no mind. "See here, Tophet! Chains upon our master's feet! Is there any doubt that he suffers unjustly? You know how Natira is!"

"Hush!" Tophet commanded. "Would you have us die?"

"Then you admit it! You know Natira is a..."

"Enough!" Tophet cried. "I know no such thing."

"Everyone knows it!" Phineas insisted. "Even Potiphera knows it in his heart!"

"There is *nothing* to know!" the butler choked. "Quiet, or you'll have us dead!"

"Aha! See, Joseph. He admits it. Why, there is no one in the house or in the entire city who wonders why Natira fills her chamber with young men. No one..."

At this, Tophet leapt across the room, grappling Phineas to the floor and throttling him.

Despite his restraints, Joseph managed to intervene and, holding the men apart, shouted, "Indeed you will both die if you are not careful. You will kill *one another*!"

The two wrestlers took heed, and as silence descended, each went to his corner.

Joseph, shaking his head, found his own cold station and closed his eyes, wondering at the insanity of his world.

* * *

The high priest's prison was not a quiet place. In the two weeks he had been held here, Joseph had become accustomed to the constant comings and goings of the place.

As high priest, Potiphera was also "captain of the royal bodyguard." This was not a military title, but a diplomatic and religious one, meaning that as minister of the sun god it followed that he was responsible for Pharaoh's welfare. Since Pharaoh was believed to be Ra in the flesh, the incarnate revelation of the divine, Potiphera was in charge of protecting him from danger.

Joseph's supposed crime was against the high priest's house, and Tophet and Phineas were considered political prisoners. Apparently the dungeons were full of such unfortunates, many accused as unjustly as these three.

Rarely did Potiphera set foot in the prison. Joseph had asked to see him many times, wishing to give his version of what had happened in Natira's room. But he knew the high priest would never receive his testimony, being blindly devoted to his vampish wife.

Day and night there was traffic outside Joseph's cell.

Pharaoh was a fickle tyrant, judging with little reference to evidence. Men and women could be locked away on the most trivial witness, or could be released on his whim.

Therefore, when Joseph heard the approaching tramp of guards, he paid it no mind. When it stopped before his door, however, and when he heard a woman's voice, he sat up and listened.

A torch was held close to the door grate, near enough to reveal the identity of a visitor, and the Hebrew's breath came sharply.

Asenath's pensive face peered through the opening, and urgently she called his name. Crossing the room, he grasped the bars, Tophet and Phineas close behind.

"My lady," Joseph cried, "what brings you to this awful place?"

"I implored my father to let me come," she said, "to deliver this to you."

Through the bars she passed a sealed letter, its parchment fine as linen. "It was the best he could bring himself to do," she added, as Joseph hastily opened the paper.

Reading the contents, his eyes widened. "What is this?" he gasped. "Potiphera is placing me in charge of the prison!"

"There is trouble in the streets," Asenath explained. "Threats of a Hyksos revolution. Father will need all the help he can get to manage this place."

Phineas clutched at Joseph's cloak. "Hyksos!" he whispered.

"In other words, Timaeus will institute a purge," Joseph guessed, his brow furrowed. "The prison will be more crowded than ever."

"It was the best my father could do," Asenath repeated.

When Joseph looked at her quizzically, she added, "The best he could do to make restitution."

"Restitution?" Joseph enthused. "Then he believes me!"

"Father was very angry," Asenath went on, "but he knows in his heart..."

She could not bring herself to accuse her mother aloud, but Phineas nudged Tophet triumphantly.

"Oh, Joseph," she asserted, "Father has not been himself since he sent you here. He has not slept or eaten. But when he learned that mother had blamed him for her 'shame,' he began to see that he had done you wrong."

"How could Natira blame Potiphera?" the Hebrew marveled.

"She told everyone that he had purposely brought you into our home to make fools of us, to make sport of her. This he could not abide, and now for the first time Father questions my mother's... goodwill. Perhaps," she apologized, "if Father were not so proud... if he would not lose

Natira forever, he would clear your name entirely and set you free."

Joseph sighed and shook his head. "Do not fret," he said. "God is with me." Then hesitating, "But the prison will be full of Semites, people of the desert...my own kind! How can I be their master?"

Phineas, for the first time openly declaring himself, stepped in front of the Hebrew.

"Consider yourself their comforter," he said. "As keeper of the prison, you will have power to ease their lot."

35

Such a colorful lot of Semites as came to occupy Joseph's prison and his time, he had never before encountered.

The revolutionaries who were incarcerated during Pharaoh's purge were of many tribes and nations. They came with countless dialects and clothing styles, and Joseph, as manager of the dungeon, allowed them to be housed according to their backgrounds.

While such people were typically earthy and freedom loving, these folk were the most outspoken of their kind. Constantly they plotted and schemed escape. And while in his heart he supported their cause, Joseph would have found it hard to love them if they had not been Hebrews.

Surly and profane, they drove him to distraction. They had heard of Joseph and of the fate which had befallen him at Natira's hands. They sympathized with his plight, but could not forgive his attachment to Potiphera.

It mattered nothing to them that he told them the priest had once saved his life. They could imagine no good in an Egyptian official.

The only reasoning which seemed to reach through their prejudice was Joseph's belief that God had brought him here, and that the full reason for his captivity in Egypt had not yet been revealed.

Joseph did not make the mistake of telling them of his youthful visions. He had learned to never again broadcast the prophecies which had sustained him all these years.

Nor did he yield to the temptation to ask after news of his father or his brothers, who were doubtless well-known in the widest of Hebrew circles. For his family's sake, he continued to keep his identity a secret. But he reveled in the Hebrews' common faith in the One God, a strain of belief which ran through their heritage, passed down from many patriarchs.

It was his unspeakable sorrow to witness Pharaoh's brutalities against his friends. Nearly every day he must stand by as men and women were led forth to execution.

So far, Tophet and Phineas had been spared, most likely because Timaeus had forgotten their minor case. But if Phineas continued to proclaim his kinship with the Hebrews, he might be taken yet.

It was early morning. Joseph had just left the guard house, where Potiphera had provided him a modest apartment, and he felt the winter sun upon his face.

All night he had been awake, his stomach knotted and his nerves frayed as group after group of captives was led forth to slaughter.

Pharaoh was on a rampage, and Joseph was helpless against it.

Bowing his head, he hastened through the prison yard on his way to the dungeon. Above, suspended from high gallows, were the swaying bodies of the dead. Mouths agape, the corpses stared at him, accusing, mocking, as all about them black crows circled, pecking at their flesh.

Time after time Joseph had wondered if he were a traitor to his kind, a coward for not throwing himself in with them and meeting the executioner's noose. But whenever he thought to do so, something caught him, some word or impression, telling him that the prophecies must be fulfilled and that his calling lay further down the road.

And so his fellow Semites sometimes hated him just as the Egyptians had hated him, just as his own brothers had. And sometimes he hated himself.

His feet leaden, he walked down the dungeon corridor, ready to check up on his remaining prisoners. As he came near the hold of Tophet and Phineas, he heard low talking within, as deathly and somber as the ache in his own heart.

Working the key in the lock, he called out to them, and entering, found them more downcast than usual, huddled together upon their blanket pile.

"What is it, friends?" he asked. "Why are your faces so sad today?"

Phineas shook his head. "We have each had dreams this night, and they are very mysterious. So clear and yet so puzzling. We have no one to tell us what they could mean."

Tophet nodded, his brow crinkled.

"The interpretation of dreams belongs to God," Joseph said, suddenly intrigued. "Tell me, please, what you dreamed."

Tophet looked askance at the Hebrew, wondering why he should share his experience with an enemy. But at last he shrugged.

"In my dream, there was a vine in front of me, and on the vine were three branches," he said. "As it was budding, its blossoms came out, and it produced ripe grapes. Now Pharaoh's cup was in my hand, so I took the grapes and squeezed them into his cup, and put it into the king's hand."

Joseph was quiet for a long while, until Tophet laughed.

"See, Phineas. What does this man know?" he mocked.

But Joseph leaned forward. "This is the interpretation," he declared. "Within three more days Pharaoh will lift up your head and restore you to your office. And you will put his cup into his hand, just as you used to do when you were his cupbearer!"

A smile lit the Hebrew's face as he shared this, and the two prisoners studied him in amazement, impressed

almost as much by his authoritative confidence as by
what he had said.

"Just keep me in mind when it goes well with you,
friend," Joseph added. "Do me the kindness of mention-
ing me to Pharaoh, and get me out of this place."

Tophet, still speechless, only stared at him. And now
Joseph was pressing him, his hand upon his knee.

"I was kidnapped out of my own country," he asserted.
"I was sold into bondage and then falsely accused before
Pharaoh. Please remember me."

Tophet sat back against the wall. "First let's see what
becomes of your prophecy," he muttered.

But Phineas was greatly moved. "Sir," he begged,
"hear my dream as well. Perhaps it is equally happy. If I
am freed, you know I would never forget you!"

"Of course," Joseph agreed.

"In my dream I carried three baskets of white bread on
my head. In the top basket there were all sorts of baked
goods for Pharaoh, and the birds were eating them out of
the basket."

The baker's eyes were round, as he anxiously awaited
the good news.

But Joseph was silent longer this time, until Phineas
grew apprehensive.

"Sir..." he whispered. "Don't toy with me. Tell me I
shall go free..."

The younger Hebrew choked back tears, trying not to
show the dread which swelled through his spirit.

Crawling over to him, Phineas implored, "Master, not
to know is worse than all my imaginings. Do not spare
me!"

Joseph looked into the eyes of his beloved friend, and
studied the dear countenance which had always warmed
him.

"God be with you, Phineas," he replied, "it is not
happy news." Seeing that Phineas would bear no refusal,
he sighed. "This is the interpretation: The three baskets

are three days. Within three days Pharaoh will lift up your head...from off you. And will hang you upon a tree."

Joseph's face was flushed, and tears spilled down his cheeks. The baker, scarcely hearing him, at first chuckled.

But his master was not joking. As the reality of the pronouncement flooded over him, he could not doubt, as Tophet had. In his heart and spirit, which belonged to Jehovah, he sensed that his kinsman spoke the truth.

"And the birds...Master. What are they doing?"

"Phineas," Joseph groaned. "You do not want to know."

"Speak, Master. Not to know is worse than all my imaginings."

Phineas shivered under Joseph's scrutiny.

"Friend, you know the interpretation," the younger surmised. "You know that in dreams, flesh and bread are the same."

"Surely, Master, you cannot mean..."

Joseph said no more, longing to embrace him.

When he reached for him, however, Phineas drew back.

"Touch me not, Master!" the baker cried. "For I am a dead man! In three days shall the birds pick the skin from off my bones!"

Joseph wept with him, and presently Phineas was clutching at him, rocking to and fro. "It is so, is it not? Tell me, so that I will think no worse!"

"It is so, Phineas," the Hebrew conceded. "In three days...in three days..."

36

Upon the third day, Pharaoh Timaeus sat in his great chair, his elbows on his knees and his chin in his hands. Never had his counselors seen him so dejected, or so troubled.

Potiphera, who had been with him through the dreadful weeks since the revolution had begun, made helpless incantations to the gods for the health of the king and for the welfare of the nation. But by the sounds of the warfare in the streets, the Hyksos were gaining the upper hand.

It was Pharaoh's birthday and should have been a merry time in the mansion. But no one was celebrating. In fact, whenever any of the king's friends tried to do him a kindness, he scowled and sent them away.

The man who had replaced Tophet as the emperor's cupbearer kept a safe distance. Often he was called upon to fill the king's cup, for Pharaoh was drinking more than usual. But the new cupbearer had never pleased him.

"Draw the blinds!" the king shouted, sending the hapless fellow to the window. Doubtless Timaeus hoped to muffle the sounds of fighting and screaming in the boulevard. But the heavy draperies did not help, and the cupbearer met with further disapproval.

"Imbecile!" the king roared. "Potiphar," he called, using the priest's nickname, "where did you get this oaf?"

"He is one of your company, sir," the high priest reminded him. "He comes from the palace in Memphis."

Pharaoh did not like to be corrected, but Potiphera was his closest ally.

Softening, he looked through bleary eyes at the priest. "Who was that fellow who used to serve me here?" he wondered. "Fine fellow. Fine. Whatever became of him?"

Potiphera was concerned for the king's mind. Rising, he stepped behind his chair and began to massage the monarch's temples. As the emperor sank back, so that his head rested in his friend's hands, he drifted sleepily, wine and worry having taken too much toll.

"Do you not recall, My Lord?" the priest said. "He angered you, he and his chief baker."

Through a fog, the memory returned. And the king sighed, his vinegar breath filling the close space between himself and Potiphera.

"Potiphar..." he said affectionately, "I incarcerated the scoundrels, didn't I?"

"Indeed," the priest affirmed, sadly remembering his own harsh judgment against Joseph.

"Well, send for him," the king decided, his tongue heavy with drink. "I would have him serve me again."

"Then, it is fitting that we should have a feast, a birthday feast, after all!" the priest suggested, determined to cheer him.

"Very well," Timaeus nodded.

"And shall I call for the baker, too?" he hoped.

"Indeed, the baker, too." Pharaoh smiled. "Let the fool think he is being restored. And then," he said, carelessly flicking his hand as though to swat at a soulless fly, "when he is merry, behead him."

* * *

Joseph stood mute in the corridor of the prison house, clutching at the ache in his chest.

Down the hall were the departing shadows of Pharaoh's guards, as they led away Tophet and Phineas.

"Remember the Lord," he had said, as Phineas was taken from him.

The butler, blithe of spirit, had gladly followed the men who came for him. But the baker, knowing they lied when they said he would be set free, had said nothing, only clinging to Joseph in terror.

Now Joseph was alone, abandoned as in the cistern, wondering how Jehovah could allow this, wondering why Phineas, kindest man in Egypt, must die.

Like a tourniquet, sorrow wrapped itself around Joseph's throat, and desperately he gasped for air. Turning, he headed for the black cell where he had spent so many hours in Phineas's presence, and once there, he threw himself upon the blanket pile where the baker had often sat.

Like a little child, he wrapped the blankets about him and tried not to cry.

But the tears would not be restrained. Weeping, he remembered all of his loved ones, and a pall of loneliness swept over him.

It was in this condition that Asenath found him hours later. Hours of seeking and asking after him.

She knew he would be mourning, for she knew the baker was his friend. And when she at last discovered him in the cell, she entered over the objections of the guards, over the objections of Joseph himself.

Sitting on the floor beside him, she drew near and cradled his head upon her breast.

This was yet another cave of Peniel. But this time, Asenath was Joseph's angel.

PART V
The Savior

37

Another full year of fighting had made the streets of On used to blood, as well as the streets of Memphis and every other Egyptian city. Peace was but a memory as victory favored first one side and then the other.

At last the stalwart Semites with their wild spirit won out over the weaker city-dwellers, and a Hyksos king took the throne.

The new Pharaoh, whose name was Salatis, had radical ideas and youthful vigor. Honoring the religion of the people, he allowed Potiphera to keep his position, but monotheism gained a foothold, and the simpler faith of the desert grew in popularity.

At his palace in Memphis, Salatis retained the best of his predecessor's servants and sent the rest away. Among those he kept for himself was Tophet, who served as his cupbearer in the stateroom of the empire's capital.

The politics of this new Pharaoh were far more liberal than those of the Theban Pharaohs. Although the conservatives had fought long and hard to retain the old ways, the people quickly came to love their new king, and by the time he was ready to celebrate his first anniversary upon the throne, the past had been forgotten.

So too had Joseph been forgotten. Tophet, in his restored position, had never seen the advantage of speaking to the old Pharaoh about the Hebrew. Though he now knew that Joseph was a prophet, and that he was gifted with unusual powers, Tophet thought it in his own best interest to let him stay where he was.

Under the new administration, there was even less reason for the cupbearer to consider the Hebrew who had served so well in Potiphera's house. Likely a Semite Pharaoh would have jumped at the chance to free him, and soon he would have been Tophet's superior again. In time, the butler conveniently forgot he had ever known such a fellow.

Pharaoh Salatis's first anniversary had just come and gone. Tophet's duties as chief cupbearer and butler in the Memphis palace were quite similar to those he had managed in On. For days he had borne a mountain of responsibility.

This morning his schedule was freer, and he was light-hearted as he headed for Pharaoh's chamber, ready to serve morning tea. Humming to himself as he passed down the hall, he considered his lot one of the happiest on earth and himself one of the most fortunate of men. No small salary was his as the king's attendant. A spacious apartment had been provided, and he always dressed in the finest of clothes. If a bit of conscience ever pricked him, he was able to suppress it; and he rarely thought on the sadder times he had seen.

As he rounded the corner of the hall nearest the king's chamber, he was not surprised to hear the sound of many voices arising from the room.

Tophet was used to finding counselors and servants in Pharaoh's bedroom. Salatis was not a shy fellow and often received visitors while still propped on his pillows.

As his valets shaved and dressed him, he would discuss matters of state at hours when the heads of other nations would have preferred to sleep.

But the people gathered today in the chamber were unfamiliar to Tophet. Strange was their appearance— long-bearded fellows garbed in flowing gowns. Their garments were covered with occult symbols, and upon their wide belts were amulets of bone, hide, gold, and wood.

Though Tophet had never met these men, he recognized instantly that they must be the caste of magicians and seers who inhabited the capital's priestly monastery.

When he entered the room, they were consulting together, heads shaking, beards wagging. Tophet noted Pharaoh's frustrated expression as he listened to their reasonings.

As soon as Salatis addressed the butler, the crowd fell silent, studying him cautiously.

"It is all right, friends," Pharaoh said. "This is my cupbearer. Come, come, Tophet, do not be shy. Perhaps you can shed some light on this matter. Heaven knows you could do no worse than these 'wise men.' "

Surprised at the flattery, Tophet set down his tray and listened.

"I have had a dream," Salatis explained. "A troublesome one, indeed. And it seems no one in all this learned company has the interpretation." At this he leaned forward. "Tell me, Tophet, do you believe dreams have significance?"

The butler's mouth went dry. Uncomfortably he remembered his own dream and the marvelous interpretation which the imprisoned Hebrew had given.

"Sir . . . I do," he admitted.

"Very well!" Salatis enthused. Then gesturing dramatically to his embarrassed magi, he smirked, "So do they! But they stumble over the meaning of my vision. Help me, Tophet."

"Why, Your Majesty," the butler deferred, feigning humility, "who am I that I should overstep these powerful men? I surely am no seer."

At this Pharaoh began to laugh, hilariously holding his sides.

"That is very good, Tophet," he said, slapping the butler on the back. "This occasion can use some humor. No, no, dear Tophet, I was hoping that perhaps since you once dwelt in the house of the high priest, you might have

heard of some seer, some wise man who has been overlooked."

Blushing, Tophet cleared his throat, feeling suddenly
foolish.

For the first time in months, Joseph haunted him as
surely as though he hovered in a corner of the room.
Guilt speared the butler's heart, and with a shudder he
tried to blunt it.

"Well, Your Highness," he stuttered, "I shall give it
some thought. Indeed, I shall."

Then, bowing, he proceeded to pour the tea, wishing
Salatis would not eye him with such curiosity.

When at last the conversation recommenced in the
room, and when Pharaoh's attention was diverted, Tophet's trembling eased and his heart slowed a bit.

Still, Joseph's face haunted him, and he recalled his
pleas to remember him when he gained his liberty.

In keeping with Tophet's nature, however, he would
consider his own interests above all others'. At first, as he
did so, it seemed risky to mention the Hebrew. But the
more he thought, the more he realized that if he could be
responsible for bringing an answer to Pharaoh's riddle,
he might be advanced as never before.

The wheels in Tophet's mind turned quickly. He would
tell this king he had once worked with the lad in Potiphera's house, and that Joseph had been thrown into
prison even though he had a reputation as a seer.

But, no. What if the king sent for Joseph, and Joseph,
in turn, mentioned Tophet's imprisonment?

The butler nervously handed the master his tea, grateful that the king was preoccupied so that he did not study
Tophet's tense face too closely.

It seemed if he spoke of Joseph at all, he must speak of
his own time in jail. But if he did, the king would surely
doubt his character altogether, strip him of his rank, and
send him away.

Back and forth he debated the matter until it struck

him that there might be a safe way to tell the truth, a way which could actually be advantageous to him.

"Sir," he said softly, "it occurs to me that I may be able to help."

"Yes?" the king said, almost having forgotten Tophet's presence.

"In doing so, I must confess my own offenses. For it involves a sorry time in my life."

Not a little surprised, the emperor and his companions were intrigued.

"You know that your predecessor was a ruthless and unjust ruler," Tophet began, as though contrasting the old administration with the new.

What could the new king do, but agree? When he nodded, Tophet went on.

"Pharaoh was furious with his servants, and he put me in confinement in the house of the captain of the bodyguard, both me and the chief baker. We both had dreams on the same night, and we were troubled by them."

"Go on," Salatis encouraged him.

"Now a Hebrew youth was with us there, a servant of the captain of the bodyguard, and we related our dreams to him, and he interpreted them for us."

Allowing suspense to build, Tophet paused.

"Amazingly, it came about that just as he interpreted for us, so it happened. Pharaoh restored me to my office, but the baker he hanged."

With this, he rolled his eyes and gripped his neck as with a noose, adding drama to the fine tale.

Momentarily the room was abuzz again, as the magi wondered over the mysterious soothsayer.

Salatis stroked his beard and looked quietly at Tophet. Pleased with the story, he announced, "If my cupbearer was an enemy to Timaeus, then he is an honest man. And if this prisoner of whom he speaks is a Hebrew, he must be a true prophet. Send for him that we may all be satisfied."

38

Slick as a Nile breeze, the wheels of a flashing carriage sped to the Memphis acropolis.

From between the parted curtains a beaming face peered, the face of the long-imprisoned Joseph.

For two years his greatest freedom had been his daily trek from the fortress apartment provided by Potiphera to the jailhouse in the prison of On. Though he had been "keeper of the prison," he had still been a ward of the state, a criminal.

Today he was on his way to Pharaoh's palace, the only mansion in Egypt greater than Potiphera's. And today he would be welcomed into the stateroom of the new Semite king.

Something told him this was the Lord's day, which he had awaited since his dreadful casting off. This was the day when the prophecies of his youth would begin to be fulfilled.

He was thirty years old and as handsome as a desert prince—for so he was, a prince of the line of Abraham. Perhaps, even this he could shortly reveal, the pride of his heritage and the faith of his fathers.

He could still smell Asenath's sweet perfume as she had hovered over him this morning, eagerly offering her assistance as he prepared to leave.

Personally bringing word of Pharaoh's summons, she had also arrived at his apartment bearing a stack of garments, fine linen embellished with finer accessories.

With her were her maids, carrying trays of male toiletries: a razor, comb, mirror, cologne, and soap.

Laughing and giggling, the women had handed him tunics and cloaks and had made him come out to them in outfit after outfit.

"There," Asenath had at last announced, "the striped one suits you best."

He had not told her he knew it would. He had not revealed that he had once worn a coat of many colors, simpler but more stunning than this.

Ahead, against capitol hill, the palace of the king loomed.

"A dream..." Joseph thought. "The king has had a dream, and he calls for me."

When Pharaoh's messengers had arrived in On, seeking Joseph, they had not mentioned Tophet. But Joseph knew there could be no other explanation for the summons. A smirk worked at Joseph's lips as he thought about the selfish butler. It must be that Tophet now served under the new administration, and that he had good personal reason to suddenly remember the Hebrew.

As the chariot dashed through the mammoth gate of the palace compound, Joseph took a deep breath. He could suddenly feel the past slipping from him, sluffed like a worn-out garment.

A bright future beckoned, and he would receive it with eager hands.

* * *

The spacious halls of Pharaoh Salatis's castle echoed about Joseph as he followed the messengers toward the king's stateroom. He had always thought the house of On must be the most magnificent on earth. But nothing could rival the majesty of this place.

Once they had passed the tight security stations which introduced the first lobbies, they entered the inner sanctums, where spilling fountains and exotic birds greeted guests, where gorgeous women lounged in garden bowers, and where music drifted on warm currents from corners and alcoves.

Rich tapestries caressed the walls and thick carpets the floors. Mirrors reflected the reality that he was indeed here, that although he was an interpreter of dreams, this was no dream.

Over and over he breathed a prayer, the same one he had repeated since leaving On. It was a prayer for wisdom and insight, a prayer that Jehovah would facilitate his calling and help him to perceive the meaning of Pharaoh's troubling vision.

Confidence in God had carried him from the dungeon, across the miles to Memphis, and through the awesome corridors of this place. Now he stood before the stateroom door. Clenching his fists, he imagined that he clung to Jehovah's unfailing hand.

It was a tall, thin man with bead-like eyes who opened the portal, greeting Joseph with a diverted gaze. Blood rushed to the visitor's face as he recognized the butler.

He knew not whether to embrace Tophet or shun him.

"Enter, Master," the man greeted, unable to face the one he should have freed from prison months before.

"It has been a long time, Tophet," Joseph returned.

Saying nothing more, he entered, walking tall and silent into the stateroom.

Ahead, upon a vast marble platform, sat the king. As Joseph was announced to him, he was not surprised to find that the new Pharaoh was a young man, younger even than himself. He had expected such a revolutionary hero to be full of youthful zeal. Nor was Joseph surprised to see that he was dark and ruddy, like the desert race from which he was descended.

In fact, the new Pharaoh could have passed for a nomad prince, which likely he was before taking the mightiest throne on earth.

Tall and dashing, he appeared bred on mountain air and stream water, and when the son of Jacob stood before him, the two men instantly recognized one another.

It was not a recognition borne of knowledge, but of spirit. They were of the same stock—Semites, Hebrews, people of the earth. And they must have cut their teeth on the same stones.

"Joseph," Salatis called out, "that is an Aramaean name, is it not?"

"Yes, Your Majesty," the Hebrew replied. "I was born in Padan-Aram."

In that instant he revealed more about his heritage than he had told anyone since setting foot in Egypt. And over the next moments he found himself revealing more.

"My people hark back to Mesopotamia," Pharaoh said.

"Mine, as well," Joseph answered. "My great-grandfather was a prince of Ur."

Stunned, the king leaned forward, studying his handsome visitor in amazement.

"I almost believe you," he marveled. "You look the part."

Joseph would have been flattered, but knew the truth of the statement and sensed Pharaoh's sincerity.

"Tell me of your tribe and your god," the king inquired.

With this, Joseph recounted his story, his lineage, and how he had come to be first a slave and then a steward in Potiphera's house. Before he knew it, he had related the encounter with Natira. All of this Salatis accepted without question.

"My God is the God of my fathers: Abraham, Isaac, and Jacob," he reverently concluded. "It is my God who has kept me all these years, and who will answer for me this day."

The king sighed, a smile lighting his face. "I have heard this kind of talk before, among the desert people. It gives me peace to hear it again."

Joseph thrilled to this confession. Suddenly he felt an even deeper bond with this man, and a desire to serve him the best he could.

"Now as to the reason I have called for you, Joseph," Salatis began, "I have had a dream, and I know it to be the kind of dream which means to tell me something. I cannot put it from mind, but no one can interpret it. I have heard it said that when *you* hear a dream you can interpret it."

Joseph bowed, feeling Tophet's eyes against his back.

"It is not in me to be so wise," he admitted. "It is God who gives me the understanding. And God will give Pharaoh a favorable answer this day."

This pleased the king greatly, relieving him of a heavy burden.

"Very well," he said. Then closing his eyes, he recounted the vision:

"In my dream, I was standing on the bank of the Nile. Suddenly seven cows, fat and sleek, came up out of the river. They grazed in the marsh grass which grew there. Then, seven other cows came up after them, poor and very ugly and gaunt, uglier than any I had ever seen in all the land of Egypt."

He shivered a little, as though the dream still terrified him.

"Then the lean, ugly cows ate up the first seven fat ones. Oh, it was horrible, Joseph! Yet when they had devoured them, it didn't look as though they had, for they were just as ugly and skinny as before."

At this, he opened his eyes and shook himself.

Joseph wondered if this were all, and began to consider an answer, but the king was not finished.

"I awoke for a space, but then fell asleep again," he went on. "And the dream continued. This time seven ears of grain, plump and good, came up on a single stalk. And then, seven more, withered, thin, and scorched by the east wind, sprouted up after them. The thin ears swallowed the seven good ears."

Pharaoh's voice trailed off, and his hands shook. Rubbing them together as though they were cold, he held them forth, desperate.

"Joseph, I told my dream to the magi, but no one could explain it to me. If you can help, I shall reward you beyond your wildest imaginings!"

Joseph understood that Salatis felt the dream portentous of the future, and that as ruler of Egypt he feared for his country.

But though the vision was deep and obscure, the meaning came to the Hebrew like a quick wind off the hills of Lebanon.

"The two parts of the dream have the same meaning," he began. "God is telling you what he is about to do."

"Truly?" the king marveled. "I have known this. Yes, yes!"

"The seven good cows are seven years," the interpreter explained. "Likewise the seven healthy ears of grain. Do you see?"

"I see, I see! Go on."

"The seven thin cows and the seven thin ears scorched by the east wind are also seven years...of famine."

The king lurched forward. "This is not good," he observed. "There will be famine in Egypt?"

"It is as I have spoken," Joseph insisted. "God has shown you what he is about to do. Now, understand. Seven years of great abundance are coming, but they shall be followed by seven more years of famine, and all of the abundance will be forgotten, for the famine will ravage the land. In fact the wealth of the first seven shall be devoured by the last."

The Hebrew let the message sink into his hearer's ears. And when he saw that Salatis resisted, he said, "You had the dream twice because God is trying to warn you. He shall bring all this to happen very soon!"

The king shook his head. "But, Joseph, you said at the beginning that God would give me a favorable interpretation. This is not favorable. It is very foreboding."

"Don't you see?" Joseph went on. "It would be unfavorable if you received no warning. This way you will have time to prepare. If I were you, O Great King, I would seek a wise and discerning man to set in charge of these matters. Put overseers in charge of the land, and let them exact a fifth of the produce of all the farmland during the seven bounteous years. Let them gather that portion into the silos of every city, under the authority of the crown. Be sure to set guards over these reserves, and let no one partake of the supply during the seven healthy years, so that when the famine comes, there will be plenty."

As the king listened to the proposal, he was dumbfounded. Studying his visitor, he motioned to his counselors, who had stood quietly by throughout the discussion.

For a few moments they consulted together, looking over their shoulders now and then and eyeing Joseph in wonder. At last Salatis stood up.

"Can we ever find such a fellow again?" he asked, gesturing to the Hebrew. "This Joseph, son of Jacob, has a divine spirit!"

Then calling Joseph forward, he proclaimed, "Since God has informed you of all this, there is no one so discerning or wise as you! I summoned you for an interpretation, and you not only gave me that, but you gave me wise counsel as well! As of this day, I put you in charge of my entire palace and all that concerns me. At your command, all my people shall do homage. Only I, in all of Egypt, shall be greater than you!"

As Joseph stood spellbound before him, the king stepped down from his platform, removed his signet ring, and put it on Joseph's hand. Then, sending for a linen cloak, he wrapped it about Joseph's shoulders and put a golden necklace about his neck.

"Zaphenath-paneah," Salatis proclaimed, kissing him on both cheeks. "So shall your name be from this day. For through you does God speak and through you he shows that he lives."

39

Joseph, prime minister of Egypt, stood in the spur of his chariot, a stinging whip flashing in his hand. Four elegant stallions, white as Hebron snow, pulled to the chase of his command.

Behind him, within the chariot, stood two princely young boys, one six years old, and one five.

Manasseh, he had named the first; and Ephraim, the youngest; for the first had helped him to forget the past and the second was proof of his fruitfulness in the land of his affliction.

Both were blessed with Joseph's ruddy good looks, but lavender glinted in their eyes, and their mother's smooth Egyptian features gave them refined dignity even at this early age.

They were the offspring of Asenath and Joseph, born in due time after Pharaoh had given her in marriage to the Hebrew.

While the union required that Asenath give up her position as priestess of Nath, Potiphera could not deny his blessing on the couple. Loving Joseph like a son and still feeling the guilt of his past treatment of him, he provided a grand wedding, one of the most elaborate ever staged in Egypt.

And as Asenath grew in her devotion to the God of Israel, Joseph knew bliss more profound than anything he dreamed could be his.

The first year of famine was upon the land, coming just

as the Hebrew had predicted after seven full years of plenty.

During the times of abundance, Joseph had traveled back and forth throughout Egypt, overseeing the fulfillment of his plan, the ingathering of a fifth of all agricultural products and the storing up of grain and dried foods in every city silo.

Because the new emperor was so popular, Joseph's edict was followed from the beginning with little resistance. And as time proved, he was indeed a prophet, for the seven fruitful years were in themselves miraculously abundant.

Today as he entered the border town of Succoth, on the east side of Egypt, he was greeted by cheers; and as he passed down the avenue, his attendants, riding on before, called out, *"Abreck! Abreck!* Attention! Attention! All bow!"

Anticipating the prime minister's arrival, the people complied, eagerly gathering along the street and in the marketplace.

All nations were represented among them, for the famine had spread throughout the known world, touching the edge of western Africa and the borders of India, the realms of southern Europe and the desert of Mesopotamia.

In all the earth, no land had food except Egypt. And Pharaoh himself would have been starving, had the wise Hebrew and his God-given prophecy not been heeded.

In every city of the land, the scene was similar when Joseph arrived. Wealthy and poor alike waited to buy food from the storehouses.

Those who had everything money could offer, except nourishment, mingled with people who had spent their last reserves just to make the journey to Egypt.

Strange dialects mixed, as well as strange clothing, the sarongs of west Africans contrasting with the streamlined robes of the Europeans and the turbans of the desert people. Black, white, and brown faces stared up at Joseph as he took his seat beneath an awning on an elevated platform and prepared to open the market.

Much of the food had set prices, but there were those people who wished to buy in such quantity that great lots of the products would be auctioned.

More than once had Joseph considered the irony of his situation: that he, once a piece of merchandise upon a slave block, should now be master of life and death in the greatest bazaar of all time.

But he took no joy in the neediness of those who came before him. Joseph knew what it was to suffer, to be poor and powerless, at the mercy of others. Day after day his heart was broken by the poverty and helplessness of the thousands who came in waves, bowing and seeking salvation.

Today, as his young sons stood by watching his attendants take silver, gold, precious stones, and personal treasures in exchange for grain and dried foods, Joseph recalled the times he had wished he might have something to offer in exchange for his freedom. As the clerks in the accounting booths kept scrupulous record of every transaction, committing it to clay tablet and parchment, he remembered the heartless men who had looked upon him as in item of barter and profit.

But most often these days, he thought of his brothers, and he wondered how they fared in the land of Canaan, so hard hit by famine.

One of Joseph's accountants had just handed him a figure-laden tablet, and after he approved it, he reached for another.

Just as he did, a certain company within the great throng caught Joseph's attention.

At first he thought his eyes deceived him, that it was only in the context of his thoughts that he would imagine such a thing. But the more he studied them, the more his heart raced.

Calling his sons to his side, he wrapped an arm around each one and, trembling, held them close. The lads, not knowing what possessed their father, surveyed the crowd but did not see what he saw.

"Papa?" Manasseh began to question him.

Joseph held a finger to his lips. "Tell me, son," he whispered, "do I look Egyptian today?"

The two boys giggled. "You will do," Manasseh teased.

"Quickly," the Hebrew told him, "go fetch my headdress."

"But, Papa," Manasseh objected, "it is too hot to wear that today."

"Quickly," Joseph spurred him.

When the boy returned with the broad, striped headpiece, Joseph donned it. "Do I look Egyptian?" he asked again.

"Yes, Papa," Ephraim assured him. "But why..."

"Run along now, sons," Joseph commanded. "Your mother should be arriving soon."

Asenath was due to join him, as she often did when he was away. But he did not want his wife and children to see him just now.

As the boys departed, their faces quizzical, Joseph turned again to his work, hoping that the men who now approached the platform would not recognize him.

There were exactly ten of them, and in the 20 years which had passed since last he saw them, they had changed little.

The leader was only more mature, his distinguished beard laced with silver. Joseph knew on the instant that he was Reuben.

Behind him came Judah, his intelligent face a little mellower with age. Then there were the two "lions," Simeon and Levi, although Joseph was surprised to find them not much taller than himself.

Benjamin, Joseph's eleventh and only full brother, was nowhere among them.

As they came forward, giving homage, tears rose in the Hebrew's eyes. The visions of the bowing sheaves and obeisant stars sprang to mind as though he had witnessed them just yesterday, and not when he was a boy.

Gripping the arms of his chair, he controlled himself, determined not to reveal his feelings.

Calling for a clean ledger, he pretended to take notes.

"Where do you come from?" he asked with the rough air of command.

Though the children of Israel knew the Egyptian tongue he spoke, it was polite to let his interpreter translate. When the question had been recast in Hebrew, it was Reuben who answered, keeping his face to the ground.

"From the land of Canaan, sir. To buy food."

"Is the famine so severe in that lush land?" Joseph tested him. Having contrived a plot to detain them, he suddenly sneered, "I suspect you are all heads of nomad tribes, here to spy out the borders of our country!"

Reuben looked up in amazement and confusion, and turning to Judah, shrugged his shoulders.

"Good sir," he said, bowing again, "permit your servant to disagree. Surely there have been many from Canaan seeking your help. The famine is very harsh in our country. We are not spies. No, my lord, but to buy food are your servants come."

"Yes, sir," Judah added, rising up and pleading, "we are all the sons of one man. We are honest men, not spies."

Joseph pretended skepticism, unwilling to expose himself, yet gleaning what information he could regarding the family.

"The sons of one man?" he laughed. "How likely is that? Look around you. Do you see so many men traveling in company? All well dressed, all strong and young? No, no. You are spies!"

At this Simeon came forth, ready to fight, his face as red as his beard.

"Sir," he argued, stupidly adding more detail, "not only are your servants ten brothers, but all together there are twelve of us, the sons of one man in Canaan!"

When the other brothers nudged him to keep quiet, Simeon only made matters worse. "The youngest is at home with our father," he stammered, "and the other... is not."

The last observation stuck in Simeon's throat, and Joseph noted how the ten men appeared uneasy with it.

Again, emotion welled within the inquisitor, but he feigned indifference.

"So, indeed, you have a father? And another brother?"

Judah, who studied the governor quizzically, sighed. "Yes, sir. It is as we have said. We have a father, an old man, and a child of his old age, a little one. And the child's brother is dead, and... his father loves him."

"Little One..." the words pricked Joseph's heart, for so had he been called by that name during all his years at home. But steeling himself against sentiment, he snorted, "Ha! A likely story! You strain my patience! It is as I suspected. You are all spies!"

At this he stood up and began to pace his platform. His attendants nervously called the guards, and the huge market crowd gasped in astonishment.

As weapon-bearing strong men surrounded the small company, fear clouded the ten faces.

"To show that I am a just man," Joseph condescended, "I shall give you a chance to prove yourselves."

Reuben gripped the edge of the platform. "Anything, sir, for we are honest men."

"Very well," Joseph continued, pacing to and fro. "This shall be your proof: By the life of Pharaoh, you shall not leave this place unless your youngest brother comes to Egypt."

The ten Israelites murmured together, shaking their heads and insisting that this was impossible, that their old father would surely die if the lad were to leave him.

But Joseph insisted. "Send one of you to fetch your brother. The rest shall be kept in confinement until I see if you are telling the truth! Otherwise, by the life of Pharaoh, you are surely spies!"

Quaking and trembling, the ten cried out as the guards bound them and hauled them away.

And Joseph left the platform, tears brimming in his eyes.

40

Asenath peeked through the flap of her husband's striped tent. Despite the searing daylight outside, the heavy shelter was dark inside, and she called softly, wondering where he was.

When he did not answer, she crept through the door and tiptoed to his couch.

The crowd of hungry marketers waited beside the platform for the prime minister to return, but Joseph had not come out of his traveling tent since committing the Israelites to prison.

A full hour had passed while heat and hunger made the people restless, and a threatening chant rose from the street.

"Husband," Asenath whispered, finding him sprawled face down upon his bed. "What are you doing here? Manasseh and Ephraim are worried. The people..."

Joseph reached for her through the dark and pulled her to him.

Still he said nothing, but when she stroked his face, she found his cheeks wet with tears.

"My lord, what has happened?" she cried. "Is there no more food? Shall the people starve?"

"No, no," he soothed her. "I am coming. Tell them I am coming."

Asenath rose to do as he asked, but he pulled her to him again.

"My heart breaks, Asenath. I have seen my brothers,

the ten who left me for dead!"

"Here? In Succoth?" she marveled.

"All the way from Cannan."

"But how can you be sure? It is so many years."

"I knew them all," he insisted. "They are so unchanged!"

Asenath sat quiet beside him a long moment, stroking his forehead and feeling what he felt.

Knowing Joseph as she did, she knew compassion would overrule vengeance. For this man, she had recanted her previous faith, giving up her devotion to the gods of Egypt and embracing the faith of Israel. Never had she regretted her choice, and never had she doubted her husband's wisdom.

"Well," she sighed, "you have power now, husband. Their lives are in your hands."

"Yes," he muttered. "Just as they should be!"

"Just as they should be," she repeated, a smile tugging at her mouth. "So what do you mean to do?"

"I have had them hauled away to prison!" he asserted, a little too strongly.

"I see," she said. "And shall they rot there forever?"

Silence, like smoke, hung between them.

"What would *you* do?" he challenged. "Surely you would do no less!"

"I would do exactly what you would do," she replied

Joseph hated the lilt in her voice, the teasing twinkle in her eye that reached through the dark into his heart.

He hated Asenath and loved her, both at once.

* * *

This was the second night that Joseph could not sleep.

Two days had passed since he had encountered his brothers, days of doling out food to strangers, of seeing fear and starvation exchanged for gratitude and hope.

But his conscience tormented him.

A luscious yellow moon hovered over the border town and some desert wolf serenaded it. Asenath breathed softly beside her husband, confident that he would make the right decision. He should have been at peace, but he was not.

Somewhere across town, in a primitive hold, his ten brothers were probably also awake, fearing for their lives and wondering if they would ever see Canaan or Jacob again.

Conflicting emotions—joy at seeing them, unresolved anger at their abuses—contended for Joseph's heart.

Several times since the Israelites had appeared he had thought to pray. But each time he had rebelled, preferring to nurse his dark memories.

As dawn approached, he knew he could not spend another day in indecision. He also knew what his move must be, for the sake of his own soul.

Before the sun had cracked the sky, Joseph was on his feet, creeping out of the tent and leaving the slumbering Asenath without a word.

Rousing his interpreter, he led him to the prison-house, which was no more than a stockade of stakes and armed guards. Shivering with desert cold, he stood outside while the bewildered spokesman called the brothers to the door.

The Israelites came forward in a huddle, rubbing their eyes and muttering together.

"Tell them I fear the same God they fear," Joseph began, nudging the servant. "Tell them that if they wish to live and if they are honest men, they must leave one of their brothers behind. The rest may carry food to their families. But they must all return as quickly as possible with their youngest brother. If they do this, they shall live."

As the men absorbed the message, Joseph watched their faces. Relief was there, but fear as well.

"We must leave one of us here?" he heard them ask. "And we must return again to Egypt?"

The interpreter nodded, and Joseph knew their quandary.

How could they single out one brother to remain? And how could they expect Jacob to release Benjamin to an unknown fate?

What, they wondered among themselves, could this Zaphenath-paneah want with the lad? And how could Jacob, aged and frail, survive such separation?

All this they discussed among themselves, not realizing that Joseph perfectly understood their tongue.

They could not seem to reach a consensus before they began to cast about for some rhyme or reason for their predicament.

Doubtless they had gone over and over it before, the peculiar treatment they were receiving, and why this strange Egyptian should suspect them as he did.

No satisfactory answer had come after two days and nights of deliberation, and now they were left with nothing but the sense that they were being divinely punished.

"Oh," Levi wailed, "it is as I have always feared. We are being repaid for our sin against Joseph!"

"You see that now?" Judah snarled. "I knew from the beginning that we should have been kinder to the lad."

"Ha!" Gad barked. "You were ready to sell him! What could be more cruel?"

"So? What about *you?*" Judah defended. "You were ready to *kill* him!"

At this Gad started, and pointing at Asher recalled how he had committed Joseph to the pit.

But Asher turned on them all. "We saw Joseph's agony when he pleaded with us, yet none of us would listen! I am no more to blame than you all!"

On and on the argument went, until Reuben spoke up. "I agree that it is because of this great sin that this evil has come upon us! Did I not warn you, 'Do not sin against the boy'? Yet you would not take heed. Now comes the reckoning for his blood!"

Joseph's chest tightened, and he grew short of breath. Turning aside, he left the compound and stood in the moonlit shadows.

Years of repressed sorrow welled from within, and like a young child, he wept until his confounded interpreter came seeking him.

"Master!" he exclaimed. "What is it?"

Shoving the man away, Joseph got control of himself and returned to the stockade, commanding the guards to let him in.

To the amazement of all, he began to bark orders.

"Since you cannot seem to choose, *I* shall do so!" he cried.

Grasping Simeon by the arms, he took a silken rope from off his own waist and proceeded to bind the big fellow's hands behind his back.

With this gesture, something close to a sense of vengeance swept over Joseph. As he recalled Simeon's sins at Shechem, his cruel and prideful destruction of the town of Shalem and his humiliation of their sister, Dinah, he bound him rudely.

"This one shall stay," he decided, "and the rest of you shall go! Bring your youngest brother with all speed, or surely you shall not live long!"

Then, storming out, he commanded the guards to free the nine, and he turned for his tent.

When he was half-way home, his interpreter racing to keep pace, Joseph suddenly felt an ache in his chest. Stopping, he braced himself against a lamppost and closed his eyes.

The anguish of conflict consumed him. Running a hand over his brow, he sighed deeply.

Overhead the moon watched as Joseph swung between hate and love.

"See to it that they are well supplied with grain," he instructed the interpreter. "And while you are at it, restore all the money that they pay. Hide it in their bags. And send them away."

41

The inn at Beer-Sheba was a desolate place. Dry breezes withered what little vegetation the desert produced, creating huge tumbleweeds that could threaten the sturdiest horse or camel.

But this was the southernmost outpost of the land of Canaan, the first true resting place for travelers crossing the Wilderness of Shur or the Wilderness of Zin from Egypt and points south.

Hundreds of people were lodged here this evening, all on their way to or from the land of Pharaoh, all going after food or bringing food back with them.

Judah pushed against a blast of desert sand on his way from the inn to the stable. He had fed his donkey the last of a bag of meal just before bedtime, but the poor beast was still hungry and he could hear it braying in the moonlit yard.

Reaching the stable, he rubbed the donkey between the ears, and chastised him gently. "Petri, your stomach is bottomless!" he complained. "I didn't want to open a new bag until morning. Shall you eat up our supplies before we reach home?"

The stubborn creature brayed again as Judah loosened the drawstring on a sack of oats and dipped his hand inside.

When the Israelite stubbed his fingers on something hard, he foraged in the bag, his brow crinkled.

"What's this?" he asked, pulling out a leather pouch.

The donkey studied it blankly as Judah shook it, listening to the jangling contents.

"My purse!" he exclaimed. "See here, Petri, it is my purse!"

Nervously, Judah opened the bag and, turning it over, found that his money was all there, the money he had paid for his supplies.

At first the realization made him giddy as he marveled at his good fortune. It seemed some oversight on the part of the stockkeepers in Succoth had fallen to his benefit.

As he considered further, however, rubbing the coins in his hands, fear seized him. Replacing the money in the pouch, he dropped it into the sack and hastily covered it over.

Like a criminal, he fled back to the inn and roused his sleeping brothers.

"My money has been returned!" he told them, his voice as low as possible. "It is in my meal bag! When the prime minister learns that the payment is missing, he will be convinced that we are thieves!"

"And spies!" Asher cried, sitting up on his pallet.

Reuben listened mutely to his brothers' reasoning, as one by one they turned to him for guidance.

"Simeon is as good as dead!" Levi moaned. "Oh, Reuben, what is this that God has done to us?"

But Reuben had no answer, sensing that the Lord's justice was on an irreversible course.

* * *

A hot night wind parched the Hebron hills and scoured the settlement at Mamre.

Jacob paced the floor of the tribal council chamber, shaking his head in outrage.

"You did *what*?" he shouted. "You left Simeon in Succoth?"

"The governor of Egypt was against us," Reuben defended. So many times had he rehearsed the story to his father that his nerves were ready to shatter.

The nine brothers, who sat in a circle on the floor, wrung their hands in frustration.

"Yes, Father," Judah interceded, "listen to Reuben. We had no choice. This strange Egyptian took a disliking to us from the outset. We have gone over and over the possible reasons but have no answer. He simply decided from the moment he saw us that we were untrustworthy."

"Spies?" Jacob cried. "How could he think you spies?"

Again, the matter had been tossed about so many times that the men tired of it. But, revering Jacob, they went over it once more.

Back and forth the elder paced, listening, dissatisfied, angry.

"Well, the man is insane!" he declared. "You are all insane if you think I shall release Benjamin to you."

Stumbling across the room, he reached for the young man, the only remaining son of Rachel, who absorbed all of this in bewildered silence. Benjamin received his father's embrace without a word, ready to offer himself for the journey, but fearful lest he break the old man's heart.

"You have bereaved me of two sons already!" Jacob cried, turning on the others. "I left Joseph to your care and he is no more. Now Simeon is gone, and you would take Benjamin? You must think me a fool!"

"Papa, Papa..." Benjamin stammered. "Perhaps it is necessary..."

But before he could complete the thought, Jacob was raving again. Staggering to a corner of the chamber, the elder reached into a cedar chest and brought out the striped coat which had once been Joseph's.

Scattered upon it were deep crimson stains, the blood of a slain beast into which the brothers had dipped the garment years before, "proof" that the vanished Joseph had met with a violent and mysterious death in the wilderness.

Clutching the coat to his breast, Jacob began to weep.

"Father," Reuben pleaded, placing an arm about the old man's shoulders, "if we do not comply, the Egyptian will surely send troops after our entire tribe! Do not worry over Benjamin. I swear, you may put my own two sons to death if I do not bring him back safely. Put him in my care, and I *will* return him to you!"

Wrenching free, Jacob stared wildly into Reuben's compassionate face.

"My son shall not go down with you!" he growled. "Joseph, his only brother, is dead, and he alone is left. If harm should befall him on the journey, you will bring my gray hair down to the grave in sorrow!"

42

It was not his sons' persuasiveness that finally convinced Jacob to release Benjamin.

It was hunger—and it was fear.

As the food supply again dwindled, someone must return to the land of Pharaoh.

The predicament was compounded by the fact that, when the food sacks which they had brought with them from Egypt had been opened, each brother discovered that, like Judah, one of his bags contained his money. To return now, appearing as a batch of thieves, would surely put their lives in peril. But to delay could bring starvation, or the army of Pharaoh against Israel.

As Jacob saw that he had no choice but to comply with the prime ministers's orders, he finally permitted Benjamin to go.

"If it must be so," he decided, "then do this: Take some of the best products of our land in your bags, and carry them down to the governor as a gift. Take a little balm and a little honey, aromatic gum and myrrh, pistachio nuts and almonds. And take double the money in your hand which was found in your sacks. Perhaps . . . we will hope that perhaps it was an oversight."

Then, clasping Benjamin to himself, he handed him over to the care of Reuben and Judah.

"May God Almighty grant you compassion in the sight of the prime minster," he prayed. "As for me, if I am bereaved of my children . . . I am bereaved."

Therefore it was with much trepidation that the sons of Israel saw the walls of Succoth on the horizon, the dread place of their imprisonment and the town where the prime minster was still headquartered.

Was Simeon still alive, confined in the stockade?

Cautiously they made their way through the town gate, the most easterly portal of Egypt.

It was early morning when they arrived. The governor was just finishing breakfast on the porch of his great tent, his wife and sons lounging beside him.

Like a spear, it went through Joseph, the sight of his returning brothers. Lurching upright on his couch, he felt his face blanch, and without explanation he sent his little family away.

"Take your maidservants and our sons, and leave the house!" he commanded Asenath. "Do not return until evening."

Wounded by his sharp command, the woman was incredulous. But when she followed his gaze down the street, she saw for the first time the faces of his notorious persecutors, and understanding his desire to be alone, she hastened to obey.

Eagerly Joseph scanned the group which approached. Yes, there he was! Benjamin! He would know him anywhere!

Ecstasy and yearning gripped him. Benjamin was handsome as a mountain cedar—his beard and hair black as bark, his skin the same golden ivory and his eyes the same lavender as Rachel's. Suddenly Joseph was 17 again, and he rode through Hebron's heathered hills beside his little brother, laughing and free.

Somehow he managed to keep back the tears. Calling to his interpreter, he commanded, "Bring the men into the house, and slay a choice fatling. Make ready, for the men are to dine with me at noon!"

Remembering his master's previous suspicions of these very characters, the servant could barely refrain from questioning the order. But with a hesitant bow, he hurried down the street.

"You are to come with me," he announced, taking Reuben by the arm. "My lord would have you dine with him."

Of course, the Israelites recognized him as the governor's aide, and they imagined the hand of doom upon their shoulders.

Quaking, Levi dared to voice their fear.

"It is because of the money that we are being brought in," he muttered. "He will fall upon us and take us for slaves!"

"Hush!" Judah snarled. And those nearest Levi elbowed him to keep silent.

Rigidly they followed the servant to the edge of the porch. Taking a deep breath, Reuben drew close behind him.

"Oh, my lord," he offered, avoiding his gaze, "we did truly come here the first time to buy food. We had no other motive. But it so happened..." Fumbling, he explained that they had found the money in their bags and quickly related that they had brought more than enough in repayment.

"We do not know who put the money in our sacks," he added sincerely.

When the man reached out to touch him on the sleeve, Reuben froze, envisioning the end.

But the interpreter only smiled.

"Peace to you," he said. "Do not be afraid. Your God and the God of your father has given you treasure in your sacks."

Then, turning for the door, he called over his shoulder, "I had your money. Relax and enjoy, for the governor...heaven knows why...has taken favor on you."

43

For the Israelites, the next few hours were like a dream.

When the ten brothers were ushered into the small enclosure which served as Joseph's traveling courtyard, they were greeted by the aromas of a succulent meal. Arrayed beneath an awning were several long tables, all laden with trays of fine food and goblets of wine.

The interpreter, who also served as Joseph's steward, went on ahead of the men, disappearing for a few moments behind a tall screen. When he returned, he led a handsome, red-bearded giant, dressed in the finest clean linen.

"Simeon!" Levi cried. Rushing to him, he embraced him fervently.

"He has been released," the steward explained, seeing their astonishment. "Do not ask me why, for I do not know."

Then, shrugging his shoulders, he led the company toward the dining area.

The prime minister, they were told, had left the house on business and would be arriving at noon. Meanwhile, they were presented with fresh water and towels with which to wash their feet, faces, and hands. They were given clean tunics to wear and were entertained with music while their cups were filled over and over with spiced tea.

When at last the governor's arrival was announced, a small trumpet blaring in the court, the Israelites rose from their couches and prostrated themselves upon the floor.

Not one dared to look up, fearing the face of the peculiar Egyptian and fearing whatever he intended for them.

As Joseph stood upon his porch, surveying the obeisant brothers, he again remembered his visions and tried valiantly to suppress his welling emotions.

"Rise," he simply said. "Take your seats."

At this, the Israelites returned to their couches, all but Reuben, who rose only to his knees.

"Your Highness," he humbly replied, "if you will be patient with your servant, we have a gift from our homeland, prepared in your honor."

Joseph easily read the tension in his brother's voice, a fear equal to his own conflict.

"Very well," he said, again through his interpreter.

Quickly Reuben called for Judah, and the two men hastened toward the stable where their donkeys were tethered. When they returned, bearing bags full of choice products from Canaan, Joseph was deeply moved.

As the gifts of ointment, exotic nuts, and perfumes were spread upon a floor tarp, the Hebrew was poignantly reminded of his country and of his life in the shepherd hills.

Barely able to contain his feelings, he thanked the men and asked, "Is your old father well, of whom you spoke? Is he still alive?"

"Your servant, our father, is well," they replied, bowing down again in homage. If they wondered at the longing in the governor's tone, they were in no position to question it and kept their eyes to the ground.

"Please stand," he repeated. "Take your seats."

Through a haze of tears, he studied their faces, one by one, until he came to Benjamin.

"Is this your youngest brother?" he inquired, knowing very well that he was.

"Yes, sir," Reuben assured him. "You commanded us to bring him to you, and this we have done."

But Joseph was not concerned for Reuben's defense. His gaze was riveted to the son of Rachel, his only full brother.

"May God be gracious to you, my son," he said, his voice breaking.

Suddenly Joseph could bear the ache of his heart no longer, and turning about, left the dining room.

To the amazement of all who were present, both Hebrews and Egyptians, the governor disappeared into his chamber, weeping.

For a long while he was gone, until the company grew restless, and the servants and steward were perplexed as to what they should do.

But at last he emerged, having washed his face and gained control of himself.

"Serve the meal," he commanded.

Receiving no explanation, the servants and the guests followed his directive. Joseph was served at his private table, the Egyptian officials at theirs, and the guests at one long spread.

But before they were served, Joseph cleared his throat, looking unhappy with the arrangement.

"Put them in order of their ages," he commanded his steward.

When the poor fellow looked baffled, Joseph rose up and pointed to the brothers, one by one.

"This is the eldest," he said, indicating Reuben, "and this the second," to Simeon.

From the firstborn, all the way down to Benjamin, he gave their rank with unfailing accuracy, adding mystery to mystery.

"How can he know?" Gad marveled.

"Quiet!" Naphtali whispered.

Obediently, the men took their designated places, looking at one another in astonishment.

When the meal began to be served, the governor still seemed dissatisfied.

Rising again from his seat, he carried platter after platter of delicacies from his own table to the table of the Israelites. And surprising everyone, he joined them.

"Here, son, have some more," he said, loading Benjamin's plate with a heap of food five times the size of his brothers'.

With a grin, Joseph began to drink with them, proposing toast after toast—to Canaan, to their father, to their welfare, to their donkeys, to anything he could name—until all were too merry to wonder, too merry to question, too merry to be mystified.

For now, they would set aside their fears. For now, they were free with the Egyptian who knew them better than they knew themselves.

44

It was the next morning before the Israelites, their caravan loaded with food and supplies, set out again for Canaan.

Their spirits heady with wine and a night full of partying, they were a lighthearted crew.

As the towers of Succoth grew smaller upon the retreating horizon, they felt free to discuss the events of the previous day.

But once again, they reached no credible conclusion regarding the prime minister's behavior. They would have written him off as an unpredictable lunatic, had it not been for his uncanny knowledge of their relative ranks and ages.

"Surely he is no madman," they concluded.

"Perhaps he is a wizard," someone suggested. "We have heard how he predicted this time of famine."

Still, this did not explain his odd treatment of their little band.

They had no reason to complain, however, and every reason to rejoice. Simeon was safely with them, no harm had befallen Benjamin, and their fears of retribution were assuaged.

The governor had seen to it that they were generously treated in the marketplace, and they had come away with enough food to see their tribe through several more months.

Not only this, but once again he had replaced their

money in their bags, not allowing them to pay a shekel for the goods.

It was not until they heard the rush of horses' hooves behind them that they grew apprehensive again.

Looking back toward the city, they saw that a forbidding group of riders pursued them, and as they came closer, they recognized the governor's steward in the lead.

"In the name of Zaphenath-paneah," he called after them, "stop in your tracks!"

Stunned, they waited on the desert highway. When the man reached them, they were speechless, for his troops leaped from their mounts and drew their swords.

"Why have you repaid evil for good?" the steward demanded.

When the Israelites only stared at him in perplexity, he commanded his men to search the train.

"The master's silver goblet has been stolen!" the steward shouted. "The one he uses for divination! You have done a great wrong in taking it!"

Judah was the first to find his voice.

"Good sir," he defended, "why does my lord speak such words as these? Far be it from your servants to do such a thing! Remember, the money which we found in our sacks we brought back to you from Canaan. How then could we steal silver or gold from your master's house?"

When the soldiers continued to search the train, Judah became even more adamant.

"You shall not find it, sir! Not with us!" he cried. "Why, if you should find it with one of us, he should be put to death! And the rest of us shall be your slaves!"

"Very well," the steward agreed. "But the one who has it shall be my slave, and the rest of you shall be innocent."

Livid, Simeon and Levi ran to the donkeys and unloaded their sacks. Each brother followed suit, and as they opened them, they laughed together, shaking their heads and cursing.

One by one, beginning with Reuben and proceeding in order of rank, the steward's men searched the bags.

Ten out of the eleven had been riffled with no sign of the cup. Only Benjamin's remained, and the elder brothers were already reloading their pack animals when a cry halted them.

"Here it is!" one of the soldiers announced. "In the bag of the youngest!"

Benjamin, his face scarlet, turned helplessly to his brothers. "I . . . I did not steal it!" he insisted.

"Then how does it come to be in your bag?" the steward growled.

Grasping the youngster by the arm, he pushed him toward one of his men.

"Bind him!" he commanded. "I have heard that Hebrews make good slaves."

45

The time of reckoning had come at last.

In fear and trembling the Israelites, the eleven sons of Jacob, were brought before the lord of Egypt.

Had they been able to share their thoughts at this moment, they would have found them remarkably similar. For every one of them, save Benjamin, bore the guilt of the past uppermost in his mind, and they all believed that the inscrutable puzzle of their time in Egypt had a direct relationship to their great and hidden sin.

How the cup had come to be in the sack of the only innocent brother, none of them could imagine. But that Zaphenath-paneah was a wizard, none of them doubted.

Surely he was an instrument of the supernatural. They felt this not only because of the knowledge he had of them, not only because the steward had said the stolen cup was used for divination, but also because the strange governor seemed capable of reading their innermost souls.

Again today, as they stood before him, they shriveled beneath his gaze, beneath the haunting torment of his eyes which stripped them of all confidence.

What magic he had to know them, they could not guess. Their theology allowed for no good power outside Jehovah, yet they did not sense that Zaphenath-paneah's gift was rooted in evil.

All this they would have discussed together, had they the chance. But they must keep silent, or they would surely not live to see tomorrow.

Before them now, upon his lofty porch, sat the prime minister, his arms outstretched along the arms of his throne, his face full of disapproval.

As one body, the Hebrews fell to the ground, prostrating themselves hopelessly.

For a long time, Joseph said nothing. When he did at last address them, it was in his most regal voice.

"What is this deed that you have done?" he demanded. "Do you not know that I am indeed a wizard?"

Quaking with resignation, Judah replied, "What can we say to my lord? How can we justify ourselves? God has discovered our iniquity. We are my lord's slaves, we and the one who had the cup."

But Joseph, feigning indignation, objected, "No, no! Far be it from me to do this. The one who had the cup shall be my slave, but as for you, return in peace to your father."

Now of course Joseph knew that this only turned the knife of their guilt more keenly. For among all of them, only Benjamin deserved to be spared.

Suddenly forgetting all propriety, Judah approached the throne, desperate to be heard. "Oh my lord," he pleaded, "may your servant please reach your heart? Do not be angry with me, for you are equal to Pharaoh!"

With this, he recounted their first conversation, reminding him of their father and his tender love for their youngest brother.

"My father told us that if we took Benjamin from him, and if harm befell the lad, we would bring the old man's gray hair down to the grave in sorrow!"

By now, Judah was on his knees, weaving to and fro, his hands clasped before him.

"If we return to our father and the lad is not with us, our father will surely die! Please, let me remain instead of the lad. I shall be your slave, but let Benjamin return with the others."

In that instant, as Joseph read Judah's despair—the agony and repentance of the very one who, years before, would have sold him into slavery—a strange thing happened.

At work within Joseph's heart was an exposing razor of memory, peeling away, ever so painfully, layer upon layer of time and resentment.

Yes, he had been here before. He had seen all of this before, not in vision, but in reality. The scene had involved different characters, but the circumstances had been the same. And as the recollection grew within him, he began to shiver.

He recalled the day his father, Jacob, had gone in fear and trembling to meet Esau. He remembered what it had felt like to see his strong Papa prostrate before the notorious hunter, the one who had sought for years to take vengeance on Jacob's selfish sin.

If anyone had the right to retribution, it was Esau. And if anyone had the right to revenge, it was Joseph.

Suddenly, the prime minister, the great lord of Egypt, could control himself no longer.

Turning to his steward, barely able to see for the tears in his eyes, he cried, "Clear the court! Send everyone away!"

Once again, the steward was faced with the conundrum of his master's behavior. But compliantly he obeyed, clapping his hands and ushering all the servants and officials away from the porch, until the governor was left alone with the Israelites.

As he stood solitary before his brothers, he began to weep so loudly that all those who occupied his compound heard him. And between convulsive sobs he revealed himself.

"I am Joseph!" he cried in his native tongue. "Is my father still alive?"

Confounded silence choked the Hebrews, and they looked upon him as though not hearing.

"Please..." Joseph pleaded, holding out his hands, "come closer to me."

As they found strength to obey, Joseph removed his striped headdress so that he might look more familiar.

"I am your brother, Joseph, whom you sold into Egypt!" he declared.

As the men tried to absorb what he was saying, a hundred questions resisted it.

Joseph? Here in Egypt? They had nearly convinced themselves, after all this time, that their brother must be dead.

But, yes—he did look somewhat like the youngster they had left in the pit, like the ghost who had haunted their dreams all these years.

Yet, how had they "sold" him? And how had he come to this high station?

They were barely beginning to accept his identity when he spoke again.

"Do not be grieved or angry with yourselves because you sold me here. For God sent me before you to preserve life...to preserve you as a remnant in the earth and to keep you alive by a great deliverance."

Still the men were speechless. As Joseph read their mystified expressions, he went on.

"Now, therefore, although you left me for dead, so that I was picked up and sold, it was not you who sent me here, but God. He has made me a guide to Pharaoh, lord of all his household, and ruler over all the land of Egypt!"

By now he was pacing before them, his arms wide. "Hurry and go to my father. Tell him what God has done. Then return with him! Do not delay! You shall live in the land of Goshen, the finest shepherd land in Egypt! And you shall be near me, you and your children and your children's children and your flocks and your herds and all that you have!"

Someone in the group began to weep, and another to

laugh. Soon the entire company was giddy with the revelation.

"There now!" Joseph cried. "Your eyes see, and the eyes of my brother Benjamin see, that it is my mouth which is speaking to you!"

He stood now directly before the youngest son, studying the lavender lights in his eyes.

"Oh," he laughed, "I could not let you go! It was I who put the cup within your sack! Anything to stop you, to bring you back to me!"

Benjamin smiled broadly, and with sudden ecstasy Joseph fell on his neck, kissing him and weeping with him.

One by one he drew his awestruck brothers to him, embracing them and kissing them:

Reuben, who had been helpless to save him; Judah, who would have sold him; Simeon and Levi, who had been lions in his life; Gad and Asher, who would have killed him . . .

One by one by one . . .

And they marveled, overcome and grateful, just as Jacob had marveled when Esau lifted him from the dirt and forgave him.

EPILOGUE

There is a friend who sticks closer than a brother.

Proverbs 18:24b NASB

Epilogue

Jacob sat upon a broad plush seat in the golden chariot of his son, the prime minister of Egypt. On either side of him were two young boys, looking much like his beloved Rachel.

Manasseh and Ephraim studied the patriarch's aged face with awe. All their lives they had heard of Israel and his great faith. But to actually sit in his presence brought them closer to the legends, closer to their father's God.

Jacob wrapped an arm around each of them, his eyes wistful and bright as he watched the passing terrain.

Joseph, who sat across from him, his lovely wife at his side, breathed softly into her ear. "That is my father, Asenath. My father, here with us!"

"Yes," she whispered, her lips parting in a smile.

She had never known her husband to be so happy, so fulfilled, and her heart glowed with joy.

The family had just taken the old patriarch to meet Pharaoh in Avaris, the king's Delta palace, and were now returning him to Goshen, where the mighty tribe of Israel was settling in.

It had been a hard thing for Jacob to leave Canaan, to come to a new land where shepherds were still often held in disdain.

But Joseph had chosen a choice site for their settlement, a fertile valley much like the Vale of Shechem and studded with oaks like Mamre.

As the chariot, driven by a court chauffeur, came

within view of the vast property, Jacob breathed deeply of the country breeze.

Warm air currents perpetually wafted over this place, passing across miles of undulating green like a caress. They bore a hint of the cooling sea as they descended from the north, and they blended with the heat of the eastern desert, creating a perfect climate.

So lush was the land of Goshen that it was also named for Raamses, one of the most renowned of the Pharaohs. This had been his favorite place, he who owned the world.

Joseph would never forget the sight of his frail father, dressed in simple nomad's robes, as he stood before the present king of Egypt. This Pharaoh, still very proud of his own shepherd roots, had welcomed him eagerly. And they had talked for a long time.

"How old are you?" the young king had asked, entranced by Jacob's wise face.

"The years of my sojourning are 130," Jacob had replied. "Few and unpleasant have been the years of my life, nor have I attained the years that my fathers lived during the days of their sojourning."

So moved had Salatis been by the venerable elder's quiet spirit, that he had actually stepped down from his throne to speak further with him.

"And your God is the God of the desert?"

"The God of the whole earth, the sea, the sky, and all that is in them," Jacob had answered.

It was easy to see that Pharaoh was touched by this. When he drew even nearer to the old man, raising Jacob's wizened hands in his own, the whole court had been breathless.

"Bless me, Father," he had said.

And so Jacob had complied, resting his hands on the young king's head and calling down the strength of Jehovah on his reign.

As the chariot traveled toward the Goshen settlement, Jacob appeared to be at peace. Joseph lifted Asenath's hand to his lips, praying privately that the old man's remaining years would be happy.

Somehow, seeing the light on Jacob's face as they pulled into camp, he knew they would be.

* * *

Joseph would return to the Avaris court in the morning. For tonight he wished to walk through Goshen Vale, to see that all was well with his father's people.

He had left Asenath and her sons with the women of the camp, and had walked some distance, marveling at the size of the tribe. Hundreds of souls were numbered among it—sons and their wives, children and grandchildren, menservants and womenservants. And despite the famine, it was a wealthy company.

As Joseph passed through the settlement, he was greeted warmly by all, and was at last hailed by one of his favorites.

Eagerly Reuben joined him, his handsome face beaming. "May I walk a little way with you?" he called.

"Please," Joseph greeted. "I would like that."

Always the younger brother had admired Jacob's first-born. And now more than ever, he was proud to be kin to the striking Reuben.

"Judah has told me that you alone, of all my brothers, tried to rescue me from the pit," Joseph said. "You always were my savior," he confessed, "from the time I was small."

Reuben smiled, remembering the lad's many tussles with Simeon, Levi, and the others.

"You had a hard way to go, Little One," he recalled.

Joseph laughed aloud. "It has been some time since I was called that!"

Suddenly Reuben blushed, hoping he had not offended. After all, this was the prime minister of Egypt to whom he spoke!

But Joseph clapped him on the back, and Reuben sighed.

"The men have been talking to me," the elder said. "They are still somewhat afraid."

"Why?" Joseph marveled. "Have I not done well by them?"

"Indeed," Reuben asserted. "But I suppose they find it hard to receive such forgiveness. They fear that you have done it for Jacob's sake, and that when our father passes on..."

Joseph stopped in the path and looked deep into his brother's eyes.

"Tell them, for me, not to be afraid. Am I in God's place? They may have meant evil against me, but God has turned it for good, in order to bring about this present result... to preserve many people."

Reuben listened in amazement, and would have objected, but could not.

"Tell them not to fear," Joseph repeated.

The elder bowed his head, his heart too full to speak, and with a nod he turned to leave.

When Joseph was alone again, he ventured to the edge of camp. Taking a seat on the rise of a little hill, he looked back over the great company and the circles of firelight which marked it against the earth.

The sun had fully set now, and night had fallen. Through Joseph's mind passed countless faces, many as familiar as his own childhood, and others whom he had never seen until this day—the faces of his father's people.

Closing his eyes, he drew his knees to his chest and recalled, as though it had never gone, his youth in the shepherd hills. For the first time in years, he communed with his God in the quiet of the wilderness.

When a shadow passed between himself and the moon above, he opened his eyes again and saw before him yet one more face.

"Papa," he sighed, "how good of you to join me!"

Stooping down, Jacob sat with him, his snowy beard gracing his lap.

"You were a good wrestler," the old Hebrew said.

"I did not let the Lord go easily," Joseph replied.

"You did not let him go until he blessed you!" the patriarch laughed.

For a long while, the two sat together—Joseph and his Papa, his mentor of the faith.

Tonight the past and the present were in harmony, and all the dreams Joseph had ever dreamed had come true.